D1494311

Please return/renew this item by the last date shown.
Items may also be renewed by the internet*

https://library.eastriding.gov.uk

* Please note a PIN will be required to access this service
- this can be obtained from your library

MICHAEL MOORCOCK

London Bone

and Other Stories

Edited by John Davey

Illustrated by Michael Moorcock

WEIDENFELD & NICOLSON

This edition first published in Great Britain in 2016
by Weidenfeld & Nicolson

An imprint of the Orion Publishing Group
Carmelite House, 50 Victoria Embankment,
London EC4Y 0DZ

An Hachette UK Company

1 3 5 7 9 10 8 6 4 2

A CIP catalogue record for this book is available
from the British Library

ISBN 978 1 473 21329 6

Typeset by Jouve (UK), Milton Keynes

Printed in Great Britain by CPI Group (UK) Ltd, Croydon, CR0 4YY

www.michaelmoorcock.co.uk
www.orionbooks.co.uk

For Linda

Contents

A Child's Christmas in the Blitz

Dear Jean-Luc,

Because you said that you were curious about my memories of growing up and celebrating Christmas during the Second World War, I'll tell you. Well, Christmas at that time had a special luminosity, a particular atmosphere which I have never been able to recapture, perhaps because I was born into a world darkened, of necessity, by conflict in which one dull day would be followed by a black, black night sometimes suddenly filled with noise and brilliant explosions.

I remember a tree whose tinsel glowed faintly in the light of a dying fire, standing in one corner of the room where I also slept. Out beyond the blackout curtains, occasionally visible as a momentary glare of yellow light or heard as a screaming drone when some plane spiralled to earth under fire, or the steady thump of the ack-ack, the war in the air pursued its course. I hardly knew why or what was happening. Bombs fell, landscapes changed, and occasionally I was even allowed to watch from a darkened room as the searchlights roamed across clouds and silvery barrage balloons, seeking targets.

I'm sure you feel little nostalgia for those times which are marked for most postwar generations by the war films which followed, whether they were stories of the Resistance or epics like *Von Ryan's Express*, but for me the War years are marked by a sense of domestic warmth and a deep, attractive melancholy which I suspect I am forever attempting to reproduce in my fiction; feelings allied to those that come from what Rose Macaulay describes as 'the Pleasure of Ruins', a romanticism not so much for the vanished splendours of the past as marked by a sense of human

1

aspiration thwarted, of beauty destroyed, of surviving memory, which is the enemy of death.

I might have been able to tell you that Germany was attacking England, but more likely I would have said something about 'dog-fights' and 'us' or 'them'. I was absorbed with my Britain's toy soldiers, miniature hollow-cast models of English Tommies, French poilus and American doughboys locked in conflict with the ultra-masculine Germans, in their pointed helmets, whom I imagined flying the planes that I passed through the beams of my battery-powered searchlights, re-enacting under our steel-strengthened dining-room table the conflict which would very much decide my family's fate.

Actually, I always liked the French infantry best, perhaps for the colour of the uniforms, then the English, then the Americans. I must have learned enough not to admire the Germans, who, of course, wore grey, for me never an attractive colour. Even my fleet of tiny battleships seemed dull and though they were distin-guished by name and type on the cigarette cards I had inherited from my father's neatly collected sets ('Modern British Warships', 'Our Modern Navy' or 'Our Maritime Heritage') I never could summon much interest in them. The planes at least had brown and green camouflage and could be given thrilling noises as they closed in on their targets.

Of course my army wasn't exactly up to date, any more than our real armies had been in 1939. It consisted chiefly of my father's boyhood collection added to by what had been presented to me at birthdays and Christmas. I had rather more cavalry than was cur-rently in action, a lot of auxiliaries dressed as cowboys or Red Indians and rather a preponderance of French zouaves, whose uniforms were considerably more romantic. There were a bunch of rather crudely cast solid metal 1914 machine-gunners. A couple of motorcycle dispatch riders. And a bunch of farm and zoo work-ers, who were ready, I suppose, as the final line of defence. There was a certain egalitarianism amongst them, I will admit. Sets of British soldiers, usually six to the box, consisted of two running men, two kneeling and firing men, two standing and firing men.

More elaborate sets would include perhaps two machine-gunners, an officer with a sword, two men lying down and firing. They had identical opposite numbers in the German, American and French armies, in identical poses. The cowboys were often armed only with pistols and the Indians with tomahawks.

Before the War began, there had been a natural tendency for manufacturers, mostly Britain's (though there were some inferior makers who tended to supply the bulk of the cannon fodder), to match both infantry, cavalry and artillery exactly one for one. There were, to be sure, no anti-aircraft gun-crews other than British. They came with each gun or searchlight, specially modelled to operate their machines. They sat in little bucket seats to wind their range-finders, or stretched their tiny arms to operate firing mechanisms. There was something of a dearth of airmen, too, all of whom were either English or American and far too big to enter the cockpits of the planes I sailed over their heads.

The dull thump of guns was echoed by my own childish imitations: *'Bam! Bam! Kerrrump!'*

The red boxes that the tiny matériel had arrived in became houses, aircraft hangars, barricades. The dark floral carpet was fields and cushions were hills. As the bombs outside whined down, I would crawl into a world bounded on four sides by heavy wire mesh into which had been let a small door. The mattress and pillows were a haven for my other comforts, the soft toys – patchwork rabbits, curly-furred dogs, Mickey and Minnie. Even then I was identifying with the Mouse. Not the middle-class, long-trousered Mouse of sanitised 1950s Disneyland, but the original, aggressive, trickster Mouse whose ancestors were Brer Rabbit and Tom Sawyer. That Mouse sported an evil grin and took cunning revenge on his enemies, mostly muscular cats and dogs in baggy pants supported by a single strap.

Christmas 1944. Home-made bunting, red, green, gold, silver, hanging in every room of the house. The candles flickering to life on the tree, wax dripping over the holders. You had to be careful. Many a house was destroyed by its Christmas candles. First a trip to Kennards, the big, grey Portland stone department store in

Croydon. They had made the most of little, as we had done at home. And suddenly I am looking in awe at an intense colour. I can't take my eyes off it. A colour I have never seen before. If it spelled a word, I wasn't aware of it. Besides, I couldn't read. It is the sign over Santa Claus's grotto. Neon, rescued from some pre-war hoard. A gorgeous, unworldly colour. A heavenly colour. I focused on it as others might have focused on gold nuggets or streaks of silver in a mine. I was looking at indigo. Glowing, pulsing indigo. Even as I passed under the sign into Santa's grotto, all scarlet and white, with a big green tree festooned with the square fruit of brightly wrapped packages, I could not take my eyes off it. Indigo. Not until I saw *Fantasia*, the following Christmas, would I ever witness such intense colour again. Indigo. And then the enveloping scarlet, soft as my mother's furs, of Santa as I sat on his knee and demanded ponies and – and something else. What is it, young man? What do you want?

I wanted indigo. I wanted to swallow or be swallowed by that colour. With Mickey Mouse and Santa Claus and a long-legged home-made Teddy Bear indigo will always mean Christmas to me. My birthstone, according to some, is Blue Zircon, Blue Topaz or Lapis Lazuli. Blue for a boy, the blues and birthdays, for a memory more vivid than flame shuddering up from a ruined house, of thick, black smoke coiling across a blue, late-summer sky. Blue for Mother's eyes. Blue for peace. Infinite indigo.

That Christmas, haunted by the memory of indigo, Mickey Mouse would be the first movie I ever saw. I woke up on Christmas Day, just after dawn, unable to sleep for the excitement. The smoke of heavy coke and what little wood we had left. Distant voices. Busy voices. Savoury smells from the kitchen. My mother was up already and my father was doing something outside. I had been dimly aware of activity. Within me built a rising chord of anticipation. I pushed back the covers. The fire in my room was no more than a glow, a few rubies glittering amongst the pale ashes. I crawled out from under the steel-strengthened table and was getting into my dressing gown and slippers just as the door opened and my mother came in. My mother. Dark eyed, loving beauty. My constant.

4

'It's a white Christmas,' she said. 'We're having a white Christmas.' It's the first I remember. She went to the big French windows and pulled back the heavy curtains so that I could see into our garden. Mrs White, our next-door neighbour, came in. She was holding a red-wrapped parcel. She was laughing. Big, heavy flakes were coming down so thick you could hardly see through them. But outside there was a shape. A dim figure moving about on the lawn, under the bare apple trees. Santa? No, it was too late for him. He would have come and gone with his sleigh and his reindeer when it was night, his passage muffled by the already settling snow. Who was it?

My mother laughed. 'It's your daddy,' she said. 'He's gone mad.'

My father was out there rolling the snow into huge balls. One for a body, one for a head. He had made a Christmas snowman. As I watched he put pieces of anthracite in for eyes, a stick of dowel for a nose and another for a cigar sticking out of his lopsided mouth. A snowman. What else? I knew what to expect from Christmas. There was no such thing as disappointment. Not then. I watched wide-eyed as my mother got me out of my pyjamas and into my little boiler suit, a miniature of the kind Mr Churchill wore (though I heard later his were silk). And then she led me into the next room, the sitting room, where the tree rose so tall to the ceiling, topped by a tinsel fairy, the branches covered with crimson balls and little, pale tinkling bells. With red, green and white candles, each in its own little tin holder, clipped to a branch.

But this I had already seen. What was new were the green, red and silver wrapped boxes. The strangely shaped thing lying on the floor beneath them. And in the grate was a fire so lively and bright, sending its light skipping from golden globe to silver bell, so that the whole room seemed full of movement, full of a warmth and a merriment, a completeness which denied everything in the world outside, where grey reality reared up through the thickening snow doing its best to hide the ruins, the anti-aircraft guns, the craters and the dull, dull blackouts, the eye-sockets of houses that would never live again. White as icing on a poisoned cake, it grew thicker and thicker while inside my father came stamping in, laughing as he did more rarely these days, his white breath rising around his head like a halo, slapping his gloved hands together, stamping his feet on the thick, wheat-coloured doormat to knock the already melting snow from his clothes, eagerly taking off his overcoat and hat as he shouted 'Merry Christmas' to Mrs White. 'Merry Christmas! Merry Christmas!'

My father, smelling of soap and brilliantine and cologne, sat down on the floor with me between his legs and helped me unwrap presents as our black-and-white Welsh collie, Pat, came running in, half dried by my mother, to sit panting by the fire and watch, half an ear cocked to the radio playing carols and dance music. 'There'll be bluebirds over, the white cliffs of Dover... I'm going to get lit up when the lights come on in London... Silent night, holy night...'

Of course, there was a box of soldiers. Red-coated ones this time, in the formal uniforms of the Scots Guards, in bearskins, marching with their shouldered guns. Not the most useful troops, but welcome nonetheless. A field gun, complete with tiny shells, fired by means of a spring-lever. A Rupert Annual from Mrs White, with that little bear always running towards some far horizon over perfect downs and welcoming woods, towards some wonderful adventure from which he would always return to the security of Mr and Mrs Bear and their beautiful cottage. Some Quality Street chocolates, wrapped in gold, silver and coloured cellophane, a picture of a dashing eighteenth-century soldier and his lady on the box, bought with carefully hoarded ration coupons, some bullseyes, bigger than my mouth, all brown and black and white stripes. And then the *pièce-de-résistance* – the mysteriously wrapped monster in red paper and tied with silver string – a scooter! A big, solid, wooden scooter, painted dark green and post-office red. A scooter like no other child I knew had ever owned. A huge, solid machine, with beautifully running rubber-tyred wheels. A scooter I could only run up and down the hall, unable to go out with it until the snow had melted. My father had made it, of course, as he made everything. It was meticulously finished, perfectly painted, aerodynamically designed as he made everything. You could smell the fresh paint on it, mingling with

6

the smell of burning wood and coke from the fire, the cooking smells to which my mother dashed every so often to supervise the lunchtime turkey.

Those are the colours of that first Christmas I remember in detail. Indigo, deep green, scarlet, gold and the blanketing white snow. I'm sure I enjoyed our Christmas lunch and was happy to show off my presents to my uncles and aunts and their American friends from the airfields who began to arrive through the afternoon. There was the smell of tobacco, of beer and whisky, gin and sherry, the loud, happy laughter of my uncles, telling mysterious jokes which made my mother and her sisters squeal with mock outrage, the radio playing Bing Crosby and Guy Lombardo's Royal Canadians, comic patter and crooning, the upbeat tempo of Harry James and Benny Goodman, of Glenn Miller. Coming in on a wing and a prayer – I'm dreaming of a White Christmas – Jingle bells – and the carpet and furniture rolled back against the walls so that my mother and father, uncles and aunts could foxtrot until the evening when one of our American guests would start to set up the movie projector and there would be Mickey Mouse again, the first movies I had ever seen, in flickering black and white projected against a slightly crumpled bedsheet. I have never since enjoyed a cartoon as much. The projector and movies were borrowed from the American base. Everyone loved them. Silently Mickey flew planes in amazing patterns, captained a steamboat, serenaded Minnie.

Only the Americans weren't in civilian clothes. They were glamorous, attractive men whose uniforms were smarter than our own, who produced chewing gum and candy at will from their infinite pockets. They had brought me Captain Marvel comics. Unlike the black-and-white English comics, these were in full colour. Captain Marvel, with his white hussar's cloak trimmed with gold, in his red suit with the yellow flash across his chest, looking exactly like Fred MacMurray whom I would later see in *Double Indemnity*, as powerful and benign an image as Santa, able to fly, to knock the evil scientist Sivana for six, given his powers by someone who actually looked a bit like Santa, the kindly old scientist Shazam. Captain Marvel was part of the Christmas pantheon. I loved Captain Marvel, who seemed pleasantly, even stupidly human, and I hated the rather pious, humourless Superman whom I had never seen, as I had seen Captain Marvel, handing out presents from the Christmas tree.

My family had opened their homes to the American flyers, some of them friends of my RAF uncle who had disappeared while ferrying a Spitfire in Rhodesia and was disappointed to be found in the Bush by rescuers. He hadn't wanted to be rescued, he admitted to me many years later, he had enjoyed his African Christmases and had several African wives, extraordinary status in the village, and no chance of being shot at. He was already burned across his face and body, from where his Spitfire had been shot down in flames and he had had to bale out. And his wife, one of my mother's many powerful sisters, he confided, was a bit of a harridan, though she had seemed very friendly, I thought, to our American visitors. He remained the most handsome man I ever knew, the living exemplar of the modestly heroic flying ace.

My father wasn't a combatant. Like most of the other men in my family he was excused military service. Some were too old or unfit or, as in his case, were doing necessary war work. I grew up in what was essentially a matriarchy. One of the first fictitious characters I ever identified with was Jo March of *Little Women*. Jo March had known how to celebrate Christmas. She's introduced to us discussing the subject. 'Christmas isn't really Christmas without presents...' I would later see Judy Garland play her. Or was it my heart-throb June Allyson? Those girls also had an absent father, away fighting for the Union in the American Civil War. Mine, of course, wasn't fighting. I think he was already involved in one of the several affairs he enjoyed as the only good-looking young man at Philips, the electrical firm where he worked on the radar which was helping us beat the apparently overwhelming Nazi forces. (A couple of Christmases later, his presents to me consisted of sheets of linen taken from his drawing offices, a box of pencils and a ruler. Looking back, I can assume he had missed the shops. It was, after all, on a Christmas Day that he had told my

8

mother he was spending the holiday with his mistress; that he was leaving her.)

I would never see my father on Christmas Day again.

I have to admit I mostly remember my father in terms of the Christmas presents he gave me – his own collection of cigarette cards, his own toy soldiers, his beautiful, multicoloured marbles, his watercolour box, the tricycle and the full-size Norton motorbike frame and untyred wheels which he told me he was working on for me. He had also given me a Hornby clockwork train set which he took back in order to trade it for the bike frame. I remember one sharp December afternoon standing beside him in his workshop at the end of our garden, near the underground shelter we hardly ever used.

'This is going to be yours,' he assured me, as I held the oil-can for him. 'You can have it for Christmas when you're sixteen.' My birthday was a week before Jesus's, I knew. But I also understood his promise to be an abstraction. I knew the bike was really his and that, even if I was old enough to ride it at that time so far, far into the distant future, I probably wouldn't. He hadn't been able to resist it. 'Your father loved bikes more than he loved us,' my mother would tell me.

Even dressed as Santa, my father would reveal himself by his neatly pressed flannels, his fastidiously clipped fingernails. In spite of my uncle, the RAF hero, my father was the embodiment of elegant masculinity for me from his neatly cut fair hair to his smartly polished brogues.

At some point in time between Christmas and New Year's, I got the train back again. I don't remember what happened to the Norton. A busy trade would often occur between the children of the neighbourhood. Some time after Boxing Day, when I swapped my tricycle with a neighbour's child for a different clockwork Hornby locomotive, my mother had stepped in and stopped the deal. After the train set was returned, I never saw the Norton again. It disappeared with the melting snow. I later wondered if this was one of the issues which had led to his leaving us on Christmas Day 1946. I had little affection for him at that time. I felt no pain at his departure, probably because he lacked the nerve to tell me he was leaving. Besides, all boys of my age had absent fathers. Many of them, like me, would grow up in mother-run homes.

But that first Christmas I remember, the bombs grew infrequent. The decorations were still up when my mother and I mounted the electric tram, whose brass rails sliced through the remains of the slushy snow, to go up to the centre of the city, to visit my Uncle Jack at 10 Downing Street. He hadn't been able to spend Christmas with us, so we went to lunch with him and my Aunt Ivy, rather pious Christians who didn't believe in too much pleasure. Uncle Jack had been on duty. He worked for Churchill. 'Happy New Year, my boy!' beamed the old warrior-drunk, puffing avuncularly on his vast cigar and smelling strongly of tobacco and brandy. I think he would have offered me a glass of brandy if my mother hadn't been with me. He did, however, give me the benefit of his wisdom that afternoon. 'Never be tempted to vote Liberal,' he said.

After tea with my uncle we went to Oxford Street and Regent Street, where the big toyshop was and where I could spend the money I had been given for birthday and Christmas. My Uncle Jack always gave me a ten-shilling note. With this and my other cash I could replenish my miniature armies. This was the equivalent of an FDR loan to the British military. My mother couldn't afford to buy me more than a box at a time, mostly restricted to infantry, though she might add the occasional tank. But with my Christmas wealth I could add to my cavalry, to my Indians and my cowboys, perhaps to my anti-aircraft batteries.

Then, as we left Hamleys or Gamages or one of the other emporia supplying my reinforcements, my heart would leap with pleasure at the sound of the aircraft siren, warning us of an attack. I knew what this meant. One of the rarest of pleasures. To my enormous delight, we were forced to descend into the Underground, to the depths of the Central Line, and join our fellow Londoners, some of whom lived there almost permanently. It would mean I could sleep on a platform with all the other people who would rather risk being buried alive or drowned than remain overhead in the dangerous, blacked-out streets. I used to hope for a bombing raid so that we could enjoy the adventure, the subterranean camaraderie and what didn't seem like a false security.

Back at home, the Christmas holidays were still in force. My father disappeared again. From Boxing Day to the first full week in January we were free not only to play with our new planes, Roy Rogers cap pistols or other treasures, we were let out, wrapped tightly in little coats and scarves and mittens, to explore the surrounding destruction, a wonderland. There was only one condition. If we heard an air-raid siren, we were to come straight home. As my father's snowman melted into the back garden, I followed older friends over ruins which became defensives, Nevada hills, the Sheriff of Nottingham's castle. We climbed through the piled snow-topped rubble filling doorways, found staircases still intact, mounted them with practised balance as they swayed beneath our feet, reaching the second storey where whole rooms remained, sliced as if with a knife, everything in perfect condition – bathrooms, bedrooms, storerooms – and if we were lucky we found unlooted booty, including toys, saucepans, kettles and books. Christmas made us greedy for more and more wealth.

We became adept as high-wire artists at crossing the beams, all that remained of destroyed floors and roofs, glancing insouciantly down at the broken rooms some of which were still decorated for Christmas, with trees and tinsel. But these did not interest us. We learned to unroll lead from roofs and gutters, which the older kids hoarded or sold to scrap-metal dealers. The dealers made us put the lead into shopping bags or baskets so that our trade went unnoted. Churches were by far the richest source of lead, especially those which had stained-glass windows. The coloured glass was sometimes picked up before Christmas to make decorations. But we searched constantly for the Holy Grail of any boy's collection – a piece of shrapnel which was more than tortured metal twisted like barley-sugar sticks, but recognisable as part of a plane. What we longed to find were whole pilots, whose goggles and parachutes, flying suits, helmets and perhaps even pistols we could scavenge.

We grew up instinctive scavengers. Vulture chicks hunting for choice titbits, for treasures we could carry home and show off to our parents and friends. We worked with busy efficiency and concentration, desperate to get the most we could before the Christmas holidays were over.

The snow never lasted for long in the city. For a while it gave a pristine, pseudo-virginity to our wrecked landscapes. As it melted, the old reminders of our situation, all the symbols of destruction, began to re-emerge. And, as school loomed, we became all the more frantic. How we longed for an unexploded anti-aircraft shell or a bomb or other ammunition to complete our Christmas collections. Shell cases were common currency and generally disdained. We had learned how to clamp the live shells and then set off the firing pins by putting a nail against them and striking them with a hammer. We tried to dig out the graphite, the powder, to make our own guns. Nobody seemed to think there was anything unwholesome in our warlike pursuits. Or perhaps their imaginations didn't stretch to how we were entertaining ourselves. Presumably, they had no idea how long the War would last. We might need those skills when we were adults.

I don't remember too many dogfights around Christmas, however. I somehow had the impression that the Nazis and the Allies broke for Christmas, much as we did for school. But I had seen some of the fiercest air-fighting. For years I thought that watching the Battle of Britain through the windows of our house, as the Spitfires and Messerschmitts wheeled and flared in a darkness speared by shafts of yellow light, had been nothing but a false memory, something inspired by watching movies. I put this to my mother a few years ago. 'Oh, no,' she said, 'you saw the Battle of Britain. We were between three airfields, Biggin Hill, Croydon and another one whose name I forget. I used to hold you up to the window to watch the dogfights. They were amazing. And they kept you quiet when you were teething or whatever.' Perhaps that's why I've never sought the distraction of war movies. The real thing was so much more exciting. And, in an almost mythical fight, we actually won command of the skies.

During those quiet Christmas times, when it seemed Hitler's

Luftwaffe was permanently beaten, we enjoyed incredible freedom which would be unknown to our own children. In our little grey suits of flannel windjammers and shorts, shirts and jerseys, twice-tied black Oxfords, ties askew and hair sticking up like the wire which jutted dangerously from the blasted remnants of reinforced concrete, we were forever dusty.

That this was the dust of the doomed and the dead never occurred to us. That bodies might still lie undiscovered in those cellars or that the rust on exposed pipes might be blood was never mentioned by our elders and therefore never considered by us. We were told it was dangerous to climb the ruined houses, but we knew anyone could learn that skill. We were told to watch for 'bad men' lurking in the wreckage or in the bushes and copses of the nearby Common and golf links, so we kept our distance from adults. But the rest of the world was ours as it never would be again. The world was unbordered. All its walls had been smashed down. We came upon large, abandoned houses with stables and outhouses. We ranged through glass-roofed conservatories. We found tools and glue in the workshops. We learned to walk on roofs. The movie *Hope and Glory* catches some of this atmosphere but seemed bland to me compared to the richness of the reality.

When the flying bombs came back the next Christmas we returned to the shelters, the reinforced tables, the dugouts. My grandmother was Jewish, my father unmistakeably Anglo-Saxon. She would sit across from him in the big communal shelter, which nobody really trusted. She would hug her thermos flask and her packet of sandwiches as we heard the drone of the Vis overhead, then the sudden silence as their engines cut out, then the shriek of their passage earthwards as they hit Dahlia Gardens and Northborough Road and Mitcham Lane and all the other suburban streets laid out by planners in the '20s, following the course of the railways to build bijou Tudor-style mansions for the upwardly mobile professional classes represented by my father and mother, the first of their families not to live by trade or the work of their hands.

My grandmother knew what would happen to her and presumably her children and grandchildren if the Nazis won. Facing my father in the cramped shelter stinking of sweat and urine she would rock back and forth as if in prayer as we listened to the dull drone of the VI engines. She had a conceit which she was too intelligent a woman to believe, but she knew it annoyed my father. Her conceit was that if the Germans won the War, then all the Jews would be rounded up, put in concentration camps and killed. But if the English won the War, she insisted, then all the Anglo-Saxons would be rounded up, put in concentration camps and killed.

So she would sit rocking, her finger wagging, grinning into my father's infuriated face. 'Better hope the Germans win, Arthur,' she would say. 'Better hope the Germans win.'

It seemed the rockets, when they came, would never stop. British pilots had discovered ways of flying close to the VIs, which were essentially drone aircraft, and nudging them out of the way, but tracing the course of the V2s was almost impossible. And it seemed we were getting more than our fair share of both.

We didn't know at the time that Churchill was deliberately misdirecting those flying bombs, that his departments would report strikes on crucial factories and aeroplane fields when actually all they were hitting were the civilians of South London. As a result of this inspired misdirection, South London received by far the greatest number of strikes. One day the house across the road was a living entity, containing people you knew, who lived much as you did, who tended little rose gardens and wisteria plants and kept their paintwork up to scratch; the next day it would be something else entirely. Something ruined and already in the process of being forgotten. Somewhere to explore, to loot, to roll the lead from. Mrs Archer and the little Archer girls, whom I still miss and dream about – removed. Their blonde pageboy haircuts and pleated grey skirts, their crisp white blouses and school hats are the originals of images I continue to find attractive. But they had gone before I noticed the intimations of sex. That would come a couple of years later when the War was over and we had moved to a timber yard. The smell of sawdust is almost as erotic for me as the smell of garlic or Mitsouko. Mr and Mrs Wall, their pebble-dashed miniature château a heap of rubble scarcely worth sifting through, forgotten. 'Auntie' Pat, who had run the corner newsagents and lent me all those wonderful books from her stock – Scott, Stevenson, Ballantine – gone one bright Sunday morning as she laid out the papers ready for delivery.

With my friends, and perhaps with my adult family, I learned never to mourn. To move on. To keep going. To act as if your number was never going to come up. Yet in all other respects we were far from stoical. We always knew, for instance, that we were luckier than the Russians, for instance. 'Mustn't grumble' became a familiar refrain. 'How are you?' *'Mustn't grumble.'* – *'Are your in-laws still living with you?'* 'Yes. Mustn't grumble…' It would be a refrain that outlasted the War and allowed restaurateurs, in particular, to get away with horror.

I was sent to infant school in Robin Hood Road, part of the estate planned in that corrupted arts-and-crafts style which is so characteristic of early-twentieth-century London, a style it shares on a larger scale with Hollywood, where I always feel immediately at home. I was at school long enough to know what boredom meant, because I could already read and write. The headmistress said she would have to have a word with my mother, because I could not concentrate on the primers. I had in fact ruined one by putting it, open, on my brilliantined little head. When she asked what I read at home I said Edgar Rice Burroughs and George Bernard Shaw, which was true. For years I believed that to be taken seriously as a writer one had to have three names.

The headmistress seemed to get even angrier at my answer but she never got to have that word. Over the weekend a V-Bomb dropped out of a pale and silent sky and eliminated the school. I was free. Hitler had saved me. The school was a leadmine and, what was more, not even the headmistress had died. Within a day, little that was valuable remained of its site.

The V2s were worse than anything we had suffered. Morale, which had remained almost hysterically high during the Blitz, began to fray. Hitler knew the power of those massive rockets which could come out of nowhere and kill you before you had time to say a word. They were a cruel weapon. Today, when I hear about the bombardments of Baghdad or other cities, I know how cruel those weapons are. No time to compose yourself for death. No time to say 'I love you' or 'Look after yourself' and no time to find the inadequate safety of those shelters. The only warning you ever had was a few seconds when the yelling tube of explosives was streaking down on your head.

My imagination, however, was informed by those early years, just as my life felt dull after the War's end. I had become used to metamorphosis, of almost constantly changing landscapes, of being able to see for miles. I had become used to the adrenaline rush of the bombing raids and the exploration of tottering ruins, of squeezing up through chimneys, of clambering walls whose only handholds were pits in the brick.

On VE Day, as if he had waited for Hitler to be defeated, my father announced that he was in love with the woman who would remain his companion for the rest of his life.

'I couldn't have loved him much,' my mother said, 'because I didn't really mind. My pride was hurt, of course, but I had what I wanted. I had you.' That was how she saw it. She never questioned her own emotions, she never wondered if her sexuality was repressed. She always vehemently defended her own father, whom some thought had 'interfered' with her and had been thus thrown out of the house by her mother. She was visibly happy throughout my childhood and would only grow miserable when the time came for me to leave home. She had what she wanted. Her brother and sister-in-law, who had come to live in our house when their own was blitzed, took advantage of my father's leaving. In those days it was not easy for a single woman with a child to rent such a house for herself. So they took over the rent and soon she had left. She went to find a job and in doing so changed my life all the more for the better. Her job was in a timber yard as a book-keeper.

Earlier, when my father had gone for good, I found a pair of those brown brogues of his and put my feet into them, feeling as masculine as I ever had, then I went outside in my Wellington boots and joined the people jumping over the fire on which effigies of Hitler and Göring burned in the half-hearted rain. I loved those shoes. I loved the smell of the polish. I found the Cherry Blossom 'Oxblood' boot cleaner and I shone them up as proudly as he ever had. I looked forward to the day when they would fit. I suppose Oedipus could not have enjoyed greater satisfaction than I had with those captured shoes.

But my mother must have discovered them, no doubt, because she presented them to him on the first birthday I had after the Blitz when he came to take me off to the toyshop on the back of his BSA. He had forgotten to get me Christmas or birthday presents, of course. Happily my nativity was only a week before the Saviour's, so he could get me both sets of presents at the same time.

I climbed onto his pillion. He gunned the engine. He kicked up the stand. There was a stink of 'mixture' as the engine fired. He told me to hold on tight to the belt of his leather jacket and then we were off, roaring through the darkening December streets to the big, usually unattainable toyshop in Streatham, close to the ice rink, which was usually far too expensive for me, even when I could get there. I don't think he ever felt so guilty again, because he let me have the pick of the store. I bought infantry. I bought imperial Indian cavalry. I bought cowboys and Indians. I bought a ranch house. I bought long-range guns and I bought light cannon. I bought another searchlight, more glorious, more powerful than any I had ever owned before. I bought planes and battleships. And I bought Mickey and Minnie Mouse, who shared my initials and for whom I had developed a profound affection.

We came back with his saddlebags loaded with treasure. My mother insisted that much of it be wrapped for Christmas Day, even though I knew what most of it was. I think it was then that she gave him the shoes. I caught a whiff of Cherry Blossom as she handed him a bag.

The yard was in the grounds of a ruined mansion. There was a small two-room cottage made of corrugated iron, heated by an old-fashioned cooking range. We moved into that. By the winter of 1947 we were still there. I remember the snow being so deep that the path cleared to the outside toilet was actually higher than my head. We made the trip to the toilet as rarely as possible. I still remember the chamber pots and the smell of them.

By the time the War ended, Britain was massively in debt to America, who had only loaned her the money to fight a war they had advised her against pursuing. She was, like the rest of the European powers, in the process of losing her empire. Her returning soldiers, determined to overturn the old order, which they blamed for their troubles, voted in vast numbers for the Labour government and nationalisation of major industries, the implementation of our National Health Service and a whole programme of reform which it would take Margaret Thatcher to dismantle some thirty years later. We could not afford immediate rebuilding and so London remained in ruins far longer than Germany, by then benefitting from the Marshall Plan.

When I was fifteen I left school, determined to become a journalist (I had not yet set my sights on being a novelist) and worked for a shipping company in the city. From there I would go down to the countless miles of docks, filled with ships, with loading cranes and warehouses for as far as the eye could see. My way back would take me through a devastated landscape only slowly recovering from the intensity of the Blitz. I could walk from the river into the depths of the city using as my points of reference the same buildings used by my eighteenth-century ancestors. It was possible to stand outside the old Billingsgate fish market, whose porters carried up to fifteen baskets of fish on their heads and were famous for their foul language, and look over to the Custom House. As you climbed the hill up towards St Paul's, you could see the Royal Mint, the Monument (to the Great Fire of London) and all the other buildings which had miraculously survived the Blitz while more recent structures, from the nineteenth century, had been totally blasted into rubble. On the artificial hills, like Celtic burial mounds, grew rosebay willowherb, imported from the slopes of Vesuvius by nineteenth-century botanists, escaped from Oxford nurseries and now growing wherever there was the ash it loved.

You can still see it, blossoming beside the railway tracks which originally carried it from Oxford to London.

You didn't need to make an effort of the imagination to feel the psychogeography of the place. I have often wondered if the Frenchman who created psychogeography and the wonderful philosophy of *dérive*, Guy Debord, had witnessed what I had witnessed in London. The very bones of the city, all her history, from Roman times to the present, were exposed and clearly visible. Here was Defoe's city and Johnson's city and Smollett's city, while the city of Dickens, who had turned London into a character, a monstrous entity, was in ruins. Where great warehouses had loomed over black water, now there were green hillocks where, at weekends, Londoners enjoyed their picnics. Where diseased warrens of slums had existed, an indictment to all civilised beings, Hitler's incendiaries had allowed the new socialist government to build attractive estates, designed by idealistic architects, not all of whom, as they later admitted, were misguided followers of Le Corbusier. Some built curving terraces, echoing the half-timbered lines of Tudor streets though without the chichi ersatz nostalgia which had characterised South London. Others erected monuments to the people, intended to bring sunlight and sanitation to all.

Even at their most brutal, the new estates were an improvement on the rat-runs thrown up in the nineteenth century to house the wage slaves servicing Britain's imperial commerce. And in those noirish times, when every young man desired nothing much more than a trenchcoat and a battered fedora, when Graham Greene, John Lodwick and the bittersweet romantics of the London literary scene came into their own. They were hard times. Poor times. It always seemed to be raining. Even in the Ealing comedies you felt that the rain had only stopped for about ninety minutes and would continue again the moment *Hue and Cry* and *Passport to Pimlico* began to roll their credits. Disenchanted men, old before their time, smoked moody cigarettes and lounged unhappily on the Thames embankment, brooding on lost love and forgotten ideals. Colour seemed almost obscene, an outrage. The late '40s and the '50s were black-and-white years of *Odd Man*

Out and *It Always Rains on Sunday*. All my girlfriends wore black and thought a lot about suicide. The novelists and playwrights, the so-called Angry Young Men, people like Kingsley Amis and John Osborne, expressed themselves with bitter laughter. They were still old enough to have swallowed the imperial myth which had betrayed them. By my generation, we had never accepted such myths in the first place and had no particular argument with our fathers, no inclination to shake our fists and yell 'Damn you, England!'. And the poets – Betjeman, Larkin and the rest – wallowed in nostalgia, in melancholy, equally disenchanted, seeking the certainties of their boyhood. Larkin in particular could not bear the idea of being rescued from the black-and-white world and when it threatened to explode into colour, as it did in the '60s, going from monochrome to Technicolor like Dorothy's transportation from Kansas to Oz, he resisted, he grumbled and he sought out the pockets of gloom which even today can be found in the remoter parts of the British provinces.

The Angries were probably not the only ones to yearn for the camaraderie of hopelessness. Many missed the years of anxiety and austerity. For my own part I was delighted to escape the grey years, when one's only choice of trousers was grey flannel or green corduroy. I embraced the '60s. From 1963 to 1976 was my (rough) decade. I knew we had discovered ourselves in a Golden Age and that it would not last. I became determined to enjoy that age while it did continue.

The metamorphosis of blitzed London became the Chaotic landscapes of Elric the Albino. As in need of his soul-drinking sword as Chet Baker was in need of his junk, he witnessed the death of his empire, even conspired in it. The adrenaline rushes of aerial bombardment and imminent death informed the Jerry Cornelius stories where London's ruins were re-created and disaster had a celebratory face. And the Holocaust became the background for the black comedies of my Colonel Pyat books. We tried to create a new literature which expressed our own experience – Ballard of his years in the Japanese civilian camp, Aldiss of the terrors of being a boy-soldier in Malaya – all the great writers who contributed to my journal NEW WORLDS were rejecting modernism not from any academic attempt to discover novelty but in order to find forms which actually described what they had witnessed, what they had felt. By 1945, Proust and Joyce and even Eliot felt as if they belonged to the nineteenth century, even if they were indeed that century's greatest products. By 1945, we knew what had happened in Auschwitz and Dachau. We did not mourn the passing of liberal humanism or indeed of our humanity. We sought new ways of expressing them. We found humour in the H-Bomb, we made jokes about Vietnam, we sought our models not in the great moderns like Mann or Faulkner, but in earlier centuries, in the work of Grimmelshausen, Smollett, even Balzac. I myself unearthed a hero in George Meredith, marginalised by the modernist literary critics because he looked back to the eighteenth century for his models and in so doing spoke to those of us who found ourselves at last in the twenty-first.

All this experience, all this fiction, all this philosophy had its origins in what for me were the Blitz years, my years of childhood, when I was as unaware of any impending doom as a newborn lamb in a field knows nothing of the slaughterhouse. Circumstances made me something of an autodidact, unable to settle at any school for very long, expelled from a couple. The schools were always glad to see me go. I learned from reading and not knowing what was respectable literature and what was not. I read everything. I became an enthusiast for the blues, in common with many of my generation, and learned some of Woody Guthrie's licks from Jack Elliott. I met Big Bill Broonzy and Muddy Waters and Howlin' Wolf. Their music was the music of hard times and though I don't pretend a white Londoner shared the same experience as that of a black Clarksdale sharecropper, that music did find an echo in my soul so that I was also privileged to enjoy the enthusiasms and pleasures of rock and roll from its earliest years. I am decidedly a child of my times. And I did inherit some enthusiasms from my father, though we saw so little of each other. It was my father, after all, who left behind the Edgar Rice Burroughs and George Bernard Shaw books, which were amongst the first I read. And he left some jazz records which ultimately led me to the blues. He then did me a great favour by leaving me to the love of my egalitarian mother and the man who fell in love with her (though I suspect never shared her bed) whose name was Jellinek.

Ernst Jellinek had helped Jews escape from Germany and Austria, going in and out of those countries to save as many as he could. Two of my friends, she a Jewish poet, he a Jamaican sculptor, had been trapped in France when the Germans arrived and, I learned from them, it had been the man who had become my unofficial guardian, Ernst Jellinek, who had helped them get across the Pyrenees and from there eventually into Portugal and back to England. If my father had been faithful, I would never have had such a model of quiet, philosophical heroism as Ernst Jellinek. I would never have understood that there is nothing wrong with sticking to one's ideals, to following one's altruistic instincts while remaining, in his case, a practical businessman. I have never ceased to be grateful to my father for finding love outside the home...

I don't remember my parents ever quarrelling, though I think I remember a few intense, whispered exchanges. One day when I opened the newspaper I found a piece cut out of it. I believe my mother must have done that. Probably a report of the separation proceedings. People avoided divorce in those days, because it was so hard to obtain.

When I was eighteen, my father came to see me on my birthday, as usual. He gave me an LP record of T-Bone Walker and we went out for a Christmas drink. Back in his car, he cleared his throat with some embarrassment and told me that he had taken out an endowment policy for me, to help with my education or perhaps marriage when I was twenty-one. I told him that I was earning good money (I was already a successful journalist) and to keep it for himself. Without another word, that's exactly what he did. My own children's birthdays he was always a bit hazy about and it never occurred to him to transfer the policy for their benefit. He remained an emotionally lazy, rather likeable man, who tended to change jobs whenever he was promoted to management, because he could not take the responsibility. But he was an obsessive record-keeper.

My father and mother never divorced. It would have involved too much trauma in those days. My father set up home with his mistress and in time she changed her name to his by deed poll. Many years later, when both were in their seventies, my father decided to apply for a divorce. He was afraid of my mother. The first I heard of it was when my mother phoned me, sobbing, to ask if I had spoken to my father recently. Although I saw more of him than she knew, I had not, as it happened, seen him for a while.

'What's the trouble, Mum?'

'He wants a divorce,' she said. 'I got the papers from his solicitor this morning. Why would he want a divorce after all this time?'

Not long afterwards came the expected call from my father. 'Um – does your mother live in Gratwicke Road?'

He had discovered what I had known for over a decade, that by chance they were living about a quarter of a mile apart in the same seaside town of Worthing. I had often wondered what would happen if they met. His solicitor, it emerged, was at the bottom of her road. And he was terrified.

They were both so emotionally overwrought by this event that I found myself acting as the mediator in my own elderly parents' divorce, calming both of them down, assuring that neither had sinister or greedy motives.

'If he thinks he's not going to give me that two pounds a week, he'll have to fight me for it,' she declared. She had settled, out of pride, for the minimum support which he had always sent late, but never missed a payment.

And so the knot was severed at last. This time I did not receive a visit to the toyshop, but he did offer to give me the family bible. I said that he should hang on to it. That I would have it when he died. I had it expensively rebound for him as a Christmas present.

As it happened, he gave the bible to my cousin, forgetting that he had promised it to me. When he died, I found photographs of all my family except my mother and myself and discovered that his father had remembered everyone in the neighbourhood in his will, but not me. I had been 'vanished'. My mother and I had been an embarrassment, evidence that he and his mistress had been living a lie. I also found every driving licence he had ever owned and, neatly stored in cardboard boxes, the stub of every postal order he had ever bought to send to the court for my mother's and my support. I also discovered that in his youth he had been a passable artist and while I had always assumed that I got my own taste for the arts from the Jewish side of the family, I also discovered, thanks to another friend, that my great-great-great-aunt Rachel Moorcock had been a passable poet who had published a book of memoirs and a book of poems in her lifetime.

Outside, the all-clear sirens begin to blast through the early-morning light. It's Christmas Day. I get up and find that my mother is already building a fire in the grate. She kisses me and wishes me a Merry Christmas. There are all my presents arranged around the bushy little tree with the candles burning on it.

'Which one shall I open first?' I ask her.

She smiles and shakes her head. 'You choose.'

I know what I want. The large box. I rip the paper off it and see the familiar maroon red beneath. Slowly I take the top from the box and stare down at the camouflage green of the long-barrelled anti-aircraft gun. I remove it from the box and begin to set it up, settling it on its stand. Soon it is pointing menacingly towards the ceiling.

Once again, Londoners will be able to rest easily in their beds tonight.

Maisie Bishop's Tic-Toc Club was in the basement of No. 21. Members included Dylan Thomas, Francis Bacon, Patrick Hamilton, Julian MacLaren-Ross, Henry Williamson and other literary luminaries of the 1940s and 1950s. The Colvin brothers (Jimmy and 'Wicksy') based their radio play *Nightmare Street* on the murder of Nigel Fox-Patterson, advertising manager of the *News Chronicle*. Fox-Patterson's body was found hanging from the area railings on 13 October, 1946. At first thought to be suicide, it soon became clear that his death was the result of foul play. Johnny Nicholson, bookmaker cousin to the notorious Walworth Nicholsons, was arrested when it was discovered that the deceased owed him a substantial sum of money. Gordon Amis, cousin of the more eminent Kingsley, was also detained and later released. After months of evidence-gathering, there was no prosecution. *Nightmare Street* remains a popular play on the repertory circuit, featuring, as it does, characters clearly based on contemporary originals. The BBC recorded a television version as a real-time experiment which was said to have influenced Hitchcock and inspired his film of Patrick Hamilton's *Rope*. See also: Dan Farson's *Hanging on Their Words* (1962) and J. Michael Harrison's *What Maisie Didn't Know* (1966).

GOLDEN PLACE, WC2

Best known for the 'Warrens' on its north side, Golden Place was notorious as a thieves' sanctuary, being technically Portuguese soil. A charter had been granted by Charles I to the Contessa d'Ecreta, an adventuress associated with *L'École des Fleures*, a secret society pursuing alchemical experiment and the search for the Emerald Stone – itself said to be a form taken by the Holy Grail (otherwise documented as the 'Roone Staffe'). Originally the haunt of quacks and 'hereticks', Golden Place degenerated into a haven for criminals. It was returned to England by the Portuguese government in 1934. The Warrens endured as a slum of evil reputation while various government agencies debated jurisdiction and responsibility. Much of the area was flattened by German incendiary bombs in 1941. The offices of the Inland Security Services (IS4) now occupy the site.

THE VENUE UNDERGROUND, LITTLE MONMOUTH STREET, WC1

Originally (1954) opened as the Jazz Cellar. In the early 1960s it changed its name to The Cellar and later to The Basement. It was where The Beatles first performed in London, but was better known for its association with the Rolling Stones and The Who. The Basement was most famous for R&B combos such as Zoot Money's Big Roll Band, Geno Washington's Ram Jam Band, Long John Baldry's Hoochie Coochie Men, Georgie Fame and the Blue Flames. Among notable early performers were the Small Faces, who would become The Faces – with Rod Stewart as their lead singer. Others associated with The Basement/the Venue Underground were Alex Harvey, Chris Farlowe, Bill 'Loud Mouth' Bailey and Robert Calvert. The Deep Fix were resident there until 1977, when the Venue decided to feature nothing but punk bands such as The Adverts, Siouxsie and the Banshees, and Needle. It is now chiefly associated with rap and hip-hop.

A Winter Admiral

AFTER LUNCH SHE woke up, thinking the rustling from the pantry must be a foraging mouse brought out of hibernation by the unusual warmth. She smiled. She never minded a mouse or two for company and she had secured anything she would not want them to touch.

No, she really didn't mind the mice at all. Their forebears had been in these parts longer than hers and had quite as much right to the territory. More of them, after all, had bled and died for home and hearth. They had earned their tranquillity. Her London cats were perfectly happy to enjoy a life of peaceful coexistence.

'We're a family.' She yawned and stretched. 'We probably smell pretty much the same by now.' She took up the brass poker and opened the firedoor of the stove. 'One big happy family, us and the mice and the spiders.'

After a few moments the noise from the pantry stopped. She was surprised it did not resume. She poked down the burning logs, added two more from her little pile, closed the door and adjusted the vents. That would keep in nicely.

As she leaned back in her chair she heard the sound again. She got up slowly to lift the latch and peer in. Through the outside pantry window, sunlight laced the bars of dust and brightened her shelves. She looked on the floor for droppings. Amongst her cat-litter bags, her indoor gardening tools, her electrical bits and pieces, there was nothing eaten and no sign of a mouse.

Today it was even warm in the pantry. She checked a couple of jars of pickles. It didn't do for them to heat up. They seemed all right. This particular pantry had mostly canned things. She only ever needed to shop once a week.

She closed the door again. She was vaguely ill at ease. She hated anything odd going on in her house. Sometimes she lost perspective. The best way to get rid of the feeling was to take a walk. Since the sun was so bright today, she would put on her coat and stroll up the lane for a bit.

It was one of those pleasant February days which deceives you into believing spring has arrived. *A cruel promise, really*, she thought. This weather would be gone soon enough. *Make the best of it*, she said to herself. She would leave the radio playing, put a light on in case it grew dark before she was back, and promise herself *The Charlie Chester Show*, a cup of tea and a scone when she got home. She lifted the heavy iron kettle, another part of her inheritance, and put it on the hob. She set her big, brown teapot on the brass trivet.

The scent of lavender struck her as she opened her coat cupboard. She had just re-lined the shelves and drawers. Lavender reminded her of her first childhood home.

'We're a long way from Mitcham now,' she told the cats as she took her tweed overcoat off the hanger. Her Aunt Becky had lived here until her last months in the nursing home. Becky had inherited Crow Cottage from the famous Great Aunt Begg. As far as Marjorie Begg could tell, the place had been inhabited by generations of retired single ladies, almost in trust, for centuries.

Mrs Begg would leave Crow Cottage to her own niece, Clare, who looked after Jessie, her half-sister. A chronic invalid, Jessie must soon die, she was so full of rancour.

A story in a Cotswold book said this had once been known as Crone's Cottage. She was amused by the idea of ending her days as the local crone. She would have to learn to cackle. The crone was a recognised figure in any English rural community, after all. She wondered if it were merely coincidence that made Rab, the village idiot, her handyman. He worshipped her. She would do anything for him. He was like a bewildered child since his wife had thrown him out: she could make more in benefits than he made in wages. He had seemed reconciled to the injustice: 'I was never much of an earner.' That apologetic grin was his response to most disappointment. It probably hadn't been fitting for a village idiot to be married, any more than a crone. Yet who had washed and embroidered the idiot's smocks in the old days?

She had been told Rab had lost his digs and was living wild in Wilson's abandoned farm buildings on the other side of the wood.

Before she opened her front door she thought she heard the rustling again. The sound was familiar, but not mice. Some folded cellophane unravelling as the cupboard warmed up? The cottage had never been cosier.

She closed the door behind her, walking up the stone path under her brown tangle of honeysuckle and through the gate to the rough farm lane. Between the tall, woven hedges she kept out of the shade as much as she could. She relished the air, the winter scents, the busy finches, sparrows, tits and yellow-hammers. A chattering robin objected to her passing and a couple of wrens fussed at her. She clicked her tongue, imitating their angry little voices. The broad meadows lay across the brow of the hills like shawls, their dark brown furrows laced with melting frost, bright as crystal. Birds flocked everywhere, to celebrate this unexpected ease in the winter's grey.

Her favourites were the crows and magpies. Such old, alien birds. So wise. Closer to the dinosaurs and inheriting an unfathomable memory. Was that why people took against them? She had learned early that intelligence was no better admired in a bird than in a woman. The thought of her father made her shudder, even out here on this wide, unthreatening Cotswold hillside, and she felt suddenly lost, helpless, the cottage no longer her home. Even the steeple on the village church, rising beyond the elms, seemed completely inaccessible. She hated the fear more than she hated the man who had infected her with it – as thoroughly as if he had infected her with a disease. She blamed herself. What good was hatred? He had died wretchedly, of exposure, in Hammersmith, between his pub and his flat, a few hundred yards away.

Crow Cottage, with its slender evergreens and lattice of willow boughs, was as safe and welcoming as always when she turned back into her lane. As the sun fell it was growing colder, but she paused for a moment. The cottage, with its thatch and its chimney, its walls and its hedges, was a picture. She loved it. It welcomed her, even now, with so little colour in the garden.

She returned slowly, enjoying the day, and stepped back over her hearth, into her dream of security, her stove and her cats and her rattling kettle. She was in good time for *Sing Something Simple* and would be eating her scones by the time Charlie Chester came on. She had never felt the need for a television here, though she had been a slave to it in Streatham. Jack had liked his sport.

He had been doing his pools when he died.

When she came back to the flat that night, Jack was in the hall, stretched out with his head on his arm. She knew he was dead, but she gave him what she hoped was the kiss of life, repeatedly blowing her warm breath through his cold lips until she got up to phone for the ambulance. She kept kissing him, kept pouring her breath into him, but was weeping almost uncontrollably when they arrived.

He wouldn't have known anything, love, they consoled her.

No consolation at all to Jack! He had hated not knowing things. She had never anticipated the anguish that came with the loss of him, which had lasted until she moved to Crow Cottage. She had written to Clare. By some miracle, the cottage had cured her of her painful grief and brought unexpected reconciliation.

It was almost dark.

Against the sprawling black branches of the old elms, the starlings curled in ranks towards the horizon, while out of sight in the tall wood the crows began to call, bird to bird, family to family. The setting sun had given the few clouds a powdering of terracotta and the air was suddenly a Mediterranean blue behind them. Everything was so vivid and hurrying so fast, as if to greet the end of the world.

She went to draw the back curtains and saw the sunset over the flooded fields fifteen miles away, spreading its bloody light into the water. She almost gasped at the sudden beauty of it.

Then she heard the rustling again. Before the light failed altogether, she was determined to discover the cause. It would be awful to start getting fancies after dark.

As she unlatched the pantry door something rose from the floor and settled against the window. She shivered, but did not retreat.

She looked carefully. Then, to her surprise: 'Oh, it's a butterfly!'

The butterfly began to beat again upon the window. She reached to cup it in her hands, to calm it. 'Poor thing.'

It was a newborn Red Admiral, its orange, red and black markings vibrant as summer. 'Poor thing.' It had no others of its kind.

For a few seconds the butterfly continued to flutter, and then was still. She widened her hands to look in. She watched its perfect, questing antennae, its extraordinary legs, she could almost smell it. *A small miracle*, she thought, *to make a glorious day complete.*

An unexpected sadness filled her as she stared at the butterfly. She carried it to the door, pushed the latch with her cupped hands, and walked into the twilight. When she reached the gate she opened her hands again, gently, to relish the vivacious delicacy of the creature. Mrs Begg sighed, and with a sudden, graceful movement lifted her open palms to let the Admiral taste the air.

In two or three wingbeats the butterfly was up, a spot of busy, brilliant colour streaming towards the east and the cold horizon.

As it gained height, it veered, its wings courageous against the freshening wind.

Shielding her eyes, Mrs Begg watched the Admiral turn and fly over the thatch, to be absorbed in the setting sun.

It was far too cold now to be standing there. She went inside and shut the door. The cats still slept in front of the stove. With the pot holder she picked up the kettle, pouring lively water over the tea. Then she went to close her pantry door.

'I really couldn't bear it,' she said. 'I couldn't bear to watch it die.'

The Third Jungle Book

O N THE DEATH of his friend Baloo, the last of his old jungle companions (who thought him immortal), Mowgli emigrated to London and took his bar exams. Thanks to a distinguished legal career representing the public interest, he was now Sir Sanjit J. Rey, respected Independent Member of Parliament for Southall South, in London. His children had grown and were now doing well in America and Australia. Occasionally, however, he grew tired of civilised life and longed for the companions he had known as a boy in his highland Indian forest.

'It is a sad day,' he said to himself, 'when the last of one's old family and friends is gone to the great Tree Above and a little frog, however happily married, is left with no-one who shares and understands his experience. O, Mother Wolf, O, Father Wolf, O, Akela, O, Baloo, O, Bagheera, how I miss thee, my mother, my father, my chief and my brothers. How I mourn for thee and long for the silence and the voices, the companionship of the forest!' Whereupon, he would lift his noble head and utter a low, pathetic howl of a kind which once issued from Sister Wolf who had died so unhappily in Regent's Park Zoological Gardens many, many years before when he had lacked the influence to have her freed from captivity.

At last came the moment of decision. Sir Sanjit divested himself of his pyjamas while his wife slept and, clad only in his underpants, crept from his window high above the traffic to run swiftly over the West London rooftops, where he eventually met a family of foxes whose yapping, panting language was easily learned, since it was cousin to that of the wolves who had first been his friends and relatives. His scent, moreover, was reassuring to them and soon he was speaking of Akela, the great pack leader, of Mother Wolf, who had known his potential as a killer of Shere Khan, the tiger; he spoke of Kaa, the python and all the others who had taught him how to survive and triumph, and told tales of the faraway jungle which somehow reminded the foxes of their own home amongst the alleys, rooftops and underground places of London.

Recognising Mowgli's sorrow, a young matron known as Makaba, with beautiful, unusually lustrous red hair, found herself comforting him. She had seen her first cubs emigrate up the Central Line of the Underground to seek their fortunes in the wealthy suburbs of Notting Hill and Bayswater, home to both Holland and Hyde Parks. Her mate had been killed a year earlier while crossing the M4 motorway to investigate a newly opened curry restaurant.

'O, beloved Mowgli,' she said. 'How I have longed to know the mind of the Big Frogs who dwell in this city. Why, for instance, do they appear to tolerate, even welcome, our presence amongst them when their brethren of the country live only to hunt and to kill us?'

Sir Sanjit thought the folk of the country might be less civilised and so have much less to occupy their minds than the city dwellers. 'But it could also be something to do with the keeping of domestic fowl which is more commonly practised in rural areas.' In the city the myth that foxes, who habitually avoided conflict with cats and dogs, caught and ate household animals had long since been contradicted by experience. 'And, though sometimes given to phases of mysterious xenophobia, city people are generally far better at absorbing new experience.' Moreover, he thought, there was a greater tolerance, an attitude of live and let live, in the city, where a more varied collection of human beings rubbed shoulders. And, finally, you could add to that the fact that the people of the city were rather proud of their foxes, which helped, among other things, to keep the city clean and free of vermin. Because foxes hunted at night, they were generally only visible during the day when sunning themselves on roofs or educating their children.

All this made considerable sense to Makaba, who was satisfied by Mowgli's answers and next asked him to tell tales of the Indian jungle, most of which can already be found in the accounts of Mr Rudyard Kipling known as *The Jungle Book* and *The Second Jungle Book*. Makaba and her people, of course, had not encountered these stories, since they did not read the 'little bugs' as they called the printed word, and had eyes which found it hard to focus on the TV screens which occasionally showed a rather stylised and senti-mental account of Mowgli's adventures. Nor did the mumbling language of the Big Frogs mean much to them. They were eager to hear Mowgli's many explanations and interpretations. In return they told him what they knew of the nocturnal goings-on in his own and neighbouring constituencies. They knew which Big Frogs seemed in need, which falsified their need, who seemed to be stealing and so on. They knew who was abusing domestic ani-mals or, indeed, hurting their own kind. By and by Mowgli built up a picture of his part of the city which, though unusual in its perspectives, was second to none. This proved very useful to Sir Sanjit in Parliament when certain issues were debated.

For the next few years, Mowgli nocturnally ranged the jungle which was the city he had made his own. Occasionally he was glimpsed by his fellow Big Frogs and became part of London's rich mythology. As well as the foxes, with whom he enjoyed the old, familiar communion of the pack, he came to know the wily cats, some of whom were of a size almost that of a small tiger, and who remained hidden during the day. Again, their language was not difficult for him to learn and they, too, told him much he would never otherwise have known, as did the feral and the domestic dogs. He even learned the simple speech of owls and night-hawks until he became as familiar and comfortable with this habitat as he had been with that Indian forest of his childhood, now a fond memory, for in common with many humans raised in the wild, Mowgli enjoyed extraordinary longevity.

Sir Sanjit meanwhile developed a very special friendship with a man whose father, an aristocrat, had given up his famous title and passed it on to him. This son spent at least part of his time on his northern English estates and often took his seat in Parliament. It was there the two had met. They had much in common, including a wish to protect the wild Waziran forest gorillas of Africa and look after the fate of wildlife in general. Sir Sanjit and the English lord also worked on health issues affecting the poorer continents. When the son and father had grown apart in the 1950s and '60s, Sir Sanjit had been instrumental in bringing the two men together until in the 1990s they had again become reconciled. The families became firm friends, taking holidays together and spending time as one another's guests in Africa and India.

The politics of the United Kingdom being what they were, a law to ban hunting with dogs was at last established, thanks in good part to the work done by Rey and his friend in the House of Lords. The urban foxes were highly relieved that their country cousins would no longer be subjected to being pursued over hill and dale by the 'unspeakable in pursuit of the uneatable', by packs of howling men and women mounted on galloping horses and accompanied by hunger-crazed dogs. But no sooner had this law been passed than another began to be mooted in the House.

Known as the Urban Vermin (Culling) Bill, it was put before Parliament by William Bale, MP, Conservative for Berking Maddely in the county of Gloucestershire in vengeful response, many on the left believed, to the success of the 'townies' who knew, he claimed, nothing of the real countryside and were merely bent on curtailing the pleasures of honest rural folk. That many honest rural folk were as disgusted by the hunts which flew willy-nilly across their lands and property, doing untold damage, followed by their supporters in massive vehicles which created further chaos, appeared to be missed by the hunters, no matter how many farmers attempted to block their paths, arguing that their livings were threatened far more by rampaging packs of dogs and riders than any number of hen-coop-raiding foxes. Not that the urban foxes approved of fowl-stealing. They had long since learned to enjoy their food well cooked, in Southall South and its surrounding locales. They were inclined to take their chicken Tandoori rather than raw.

The Bill began to gather momentum across party lines when the London *Daily Mail* determined that its falling readership could be stimulated by supporting Mr Bale's entirely apocryphal stories of city foxes carrying off infants, feasting on cats and smaller dog breeds and generally behaving like packs of, as an editorial put it, 'canine Huns'. When a woman in Hackney was found to swear that her husband, returning intoxicated from the Hoop and Hooligan, had woken in the gutter to find his hand being gnawed by two monstrous red foxes, even *The Times*, at the instigation of Rupert Murdoch, its proprietor, felt obliged to carry several features asking if the 'fox epidemic' was threatening the health and welfare of citizens everywhere.

A Birmingham man claimed that his wife had been set upon by mad foxes and run in terror to the canal, where she had drowned. Another in Manchester told of walking home with his Indian takeaway in a carrier bag, only to have the food snatched from him by what he called 'an organised pack' of ten or a dozen 'gigantic foxes'. Some youths in Lewisham told how they were attacked by rabid foxes 'foaming at the mouth', though no case of rabies had been recorded in England for the past several years. Another story linked the taste of foxes for geese, ducks, chickens and other farmyard fowl with the possibility of their spreading some form of avian influenza, now being called 'Mad Parrot Disease' by the tabloids.

Needless to say all these stories were proven false by investigators, but they swiftly entered the mythology of public life. As every journalist knows, truth is never really the issue in the public mind. The dominant story is what concerns readers of tabloids and broadsheets alike, and anything which contradicts it, no matter how convincing the evidence, merely becomes a marginalised alternative.

Thus it was that the urban foxes, who had enjoyed so much approval from the average city dweller, now suddenly found themselves likened to the wolves which had allegedly pursued troikas in Old Russia or the dingoes said to have carried off children in the Australian outback. No longer was 'cunning Reynard' an affectionate term, nor was 'Old Rufus' playing a useful rôle in the urban ecology. Opinions would change, of course, as they always did, but in the media-engendered hysteria of the moment foxes had become 'a pressing problem' and a 'social menace'.

All the outrage and fear which the tabloid press had once turned on asylum-seeking immigrants and those looking for work from the old English colonies became focused on the foxes. The voices of liberalism and reason were drowned by the tabloid shout. Fox News even considered changing its name for the UK market where, anyway, it was better known as 'Sky News'. Murdoch had rather enjoyed the soubriquet of 'The Sky Fox' until now.

Not that the immigrants and Commonwealth citizens were unhappy with this turn of events, which led them, sad to say, to join in the general outcry against Makaba and her relations, just as Jews had been happy to condemn Jamaican and Indian newcomers to the British Isles in the 1950s and Pakistanis claimed that Poles were threatening their jobs. There seems to be no end to the human capacity for prejudice, however temporary, especially where it helps avoid any self-blame and allows them to feel that they are siding with the majority. Indeed, some people who might otherwise have been expected to speak up for the vulpine cause were so glad to see different groups of human beings joining ranks against a common non-human enemy that they were either silent or echoed the general condemnation.

Sir Sanjit and his cousins of the urban jungle viewed all these developments with considerable trepidation. Had it not been for Mowgli's eloquence in Parliament and the Press, together with the humanity of some of his political colleagues of all political stripes, we might even have witnessed parties of anti-vulpine vigilantes prowling the streets with nets and other implements, though not, happily, with shotguns or any firearms, these still being illegal in the hands of private citizens. Nonetheless, it seemed touch and go when Bale and his fellow 'cullers' suggested arming the bobby on the beat with dart guns and Tasers designed to stun all large urban vermin. Luckily Sir Sanjit's friend Anthony Wellington (Labour, Fulham W) pointed out that people were as likely to find their dogs victims of the puffing policemen as any fox, and the idea was dropped.

The Bill itself was not. While no-one accepted Percy Effingham-Harde's suggestion that 'experienced country people' be bused into town and given sturdy 'hunting bicycles' to pursue the foxes with the packs of no-longer-employed hounds, it was becoming increasingly likely that innocent foxes actually spotted during the day when lying out on roofs and patches of waste ground or, indeed, enjoying the security of whatever dens they had made for themselves, were likely to be attacked by members of a specially formed Animal Security Service, whose job would be to kill them, in whatever way was most practical. The old, amiable balance between Fox and Man seemed about to come to an end.

Makaba foresaw the necessity of returning to the country where, because they would so swell the ranks of rural foxes, they would suffer as badly from being shot, poisoned or trapped. There seemed no hope for any of the packs who had so recently been the pride of their adopted boroughs and suburbs.

'O, Mowgli, dear cousin,' said Makaba, at the great gathering of foxpacks which she and he had called in Holland Park after closing hours (and which itself was nowadays much riskier than it had been), 'it seems we are fated never to be at peace, thy tribe and mine. Is there anything which can be done to return us to the condition of mutual respect we shared until recently?'

'Honoured Mother of Many,' replied Mowgli, 'know that I am doing everything I can in the councils of the Big Frogs to persuade them that their fears are without substance and their tales the mere baying of mad beasts, but that madness which was once confined to a few country dwellers is now bent on spreading itself to all the manpacks. Soon a vote will be taken amongst their representatives and the fate of my cousins will be sealed. I have to tell thee that this madness of theirs is running very high and though it must eventually subside and, given time, relations return to normal between thy folk and mine, there is every likelihood that it might meanwhile become a formula for attacking thee, who dwell in the deep valleys and high peaks of the city, and have done nothing but good for the manpacks.'

'Has your voice no weight in these councils, O, Mowgli?' asked grey-muzzled Woova, sent from across the Great River from far Norbury. 'Have you not told thy fellows that we mean them no harm and do them no harm?'

'Many times have I told them this, Brother Woova, but I fear they have become hysterical, thanks to the yapping and shrilling of their talking papers and pictures. I know that by and by I would be able to persuade them of the truth, but there is no time. They are infected as some are infected by the movements of the moon. When that madness dies out, the evil will have been done.'

Therefore by and by the fox-leaders returned to their respective packs to report this terrible news, while Mowgli continued his work on their behalf. He knew that even if a majority of his fellow parliamentarians passed the Bill, as they might in their wish to placate the yellow press and ensure their re-election, the House of Lords would not be so ready to validate it. It only needed a majority of one against the Bill for it to be put back to a later session or probably killed for ever, when the hysteria would have died and the whole matter have been forgotten, replaced by some other equally fashionable and empty cause. The Lords, however, were themselves being accused of ruralophobia. Many hereditary peers were also being 'culled' by New Labour's war against tradition, which aimed to replace peers with 'senators'. They wondered if it would not be better to pass this Bill, sacrificing the foxes for what many believed were more important issues. When Bale was supported by Baron Wessex and Lady Hatchet and their various followers, things looked decidedly black for the urban foxes.

Sir Sanjit and his supporters urgently took a survey of the Upper House and to their horror it seemed that opinions, for an assortment of reasons, were pretty evenly divided. If all those who were going to be sitting when the Bill came before the Lords voted as they said they would, the Bill would pass by two votes. Sir Sanjit then took Viscount Earlybird to lunch and persuaded him that his own estates would be flooded by returning foxes, but had a hard time convincing the noble lord to vote against the proposal. Only when Sir Sanjit pointed out that the urban foxes had become increasingly intelligent and would soon learn how to open up Earlybird's massive battery-chicken hutches and make meals of such easy prey did the peer, who had been elevated for his services to British chain-groceries, agree to vote against the Bill.

Now, it seemed, the vote would reach stalemate, for several peers had either absented themselves deliberately or would be away for other reasons. The friend who might have swung the Lords to Sir Sanjit's point of view had disappeared into the deep African jungles and an e-mail, addressed to him in Wazira, had been read neither by him nor by his father. Sir Sanjit guessed that the two had gone together to the secret source of their wealth in the far mountains. This wealth had increasingly been turned to the good of the poorer African countries and was currently much needed.

'O, Mowgli,' said Makaba on hearing this news, 'while I have sympathy for the plight of the unfortunate African Big Frogs, what will become of my own folk if they are driven from their dens and forced to fend for themselves in the inhospitable wild? If only I could appear before thy Great Gathering and speak the truth, telling them how we mean our Big Frog cousins nothing but good! Canst thou not achieve this for me?'

'Aunt Makaba,' said Mowgli sadly, 'thy voice would not be heard for its wisdom, even if thou spoke words they would understand. They would marvel at the wonder of thy talent but hear nothing of thy logic. All, I fear, is lost, for it has become our Law that if a Bill is passed by the House of Commons and not actively dismissed by a majority in the House of Lords, then that Bill shall be instated.'

And so both Mowgli and his cousins became drowned in misery, facing the prospect of doom as, in Mowgli's old homeland, the inevitability of seasonal rain had been faced. The Bill would be the last one voted upon before the Lords broke for their Christmas recession. The night before this final debate, Mowgli could not bear to divest himself of his pyjamas and race across the rooftops to commune with his friends of the urban jungle, but instead went to bed with only a mug of cocoa for company, his wife being called away to visit a sick sister. Before she went, she tried to console him. 'This is only a storm in a teacup, dear husband. The Bill cannot be applied in any practical sense. Eventually they will forget about it and the foxes will be able to return to their city again.'

'Sadly,' he had replied, 'they are poorly adapted for rural life. Too many will suffer since winter is almost upon us. It will be an unhappy time for all concerned.'

With a tear in her eye, Lady Rey left to catch her train. She knew her husband spoke the truth, for she had learned to trust him on all such matters. She did not look forward to enjoying the Season of Good Will.

She was away for a week and during that time she had no opportunity to read the newspapers or watch the television. Her sister had forbidden both from her hospital room and her nurses and doctors were convinced that this action had seriously helped her recovery. When Lady Rey took the train back to Euston and from there to Southall South, her sister was sitting up in bed waiting to be returned to her own flat.

Of course, though she was pleased at her sister's recovery, it was with heavy heart that she got out of the taxi and wheeled her little suitcase up the path to her delightful detached residence. She had, after all, been told to expect the worst. The Urban Vermin (Culling) Bill would have gone through the House of Lords that very night, and she expected to find her husband in the depths of misery that he had been unable to help his many cousins. She was all the more concerned when she saw that he had left her a note on the hall table. He explained that he would not be back until after midnight and that she was to go to bed without him.

Lady Rey decided in this case that she would wait up for her husband, but it was not until three in the morning that she heard the noise of the dormer window opening and knew he was home.

She climbed the stairs, hoping that he had not been drinking or otherwise trying to drown his misery. The door of the attic room opened and he stood there in his underpants, his muscled, brown body almost as attractive as it had been on the day, so many years ago, when they were first married. She looked at his eyes. They were glistening. Had he been crying?

And then he jumped forward and picked her up. She felt the thrill she had always known at his embrace. There was still something of the wild about him. It was why she had never objected to these night-time adventures. But was he hiding his misery?

When he smiled, she knew that he was not. Had the impossible, after all, happened?

'The Bill?' she said. 'Didn't it get its final reading?'

'Oh, indeed, it did, my dear, dear Ayesha.'

'So somebody changed their mind?'

'They all voted exactly as they were expected to vote.'

'Mowgli, my darling, you must not keep me in suspense. What happened tonight?'

He threw up his handsome head and laughed, his hair falling straight as a wolf's mane behind him. 'My friend came back from Africa! Korak heard the news on the BBC World Service in New Tarzana. He checked my e-mail. He borrowed his father's aeroplane and flew as far as Nairobi. From Nairobi he got a jet directly to London. From London he took a taxi to the House of Lords and was just in time to vote against the Bill. It is over, Ayesha. The foxes are safe. All this nonsense will die down over the Christmas holidays, and Bale's party won't let him bring the Bill again.'

There was a sound from the room above. A window opened. A window shut. A movement on the stairs from the attic and the door opened for a second time. There, his blue eyes twinkling, also wearing nothing but a pair of underpants, his long hair tousled, his body tanned almost as brown as Mowgli's, stood Jack Clayton, Lord Greystoke, the son of Tarzan. He bowed with easy grace. 'Good evening. Lady Ayesha. What a pleasure to see you. I gather Mowgli has told you that we won?'

'Indeed he has. We must certainly celebrate, late as it is.' She returned to the stairs and went to make them all a cup of tea. 'Can I get you anything to eat?'

'Awfully kind of you, Ayesha,' he said, 'but I'm not hungry. However, if you have any Tandoori chicken in the refrigerator I have a friend who would love to help us celebrate. She does not as a rule drink tea.' Clayton sprang down the stairs after Lady Rey and opened the front door.

There on the step, her dark eyes shining, her pink tongue lolling with happiness, her greying red hair bristling from ears to brush, stood Makaba the vixen.

Unfortunately, Lady Rey did not understand the language of foxes or she would have heard Makaba say: 'Good evening to thee, cousin. I am so pleased we are able to meet at last. It seems the Big Frogs are not going to make war on us, after all. We have thy husband to thank for that.'

But Mowgli shook his head. 'Oh, no, indeed,' he said in English, 'it's Jack Clayton who saved the day.'

At which the English lord let out a sharp, self-deprecating yap of denial.

THE FRENCH BOOKSHOP, CHARING CROSS ROAD, WCI

Founded by Pierre Quirole in 1905, this small but well-stocked shop became, during the Second World War, the meeting place of various exiled French citizens, chiefly writers and journalists, including Georges Bataille, Jean-Luc Fromental, Louis Murail, Boris Vian – and, briefly, Françoise Stein. From this address was published the weekly journal *Refusé*. After the liberation the shop continued to flourish, thanks to the interest of English readers in certain aspects of continental writing. The business was taken over by Colletts and absorbed into their main shop in 1967, by which time few readers could be found for untranslated literature. Quirole himself had returned to France in 1925 and later emigrated to the US, where he was to die in the Chicago bombing, while observing a meeting of the German–American Bund (9 September, 1933).

London Blood

THERE ARE CERTAIN memories that never really reach your brain. They stay in your blood like a dormant virus. Then something triggers them and you don't remember the moment; instead, you relive every detail. It's the reliving, not the original experience, that your brain registers. I think this happens to you more as you get older. And you don't always welcome it, either, however ordinary. Last week I was just looking out of the window and suddenly I was back at Gloria's funeral, with all the family there and Mum still alive. It's when it stays on as a memory that it hurts. Nine of us survived childhood out of thirteen. Three boys and six girls. Little Jimmy, named after Dad, Freddy, Ellie, Sammy, Nora, Lilly, Nellie, me and Gloria. Everyone but Mum and Gloria is still with us. We're a bit too crotchety to travel much; but we stay in touch on the phone.

I had a flashback the other day of what we called Mum's grieving chair. It was a funny name for such a big, comfortable bit of furniture, but usually she only sat there when somebody had died. An old-fashioned Victorian easy with dark flower patterns and enclosing wings. You could divide a chair like that into flats, these days. Of course, there'd be nowhere to put it in a place this size. The chair survived the Blitz but not the '50s. Mum's buildings were knocked down as part of the Battersea project and we sold everything to a dealer. Ellie, who was staying at Mum's then, didn't want it. She was moving to Australia to live with her son.

Gloria died of cancer in Bournemouth within a year of her husband. It was a real shock. We'd never had anyone with cancer before. It was just before Mum moved to Lilly's, so it was probably the last time she used her chair.

We were all sorry Ellie missed the Coronation and the Festival of Britain. Mum visited the South Bank eventually, though she blamed it for knocking down her flats. She really enjoyed herself when she got there, especially at the funfair. Outside the Skylon she helped an old man. He'd collapsed with heatstroke and she looked after him till the St John's Ambulance Brigade turned up. She took care of everything. She did all the right things. They said she probably saved his life. We couldn't help feeling proud of her, even though we were a bit embarrassed by all the attention. And then, of course, it was too late to do anything else. We never did get to the Dome of Discovery.

Lilly's kids adored Mum. She was a perfect grandma. She couldn't have done better than Lilly who was married to a GP. They made her a lovely little flat of her own in their really posh old house looking out over the Common. But she still missed her chair.

It's one of my first memories, that chair. I couldn't have been more than six, 1924 at the latest, when our little Gus went down with TB. After Gus's final illness, when all the funeral arrangements had been made and the rest of the formalities were over, Mum sat in that chair for five days. Hardly spoke a word. Most of us were still at home. We knew what to expect. We were all old enough by then to look after ourselves.

Of course, she didn't sit for five days solid. She ate a bit and slept a bit and so on. She was very sweet to us when we had to speak. But distant. She sat there nights, too, with her favourite cat on her lap.

Tizer was a massive green-eyed African orange brindle Mr Simpson the missionary gave Mum when he had to go into Sunnydales. Tizer loved her as much as she loved him. He'd mope when she was away and he'd shake with a deep vibrant purr whenever she came back. He was the boss cat but he had a kind, dignified nature.

Half our cats were from other homes, not always with their owners' knowledge. Mum would send us out to find them; then she'd pick the best and make us put the others back. It was the only crime she'd condone. Of course, she didn't see it as crime. She knew she could look after cats better than anyone. She could double their life-spans. She understood them. Everything about them. She'd always talk to them in her ordinary voice and you had the feeling they answered back the same. She could tell you if a cat was going to get sick or leave or pine. And she wouldn't have it she was psychic.

Another ordinary memory. A family story, really. One frosty Boxing Day we were out on Tooting Common with Sammy's new roller skates and we found this skinny dog we took home. Mum was horrified. 'Look at his poor ribcage!' She offered him a huge plate of goose and chicken scraps. He wolfed them down, grinning and wagging and panting for more. So, while Tizer twitched his tail in outrage, she gave the dog seconds. Eventually the owner was found and arrived glad to see his dog again, if a bit glum.

Mum was relieved. He seemed a decent sort of bloke. The animal clearly liked him. 'He was so hungry when he got here.' Looking fondly down at the contented dog, Mum folded her arms in a gesture of self-satisfaction. Mum was tall, with a nose that could cut concrete, thick raven hair and blue X-ray eyes. People didn't often argue with her. 'He must have been lost for days. I bet you're glad to have him back. You keep him well. Greyhound, is he?'

'Yes,' the man replied sadly. 'He was due to run at Summerstown this afternoon. We rather fancied he'd win.'

Mum didn't say anything then but after she closed the door on him she said she thought it was wicked to starve animals for sport. Let the skinny little bugger have a good sleep instead. It was Christmas, wasn't it? Nobody should have to work over Christmas. She offered me a secret wink. God, I loved my mum.

She could pick horses, too, even though she had a feeling steeplechasing might be cruel. When she got the chance she'd have a couple of bob each way on the National and she'd always win. She'd never put too much on, and she never told Dad. I often took her bets to Mr Phelps in the greengrocers, there being no betting shops in those days. He was what they used to call a bookie's runner. But only a couple of bob. Always each way. She felt it would break her luck otherwise. Dad used to try to get her to pick a name off his card, but she wouldn't.

Mum's room was the long narrow one at the back. It was the noisiest but that didn't matter too much to her since she was going a bit deaf and she had the wireless by then. She'd made the room her own after Jim married. Nellie, Gloria and me all got her big bedroom to share. Me and Nellie were best friends. We loved it. But Gloria thought we were horrible tomboys and kept her little bed neatly to herself in the corner. Nellie got prissy like that. Lives in Hove. Won't relax and have a laugh. All health food and perms, these days. Disapproves when I have a gin.

People thought we were Irish because we had red hair and green eyes like Nellie or black hair and blue eyes, like me. They always described us as vivacious or full of life. They'd have called us slappers if we'd been ugly. But we were the famous Lee girls. We were never short of mashers. And Mum saw to it we didn't fall in love with anyone unsuitable. My first husband was a civil engineer. More engineer than civil, I must say. While I was entertaining the troops, he was entertaining the girls they'd left behind.

After our Gus died I was the youngest but one. I was born at Stone Cottages, Mitcham, when there was a village green and one pump, and the tram link with Streatham went across lavender fields. That was at the end of the first German war. But I was brought up in Tooting, which we thought of as proper South London. You could take the tram direct to Vauxhall.

Ours was a big flat. We had the first and second floors above a furniture showroom. Their warehouse was over in Figges Marsh, so most of the flat was never too noisy. We were at the pointed end of a parade of shops, handy for the market. Our building was wedge-shaped because it was on the corner where the trams turned down towards Mitcham Cricketers. 'The prow', Dad called it. 'Ahoy, ahoy, I'm captain of the clipper,' he'd sing when in a good mood. Then Mum would tell him off when he mumbled the rest of the words and he'd laugh that infectious, dirty laugh of his. He drew you in to stuff like that, even if you didn't like it much.

When I lay in bed I could see the spiderweb of tramlines

reflecting the light of the shops sparkling through our net curtains. I thought those lines were roads through fairyland. On the whole we weren't very imaginative as a family. Probably that's why almost everyone but me went into politics. I used to lie there, hearing Mum and Dad in hissing argument. I'd actually teach myself to go somewhere else – into a fantasy so vivid I almost remembered it as real. I kept it all to myself, even from Nellie. Dad would have laughed himself silly if he'd have guessed. Especially if he'd had a few of his 'noggins'.

Even early on Mum would sometimes lock Dad out until his pleading and oaths threatened to involve the neighbours. Then she'd let him back in on promises to stop drinking and playing the horses. He'd cheer up for a few days and stay around the house. 'Bai Jove, bai Jove,' he'd sing, 'Our Jimmy's a jolly old cove!' But sooner or later the kids would drive him out to the pub or the racecourse. He complained she didn't discipline us.

Mum kept us in order all right. I don't remember her ever raising her hand. And when she was grieving you didn't feel you had to behave any differently. You only heard her going to the lavatory or having a wash, but you were always aware of her, there in her room, sitting in her chair. Doing nothing but staring and thinking. I think it was her way of praying. And the respect we automatically gave her was our way of joining in.

She wasn't a religious woman. Though she'd been a suffragette her hero was still Lloyd George, whom she saw as the people's prime minister. She believed fiercely – and fierce was the word if she heard you putting down some underdog – in equality, liberty and all that other stuff. With a couple of exceptions, she bred a family of men and women who could stand rock-solid on their own feet and look anyone in the eye as an equal. But natural arguers. We had the lot, from Tories to Trots.

Tooting's changed since our day, naturally, because of the bombing. What you see now that isn't concrete is a collection of ancient and modern: the old blood-red brick of South London or that new hard-fired pale brick which they used so much in the '50s, when they thought it looked clean and contemporary. There's no warmth to it, except what you can write with a spray can. The people who painted messages on walls in my day were communists and fascists. This new stuff's prettier and wittier.

We're now in our nineties, except for Ellie and Nora who are 104 and 105 respectively. That's London blood for you. You can't find a gene pool like that any more. Antibiotics is what I blame. Wiping out the cheap and natural and replacing it with the pricey and artificial. You see it everywhere, don't you? The only time you looked for bottled water when I was a kid was when there was a cholera scare. And a scare was all it was.

I've had two penicillin shots in my life and benefited from both of them. And apart from the junior aspirin I take every day, that's all I've ever needed or wanted. I've got kids, grandkids and great-grandkids and we're all the same in the main: healthy as horses. Four of them are actors now, all doing well. Better than me. I still do some radio stuff and get good offers, and I'm in that new red-grapefruit commercial. Apart from the home help once a week I'm as completely self-sufficient as ever. At this rate our family will survive a nuclear holocaust. It's survived most other kinds.

Anyone the gypsies admired they'd say had gypsy blood. It was their way of praising you. My mother used to say that you had to give *yourself* deep roots. If you didn't know what your original roots were, if they were lost somehow, you made up a set of rules and a history to go with them. Find them in a book. A novel. Anything. The best you could be. The best your people could have been. People you admired. You invented your ancestors if you didn't have any. And those were the roots you kept alive and they kept you alive. It was nothing to do with staying in the same place, she said, though that helped. It was to do with being the same, whatever else changed. Listening to your blood, Mum called it. Being yourself and as good as you could be. It sounded like gypsy lore to us, so we took it seriously. You stuck to your word for your own sake, she said. You didn't let anyone tell your story for you. You trusted yourself because your private behaviour matched your public conversation. She told us never to lie knowingly, except sometimes to authority, and never to give too much away either. Sometimes a little white lie was all right because it wasn't so much the lie in that case as who you told it to.

By the time Jim came back from the War, Mum had four lots of money coming in. Jim's, Freddy's, Ellie's and Sammy's. Ellie was a book-keeper at the Home & Colonial. The boys went into the Civil Service and all did very well. The Depression was looming. They kept jobs that were certain and steady and unaffected by lay-offs and bankruptcies. They could give Mum money regularly. And she was still manageress at the Sunlight Laundry.

For a while she must have taken over Dad's money, too, when he earned at all. He was a master tailor, but he couldn't hold a job. She'd told him enough times about his drinking and gambling. You could say she waited until she was no longer in any way finan-cially dependent on him before exerting her power. The boys were leaving home, getting married, and she'd come to rely on them. She was probably a bit scared of what might happen. Though my brothers all worshipped her, they knew she wouldn't have wanted them to stay. They had their own lives.

She worked late on Mondays and sometimes Fridays to pay for her pleasures. She liked the pictures but would never go in seats any more expensive than the one-and-threes. She also went to the music hall once a month, in the evening. She complained about the new acts but loved Max Miller, of all people. She thought it was narrow-minded of the BBC to keep banning him. She'd always insisted on her nights out. Which meant sometimes only Dad was home when we got back from school.

Dad said I was his favourite, and I think it was true. I couldn't easily resist his crooked charm any more than Mum had been able to. He could make me squirm, half embarrassed, half delighted. Like her I was a bit unsure of him. There was some-thing aggressive and needy under the jokes. He said I was the only one who understood him. I knew he wasn't really misunderstood. I'd noticed the difference between him and ordinary people. And when he was away life became more secure, more predictable. The house cheered up quietly.

Mum never seemed to miss him. To be honest, I missed his

attention, the flattery. I knew he was a drunkard, a gambler and a con man, and nasty sometimes, too. As Mum grimly said to me around the time Gloria died, it wasn't his charm that gave her thirteen kids.

When they were courting, my dad promised her the earth. Jimmy Lee was considered a catch. He was finishing his tailoring apprenticeship. Nothing safer than the rag trade, he said. He'd told her he was well connected. Marks & Spencer's, I think. Of course, all he was really attached to was the track and the saloon bar.

Dad had inherited half a gents' outfitters in Streatham Hill. The family he sold it to kept the name. You could see it for years. *Lee and Green, Bespoke Tailor*. Green was his cousin who went to America. My brother Jimmy, who wound up in the Foreign Office, met him out there.

Mum saved what she could from the sale. She had three boys to educate into good jobs and six girls who had to be properly schooled so as to be married to professional men. That was six weddings just there. And six dowries. She hid the money from Dad, of course. He never knew, as he worried how to pay his bookie, that he was sleeping over a chest of sovereigns.

There's a story how later, when Dad had gone and Nellie was thinking of getting married, there was some dispute between the families. Someone had suggested Nellie was marrying for money. Mum dragged her box out and showed it to the intended in-laws to prove we weren't poor just because we didn't live in a road with trees. 'That's my Jewish side,' she said. 'Romany, too, I suppose.'

Mum had an insurance policy to pay for her funeral, small endowments for us when we were twenty-one, but nothing else. She nurtured a deep suspicion of 'paper promises'. She and her family had been through what they called the Great Depression which had lasted well into the 1890s. When she'd met my dad she was reluctantly going into service.

She was too much of an egalitarian to show respect for author-ity just for the sake of it, and she defied respectability, too. From the first year she was married, she regularly took the tram up to the Corinthians in New Jewry. Mostly to see Marie Lloyd, whom she adored. She always went on her own. I suspect she reckoned it wasn't right to bring kids. They had a Ladies Only bar by then. And she'd always have a pint of Guinness in the course of the evening, coming home a little jolly. Otherwise she generally drank half a pint, but no more, at suppertime. To keep up her strength, she said.

We ate well. Most of our stuff was home-made. Mum was a dedicated putter-up of pickles, pies and preserves. She had routines. We always knew when the times came round for beetroot jars or salt beef or apple butter or plum puddings. And we had a huge pantry, which she tended to keep locked, to stop us pinching the pickles and crystallised fruit. She refused to use the butcher two doors down because she'd seen rats in their yard. The same went for the baker's. She wouldn't accept that most yards had rats. Ours didn't, she said, because she kept enough cats.

Really she just had a passion for moggies. When Tizer died of kidney failure, she sat in her chair with him in her lap for over twenty-four hours, then took him to the pet cemetery at Streatham and had him buried. It wasn't cheap. His stone said *TIZER: Born Nairobi, 1909. Died Tooting, 1930*. You can go and see it. It's still there, if it hasn't been vandalised. He was a wonderful old cat, that Tizer.

One day I came home and Dad was sitting in Mum's room, on his own, drunk. It was probably Monday. Everyone else was out doing something, including Nellie who was round at Aunty Rachel's getting her piano lesson. The worst thing was he was sitting in Mum's grieving chair.

'And how's my little princess?' he said. He knew he shouldn't be in that chair. I was alarmed, but fascinated by his effrontery, what might be his courage. He told me to come and give my old dad a peck on the cheek. Then he sat me up on his knee and bounced me and kissed me and I was a bit startled, because I was too old for it and he'd never done it much before. I wanted to go to the lavatory. I was praying I wouldn't pee on his leg. Then Mum bustled into the hall with Nellie, shouting for me, saw him and he turned very funny. Very placatory. Put me down with his hands round my waist. It hurt. I stood there for a moment in the silence. Then I was sent out with Nellie to get some butter Mum had forgotten.

Next day Dad was gone for good. Almost without trace. I don't think it had anything to do with me. I knew he'd overstepped the mark at last, sitting in her special chair. She had the locks changed right away. I heard her talking to her sister, who had come up from Brighton. 'I sometimes think I prefer the company of the dead,' she said. 'It's the peace. They stop struggling.' I didn't understand her. I probably heard wrong. But she'd sat out her share of death, one way or another.

Not many remember the big tram crash of 1929, partly because of the City news. The tram came off the rails on the corner and almost smashed through our front windows. It was a terrible accident. Mum had been on her way home. She was one of the first there. She helped a dozen people until the ambulances started turning up. This old lady died in her arms, blood running down her head. Mum said she couldn't get the stench of death out of her nostrils for months, though Freddy said it was probably the butcher's she was smelling.

Mum wouldn't let us come near. There were two dead little boys whose heads had been crushed. Twins. Nobody in Tooting saw worse in the War. It was pretty gruesome. Sammy told me the details later. It made me queasy. I nearly passed out. I've always had a weak stomach. I can't watch the news. I won't let people tell me things like that any more. Why fill your head with horror you can't do anything about? You just worry all the time. Mum sat through her personal storms in her chair, I suppose. I'd need a drink at that point. But Mum didn't drink, except for her usual Guinness. Nora said Dad had done enough boozing for all of us.

I was the only one who occasionally missed Dad. Mum joked that I was always flirting, but I don't think I really was. I just didn't like to offend anyone. Everyone said I was highly strung. It wasn't attention I needed, it was approval, security to be left alone. So I don't think I loved him. I just trusted him in a way. It was as if I could make a deal with him. I've tried to explain it in the past. As if I could buy privacy by giving in to him for a little while. He wanted to know the old smile worked for him. I wanted to be daydreaming in my own world. But the reality was nasty.

When Dad left we were all upset. Mum told us under no circumstances to let him in if he came round to the flat. And he did come round. Usually in the evening when he'd had a few. She instructed us not to answer the door and went into her room. Can you imagine? Not answering the door to your own dad? But Mum wouldn't have it different, and we cared a lot more for her approval than his.

Do you know how hard it is to disobey your dad? Particularly back in those days. I remember shivering on the other side of the big, curtained door and crying. 'I can't, Dad. I can't. Don't, Dad. Don't.' I didn't dare shout at him to go away and leave me in peace.

'Come on, darling, open it for me. It's just your daddy.'

My stomach turned over and I continued to cry silently as he cajoled me through the letterbox. 'Come on, princess. Come on, little 'un.' I used to dread it and would try to be somewhere else in the house at any time he was likely to arrive, just so I wouldn't have to say no to him. Mum would let Nellie off, but I was part of her anti-Dad guard. I never blamed her. I was always on her side. But I just hated doing it.

I was congratulating myself that I'd got avoiding him down to a fine art when I came out of school one day after gym, and there he was, all glittering false teeth and cosmetic dash. He was wearing that cream suit of his with a straw hat. His new moustache gave him a bit of a Ronald Colman look from a distance. He said he was passing and did I mind if he joined me on the tram home. What could I say? Apart from his face, which close up was a map of Mars, he looked dapper and genial as ever. He always wore a fresh pink rosebud in his lapel. On Armistice Day he wore a poppy. 'Call me old-fashioned,' he'd say, 'but I'm a bit of a patriot.'

When the tram came Dad bowed me aboard like a lady. He knew the tram conductor by name. He paid my fare. I was already in profit. He made a friendly enquiry about the conductor's wife. I loved those trams, rattling, bouncing, sparking and swaying, with their scarlet and brass, their reversible wooden seats varnished almost orange. There was always a chance they'd go somewhere new. When the tram reached the terminus you ran along the grooved wooden floors, thumping the seats back on their big oiled brass hinges. All the metal was worn and golden, and everything had that strange metallic smell of electricity.

I got off at the usual stop and he went on. And that was all. Of course, he told me not to tell Mum, but that suited me. I'd rather have felt a bit guilty and still been able to see them both. I cheered up. He started taking the tram with me a couple of times a week.

Once he bought me a quarter of toffees, which I had to stuff down before I got home. Then I couldn't eat my tea and was sick, and Mum was cautious and let me have the next morning off. Dad had that way of 'not wanting to worry people' with too much information. Soon he'd meet me almost every day. I had to make up delayed trams and late chats with teachers at school to explain the odd half-hour. Once or twice Mum noticed chocolate on me, and I said another kid had given me some. I remember telling my first conscious lie to her and how easy it was and how she believed me and there were no consequences. It worked. Life became easier.

One Monday Dad said he was going to show me where he lived. Would I like that? I was really curious. It might put the picture together for me, I thought. Maybe explain why he'd left. He said he'd have me home in an hour, long before Mum got back. My knees were knocking, but I felt excited, too. I'd know something even Mum didn't know about him.

So we stayed on the tram for another two stops and got off at Mitcham Road. His road was called Undine Street and he was about halfway down on the left. A nice road, I thought, with trees in it. I was impressed when we went into a proper garden but then wondered why we had to go up so many stairs to the top of the house. 'My little hideaway,' Dad laughed. 'Bai Jove, bai Jove, Ai'm a comical cove!'

I think it was what they used to call a bed-dinette. All one room, with a kitchen area curtained off. It had a cold feel and stank of grease, tobacco and beer. There was a big wardrobe, a single bed covered with a green silk counterpane, a table and chair and an old horsehair sofa. A bit of faded carpet on cracked lino. Mum wouldn't have tolerated it. She set high store by appearances. Sporting papers and racecards were everywhere. And empty bottles. I didn't want to stay, but he said I'd hurt his feelings if I didn't accept his hospitality. So I sat on the edge of his bed and drank some tea I didn't like and ate a piece of stale buttered bun that looked as if he'd brought it home from a Lyons tea shop in his pocket.

Dad was in a very sentimental mood. I knew from the familiar smell that his cup didn't have tea in it. That smell made me feel sick, and it was so close and nasty in there. I got a headache. I think I must have fainted. My weak stomach was always my worst enemy. I probably threw up. The next thing is I'm going out his door and I'm in Garratt Lane, still feeling weak, while he tells me I need some fresh air. Maybe a glass of lemonade? I say I want Mum. He thinks there must be a gas-leak in his room. 'Just say I met you from school,' he keeps telling me. 'Say you were sick before I saw you.'

I remember him delivering me back home and Mum not talking much to him. He didn't seem to want to come in.

I'm not sure what she said, because she went out onto the landing to say it, but I never saw him at my school or on the tram again. I think I caught a glimpse of him once or twice in the street. I waved but he never said hello.

The next day there was a funny question about my clothes. Mum'd found a spot of blood and wanted to know if I'd been scratching myself. I couldn't remember, I said. I really couldn't. She started asking more questions. And then I lied. I don't know why. I said, oh, yes, I'd been climbing a tree. I'd put some iodine on a graze. But this time Mum didn't seem reassured. I said I had to go to the toilet. I used a pin to scrape my leg in case she wanted to see it. But I never really knew why she'd mentioned the blood.

Funnily enough, Mum sat in her chair for a day or two after that, even though nobody was dead. It was more like she was thinking, as well as praying. Something about Dad, maybe? She was nice to me, so it couldn't have been about the lies. Later she talked to me a bit. How telling the truth sometimes was harder than not. And the difference between pretending and deceiving. For instance, she said, Dad didn't know the difference between a game and reality. It meant nothing much to me, although it probably helped me get the idea of going into the theatre.

By then I'd started reading those *Playgoer* magazines Lilly gave me, and it was dreamland for years and years. I got in with a crowd Nellie knew. They did local theatricals and things. I told them all sorts of stuff and they believed me. I told them I'd been schooled by nuns in Portugal. That my father was an exiled Spanish count. I fell out with Nellie for a while, because she wouldn't back me up. It was only for fun. Just white lies. They didn't do anyone any harm.

I was married and twenty when I got my first real job in Dicky Diamond's Pierrots. At first Mum wasn't sure about it, but she spoke to Dicky himself who offered all sorts of guarantees and contracts. No mixed accommodation or facilities, I heard him tell her. Entertainers were in demand. It paid to stay wholesome. I'd hear him say that a few times in the coming years. Les was all right about it, too. Of course, I didn't know why. Then I got into films and was offered the Jessie Matthews parts she didn't want, because I looked quite a lot like her apparently, though I could only see it when dressers posed me in her style. I could dance like her, that sort of slinky stepping and kicking that went out when American dancing came in.

Like Jessie, I didn't have luck with men. I expected too much of them, I suppose. All I've wanted for years is my cats and my little garden. A comfortable easy chair. Something decent on the telly. I think it's really all Mum ever wanted, too. Most of my career, though, there was something in me that really craved a chap's approval, even when I was starring in the West End. Well, obviously that kind of approval's the easiest thing in the world to get. So you wind up never valuing it for long. Chaps aren't a lot different, are they?

We were touring the South Coast that wonderful summer of

1939 and I was still married to Les Andrews when I heard that Dad had died. It was a stroke, apparently. They found him on the steps of the Horse and Groom. We were finishing the season, so I was able to pop up from Worthing to see Mum and help with the arrangements. I stayed two or three nights in my old room. What surprised me was that while she was withdrawn and briskly sad, she never once sat in her chair. It was as if she was avoiding it.

After we buried him in Streatham Cemetery with the other Lees, Mum didn't want to go home. We were with her, all nine of us. Jimmy was over from Washington. Ellie came on the boat train from Paris, where she was living with an Italian count who couldn't get a divorce. Everyone else still lived nearby, then, in Norbury and Streatham. Sammy was furthest in West Kensington. We had a brief reception at Auntie Rachel's in Khartoum Road. Then Mum took us up to Streatham Hill on the tram. Her treat, she said. We were going to the pictures. Not the old ABC or the State, but the new Astoria. These days they'd call it a luxury cinema. They charged top prices because the posh films were first shown there after they left the West End. Mum had a big white five-pound note. She paid for everything, including ice creams. It was like being kids again, only better. This time we sat in the half-crown seats, which were wonderful, almost like sitting at home. We watched *Dark Victory* with Bette Davis, George Brent and Humphrey Bogart.

Mum cried all the way through.

A Portrait in Ivory

Chapter One
An Encounter with a Lady

E LRIC, WHO HAD slept well and revived himself with fresh-brewed herbs, was in improved humour as he mixed honey and water into his glass of green breakfast wine. Typically, his night had been filled with distressing dreams, but any observer would see only a tall, insouciant 'silverskin' with high cheekbones, slightly sloping eyes and tapering ears, revealing nothing of his inner thoughts.

He had found a quiet hostelry away from the noisy centre of Séred-Öma, this city of tall palms. Here, merchants from all over the Young Kingdoms gathered to trade their goods in return for the region's most valuable produce. This was not the dates or live-stock, on which Séred-Öma's original wealth had been founded, but the extraordinary creations of artists famed everywhere in the lands bordering the Sighing Desert. Their carvings, especially of animals and human portraits, were coveted by kings and princes. It was the reputation of these works of art which brought the crimson-eyed albino out of his way to see them for himself. Even in Melniboné, where barbarian art for the most part was regarded with distaste, the sculptors of Séred-Öma had been admired.

Though Elric had left the scabbarded runesword and black armour of his new calling in his chamber and wore the simple chequered clothing of a regional traveller, his fellow guests tended to keep a certain distance from him. Those who had heard little of Melniboné's fall had celebrated the Bright Empire's destruction with great glee until the implications of that sudden defeat were understood. Certainly, Melniboné no longer controlled the world's trade and could no longer demand ransom from the Young Kingdoms, but the world was these days in confusion as upstart nations vied to seize the power for themselves. And meanwhile, Melnibonéan mercenaries found employment in the armies of rival countries. Without being certain of his identity, they could tell at once that Elric was one of those misplaced unhuman warriors, infamous for their cold good manners and edgy pride.

Rather than find themselves in a quarrel with him, the customers of the Rolling Pig kept their distance. The haughty albino too seemed indisposed to open a conversation. Instead, he sat at his corner table staring into his morning wine, brooding on what could not be forgotten. His history was written on handsome features which would have been youthful were it not for his thoughts. He reflected on an unsettled past and an uneasy future. Even had someone dared approach him, however sympathetically, to ask what concerned him, he would have answered lightly and coldly, for, save in his nightmares, he refused to confront most of those concerns. Thus, he did not look up when a woman, wearing the conical russet hat and dark veil of her caste, approached him through the crowd of busy dealers.

'Sir?' Her voice was a dying melody. 'Master Melnibonéan, could you tolerate my presence at your table?' Falling rose petals, sweet and brittle from the sun.

'Lady,' said Elric, in the courteous tone his people reserved for their own high-born kin, 'I am at my breakfast. But I will gladly order more wine…'

'Thank you, sir. I did not come here to share your hospitality. I came to ask a favour.' Behind the veil her eyes were grey-green. Her skin had the golden bloom of the Na'äne, who had once ruled here and were said to be a race as ancient as Elric's own. 'A favour you have every reason to refuse.'

The albino seemed almost amused, perhaps because, as he looked into her eyes, he detected beauty behind the veil, an unexpected intelligence he had not encountered since he had left

Imrryr's burning ruins behind him. How he had longed to hear the swift wit of his own people, the eloquent argument, the careless insults. All that and more had been denied him for too long. To himself he had become sluggish, almost as dull as the conniving princelings and self-important merchants to whom he sold his sword. Now, there was something in the music of her speech, something in the lilt of irony colouring each phrase she uttered, that spoke to his own sleeping intellect. 'You know me too well, lady. Clearly, my fate is in your hands, for you're able to anticipate my every attitude and response. I have good reason not to grant you a favour, yet you still come to ask one, so either you are prescient or I am already your servant.'

'I would serve you, sir,' she said gently. Her half-hidden lips curved in a narrow smile. She shrugged. 'And, in so doing, serve myself.'

'I thought my curiosity atrophied,' he answered. 'My imagination a petrified knot. Here you pick at threads to bring it back to life. This loosening is unlikely to be pleasant. Should I fear you?' He lifted a dented pewter cup to his lips and tasted the remains of his wine. 'You are a witch, perhaps? Do you seek to revive the dead? I am not sure...'

'I am not sure, either,' she told him. 'Will you trust me enough to come with me to my house?'

'I regret madam, I am only lately bereaved –'

'I'm no sensation-seeker, sir, but an honest woman with an honest ambition. I do not tempt you with the pleasures of the flesh, but of the soul. Something which might engage you for a while, even ease your mind a little. I can more readily convince you of this if you come to my house. I live there alone, save for servants. You may bring your sword, if you wish. Indeed, if you have fellows, bring them also. Thus I offer you every advantage.'

The albino rose slowly from his bench and placed the empty goblet carefully on the well-worn wood. His own smile reflected hers. He bowed. 'Lead on, madam.' And he followed her through a crowd which parted like corn before the reaper, leaving a momentary silence behind him.

Chapter Two
The Material

S HE HAD BROUGHT him to the depth of the city's oldest quarter, where artists of every skill, she told him, were licensed to
work unhindered by landlord or, save in the gravest cases, the law.
This ancient sanctuary was created by time-honoured tradition
and the granting of certain guarantees by the clerics whose great
university had once been the centre of the settlement. These
guarantees had been strengthened during the reign of the great
King Alo'ofd, an accomplished player of the nine-stringed *mur-
merlan*, who loved all the arts and struggled with a desire to throw
off the burdens of his office and become a musician. King Alo'ofd's
decrees had been law for the past millennium and his successors
had never dared challenge them.

'Thus, this quarter harbours not only artists of great talent,'
she told him, 'but many who have only the minimum of talent.
Enough to allow them to live according to our ancient freedoms.
Sadly, sir, there is as much forgery practised here, of every kind, as
there is originality.'

'Yours is not the only such quarter.' He spoke absently, his eyes
inspecting the colourful paintings, sculptures and manuscripts displayed on every side. They were of varied quality, but only a few
showed genuine inspiration and beauty. Yet the accomplishment
was generally higher than Elric had usually observed in the Young
Kingdoms. 'Even in Melniboné we had these districts. Two of my
cousins, for instance, were calligraphers. Another composed for
the flute.'

'I have heard of Melnibonéan arts,' she said. 'But we are too
distant from your island home to have seen many examples. There
are stories, of course.' She smiled. 'Some of them are decidedly
sinister…'

'Oh, they are doubtless true. We had no trouble if audiences, for instance, died for an artist's work. Many great composers would experiment, for instance, with the human voice.' His eyes again clouded, remembering not a crime but his lost passion.

It seemed she misinterpreted him. 'I feel for you, sir. I am not one of those who celebrated the fall of the Dreaming City.'

'You could not know its influence, so far away,' he murmured, picking up a remarkable little pot and studying its design. 'But those who were our neighbours were glad to see us humiliated. I do not blame them. Our time was over.' His expression was again one of cultivated insouciance. She turned her own gaze towards a house which leaned like an amiable drunkard on the buttressed walls of two neighbours, giving the impression that if it fell, then all would fall together. The house was of wood and sandy brick, of many floors, each at an angle to the rest, covered by a waved roof.

'This is the residence,' she told him, 'where my forefathers and myself have lived and worked. It is the House of the Th'ee and I am Rai-u Th'ee, last of my line. It is my ambition to leave a single great work of art behind, carved in a material which has been in our possession for centuries, yet until now always considered too valuable to use. It is a rare material, at least to us, and possessed of a number of qualities, some of which our ancestors only hinted at.'

'My curiosity grows,' said Elric, though now he found himself wishing that he had accepted her offer and brought his sword. 'What is this material?'

'It is a kind of ivory,' she said, leading him into the ramshackle house which, for all its age and decrepitude, had clearly once been rich. Even the wall hangings, now in rags, revealed traces of their former quality. There were paintings from floor to ceiling which, Elric knew, would have commanded magnificent prices at any market. The furniture was carved by genuine artists and showed the passing of a hundred fashions, from the plain, somewhat austere style of the city's secular period, to the ornate enrichments of her pagan age. Some were inset with jewels, as were the many mirrors, framed with exquisite and elaborate ornament. Elric was surprised, given what she had told him of the quarter, that the House of Th'ee had never been robbed.

Apparently reading his thoughts, she said: 'This place has been afforded certain protections down the years.' She led him into a tall studio, lit by a single, unpapered window through which a great deal of light entered, illuminating the scrolls and boxed books lining the walls. Crowded on tables and shelves stood sculptures in every conceivable material. They were in bone and granite and hardwood and limestone. They were in clay and bronze, in iron and sea-green basalt. Bright, glinting whites, deep, swirling blacks. Colours of every possible shade from darkest blue to the lightest pinks and yellows. There was gold, silver and delicate porphyry. There were heads and torsos and reclining figures, beasts of every kind, some believed extinct. There were representations of the Lords and Ladies of Chaos and of Law, every supernatural aristocrat who had ever ruled in heaven, hell or limbo. Elementals. Animal-bodied men, birds in flight, leaping deer, men and women at rest, historical subjects, group subjects and half-finished subjects which hinted at something still to be discovered in the stone. They were the work of genius, decided the albino, and his respect for this bold woman grew.

'Yes.' Again she anticipated a question, speaking with firm pride. 'They are all mine. I love to work. Many of these are taken from life…'

He thought it impolitic to ask which.

'But you will note,' she added, 'that I have never had the pleasure of sculpting the head of a Melnibonéan. This could be my only opportunity.'

'Ah,' he began regretfully, but with great grace she silenced him, drawing him to a table on which sat a tall, shrouded object. She took away the cloth. 'This is the material we have owned down the generations but for which we had never yet found an appropriate subject.'

He recognised the material. He reached to run his hand over its warm smoothness. He had seen more than one of these in the old caves of the Phoorn, the dragons to whom his folk were related.

He had seen them in living creatures who even now slept in Melniboné, wearied by their work of destruction, their old master made an exile, with no-one to care for them save a few mad old men who knew how to do nothing else.

'Yes,' she whispered, 'it is what you know it is. It cost my forefathers a great fortune for, as you can imagine, your folk were not readily forthcoming with such things. It was smuggled from Melniboné and traded through many nations before it reached us, some two and a half centuries ago.'

Elric found himself almost singing to the thing as he caressed it. He felt a mixture of nostalgia and deep sadness.

'It is dragon ivory, of course.' Her hand joined his on the hard, brilliant surface of the great curved tusk. Few Phoorn had owned such fangs. Only the greatest of the patriarchs, legendary creatures of astonishing ferocity and wisdom, who had come from their old world to this, following their kin, the humanlike folk of Melniboné. The Phoorn, too, had not been native to this world, but had fled another. They, too, had always been alien and cruel, impossibly beautiful, impossibly strange. Elric felt kinship even now for this piece of bone. It was perhaps all that remained of the first generation to settle on this plane.

'It is a holy thing.' His voice was growing cold again. Inexplicable pain forced him to withdraw from her. 'It is my own kin. Blood for blood, the Phoorn and the folk of Melniboné are one. It was our power. It was our strength. It was our continuity. This is ancestral bone. Stolen bone. It would be sacrilege...'

'No, Prince Elric, in my hands it would be a unification. A resolution. A completion. You know why I have brought you here.'

'Yes.' His hand fell to his side. He swayed, as if faint. He felt a need for the herbs he carried with him. 'But it is still sacrilege...'

'Not if I am the one to give it life.' Her veil was drawn back now and he saw how impossibly young she was, what beauty she had: a beauty mirrored in all the things she had carved and moulded. Her desire was, he was sure, an honest one. Two very different emotions warred within him. Part of him felt she was right, that she could unite the two kinsfolk in a single image and

69

bring honour to all his ancestors, a kind of resolution to their mutual history. Part of him feared what she might create. In honouring his past, would she be destroying the future? Then some fundamental part of him made him gather himself up and turn to her. She gasped at what she saw burning in those terrible, ruby eyes.

'Life?'

'Yes,' she said. 'A new life honouring the old. Will you sit for me?' She too was caught up in his mood, for she too was endangering everything she valued, possibly her own soul, to make what might be her very last great work. 'Will you allow me to create your memorial? Will you help me redeem that destruction whose burden is so heavy upon you? A symbol for everything that was Melniboné?'

He let go of his caution but felt no responsive glee. The fire dulled in his eyes. His mask returned. 'I will need you to help me brew certain herbs, madam. They will sustain me while I sit for you.'

Her step was light as she led him into a room where she had lit a stove and on which water already boiled, but his own face still resembled the stone of her carvings. His gaze was turned inward, his eyes alternately flared and faded like a dying candle. His chest moved with deep, almost dying breaths as he gave himself up to her art.

Chapter Three
The Sitting

H OW MANY HOURS did he sit, still and silent in the chair? At
one time she remarked on the fact that he scarcely moved.
He said that he had developed the habit over several hundred
years and, when she voiced surprise, permitted himself a smile.
'You have not heard of Melniboné's dream couches? They are
doubtless destroyed with the rest. It is how we learn so much
when young. The couches let us dream for a year, even centuries,
while the time passing for those awake was but minutes. I appear
to you as a relatively young man, lady. But actually I have lived for
centuries. It took me that time to pursue my dream-quests, which
in turn taught me my craft and prepared me for...' And then he
stopped speaking, his pale lids falling over his troubled, unlikely
eyes.

She drew breath, as if to ask a further question, then thought
better of it. She brewed him cup after cup of invigorating herbs
and she continued to work, her delicate chisels fashioning an extraordinary likeness. She had genius in her hands. Every line of the
albino's head was rapidly reproduced. And Elric, almost dreaming
again, stared into the middle distance. His thoughts were far away
and in the past, where he had left the corpse of his beloved Cymoril to burn on the pyre he had made of his own ancient home, the
great and beautiful Imrryr, the Dreaming City, the Dreamers' City,
which many had considered indestructible, had believed to be
more conjuring than reality, created by the Melnibonéan Sorcerer
Kings into a delicate reality, whose towers, so tall they disappeared
amongst clouds, were actually the result of supernatural will
rather than the creation of architects and masons.

Yet Elric had proven such theories false when Melniboné
burned. Now all knew him for a traitor and none trusted him,

even those whose ambition he had served. They said he was twice a traitor, once to his own folk, second to those he had led on the raid which had razed Imrryr and upon whom he had turned. But in his own mind he was thrice a traitor, for he had slain his beloved Cymoril, beautiful sister of cousin Yyrkoon, who had tricked Elric into killing her with that terrible black blade whose energy both sustained and drained him.

It was for Cymoril, more than Imrryr, that Elric mourned. But he showed none of this to the world and never spoke of it. Only in his dreams, those terrible, troubled dreams, did he see her again, which is why he almost always slept alone and presented a carefully cultivated air of insouciance to the world at large.

Had he agreed to the sculptress's request because she reminded him of his cousin?

Hour upon tireless hour she worked with her exquisitely made instruments until at last she had finished. She sighed and it seemed her breath was a gentle witch-wind, filling the head with vitality. She turned the portrait for his inspection.

It was as if he stared into a mirror. For a moment he thought he saw movement in the bust, as if his own essence had been absorbed by it. Save for the blank eyes, the carving might have been himself. Even the hair had been carved to add to the portrait's lifelike qualities.

She looked to him for his approval and received the faintest of smiles. 'You have made the likeness of a monster,' he murmured. 'I congratulate you. Now history will know the face of the man they call Elric Kinslayer.'

'Ah,' she said, 'you curse yourself too much, my lord. Do you look into the face of one who bears a guilt-weighted conscience?'

And of course, he did. She had captured exactly that quality of melancholy and self-hatred behind the mask of insouciance which characterised the albino in repose.

'Whoever looks on this will not say you were careless of your crimes.' Her voice was so soft it was almost a whisper now.

At this he rose suddenly, putting down his cup. 'I need no sentimental forgiveness,' he said coldly. 'There is no forgiveness, no understanding, of that crime. History will be right to curse me for a coward, a traitor, a killer of women and of his own blood. You have done well, madam, to brew me those herbs, for I now feel strong enough to put all this and your city behind me!'

She watched him leave, walking a little unsteadily like a man carrying a heavy burden, through the busy night, back to the inn where he had left his sword and armour. She knew that by morning he would be gone, riding out of Séred-Öma, never to return. Her hands caressed the likeness she had made, the blind, staring eyes, the mouth which was set in a grimace of self-mocking carelessness.

And she knew he would always wonder, even as he put a thousand leagues between them, if he had not left at least a little of his yearning, desperate soul behind him.

THE PORCHESTER TOWER, WESTBOURNE GROVE, WII

This Gothic folly was built in 1820 by Sir Hector Reed, who owned large tracts of land on both sides of the West Bourne River. The Tower's most famous resident was Paul Black, known as the 'London Spymaster'. Operating from an antique shop in Kensington Old Church Street, Black ran a complex intelligence operation for his Soviet paymasters, but was also a double agent working for MI6. He sold limited editions of Ezra Pound to James Jesus Angleton and Victorian detective fiction and pornography to Graham Greene. An affable man of ambiguous sexuality, Black was implicated in the IRA bombing of the Kensington Café in 1971. The restaurant, he later revealed, was never the intended target. A runner, dealing in fantastically inventive and obscene drawings of 1940s film divas, had left his shop with the wrong parcel. Black wrote his memoirs in 1982 and returned to Kiev in 1996, where he still runs a successful business, trading in icons. His house, in some disrepair, was given to the National Trust shortly before he left England for the last time. Fully restored, the Tower is once more in private ownership, rented by the Trust to Prince Omar bin Faud.

THE ZODIAC HOUSE, ORMINGTON PLACE, SWI

Residence of the Variety, stage and cabaret performer known as 'Monsieur' (sometimes 'Count') Zodiac. This illusionist and conjuror was an albino, unusual among human beings for his crimson eyes and his bone-white hair. He was said to be an Austro-Hungarian aristocrat who lost his estates after the First World War; or perhaps a Serb whose lands were divided in the formation of Yugoslavia. Another rumour associated him with 'Crimson Eyes' (the 'Mirenburg Ripper').

Known for his elegance and courtesy, Zodiac was fictionalised by Anthony Skene as 'Monsieur Zenith', an opponent of his 'metatemporal detective', Sir Seaton Begg. He is thought to have died in a direct hit during a London air raid in September 1941, at the Kennington Empire, while performing his famous Bronze Basilisk illusion. The police became suspicious and searched the house in Ormington Place, near Victoria Station, finding a considerable quantity of opium and arresting Zodiac's Japanese manservant, who was subsequently interned on the Isle of Man.

The house is now a museum of things occult, magical and illusory. It can be visited in the summer months between 11 a.m. and 5 p.m. and during the winter months between 10.30 a.m. and 4 p.m. The museum displays some of Zodiac's illusions, as well as a full set of his evening clothes.

DERRY & TOMS ROOF GARDEN, W8

This elaborate roof garden was created in 1938 when the department store was first opened. Consisting of an aviary and themed gardens – such as the Tudor Garden, the Spanish Garden, the Old English Garden and the Japanese Garden – it also featured a large tea room, on whose terrace customers frequently arranged to meet. Lady Shapiro was said to have favoured the roof garden for her assignations with Sir Frank Cornelius, the postwar property developer. A liaison which was brought to light in the 1950 divorce case with its lurid testimonies from valets and maidservants, its torn photographs of headless men in hotel rooms. The episode marked the beginning, some media scholars assert, of tabloid journalism and the cult of celebrity exposure.

Mary Quant and Sir Richard Branson are among the better-known custodians of the garden in recent times. Now the property of a private club, the roof gardens are occasionally opened to the public. Times and details of visits are announced on the relevant website.

Doves in the Circle

Situated between Church Street and Broadway, several blocks
from Houston Street, just below Canal Street, *Houston Circle* is
entered via Houston Alley from the North, and *Lispenard*, *Walker*
and *Franklin* Streets from the West. The only approach from the
South and East is via *Courtland Alley*. Houston Circle was known
as *Indian Circle* or *South Green* until about 1820. It was populated
predominantly by Irish, English and, later, Jewish people and
today has a poor reputation. The circle itself, forming a green,
now an open market, had some claims to antiquity. Aboriginal
settlements have occupied the spot for about five hundred years
and early travellers report finding non-indigenous standing
stones, remarkably like those erected by the Ancient Britons.
The *Kakatanawas*, whom early explorers first encountered,
spoke a distinctive Iroquois dialect and were of a high standard
of civilisation. Captain Adriaen Block reported encountering the
tribe in 1612. Their village was built around a stone circle 'whych
is their *Kirke*'. When, under the Dutch, Fort Amsterdam was
established nearby, there was no attempt to move the tribe
which seems to have become so quickly absorbed into the
dominant culture that it took no part in the bloody Indian War
of 1643–5 and had completely disappeared by 1680. Although of
considerable architectural and historical interest, because of its
location and reputation Houston Circle has not attracted
redevelopment and its buildings, some of which date from the
18th century, are in poor repair. Today the Circle is best known for
'The Three Sisters', which comprise the Catholic Church of *St
Mary the Widow* (one of Huntingdon Begg's earliest commissions),
the Greek Orthodox Church of *St Sophia* and the Orthodox

Jewish Synagogue which stand side by side at the East end, close to *Doyle's Ale House*, built in 1780 and still in the same family. Next door to this is *Doyle's Hotel* (1879), whose tariff reflects its standards. Crossed by the Elevated Railway, which destroys the old village atmosphere, and generally neglected now, the Circle should be visited in daylight hours and in the company of other visitors. *Subway:* White Street IRT. *Elevated:* 6th Ave. El. at Church Street, *Streetcar:* B & 7th Ave., B'way & Church.

– R.P. Downes,
New York: A Traveller's Guide,
Charles Kelly, London, 1924

Chapter One

I F THERE IS such a thing as unearned innocence, then America has it, said Barry Quinn mysteriously lifting his straight glass to the flag and downing the last of Corny Doyle's passable porter. Oh, there you go again, says Corny, turning to a less contentious customer and grinning to show he saw several viewpoints. Brown as a tinker, he stood behind his glaring pumps in his white shirt-sleeves, his skin glowing with the bar work, polishing up some silverware with all the habitual concentration of the rosary.

Everyone in the pub had an idea that Corny was out of sorts. They thought, perhaps, he would rather not have seen Father McQueeny there in his regular spot. These days the old priest carried an aura of desolation with him so that even when he joined a toast he seemed to address the dead. He had never been popular and his church had always chilled you but he had once enjoyed a certain authority in the parish. Now the Bishop had sent a new man down and McQueeny was evidently retired but wasn't admitting it. There'd always been more faith and Christian charity in Doyle's, Barry Quinn said, than could ever be found in that damned church. Apart from a few impenetrable writers in the architectural journals, no-one had ever liked it. It was altogether too modern and Spanish-looking.

Sometimes, said Barry Quinn putting down his glass in the copper stand for a refill, there was so much good will in Doyle's Ale House he felt like he was taking his pleasure at the benign heart of the world. And who was to say that Houston Circle, with its profound history, the site of the oldest settlement on Manhattan, was not a centre of conscious grace and mystery like Camelot or Holy Island or Dublin, or possibly London? You could find all the inspiration you needed here. And you got an excellent confessional. Why freeze your bones talking to old McQueeny in the box when you might as well talk to him over in that booth. Should you want to.

The fact was that nobody wanted anything at all to do with the old horror. There were some funny rumours about him. Nobody was exactly sure what Father McQueeny had been caught doing, but it must have been bad enough for the Church to step in. And he'd had some sort of nasty secretive surgery. Mavis Byrne and her friends believed the Bishop made him have it. A popular rumour was that the Church castrated him for diddling little boys. He would not answer if you asked him. He was rarely asked. Most of the time people tended to forget he was there. Sometimes they talked about him in his hearing. He never objected.

She's crossed the road now, look. Corny pointed through the big, green-lettered window of the pub to where his daughter walked purposefully through the wrought-iron gates of what was nowadays called Houston Park on the maps and Houston Green by the realtors.

She's walking up the path. Straight as an arrow. He was proud of her. Her character was so different from his own. She had all her mother's virtues. But he was more afraid of Kate than he had ever been of his absconded spouse.

Will you look at that? Father McQueeny's bloody eyes stared with cold reminiscence over the rim of his glass. She is about to ask Mr Terry a direct question.

He's bending an ear, says Barry Quinn, bothered by the priest's commentary, as if a fly interrupted him. He seems to be almost smiling. Look at her coaxing a bit of warmth out of that grim old mug. And at the same time she's getting the info she needs, like a bee taking pollen.

Father McQueeny runs his odd-coloured tongue around his lips and says, shrouded safe in his inaudibility, his invisibility: What a practical and down-to-earth little creature she is. She was always that. What a proper little madam, eh? She must have the truth, however dull. She will not allow us our speculations. She is going to ruin all our fancies!

His almost formless body undulates to the bar, settles over a stool and seems to coagulate on it. Without much hope of a quick response, he signals for a short and a pint. Unobserved by them, he consoles himself in the possession of some pathetic and unwholesome secret. He marvels at the depths of his own depravity, but now he believes it is his self-loathing which keeps him alive. And while he is alive, he cannot go to Hell.

Chapter Two

'WELL,' SAYS KATE Doyle to Mr Terry McLear, 'I've been sent out and I beg your pardon but I am a kind of deputation from the whole Circle, or at least that part of it represented by my dad's customers, come to ask if what you're putting up is a platform on which you intend to sit, to make, it's supposed, a political statement of some kind? Or is it religious? Like a pole?'

And when she has finished her speech, she takes one step back from him. She folds her dark expectant hands before her on the apron of her uniform. There is a silence, emphasised by the distant, constant noise of the surrounding city. Framed by her bobbed black hair, her little pink oval face has that expression of sardonic good humour, that hint of self-mockery, which attracted his affection many years ago. She is the picture of determined patience, and she makes Mr Terry smile.

'Is that what people are saying these days, is it? And they think I would sit up there in this weather?' He speaks the musical, old-fashioned convent-educated, precisely pronounced English he learned in Dublin. He'd rather die than make a contraction or split an infinitive. He glares up at the grey, Atlantic sky. Laughing helplessly at the image of himself on a pole he stretches hard-worn fingers towards her to show he means no mockery or rudeness to herself. His white hair rises in a halo. His big old head grows redder, his mouth rapidly opening and closing as his mirth engulfs him. He gasps. His pale blue eyes, too weak for such powerful emotions, water joyfully. Kate Doyle suspects a hint of senile dementia. She'll be sorry to see him lose his mind, it is such a good one, and so kind. He never really understood how often his company had saved her from despair.

Mr Terry lifts the long thick dowel onto his sweat-shirted shoulder. 'Would you care to give me a hand, Katey?'

She helps him steady it upright in the special hole he had prepared. The seasoned pine dowel is some four inches in diameter and eight feet tall. The hole is about two feet deep. Yesterday, from the big bar, they had all watched him pour in the concrete.

The shrubbery, trees and grass of the Circle nowadays wind neatly up to a little grass-grown central hillock. On this the City has placed two ornamental benches. Popular legend has it that an Indian chief rests underneath, together with his treasure.

When Mr Terry was first seen measuring up the mound, they thought of the ancient redman. They had been certain, when he had started to dig, that McLear had wind of gold.

All Doyle's regulars had seized enthusiastically on this new topic. Corny Doyle was especially glad of it. Sales rose considerably when there was a bit of speculative stimulus amongst the customers, like a sensational murder or a political scandal or a sporting occasion.

Katey knew they would all be standing looking out now, watching her and waiting. They had promised to rescue her if he became unpleasant. Not that she expected anything like that. She was the only local that Mr Terry would have anything to do with. He never would talk to most people. After his wife died he was barely civil if you wished him 'good morning'. His argument was that he had never enjoyed company much until he met her and now precious little other company satisfied him in comparison. Neither did he have anything to do with the Church. He'd distanced himself a bit from Katey when she started working with the Poor Clares. This was the first time she'd approached him in two years. She's grateful to them for making her come but sorry that it took the insistence of a bunch of feckless boozers to get her here.

'So,' she says, 'I'm glad I've cheered you up. And if that's all I've achieved, that's good enough for today, I'm sure. Can you tell me nothing about your pole?'

'I have a permit for it,' he says. 'All square and official.' He pauses and watches the Sears delivery truck which has been droning round the Circle for the last fifteen minutes, seeking an exit.

Slumped over his wheel, peering about for signs, the driver looks desperate.

'Nothing else?'

'Only that the pole is the start of it.' He's enjoying himself. That heartens her.

'And you won't be doing some sort of black magic with the poor old Indian's bones?'

'Magic, maybe,' he says, 'but not a bit black, Katey. Just the opposite, you will see.'

'Well, then,' she says, 'then I'll go back and tell them you're putting up a radio aerial.'

'Tell them what you like,' he says. 'Whatever you like.'

'If I don't tell them something, they'll be on at me to come out again,' she says.

'You would not be unwelcome,' he says, 'or averse, I am sure, to a cup of tea.' And gravely he tips that big head homeward, towards his brownstone basement on the far side of the Circle.

'Fine,' she says, 'but I'll come on my own when I do and not as a messenger. Good afternoon to you, Mr Terry.'

He lifts an invisible hat. 'It was a great pleasure to talk with you again, Katey.'

She's forgotten how that little smile of his so frequently cheers her up.

Chapter Three

'OKAY, KATEY, SO what's the story?' says Father McQueeny wearing his professional cheer like an old shroud, as ill-smelling and threadbare as his clerical black. The only life on him is his sweat, his winking veins. The best the regulars have for him these days is their pity, the occasional drink. He has no standing at all with the Church or the community. But, since Father Walsh died, that secret little smirk of his always chills her. Knowing that he can still frighten her is probably all that keeps the old shit alive. And since that knowledge actually informs the expression which causes her fear, she is directly feeding him what he wants. She has yet to work out a way to break the cycle. Years before, in her fiercest attempt, she almost succeeded.

To the others, the priest remains inaudible, invisible. 'Did he come out with it, Katey?' says Corny Doyle, his black eyes and hair glinting like pitch, his near-fleshless body and head looking as artificially weathered as those shiny, smoked hams in Belladonna's. 'Come on, Kate. There's real money riding on this now.'

'He did not tell me,' she says. She turns her back on Father McQueeny but she cannot control a shudder as she smiles from behind the bar where she has been helping out since Christmas, because of Bridget's pneumonia. She takes hold of the decorated china pump-handle and turns to her patient customer. 'Two pints of Mooney's was it, Mr Gold?'

'You're an angel,' says Mr Gold. 'Well, Corny, the book, now how's it running?' He is such a plump, jolly man. You would never take him for a pawnbroker. And it must be admitted he is not a natural profiteer. Mr Gold carries his pints carefully to the little table in the alcove, where Becky, his secretary, waits for him. Ageless, she is her own work of art. He dotes on her. If it wasn't for her he would be a ruined man. They'll be going out this evening.

You can smell her perm and her Chantilly from here. A little less noise and you could probably hear her mascara flake.

'Radio aerial's still number one, Mr Gold,' says Katey. Her father's attention has gone elsewhere, to some fine moment of sport on the box. He shares his rowdy triumph with his fellow aficionados. He turns back to her, panting. 'That was amazing,' he says.

Kate Doyle calls him over with her finger. He knows better than to hesitate. 'What?' he blusters. 'What? There's nothing wrong with those glasses. I told you it's the dishwasher.'

Her whisper is sharp as a needle in his wincing ear. She asks him why, after all she's spoken perfectly plainly to him, he is still letting that nasty old man into the pub?

'Oh, come on, Katey,' he says, 'where else can the poor devil go? He's a stranger in his own church these days.'

'He deserves nothing less,' she says. 'And I'll remind you, Dad, of my original terms. I'm off for a walk now and you can run the bloody pub yourself.'

'Oh, no!' He is mortified. He casts yearning eyes back towards the television. He looks like some benighted sinner in the picture books who has lost the salvation of Christ. 'Don't do this to me, Kate.'

'I might be back when he's gone,' she says. 'But I'm not making any promises.'

Every so often she has to let him know he is going too far. Getting her father to work was a full-time job for her mother but she's not going to waste her own life on that non-starter. He's already lost the hotel next door, to his debts. Most of the money Kate allows him goes in some form of gambling. Those customers who lend him money soon discover how she refuses to honour his IOUs. He's lucky these days to be able to coax an extra dollar or two out of the till, usually by short-changing a stranger.

'We'll lose business if you go, Kate,' he hisses. 'Why cut off your nose to spite your face?'

'I'll cut off *your* nose, you old fool, if you don't set it to that grindstone right now,' she says. She hates sounding like her mother.

Furiously, she snatches on her coat and scarf. 'I'll be back when you get him out of here.' She knows Father McQueeny's horrible eyes are still feeding off her through the pub's cultivated gloom.

'See you later, Katey, dear,' her father trills as he places professional fingers on his bar and a smile falls across his face. 'Now, then, Mrs Byrne, a half of Guinness, is it, darling?'

Chapter Four

THE CIRCLE WAS going up. There were all kinds of well-heeled people coming in. You could tell by the brass door-knockers and the window boxes, the dark green paint. With the odd *boutique* and *croissanterie*, these were the traditional signs of gentrification. Taking down the last pylons of the ugly elevated had helped, along with the hippies who in the '60s and '70s had made such a success of the little park, which now had a playground and somewhere for the dogs to go. It was lovely in the summer.

It was quiet, too, since they had put in the one-way system. Now the only strange vehicles were those which thought they could still make a short cut and wound up whining round until, defeated, they left the way they had entered. You had to go up to Canal Street to get a cab. They wouldn't come any further than that. There were legends of drivers who had never returned.

This recent development had increased the sense of the Circle's uniqueness, a zone of relative tranquillity in one of the noisiest parts of New York City. Up to now they had been protected from a full-scale yuppie invasion by the nearby federal housing. Yet nobody from the projects had ever bothered the Circle. They thought of the place as their own, something they aspired to, something to protect. It was astonishing the affection local people felt for the place, especially the park, which was the best-kept in the city.

She was on her brisk way, of course, to take Mr Terry McLear up on his invitation but she was not going there directly for all to see. Neither was she sure what she'd have to say to him when she saw him. She simply felt it was time they had one of their old chats.

Under a chilly sky, she walked quickly along the central path of the park. Eight paths led to the middle these days, like the arms of a compass, and there had been some talk of putting a sundial on the knoll, where Mr Terry had now laid his discreet foundations. She paused to look at the smooth concrete of his deep, narrow hole. A flag, perhaps? Something that simple? But this was not a man to fly a flag at the best of times. And even the heaviest banner did not need so sturdy a pole. However, she was beginning to get a notion. A bit of a memory from a conversation of theirs a good few years ago now. *Ah*, she thought, *it's about birds, I bet.*

Certain some of her customers would still be watching her, she took the northern path and left the park to cross directly over to Houston Alley, where her uncle had his little toy-soldier shop where he painted everything himself and where, next door, the Italian shoe-repairer worked in his window. They would not be there much longer now that the real-estate people had christened the neighbourhood 'Houston Village'. Already the pub had had a sniff from Starbucks. Up at the far end of the alley the street looked busy. She thought about going back, but told herself she was a fool.

The traffic in Canal Street was unusually dense and a crew-cut girl in big boots had to help her when she almost fell into the street, shoved aside by some thrusting Wall Street stockman in a vast raincoat which might have sheltered half the Australian outback. She thought she recognised him as the boy who had moved into No. 91 a few weeks ago and she had been about to say hello.

She was glad to get back into the quietness of the Circle, going round into Church Street and then through Walker Street which would bring her out only a couple of houses from Mr Terry's place.

She was still a little shaken up but had collected herself by the time she reached the row of brownstones. No. 27 was in the middle and his flat was in the basement. She went carefully down the iron steps to his area. It was as smartly kept up as always, with the flower baskets properly stocked and his miniature greenhouse raising tomatoes in their gro-bags. And he was still neat and clean. No obvious slipping of standards, no signs of senile decay. She took hold of the old black lion knocker and rapped twice against the dented plate. That same vast echo came back, as if she stood at the door to infinity.

He was slow as Christmas unbolting it all and opening up. Then everything happened at once. Pulling back the door he embraced her and kicked it shut at the same time. The apartment was suddenly very silent. 'Well,' he said, 'it has been such a long time. All my fault, too. I have had a chance to pull myself together and here I am.'

'That sounds like a point for God for a change.' She knew all the teachers had been anarchists or pagans or something equally silly in that school of his. She stared around at the familiar things, the copper and the oak and the big ornamental iron stove which once heated the whole building. 'You're still dusting better than a woman. And polishing.'

'She had high standards,' he says. 'I could not rise to them when she was alive, but now it seems only fair to try to live up to them. You would not believe what a slob I used to be.'

'You never told me,' she says.

'That is right. There is quite a bit I have not told you,' he says.

'And us so close once,' she says.

'We were good friends,' he agreed. 'The best of company. I am an idiot, Kate. But I do not think either of us realised I was in a sort of shock for years. I was afraid of our closeness, do you see? In the end.'

'I believe I might have mentioned that.' She went to put the kettle on. Filling it from his deep old-fashioned stone sink with its great brass faucets she carried it with both hands to the stove while he got out the teacakes and the toasting forks. He must have bought them only today from Van Beek's Bakery on Canal, the knowing old devil, and put them in the icebox. They were still almost warm. She fitted one to the fork. 'It doesn't exactly take Sigmund Freud to work that out. But you made your decisions,

Mr Terry. And it is my general rule to abide by such decisions until the party involved decides to change. Which in my experience generally happens at the proper time.'

'Oh, so you have had lots of these relationships, have you, Kate?'

She laughed.

Chapter Five

'I WAS SIXTEEN when I first saw her. In the Circle there she was, coming out of No. 10, where the dry-cleaners is now. I said to myself, that is whom I am going to marry. And that was what I did. We used to sing quite a bit, duets together. She was a much better and sweeter singer than I, and she was smarter, as well.' Mr Terry looks into the fire and slowly turns his teacake against the glare. 'What a little old snob I was in those days, thinking myself better than anyone, coming back from Dublin with an education. But she liked me anyway and was what I needed to take me down a peg or two. My father thought she was an angel. He spoke often of the grandchildren he would care for. But both he and she died before that event could become any sort of reality. And I grew very sorry for myself, Kate. In those first days, when we were having our chats, I was selfish.'

'Oh, yes,' she says, 'but you were more than that. You couldn't help being more than that. That's one of the things hardest to realise about ourselves sometimes. Even in your morbid moments you often showed me how to get a grip on things. By example, you might say. You cannot help but be a good man, Mr Terry. A protector, I think, rather than a predator.'

'I do not know about that.'

'But I do,' she says.

'Anyway,' he flips a teacake onto the warming plate, 'we had no children and so the McLears have no heirs.'

'It's a shame,' she says, 'but not a tragedy, surely?' For an instant it flashes through her head, *Oh, no, he doesn't want me to have his bloody babies, does he?*

'Not in any ordinary sense, I quite agree. But you see there is an inheritance that goes along with that. Something which must be remembered accurately and passed down by word of mouth. It is our family tradition and has been so for quite a time.'

'My goodness,' she says. 'You're Brian Boru's rightful successor to the high throne of Erin, is that it?' With deft economy she butters their teacakes.

He takes some jelly from the dish and lays it lightly on top. 'Oh, these are good, eh?'

When they are drinking their last possible cup of Assam he says very soberly: 'Would you let me share this secret, Kate? I have no-one else.'

'Not a crime, is it, or something nasty?' she begs.

'Certainly not!' He falls silent. She can sense him withdrawing and laughs at his response. He sighs.

'Then get on with it,' she says. 'Give me a taste of it, for I'm a busy woman.'

'The story does not involve the Irish much,' he says. 'Most of the Celts involved were from southern England, which was called Britannia in those days, by the Romans.'

'Ancient history!' she cries. 'How long, Mr Terry, is your story?'

'Not very long,' he says.

'Well,' she says, 'I will come back another time to hear it.' She glances at her watch. 'If I don't go now I'll miss my programme.'

As he helps her on with her coat she says: 'I have a very low tolerance for history. It is hard for me to see how most of it relates to the here and now.'

'This will mean something to you, I think, Kate.'

They exchange light kisses upon the cheek. There is a new warmth between them which she welcomes.

'Make it scones tomorrow,' she says. 'Those big juicy ones they do, with the raisins in them, and I will hear your secret. We'll have Darjeeling, too. I'll bring some if you don't have any.'

'I have plenty,' he says.

'Bye, bye for now,' she says.

Chapter Six

'ALL THE GOODNESS is in the marrow!' declares Mrs Byrne, waving her bones at the other customers. 'But these days the young people all turn their noses up at it.'

'That's not the problem at all, Mavis. The plain truth is you're a bloody noisy eater,' says Corny Doyle, backing up the other diners' complaints. 'And you've had one too many now. You had better go home.'

With her toothless mouth she sucks at her mutton.

'They don't know what they're missing, do they, Mavis?' says Father McQueeny from where he sits panting in a booth.

'And you can fuck off, you old pervert.' Mavis rises with dignity and sails towards the Ladies'. She has her standards.

'Well, Kate, how's the weather out there?' says Father McQueeny.

'Oh, you are here at last, Kate. It seems Father McQueeny's been locked out of his digs.' In other circumstances Corny's expression of pleading anxiety would be funny.

'That doesn't concern me,' she says, coming down the stairs. 'I just popped in for something. I have told you what I want, Dad.' She is carrying her little bag.

He rushes after her, whispering and pleading. 'What can I do?'

'I have told you what you can do.'

She looks back into the shadows. She knows he is staring at her. Often she thinks it is not exactly him that she fears, only what is in him. What sense does that make? Does she fear his memories and secrets? Of course Father Walsh, her confessor, had heard what had happened and what she had done and she had been absolved. What was more, the Church, by some means of its own, had discovered at least part of the truth and taken steps to curb him. They had sent Father Declan down to St Mary's. He was a tough old bugger but wholesome as they come. McQueeny was supposed to assist Declan who had found no use for him. However, since Father Walsh died, McQueeny revelled in their hideous secret, constantly hanging around the pub even before she started working there, haunting her, threatening to tell the world how he had come by his horrid surgery.

She is not particularly desperate about it. Sooner or later she knows her father will knuckle down and ban the old devil. It must be only a matter of time before the priest's liver kills him. She's never wished anyone dead in her life, save him, and her hatred of him is such that she fears for her own soul over it.

This time she goes directly across the park to Mr Terry McLear's. It might look as if she plans to spend the night there but she does not care. Her true intention is to return eventually to her own flat in Delaware Court and wait until her father calls. She gives it twenty-four hours from the moment she stepped out of the pub.

But when she lifts the lion's head and lets it fall there is no reply. She waits. She climbs back up the steps. She looks into the park. She is about to go down again when an old chequer cab pulls up and out of its yellow-and-black depths comes Mr Terry McLear with various bags and bundles. 'Oh, what luck!' he declares. 'Just when I needed you, Kate.'

She helps him get the stuff out of the cab and down into his den. He removes his coat. He opens the door into his workshop and switches on a light. 'I was not expecting you back today.'

'Circumstances gave me the opportunity.' She squints at the bags. 'Who is Happy the Hammer?'

'Look on the other side. It is Stadtler's Hardware. Their mascot. Just the last bits I needed.'

'Is it a bird-house of some kind that you are building?' she asks.

'And so you are adding telepathy to your list of extraordinary qualities, are you, Katey?' He grins. 'Did I ever mention this to you?'

'You might have done. Is it pigeons?'

'God bless you, Katey.' He pulls a bunch of small dowels out of a bag and puts it on top of some bits of plywood. 'I must have told you the story.'

'Not much of a secret, then,' she says.

'This is not the secret, though I suppose it has something to do with it. There used to be dovecotes here, Katey, years ago. And that is all I am building. Have you not noticed the little doves about?'

'I can't say I have.'

'Little mourning doves,' he says. 'Brown and cream. Like a kind of delicate pigeon.'

'Well,' she says, 'I suppose for the non-expert they'd be lost in the crowd.'

'Maybe, but I think you would know them when I pointed them out. The City believes me, anyhow, and is anxious to have them back. And it is not costing them a penny. The whole thing is a matter of fifty dollars and a bit of time. An old-fashioned dovecote, Katey. There are lots of accounts of the dovecotes, when this was more or less an independent village.'

'So you're building a little house for the doves,' she says. 'That will be nice for them.'

'A little house, is it? More a bloody great hotel.' Mr Terry erupts with sudden pride. 'Come on, Kate. I will take you back to look.'

Chapter Seven

S HE ADMIRES HIM turning the wood this way and that against the whirling lathe he controls with a foot pedal.

'It is a wonderful smell,' she says, 'the smell of shavings.' She peers with casual curiosity at his small, tightly organised workshop. Tools, timber, electrical bits and pieces, nails, screws and hooks are neatly stowed on racks and narrow shelves. She inspects the white-painted sides of the near-completed bird-house. In the room, it seems massive, almost large enough to hold a child. She runs her fingers over the neatly ridged openings, the perfect joints. Everything has been finished to the highest standard, as if for the most demanding human occupation. 'When did they first put up the dovecotes?'

'Nobody knows. The Indians had them when the first explorers arrived from Holland and France. There are sketches of them in old books. Some accounts call the tribe that lived here "the Dove Keepers". The Iroquois respected them as equals and called them the Ga-geh-ta-o-no, the People of the Circle. But the phrase also means People of the Belt.

'The Talking Belts, the "wampum" records of the Six Nations, are invested with mystical meanings. Perhaps our tribe were the Federation's record-keepers. They were a handsome, wealthy, civilised people, apparently, who were happy to meet and trade with the newcomers. The famous Captain Block was their admirer and spoke of a large stone circle surrounding their dovecotes. He believed that these standing stones, which were remarkably like early European examples, enclosed their holy place and that the doves represented the spirit they worshipped.

'Other accounts mention the stones, but there is some suspicion that the writers simply repeated Block's observations. Occasionally modern construction work reveals some of the granite, alien rock driven into the native limestone like a knife, and there is a suspicion the rock was used as part of a later stockade. The only Jesuit records make no mention of the stones but concentrate on the remarkable similarity of Kakatanawa (as the Europeans called them) myths to early forms of Christianity.'

'I have heard as much myself,' she agrees, more interested than she expected. 'What happened to the Indians?'

'Nothing dramatic. They were simply and painlessly absorbed, mainly through intermarriage and mostly with the Irish. It would not have been difficult for them, since they still had a considerable amount of blood in common. By 1720 this was a thriving little township, built around the green. It still had its dovecotes. The stones were gone, re-used in walls of all kinds. The Kakatanawa were living in ordinary houses and intermarrying. In those days it was not fashionable to claim native ancestry. But you see the Kakatanawa were hardly natives. They resembled many of the more advanced Iroquois peoples and spoke an Iroquois dialect, but their tradition had it that their ancestors came from the other side of the Atlantic.'

'Where did you read all this?' she asks in some bewilderment.

'It is not conventionally recorded,' he says. 'But this is my secret.'

And he told her of Trinovante Celts, part of the Boudicca uprising of AD 69, who had used all their wealth to buy an old Roman trading ship with the intention of escaping the emperor's cruel justice and sailing to Ireland. They were not navigators but good fortune eventually took them to these shores where they built a settlement. They chose Manhattan for the same reason as everyone else, because it commanded a good position on the river, had good harbours and could be easily defended.

They built their village inland and put a stockade around it, pretty much the same as the villages they had left behind. Then they sent the ship back with news and to fetch more settlers and supplies. They never heard of it again. The ship was in fact wrecked off Cornwall, probably somewhere near St Ives, but there were survivors and the story remained alive amongst the Celts, even as they succumbed to Roman civilisation.

When, some hundreds of years later, the Roman legions were withdrawn and the Saxon pirates started bringing their families over, further bands of desperate Celts fled for Ireland and the land beyond, which they had named Hy Braseal. One other galley reached Manhattan and discovered a people more Senecan than Celtic.

This second wave of Celtic immigrants were the educated Christian stone-raisers, Romanised astronomers and mystics, who brought new wisdom to their distant cousins and were doubtless not generally welcomed for it. For whatever reasons, however, they were never attacked by other tribes. Even the stern Iroquois, the Romans of these parts, never threatened them, although they were nominally subject to Hiawatha's Federation. By the time the Dutch arrived, the dominant Iroquois culture had again absorbed the Celts, but they retained certain traditions, stories and a few artefacts. Most of these appear to have been sold amongst the Indians and travelled widely through the Northeast. They gave rise to certain rumours of Celtic civilisations (notably the Welsh) established in America.

'But the Kakatanawa spoke with the same eloquence and wore the finery and fashions of the Federation. Their particular origin-legend was not remarkable. Other tribes had far more dramatic conceptions, involving spectacular miracles and wildly original plots. So nobody took much notice of us and so we have survived.'

'Us?' says Kate Doyle. 'We?'

'You,' he says, 'represent the third wave of Celtic settlement of the Circle during the nineteenth and twentieth centuries. And I represent the first and second. I am genuinely, Katey, and it is embarrassing to say so, the Last of the Kakatanawas. That was why my father looked forward to an heir, as did I. I suppose I was not up to the burden, or I would have married again.'

'You'd be a fool to marry just for the sake of some old legend,' she says. 'A woman deserves more respect than that.'

'I agree.' He returns to his work. Now he's putting the fine little touches to the dowels, the decorations. It's a wonder to watch him.

'Do you have a feathered headdress and everything? A peace pipe and a tomahawk?' Her mockery has hardly any scepticism in it.

'Go over to that box just there and take out what is in it,' he says, concentrating on the wood.

She obeys him.

It is a little modern copper box with a Celtic motif in the lid. Inside is an old dull coin. She picks it up between wary fingers and fishes it out, turning it to try to read the faint letters of the inscription. 'It's Constantine,' she says. 'A Roman coin.'

'The first Christian Emperor. That coin has been in New York, in our family, Katey, since the sixth century. It is pure gold. It is what is left of our treasure.'

'It must be worth a fortune,' she says.

'Not much of one. The condition is poor, you see. And I am sworn never to reveal its provenance. But it is certainly worth a bit more than the gold alone. Anyway, that is it. It is yours, together with the secret.'

'I don't want it,' she says, 'can't we bury it?'

'Secrets should not be buried,' he says, 'but kept.'

'Well, speak for yourself,' she says. 'There are some secrets best buried.'

While he worked on, she told him about Father McQueeny. He turned the wood more and more slowly as he listened. The priest's favourite joke that always made him laugh was 'Little girls should be screwed and not heard'. With her father's half-hearted compliance, the old wretch had enjoyed all his pleasures on her until one day when she was seventeen she had taken his penis in her mouth and, as she had planned, bitten down like a terrier. He had torn her hair out and almost broken her arm before he fainted.

'And I did not get all the way through. You would not believe how horrible it feels – like the worst sort of gristle in your mouth and all the blood and nasty crunching, slippery stuff. At first, at least, everything in you makes you want to stop. I was very sick afterwards, as you can imagine, and just able to dial 911 before I left him there. He almost died of losing so much blood. I hadn't expected it to spurt so hard. I almost drowned. I suppose if I had thought about it I should have anticipated that. And had a piece of string ready, or something. Anyway, it stopped his business. I was never reported. And I don't know how confessors get the news out, but the Church isn't taking any chances with him, so all he has now are his memories.'

'Oh, dear,' says Mr Terry gravely. 'Now there is a secret to share.'

'It's the only one I have,' she said. 'It seemed fair to reciprocate.'

Chapter Eight

Two days later, side by side, they stand looking up at his magnificent bird-house, complete at last. He's studied romantic old plans from the turn of the century, so it has a touch or two of the Charles Rennie Mackintosh about it in its white austerity, its sweeping gables. There are seven fretworked entrances and eight beautifully turned perches, black as ebony, following the lines of the park's paths. He's positioned and prepared the cote exactly as instructed in Tiffany's *Modern Gardens* of 1892 and has laid his seed and corn carefully. At her request, and without much reluctance, he's buried the Roman coin in the pole's foundation. Now we must be patient, he says. And wait. As he speaks a whickering comes from above and a small dove, fawn and pale grey, settles for a moment upon the gleaming roof, then takes fright when she sees them.

'What a pretty thing. I will soon have to get back to my flat,' she says. 'My father will be going frantic by now. I put the machine on, but if I know him he'll be too proud to leave a message.'

'Of course.' He stoops to pick up a delicately coloured wing feather. It has a thousand shades of rose, beige, pink and grey. 'I will be glad to come with you if you want anything done.'

'I'll be all right,' she says. But he falls in beside her.

As they turn their backs on the great bird-house three noisy mourning doves land on the perches as if they have been anticipating this moment for a hundred and fifty years. The sense of celebration, of relief, is so tangible it suffuses Kate Doyle and Mr Terry McLear even as they walk away.

'This calls for a cup of coffee,' says Mr Terry McLear. 'Shall we go to Belladonna's?'

They are smiling when Father McQueeny, evicted at last, comes labouring towards them along the path from the pub and pauses, suddenly gasping for his familiar fix, as if she has turned up in the nick of time to save his life.

'Good morning, Katey, dear.' His eyes begin to fill with powerful memories. He speaks lovingly to her. 'And Terry McLear, how are you?'

'Not bad, thank you, Father,' says Mr Terry, looking him over.

'And when shall we be seeing you in church, Terry?' The priest is used to people coming back to the faith as their options begin to disappear.

'Oh, soon enough, Father, I hope. By the way, how is Mary's last supper doing? How is the little hot-dog?' And he points.

It is a direct and fierce attack. Father McQueeny folds before it. 'Oh, you swore!' he says to her.

She tries to speak but she cannot. Instead she finds herself laughing in the old wretch's face, watching him die, his secret, his sustenance lost for ever. He knows at once, of course, that his final power has gone. His cold eyes stare furiously into inevitable reality as his soul goes at last to the Devil. It will be no more than a day or two before they bury him.

'Well,' says Katey, 'we must be getting on.'

'Goodbye, Father,' says Mr Terry McLear, putting his feather in his white hair and grinning like a fool.

When they look back the priest has disappeared, doubtless scuttling after some mirage of salvation. But the dovecote is alive with birds. It must have a dozen on it already, bobbing around in the little doorways, pecking up the seed. They glance around with equanimity. You would think they had always been here. The distant noise of New York's traffic is muffled by their excited voices, as if old friends meeting after years. There is an air of approving recognition about their voices.

'They like the house. Now we must see if, when they have eaten the food, they will stay.' Mr Terry McLear offers a proud arm to his companion. 'I never expected it to happen so quickly. It was as if they were waiting to come home. It is a positive miracle.'

Amused, she looks up at him. 'Come on now, a grown man like you with tears in his eyes!

'After all, Mr Terry.' She takes his arm as they continue down the path towards Houston Alley. 'You must never forget your honour as the Last of the Kakatanawas.'

'You do not believe a word of it, do you, Kate?' he says.

'I do,' she says. 'Every word, in fact. It's just that I cannot fathom why you people went to so much trouble to keep it dark.'

'Oh, you know all right, Kate,' says Mr Terry McLear, pausing to look back at the flocking doves. 'Sometimes secrecy is our only means of holding on to what we value.'

Whistling, she escorts him out of the Circle.

A Twist in the Lines

1

Cornelius got off at Tottenham Court Road again. Not for the first time he hesitated by the doors, only jumping out when they hissed at him. Something was sodding with the system. Reality was haywire. Subtly rearranged, the mosaic was affecting the passengers. People shielded their eyes or stared at the tarmac. Some were already shocked, shaking, vomiting. In a frightened self-conscious silence they hurried through connecting tunnels and up flights of steps. The station had the atmosphere of a cathedral at the end of a long service. Slipping his hands from the pockets of his black car coat Jerry pulled on his gloves. He checked his wrists. Both watches had stopped.

The escalator still carried him up to Notting Hill Gate, the station he'd started from. On the big map outside an arrow pointed at Tottenham Court Road. **You Were Here**. Should he buy a fresh ticket?

2

The mass disappearance of some seven hundred passengers from Kasuga Kōrakuen, a busy Tokyo interchange, was only noticed by the Press when some passengers started reappearing at Montparnasse and Knightsbridge. After frantically shopping in Galeries Lafayette and Harrods, they got back on trains terminating at Pelham Bay Park, Van Cortlandt Park and other unfamiliar suburbs of New York where they generally became hysterical.

3

'Bloody 'ell,' Jerry's old mum wheezed up to him on the west-bound platform while he stared at another map. 'Slow darn, Jer, don't wanna overdo it, love. I'm tryin' ter reach Victoria. While I've got yer…' Dragging a great lump of dirty knitting from her horrible bag she held it by its needles to his chest. 'Makin' sure it's yer colour. You've gorn red.'

Jerry had given up protesting. 'Try yellow.' He pointed. 'Or green.' He tapped the District Line. 'I'll meet you there, Mum.' He legged it, working out his options. *Try something more oblique. Change at Oxford Circus, approach from Warren Street.*

4

Shakey Mo Collier saluted Jerry waiting for the Northern Line train. Mo wore his own navy-blue security stuff. Uniforms made him feel safe. A big chromed steel Banning 0.27 rested across his scrawny chest.

He loved Jerry. He hated Jerry. What could you do? 'Aren't you barred from Tottenham Court Road, Mr C?'

Almost mockingly the doors closed and opened quickly. They leapt aboard. Mo cocked the gun: 'There's a simple way to deal with this. Ouch.' He had caught his beard in the selector lever. 'I'm thinking of getting out of this game.' The train slowed. They had arrived at Châtelet–Les Halles. 'Oh, blimey, not bloody Paris again.'

Mo tugged the gun free and tried to fire a random burst but he'd left too much hair on the charging handle. The Banning muttered for a few seconds then seized up completely. The gun's neurotic electronics were notorious. He followed Jerry out to the nearest Vélib' stand.

Choosing a bike Jerry wondered if he could pick up the plans and crack the codes intratemporally. He must give Mo the slip, meet his contacts and make it back to 1982, before the first cement was up. 'When in doubt, twist and shout.' $Z^2 + c$? The maths on this one was a step ahead of Mandelbrot. Jerry grinned. Self-similarity? A slightly different equation. But logic he could live with. Altschuler's radiant time: $R^2 + c = m$. Pedalling rapidly towards République he asked his iWatch for some quick calculations but it, too, was baffled. Losing Mo at the Cirque d'Hiver, Jerry ducked down into Les Filles du Calvaire and bought some tickets at the machine.

Meanwhile, phone Alvarez. He tapped his wrist. He mapped out his own circuit. If he made it to Madeleine he might get his memory back.

5

Albertine Pardon waited for Jerry by the Canal St Martin lock across from *La Grisette*. She was elegant in her old cashmere overcoat, astrakhan collar, black homburg. She pulled off her glove as Jerry approached. Jerry wore a dark green bluegrass jacket with yoke shoulders, Peruvian Levis and black snakeskin and silver boots. He had changed during his walk down from Belleville. They shook hands. Crossing to a café modern, they sat outside.

'The maths you asked for was in Munich. I took the U-bahn from Karlsplatz and here I am. Thanks.'

'Just a hunch.' Jerry studied the figures. 'So this is what we need. A conceptual delivery system. The original circuit board. Beck's Tube map.'

'The disappearances and reappearances are widespread. Nobody wants to use the Underground, autoroutes, trains. As for Eurostar…' Mme Pardon's small nose jabbed like a finger. 'Why Altschuler?'

'Space as a dimension of Time.'

'And Mandelbrot?'

'Self-similarity.'

'The mosaic?'

'Caroll's new model of the multiverse. A deck of cards. It

works well enough. It's almost my favourite. Echoes, resonances, circuits, tiles. The existentialist's panto.'

'Someone's forever falling into a black hole and popping out of one, is that it?' Pardon reached for her *pressé* as a chubby, turbaned Hindu paused smiling at their table. Jerry rose comfortably. '*Kita kore*! This is my old Sri Lankan friend.' He made introductions. 'Things in Colombo okay, prof?'

'Surprisingly stable.' With his back to the view, Professor Hira sat down and ordered an *américain*. 'This is a matter of gravity, eh?' Hira loved dry, academic jokes. He couldn't help himself. 'Well, Mr Cornelius, it's just as you suspected. The problem is focused at Tottenham Court.' His tone was fruity rich.

'Art is science. Science is art. We have reached that point again. All great works of art are re-created across the multiverse, of course. Recently we've had a fresh phenomenon: art is no longer echoing reality but redefining it. Since 1984 the model of existence we share and prefer, the whole of radiant time, version upon version of constructed reality, has depended for its survival on a certain artistic pattern, an essential mechanism for order. Alter that pattern and you get rather closer to chaos than most people would like. Every other design begins to follow the disturbance, adjusting itself.

'Black holes, dark matter, dark flow. The system constantly evolves and devolves, is destroyed and re-created. Our universes are best described in terms of size and mass extending, unseen one by the other, through something like eternity. We're a tiny mote of dust in comparison to the expanding multiverse and there are zillions of still tinier motes. Size is completely relative. But those almost identical patterns are repeated to near-infinity. They are delicate, you see. Disturb a single pattern and you disturb them all. Everything starts vibrating and eventually things fall apart. The Central Line is the first to go. Chaos. But then we have Altschuler. Radiant time.' Professor Hira smacked his lips. 'Oh, indeed!'

Mme Pardon studied the papers.

'It would take –'

'A fool!' Panicking, Jerry noticed the canal's waters slowly rising, overflowing its banks and running backwards. 'Is the Eiffel hangar still open?'

6

There was nothing else for it. He could only get to 1982 by driving his mum to Eel Pie Island and the Time Centre. He should have known she was part of the equation. Breakdown was almost complete. Worldwide, millions of commuters found themselves emerging from the wrong stations, getting off buses in alien nations, finding they had arrived in tiny Cuban villages or taking an interstate flyover in Ohio and going north into St Petersburg with only the Cyrillic signs offering any clue to their whereabouts. Could the pattern be restored?

7

At the Time Centre Sergeant Alvarez soothed his black beard. 'All we have between ourselves and disintegration are some Pound and a couple of Firbank novels. Oh, and a bit of Mozart. That's it. Not a perfect fit.' He leaned back in his chair, brooding up at his screens, accepting the packet Jerry handed him. Smoothing out the contents he smiled. 'Ha, ha! Munich turned up trumps. This scrap of paper might just save the world. All I needed was the resolution.' He tapped in some numbers. 'But you'll have to get back there and check the data as it reassembles itself. Hello, Mrs C. Could I have a quick look at your casting off?'

Cocking her head like a budgie, she reluctantly passed him her mephitic wool.

8

With Beck's map in one hand, Paolozzi's plans at eye level, Jerry glued in the last tile, standing with his thumb on it until it dried. A quietening of the dissonance. The Tottenham Court Road circuits were now restored, the resonances balanced.

Mrs C. remained unimpressed by the pattern. 'Fair Isle, innit? A Scotchman, was 'e? Sort o' fing they'd play golf in.'

Jerry checked his watches. 6 p.m. Rush hour. Only one way to test it. Philosophically, he boarded the homebound Central Line train. Even the muzak was restored to default.

'Is that Vera Lynn or Bob Dylan?' Giggling, his mum squeezed in behind him. 'Cosy, eh? Reminds yer o' the War.'

Running between Leather Lane and Brookgate Market, Livesey Walk is best known for its eighteenth-century inn, the Three Jolly Dragoons – where, legend has it, Dick Turpin and Tom King held court during the Golden Age of the Tobymen (mounted highway-robbers whose exploits were finally brought to an end by the introduction of the electric tram). A few tobymen continued to waylay trams run by the London Universal Transport Co., though the famous cry of 'Throw down your lever' was a myth propagated in such boys' papers as *Thrilling Tramway Yarns* and *The Dick Turpin Library*. Livesey Walk was later the residence of Edward Holmes, Desmond Reid and a number of authors, all of whom worked for the Amalgamated Press, which was situated nearby. Between 1910 and 1914, the Walk was the fictitious address of the 'office boy's Sherlock Holmes', Sexton Blake. Arnold Bennett lived here for a short time, after his return from France in 1912.

COVENEY'S YARD, EC3

Although the Elizabethan courtyard has now disappeared, the name is still attached to the Brookgate flats (built in 1990). Until the early years of the twentieth century the Yard was best known for Coveney & Child's Medical Supply Stores – the chief importers of opium and morphine, suppliers to London society (including many theatrical celebrities). George Grossmith refers to 'Coveney the Younger, the Happiness Monger' in one of his comic songs. De Quincey mentions 'Coveney's Comfort' in a footnote to his second revision of *Confessions of an English Opium Eater*. For a short time, in the 1870s, Coveney & Child enjoyed the prestige of a royal warrant.

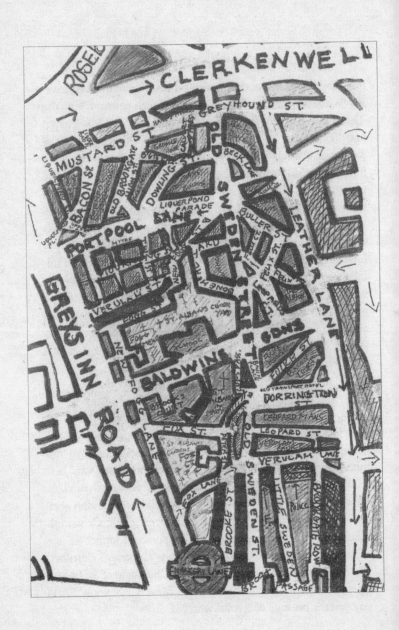

Named for Sir John Moustiere, the first Huguenot judge in London, the Old Moon & Stars was originally a coffee shop. It is mentioned by Goldsmith in an essay published in the *Monthly Review* (1758). (The New Moon & Stars is located in Dykes Street, Smithfield, and is notable for its 'bloodworms' – the black sausages that are still sold, on request, in the teeth of Euro regulations.)

The Old Moon & Stars became a public house during the middle part of the nineteenth century and was noticed by Dickens in several articles for *Once a Week*. The association with *Master Humphrey's Clock* is recalled in dubious memorabilia. A framed document claims that in the first draft of the tale Dickens portrays Adjutant Slate holding court in the pub.

The house sustained some damage during the Blitz but was restored in 1965. The proprietor, Tommy Mendes, had a reputation in the East End as a bare-knuckle boxer. He can still be brought downstairs to talk to customers who are making a disturbance. In recent years, thanks to a relaxation in the licensing laws, fifty kinds of absinthe have been made available – including the famous 'Red and Yellow' (95 p.c. proof).

TALES of the TRAMWAYS

**A Monthly Magazine of Adventure, Mystery and Education
featuring the famous
'Knight of the Line' -- DICK TURPIN**

JULY 1976   PRICE ONE SHILLING   Vol. VIX No. 3

DICK TURPIN SOLVES THE MYSTERY OF THE

*MURDER on the
ORPINGTON EXPRESS!!
By Agatha Colvin*

A Tale of the Romney Marsh lines

The final issue of *Tales of the Tramways*. 'A kind of popular fiction unique to London' – Cyril Connolly. Hugely popular in the 1920s and 1930s, *Tales* had by 1970 become primarily a comic book.

The Clapham Antichrist

Begg Mansions,
Sporting Club Square
London, W14

The Editor,
Fulham & Hammersmith Telegraph,
Bishops Palace Avenue,
London W14

13th October 1992

Sir,

SPIRIT OF THE BLITZ

It is heartening to note, as our economy collapses perhaps for the last time, a return to the language and sentiments of mutual self-interest. London was never the kindest of English cities but of late her cold, self-referential greed has been a watchword around the world. Everything we value is threatened in the name of profit.

I say nothing original when I mourn the fact that it took the Blitz to make Londoners achieve a humanity and heroism they never thought to claim for themselves and which no-one expected or demanded of them!

Could we not again aspire to achieve that spirit, without the threat of Hitler but with the same optimistic courage? Can we not, in what is surely an hour of need, marshal what is best in us and find new means of achieving that justice, equity and security for which we all long? The existing methods appear to create as many victims as they save.

Yours faithfully, Edwin Begg,
former vicar of St. Odhran's, Balham.

HEAR! HEAR! says the Telegraph. This week's Book Token to our Letter of the Week! Remember, your opinions are important to us and we want to see them! A £5.00 Book Token for the best!

Chapter One

My First Encounter with the Clapham Antichrist;
His Visions & His Public Career;
His Expulsion from the Church & Subsequent Notoriety;
His Return to Society & Celebrity as a Sage;
His Mysterious & Abrupt Departure into Hermitage;
His Skills in the Kitchen.

'SPIRIT OF THE Blitz' (a sub-editor's caption) was the last public statement of the Clapham Antichrist.

Until I read the letter at a friend's I believed Edwin Begg dead some twenty years ago. The beloved TV eccentric had retired in the 1950s to live as a recluse in Sporting Club Square, West Kensington. I had known him intimately in the '60s and '70s and was shocked to learn he was still alive. I felt a conflicting mixture of emotions, including guilt. Why had I so readily accepted the hearsay of his death? I wrote to him at once. Unless he replied to the contrary I would visit him on the following Wednesday afternoon.

I had met Begg first in 1966 when as a young journalist I interviewed him for a series in the *Star* about London's picturesque obscurities. Then too I had contacted him after reading one of his letters to the *Telegraph*. The paper, still a substantial local voice, was his only source of news, delivered to him weekly. He refused to have a telephone and communicated mostly through the post.

I had hoped to do a few paragraphs on the Antichrist's career, check a couple of facts with him and obtain a short, preferably amusing, comment on our Fab Sixties. I was delighted when, with cheerful courtesy, Edwin Begg had agreed by return to my request. In a barely legible old-fashioned hand he invited me to lunch.

My story was mostly drafted before I set off to see him. Research had been easy. We had half a filing drawer on Edwin Begg's years of notoriety, first before the War then afterwards as a radio and early TV personality. He had lived in at least a dozen foreign cities. His arguments were discussed in every medium and he became a disputed symbol. Many articles about him were merely sensa-tional, gloating over alleged black-magic rites, sexual deviation, miracle-working, blasphemy and sorcery. There were the usual photographs and also drawings, some pretending to realism and others cruel cartoons: the Clapham Antichrist as a monster with blazing eyes and glittering fangs, architect of the doom to come. One showed Hitler, Stalin and Mussolini as his progeny.

The facts were pretty prosaic; in 1931 at the age of twenty-four Begg was vicar of St Odhran's, Balham, a shabby South London living where few parishioners considered themselves respectable enough to visit a church and were darkly suspicious of those who did. The Depression years had almost as many homeless and hun-gry people on the streets as today. Mosley was gathering a more militant flock than Jesus, and those who opposed the fascists looked to Oxford or the secular left for their moral leadership. Nonetheless the Reverend Begg conscientiously performed his duty, offering the uncertain comforts of his calling to his flock.

Then quite suddenly in 1933 the ordinary hard-working cleric became an urgent proselytiser, an orator. From his late Victorian pulpit he began preaching a shocking message urging Christians to act according to their principles and sacrifice their own material ambitions to the common good, to take a risk on God being right, as he put it. This Tolstoyan exhortation eventually received enough public attention to make his sermons one of London's most popular free attractions from Southwark to Putney, which of course brought him the attention of the famous Bermondsey barrackers, the disapproval of his establishment and the closer interest of the Press.

The investigators the Church sent down heard a sermon touching mainly on the current state of the Spanish Republic, how anarchists often acted more like ideal Christians than the priests, how people seemed more willing to give their lives to the anarchists than to the cause of Christ. This was reported in *Reynolds News*, tipped off that the investigators would be there, as Begg's urging his congregation to support the coming Antichrist. The report was more or less approving. The disapproving church investigators, happy for a lead to follow, confirmed the reports. Overnight, the Reverend Edwin Begg, preaching his honest Christian message of brotherly love and equity under the law, became the Clapham Antichrist, Arch-Enemy of British Decency, Proud Mocker of All Religion and Hitler's Right Hand, a creature to be driven from our midst.

In the course of a notoriously hasty hearing Edwin Begg was unfrocked, effectively by public demand. In his famous defence Begg confirmed the general opinion of his guilt by challenging the commission to strip itself naked and follow Christ, if they were indeed Christians! He made a disastrous joke: and if they were an example of modern Christians, he said, then after all he probably was the Antichrist!

Begg never returned to his vicarage. He went immediately to Sporting Club Square. Relatives took him in, eventually giving him his own three-roomed flat where it was rumoured he kept a harem of devil-worshipping harlots. The subsequent Siege of Sporting Club Square in which the *News of the World* provoked a riot causing one near-fatality and thousands of pounds' worth of damage was overshadowed by the news of Hitler's massacre of his storm troopers, the SA.

Goebbels's propaganda became more interesting and rather

more in the line of an authentic harbinger of evil, and at last Edwin Begg was left in peace.

Usually attached to a circus or a fair and always billed as 'Reverend' Begg, The Famous Clapham Antichrist! he began to travel the country with his message of universal love. After his first tours he was never a great draw since he disappointed audiences with urgent pleas for sanity and the common good and never rose to the jokes or demands for miracles, but at least he had discovered a way of making a living from his vocation. He spent short periods in prison and there were rumours of a woman in his life, someone he had mentioned early on, though not even the worst of the Sundays found evidence to suggest he was anything but confirmed in his chastity.

When the War came Edwin Begg distinguished himself in the ambulance service, was wounded and decorated. Then he again disappeared from public life. This was his first long period of seclusion in Begg Mansions until suddenly on 1 May, 1949, encouraged by his nephew Robert in BBC Talks, he gave at 9.45 p.m. on the Home Service the first of his Fireside Observer chats.

No longer the Old Testament boom of the pulpit or the sideshow, the Fireside Observer's voice was level, reassuring, humorous, a little sardonic sometimes when referring to authority. He reflected on our continuing hardships and what we might gain through them if we kept trying – what we might expect to see for our children. He offered my parents a vision of a wholesome future worth working for, worth making a few sacrifices for, and they loved him.

He seemed the moral spirit of the Festival of Britain, the best we hoped to become, everything that was decent about being British. An entire book was published proving him the object of a plot in 1934 by a Tory bishop, a fascist sympathiser, and there were dozens of articles, newsreels and talks describing him as the victim of a vicious hoax or showing how Mosley had needed a scapegoat.

Begg snubbed the Church's willingness to review his case in the light of his new public approval and continued to broadcast the reassuring ironies which lightened our 1950s darkness and helped us create the golden years of the 1960s and '70s. He did not believe his dream to be illusory.

By 1950 he was on television, part of the *Thinkers' Club* with Gilbert Harding and Professor Joad, which every week discussed an important contemporary issue. The programme received the accolade of being lampooned in *Radio Fun* as *The Stinker's Club* with Headwind Legg which happened to be one of my own childhood favourites. He appeared, an amiable sage, on panel games, quiz shows, programmes called *A Crisis of Faith* or *Turning Point* and at religious conferences eagerly displaying their tolerance by soliciting the opinion of a redeemed antichrist.

Suddenly, in 1955, Begg refused to renew all broadcasting contracts and retired from public life, first to travel and finally to settle back in Begg Mansions with his books and his journals. He never explained his decision and then the public lost interest. New men with brisker messages were bustling in to build utopia for us in our lifetime.

Contenting himself with a few letters mostly on parochial matters to the Hammersmith *Telegraph*, Edwin Begg lived undisturbed for a decade. His works of popular philosophy sold steadily until British fashion changed. Writing nothing after 1955, he encouraged his books to go out of print. He kept his disciples, of course, who sought his material in increasingly obscure places and wrote to him concerning his uncanny understanding of their deepest feelings, the ways in which he had dramatically changed their lives, and to whom, it was reported, he never replied.

The first Wednesday I took the 28 from Notting Hill Gate down North Star Road to Greyhound Gardens. I had brought my *A–Z*. I had never been to Sporting Club Square before and was baffled by the surrounding network of tiny twisting streets, none of which seemed to go in the same direction for more than a few blocks, the result of frenzied rival building work during the speculative 1880s when developers had failed to follow the plans agreed between themselves, the freeholder, the architect and the authorities. The consequent recession ensured that nothing was ever done to remedy the mess. Half-finished crescents and abrupt cul-de-sacs, odd patches of wasteland, complicated rights of way involving narrow alleys, walls, gates and ancient pathways were interrupted, where bomb damage allowed, by the new council estates, totems of clean enlightenment geometry whose erection would automatically cause all surrounding social evils to wither away. I had not expected to find anything quite so depressing and began to feel sorry for Begg ending his days in such circumstances, but turning out of Margrave Passage I came suddenly upon a cluster of big unkempt oaks and cedars gathered about beautiful wrought-iron gates in the baroque oriental regency style of Old Cogges, that riot of unnatural ruin, the rural scat of the Beggs which William the Goth remodelled in 1798 to rival Strawberry Hill. They were miraculous in the early-afternoon sun: the gates to paradise.

The Square now has a preservation order and appears in international books of architecture as the finest example of its kind. Sir Hubert Begg, its architect, is mentioned in the same breath as Gaudí and Norman Shaw, which will give you some notion of his peculiar talent. Inspired by the fluid aesthetics of the *fin de siècle* he was loyal to his native brick and fired almost every fancy from Buckingham clay to give his vast array of disparate styles an inexplicable coherence. The tennis courts bear the motifs of some Mucha-influenced smith, their floral metalwork garlanded with living roses and honeysuckle from spring until autumn: even the benches are on record as one of the loveliest expressions of public art nouveau.

Until 1960 there had been a black chain across the Square's entrance and a porter on duty day and night. Residents' cars were never seen in the road but garaged in the little William Morris cottages originally designed as studios and running behind the eccentrically magnificent palaces, which had been Begg's Folly until they survived the Blitz to become part of our heritage. When

I walked up to the gates in 1966 a few cars had appeared in the gravel road running around gardens enclosed by other leafy iron-work after Charles Rennie Mackintosh, and the Square had a bit of a shamefaced seedy appearance.

There were only a few uniformed porters on part-time duty by then and they too had a slightly hangdog air. The Square was wea-thering one of its periodic declines, having again failed to connect with South Kensington during a decade of prosperity. Only the bohemian middle classes were actually proud to live there, so the place had filled with actors, music-hall performers, musicians, singers, writers, cheque-kiters and artists of every kind, together with journalists, designers and retired dance instructresses, hair-dressers and disappointed legatees muttering bitterly about any blood not their own, for the Square had taken refugees and immi-grants. Others came to be near the tennis courts maintained by the SCS Club affiliated to nearby Queen's.

Several professionals had taken apartments in Wratislaw Villas, so the courts never went down and neither did the gardens which were preserved by an endowment from Gordon Begg, Lord Mauleverer, the botanist and explorer, whose elegant vivarium still pushed its flaking white girders and steamy glass above exotic shrubbery near the Mandrake Road entrance. Other examples of his botanical treasures, the rival of Holland's, flourished here and there about the Square and now feathery exotics mingled with the oaks and hawthorn of the original Saxon meadow.

Arriving in this unexpected tranquillity on a warm September afternoon when the dramatic red sun gave vivid contrast to the terracotta, the deep greens of trees, lawns and shrubbery, I paused in astonished delight. Dreamily I continued around the Square in the direction shown me by the gatehouse porter. I was of a generation which enthused over Pre-Raphaelite paint and made Beardsley its own again, who had bought the five-shilling Mackin-tosh chairs and sixpenny Muchas and ten-bob Lalique glass in Portobello Road to decorate Liberty-oriental pads whose fragrant patchouli never disguised the pungent dope. They were the best examples we could find in this world to remind us of what we had seen on our acid voyages.

To my father's generation the Square would be unspeakably old-fashioned, redolent of the worst suburban pretension, but I had come upon a gorgeous secret. I understood why so few people mentioned it, how almost everyone was either enchanted or repelled. My contemporaries, who thought 'Georgian' the absolute height of excellence and imposed their stern developments upon Kensington's levelled memory, found Sporting Club Square hideously 'Victorian' – a gigantic, grubby whatnot. Others dreamed of the day when they would have the power to be free of Sporting Club Square, the power to raze her and raise their fake Le Corbusier mile-high concrete in triumph above the West London brick.

I did not know, as I made my way past great mansions of Caligari Tudor and Kremlin De Mille, that I was privileged to find the Square in the final years of her glory. In those days I enjoyed a wonderful innocence and could no more visualise this lovely old place changing for the worse than I could imagine the destruction of Dubrovnik.

Obscured, sometimes, by her trees, the mansion apartments of Sporting Club Square revealed a thousand surprises. I was in danger of being late as I stared at Rossettian gargoyles and Blakean caryatids, copings, gables, corbels of every possible stamp yet all bearing the distinctive style of their time. I was filled with an obscure sense of epiphany.

In 1886, asymmetrical Begg Mansions was the boldest expression of modernism, built by the architect for his own family use, for his offices and studios, his living quarters, a suite to entertain clients, and to display his designs, accommodation for his draughts- and crafts-people whose studios in attics and basements produced the prototype glass, metal, furniture and fabrics which nowadays form the basis of the V&A's extraordinary collection. By the 1920s after Hubert Begg's death the Square became unfashionable. Lady Begg moved to Holland Park and Begg Mansions filled up with the poorer Beggs who paid only the communal fee for general upkeep and agreed to maintain their own flats in good condition. Their acknowledged patron was old Squire Begg, who had the penthouse. By 1966 the building was a labyrinth of oddly twisting corridors and stairways, unexpected landings reached by two old oak-and-copper cage elevators served by their own generator, which worked on an eccentric system devised by the architect and was always going wrong. Later I learned that it was more prudent to walk the six flights to Edwin Begg's rooms but on that first visit I got into the lift, pressed the stud for the sixth floor and was taken up without incident in a shower of sparks and rattling brass to the ill-lit landing where the Antichrist himself awaited me.

I recognised him of course but was surprised that he seemed healthier than I had expected. He was a little plumper and his bone-white hair was cropped in a self-administered pudding-basin cut. He was clean-shaven, pink and bright as a mouse, with startling blue eyes, a firm rather feminine mouth and the long sharp nose of his mother's Lowland Presbyterian forefathers. His high voice had an old-fashioned Edwardian elegance and was habitually rather measured. He reminded me of a Wildean *grande-dame*, tiny but imposing. I was dressed like most of my Ladbroke Grove peers and he seemed pleased by my appearance, offering me his delicate hand, introducing himself and muttering about my good luck with the lift. He had agreed to this interview, he said, because he'd been feeling unusually optimistic after playing the new Beatles album. We shared our enthusiasm.

He guided me back through those almost organic passages until we approached his flat and a smell so heady, so delicious that I did not at first identify it as food. His front door let directly onto his study which led to a sitting room and bedroom. Only the dining room seemed unchanged since 1900 and still had the original Voysey wallpaper and furniture, a Henry dresser and Benson copperware. Like many reclusive people he enjoyed talking. As he continued to cook he sat me on a sturdy Wilson stool with a glass of wine and asked me about my career, showing keen interest in my answers.

'I hope you don't mind home cooking,' he said. 'It's a habit I cultivated when I lived on the road. Is there anything you find disagreeable to eat?'

I would have eaten strychnine if it had tasted as that first meal tasted. We had mysterious sauces whose nuances I can still recall, wines of exquisite delicacy, a dessert which contained an entire orchestra of flavours, all prepared in his tiny perfect 1920s 'modern' kitchenette to one side of the dining room.

After we had eaten he suggested we take our coffee into the bedroom to sit in big wicker chairs and enjoy another wonderful revelation. He drew the curtains back from his great bay window to reveal over two miles of almost unbroken landscape all the way to the river with the spires and roofs of Old Putney beyond. In the far distance was a familiar London skyline but immediately before us were the Square's half-wild communal gardens and cottage garages, then the ivy-covered walls of St Mary's Convent, the Convent School sports field and that great forest of shrubs, trees and memorial sculptures, the West London Necropolis, whose Victorian angels raised hopeful swords against the ever-changing sky. Beyond the cemetery was the steeple of St Swithold's and her churchyard, then a nurtured patchwork of allotments, some old alms cottages and finally the sturdy topiary of the Bishop's Gardens surrounding a distant palace whose Tudor dignity did much to inspire Hubert Begg. The formal hedges marched all the way to the bird sanctuary on a broad, marshy curve where the Thames approached Hammersmith Bridge, a mediaeval fantasy.

It was the pastoral and monumental in perfect harmony which some cities spontaneously create. Edwin Begg said the landscape was an unfailing inspiration. He could dream of Roman galleys beating up the river cautiously alert for Celtic war parties or Vikings striking at the Bishop's Palace leaving flames and murder behind. He liked to think of other more contemplative eyes looking on a landscape scarcely changed in centuries. 'Hogarth, Turner and Whistler amongst them. Wheldrake, writing *Harry Wharton*, looked out from this site when staying at the Sporting Club Tavern and earlier Augusta Begg conceived the whole of *The*

Bravo of Bohemia and most of *Yamboo; or, The North American Slave* while seated more or less where I am now! Before he went off to become an orientalist and London's leading painter of discreet seraglios James Lewis Porter painted several large landscapes which show market gardens where the allotments are, a few more cottages, but not much else has changed. I can walk downstairs, out of the back door, through that gate, cross the convent field into the graveyard, take the path through the church down to the allotments all the way to the Bishop's Gardens and be at the bird sanctuary within half an hour, even cross the bridge into Putney and the Heath if I feel like it and hardly see a house, a car or another human being!' He would always stop for a bun, he said, at the old Palace Tea Rooms and usually strolled back via Margrave Avenue's interesting junkyards. Mrs White, who kept the best used bookshop there, told me he came in at least twice a week.

He loved to wake up before dawn with his curtains drawn open and watch the sun gradually reveal familiar sights. 'No small miracle, these days, dear! I'm always afraid that one morning it won't be there.' At the time I thought this no more than a mildly philosophical remark.

For me he still had the aura of a mythic figure from my childhood, someone my parents had revered. I was prepared to dislike him but was immediately charmed by his gentle eccentricity, his rather loud plaid shirts and corduroys, his amiable vagueness. The quality of the lunch alone would have convinced me of his virtue!

I was of the 1960s, typically idealistic and opinionated and probably pretty obnoxious to him but he saw something he liked about me and I fell in love with him. He was my ideal father.

I returned home to rewrite my piece. A figure of enormous wisdom, he offered practical common sense, I said, in a world ruled by the abstract sophistries and empty reassurances heralding the new spirit of competition into British society. It was the only piece of mine the *Star* never used, but on that first afternoon Edwin Begg invited me back for lunch and on almost every Wednesday for the next eight years, even after I married, I would take the 28 from the Odeon, Westbourne Grove, to Greyhound Gardens and walk through alleys of stained concrete, past shabby red terraces and doorways stinking of rot until I turned that corner and stood again before the magnificent gates of Sporting Club Square.

My friend kept his curiosity about me and I remained flattered by his interest. He was always fascinating company, whether expanding on some moral theme or telling a funny story. One of his closest chums had been Harry Lupino Begg, the music-hall star, and he had also known Al Bowlly. He was a superb and infectious mimic and could reproduce Lupino's patter by heart, making it as topical and fresh as the moment. His imitation of Bowlly singing 'Buddy, Can You Spare a Dime' was uncanny. When carried away by some amusing story or conceit his voice would rise and fall in rapid and entertaining profusion, sometimes taking on a birdlike quality difficult to follow. In the main however he spoke with the deliberate air of one who respected the effect of words upon the world.

By his own admission the Clapham Antichrist was not a great original thinker but he spoke from original experience. He helped me look again at the roots of my beliefs. Through him I came to understand the innocent intellectual excitement of the years before political experiments turned one by one into tyrannical orthodoxies. He loaned me my first Kropotkin, the touching *Memoirs of a Revolutionist*, and helped me understand the difference between moral outrage and social effect. He loved works of popular intellectualism. He was as great an enthusiast for Huxley's *The Perennial Philosophy* as he was for Winwood Reade's boisterously secular *Martyrdom of Man*. He introduced me to the interesting late work of H.G. Wells and to Elizabeth Bowen. He led me to an enjoyment of Jane Austen I had never known. He infected me with his enthusiasm for the more obscure Victorians who remained part of his own living library and he was generous with his books. But, no matter how magical our afternoons, he insisted I must always be gone before the BBC broadcast *Choral Evensong*. Only in the dead of winter did I ever leave Sporting Club Square in darkness.

Naturally I was curious to know why he had retired so abruptly from public life. Had he told the church of his visions? Why had he felt such an urgent need to preach? To risk so much public disapproval? Eventually I asked him how badly it had hurt him to be branded as the premier agent of the Great Antagonist, the yapping dog as it were at the heels of the Son of the Morning. He said he had retreated from the insults before they had grown unbearable. 'But it wasn't difficult to snub people who asked you questions like "Tell me, Mr Begg, what does human blood taste like?" Besides, I had my Rose to sustain me, my vision…'

I hoped he would expand on this but he only chuckled over some association he had made with an obscure temptation of St Anthony and then asked me if I had been to see his cousin Orlando Begg's *Flaming Venus*, now on permanent display at the Tate.

Though I was soon addicted to his company, I always saw him on the same day and time every week. As he grew more comfortable with me he recounted the history of his family and Sporting Club Square. He spoke of his experiences as a young curate, as a circus entertainer, as a television personality, and he always cooked. This was, he said, the one time he indulged his gourmet instincts. In the summer we would stroll in the gardens or look at the tennis matches. Sitting on benches we would watch the birds or the children playing. When I asked him questions about his own life his answers became fuller, though never completely unguarded.

It was easy to see how in his determined naïveté he was once in such frequent conflict with authority.

'I remember saying, my dear, to the magistrate – Who does not admire the free-running, intelligent fox? And few, no matter how inconvenienced, begrudge him his prey which is won by daring raiding and quick wits, risking all. A bandit, your honour, one can admire and prepare against. There is even a stirring or two of romance for the brigand chief. But once the brigand becomes a baron that's where the balance goes wrong, eh, your honour? It gets unfair, I said to him. Our sympathies recognise these differences so why can't our laws? Our courts make us performers in pieces of simplistic fiction! Why do we continue to waste so much time? The magistrate said he found my last remark amusing and gave me the maximum sentence.'

Part of Edwin Begg's authority came from his vivacity. As he sat across from me at the table, putting little pieces of chicken into his mouth, pausing to enjoy them, then launching off onto a quite different subject, he seemed determined to relish every experience, every moment. His manner offered a clue to his past. Could he be so entertaining because he might otherwise have to confront an unpleasant truth? Anyone raised in a post-Freudian world could make that guess. But it was not necessarily correct.

Sometimes his bright eyes would dart away to a picture or glance through a window and I learned to interpret this fleeting expression as one of pain or sadness. He admitted readily that he had retreated into his inner life, feeling he had failed in both his public and private missions. I frequently reassured him of his value, the esteem in which he was still held, but he was unconvinced.

'Life isn't a matter of linear consequences,' he said. 'We only try to make it look like that. Our job is not to force grids upon the world but to achieve harmony with nature.'

At that time in my life such phrases made me reach for my hat, if not my revolver, but because I loved him so much I tried to understand what he meant. He believed that in our terror we imposed perverse linearity upon a naturally turbulent universe, that our perceptions of time were at fault since we saw the swirling cosmos as still or slow-moving just as a gnat doubtless sees us. He thought that those who overcame their brute terror of the truth soon attained the state of the angels.

The Clapham Antichrist was disappointed that I was not

more sympathetic to the mystical aspects of the alternative society but because of my familiarity with its ideas was glad to have me for a devil's advocate. I was looking for a fast road to utopia and he had almost given up finding any road at all. Our solutions were wrong because our analysis was wrong, he said. We needed to rethink our fundamental principles and find better means of applying them. I argued that this would take too long. Social problems required urgent action. His attitude was an excuse for inaction. In the right hands there was nothing wrong with the existing tools.

'And what are the right hands, dear?' he asked. 'Who makes the rules? Who keeps them, my dear?' He ran his thin fingers through hair which became a milky halo around his earnest face. 'And how is it possible to make them and keep them when our logic insists on such oppressive linearity? We took opium into China and bled them of their silver. Now they send heroin to us to lay hands upon our currency! Am I the only one enjoying the irony? The Indians are reclaiming the south-western United States in a massive migration back into the old French and Spanish lands. The world is never still, is it, my dear?'

His alert features were full of tiny signals, humorous and anxious, enquiring and defiant, as he expanded on his philosophy one autumn afternoon. We strolled around the outer path enjoying the late roses and early chrysanthemums forming an archway roofed with fading honeysuckle. He wore his green raglan, his yellow scarf, his hideous turf-accountant's trilby, and gestured with the blackthorn he always carried but hardly used. 'The world is never still and yet we continue to live as if turbulence were not the natural order of things. We have no more attained our ultimate state than has our own star! We have scarcely glimpsed any more of the multiverse than a toad under a stone! We are part of the turbulence and it is in turbulence we thrive. Once that's understood, my dear, the rest is surely easy? Brute warfare is our crudest expression of natural turbulence, our least productive. What's the finest? Surely there's no evil in aspiring to be our best? What do we gain by tolerating or even justifying the worst?'

I sat down on the bench looking the length of a bower whose pale golds and browns were given a tawny burnish by the sun. Beyond the hedges was the sound of a tennis game. 'And those were the ideas which so offended the Church?' I asked.

He chuckled, his face sharp with self-mockery. 'Not really. They had certain grounds, I suppose. I don't know. I merely suggested to my congregation, after the newspapers had begun the debate, that perhaps only through Chaos and Anarchy could the Millennium be achieved. There were after all certain clues to that effect in the Bible. I scarcely think I'm to blame if this was interpreted as calling for bloody revolution, or heralding Armageddon and the Age of the Antichrist!'

I was diplomatic. 'Perhaps you made the mistake of overestimating your audiences?'

Smiling he turned where he sat to offer me a reproving eye. 'I did not overestimate them, my dear. They underestimated themselves. They didn't appreciate that I was trying to help them become one with the angels. I have experienced such miracles, my dear! Such wonderful visions!'

And then quite suddenly he had risen and taken me by my arm to the Duke's Elm, the ancient tree which marked the border of the larger square in what was really a cruciform. Beyond the elm were lawns and well-stocked beds of the cross's western bar laid out exactly as Begg had planned. Various residents had brought their deckchairs here to enjoy the last of the summer. There was a leisurely good-humoured holiday air to the day. It was then, quite casually and careless of passers-by, that the Clapham Antichrist described to me the vision which converted him from a mild-mannered Anglican cleric into a national myth.

'It was on a similar evening to this in 1933. Hitler had just taken power. I was staying with my Aunt Constance Cunningham, the actress, who had a flat in D'Yss Mansions and refused to associate with the other Beggs. I had come out here for a stroll to smoke my pipe and think over a few ideas for the next Sunday's sermon which I would deliver, my dear, to a congregation consisting mostly of the miserably senile and the irredeemably small-minded who came to church primarily as a signal to neighbours they believed beneath them...

'It was a bloody miserable prospect. I have since played better audiences on a wet Thursday night in a ploughed field outside Leeds. No matter what happened to me I never regretted leaving those dour ungiving faces behind. I did my best. My sermons were intended to discover the smallest flame of charity and aspiration burning in their tight little chests. I say all this in sad retrospect. At the time I was wrestling with my refusal to recognise certain truths and find a faith not threatened by them.

'I really was doing my best, my dear.' He sighed and looked upward through the lattice of branches at the jackdaw nests just visible amongst the fading leaves. 'I was quite agitated about my failure to discover a theme appropriate to their lives. I wouldn't give in to temptation and concentrate on the few decent parishioners at the expense of the rest.' He turned to look across the lawns at the romantic rococo splendour of Moreau Mansions. 'It was a misty evening in the Square with the sun setting through those big trees over there, a hint of pale gold in the haze and bold comforting shadows on the grass. I stood here, my dear, by the Duke's Elm. There was nobody else around. My vision stepped forward, out of the mist, and smiled at me.

'At first I thought that in my tiredness I was hallucinating. I'd been trained to doubt any ecstatic experience. The scent of roses was intense, like a drug! Could this be Carterton's ghost said to haunt the spot where he fell to his death, fighting a duel in the branches after a drunken night at Begg's? But this was no young duke. The woman was about my own height, with graceful beauty and the air of peace I associated with the Virgin. My unconventional madonna stood in a mannish confident way, a hand on her hip, clearly amused by me. She appeared to have emerged from the earth or from the tree. Shadows of bark and leaves still clung to her. There was something plantlike about the set of her limbs, the subtle colours of her flesh, as if a rose had become human and yet remained thoroughly a rose. I was rather frightened at first, my dear.

'I'd grown up with an Anglicanism permitting hardly a hint of the Pit, so I didn't perceive her as a temptress. I was thoroughly aware of her sexuality and in no way threatened by it or by her vitality. After a moment the fear dissipated, then after a few minutes she vanished and I was left with what I could only describe as her inspiration which led me to write my first real sermon that evening and present it on the following Sunday.'

'She gave you a message?' I thought of Jeanne D'Arc.

'Oh, no. Our exchange was wordless on that occasion.'

'And you spoke of her in church?'

'Never. That would have been a sort of betrayal. No, I based my message simply on the emotion she had aroused in me. A vision of Christ might have done the same. I don't know.'

'So it was a Christian message? Not anti-Christian?'

'Not anti-religious, at any rate. Perhaps, as the bishop suggested, a little pagan.'

'What brought you so much attention?'

'In the church that Sunday were two young chaps escorting their recently widowed aunt, Mrs Nye. They told their friends about me. To my delight when I gave my second sermon I found myself with a very receptive congregation. I thanked God for the miracle. It seemed nothing else, my dear. You can't imagine the joy of it! For any chap in my position. I'd received a gift of divine communication, perhaps a small one, but it seemed pretty authentic. And the people began to pack St Odhran's. We had money for repairs. They seemed so willing suddenly to give themselves to their faith!'

I was mildly disappointed. This Rose did not seem much of a vision. Under the influence of drugs or when overtired I had experienced hallucinations quite as elaborate and inspiring. I asked him if he had seen her again.

'Oh, yes. Of course. Many times. In the end we fell in love. She taught me so much. Later there was a child.'

He stood up, adjusted his overcoat and scarf and gave his stick a little flourish. He pointed out how the light fell through the parade of black gnarled maples leading to the tennis courts. 'An army of old giants ready to march,' he said. 'But their roots won't let them.'

The next Wednesday when I came to lunch he said no more about his vision.

Chapter Two

A Brief History of the Begg Family
& of Sporting Club Square

IN THE COURSE of my first four hundred lunches with the Clapham Antichrist I never did discover why he abandoned his career but I learned a great deal about the Begg family, its origins, its connections and its property, especially the Square. I became something of an expert and planned a monograph until the recent publication of two excellent Hubert Begg books made my work only useful as an appendix to real scholarship.

Today the Square, on several tourist itineraries, has lost most traces of its old unselfconscious integrity. Only Begg Mansions remains gated and fenced from casual view, a defiantly private museum of human curiosities. The rest of the Square has been encouraged to maximise its profitability. Bakunin Villas is now the Hotel Romanoff. Ralph Lauren for some time sponsored D'Yss Mansions as a fashion gallery. Beardsley Villas is let as company flats to United Foods, while the Council (which invested heavily in BBIC) took another building, the Moorish fantasy of Flecker Mansions, as offices. There is still some talk of an international company 'theme-parking' Sporting Club Square, running commercial tennis matches and linking it to a television soap. Following the financial scandals involving Begg Belgravia International and its associate companies, the Residents' Association has had some recent success in reversing this progress.

When I visited Edwin Begg in 1992, he welcomed me as if our routine had never been broken. He mourned his home's decline into a mere fashion, an exploitable commodity instead of a respected eccentricity, and felt it had gone the way of the Château Pantin or Derry & Toms Famous Roof Garden, with every feature displayed as an emphatic curiosity, a sensation, a mode, and all her old charm a wistful memory. He had early on warned them about these likely consequences of his nephew's eager speculations. 'Barbican wasn't the first to discover what you could do in a boom economy with a lick of paint, but I thought his soiling of his own nest a remote chance, not one of his first moves! The plans of such people are generally far advanced before they achieve power. When they strike, you are almost always taken unawares, aren't you, dear? What cold, patient dreams they must have.'

He derived no satisfaction from any prospect of Barbican Begg's future ruin but felt deep sympathy for his fellow residents hopelessly trying to recover their stolen past.

'It's too late for us now and soon it won't matter much, but it's hard to imagine the kind of appetite which feeds upon souls like locusts on corn. We might yet drive the locust from our field, my dear, but he has already eaten his fill. He has taken what we cannot replace.'

Sometimes he was a little difficult to follow and his similes grew increasingly bucolic.

'The world's changing physically, dear. Can't you feel it?' His eyes were as bright a blue and clear as always, his pink cheeks a little more drawn, his white halo thinner, but he still pecked at the middle distance when he got excited, as if he could tear the truth from the air with his nose. He was clearly delighted that we had resumed our meetings. He apologised that the snacks were things he could make and microwave. They were still delicious. On our first meeting I was close to tears, wondering why on earth I had simply assumed him dead and deprived myself of his company for so long. He suggested a stroll if I could stand it.

I admitted that the Square was not improving. I had been appalled at the gaudy golds and purples of the Hotel Romanoff. It was, he said, currently in receivership, and he shrugged. 'What is it, my dear, which allows us to become the victims of such villains, time after time! Time after time they take what is best in us and turn it to our disadvantage. It's like being a conspirator in one's own rape.'

We had come up to the Duke's Elm again in the autumn twilight and he spoke fondly of familiar ancestors.

Cornelius Van Beek, a Dutch cousin of the Saxon von Beks, had settled in London in 1689, shortly after William and Mary. For many Europeans in those days England was a haven of relative enlightenment. A daring merchant banker, Van Beek financed exploratory trading expeditions, accompanying several of them himself, and amassed the honourable fortune enabling him to retire at sixty to Cogges Hall, Sussex. Amongst his properties when he died were the North Star Farm and tavern, west of Kensington, bought on the mistaken assumption that the area was growing more respectable and where he had at one time planned to build a house. This notorious stretch of heath was left to Van Beek's nephew, George Arthur Begg who had anglicised his name upon marriage to Harriet Vernon, his second cousin, in 1738. Their only surviving grandson was Robert Vernon Begg, famous as Dandy Bob Begg and ennobled under the Prince Regent.

As financially impecunious as his patron, Dandy Bob raised money from co-members of the Hellfire, took over the old tavern at North Star Farm, increased its size and magnificence, entertained the picaro captains so they would go elsewhere for their prizes, ran bare-knuckle fights, bear-baitings and other brutal spectacles, and founded the most notorious sporting establishment of its day. Fortunes were commonly lost and won at Begg's; suicides, scandals and duels no rarity. A dozen of our oldest families spilled their blood in the meadow beneath the black elm, and perhaps a score of men and women drowned in the brook now covered and serving as a modern sewer.

Begg's Sporting Club grew so infamous, the activities of its members and their concubines such a public outrage, that when the next William ascended, Begg rapidly declined. By Victoria's crowning the great dandy whom all had courted had become a souse married into the Wadhams for their money, got his wife Effie pregnant with male twins and died, whereupon she somewhat boldly married his nephew Captain Russell Begg and had three more children before he died a hero and a colonel in the Crimea. The twins were Ernest Sumara and Louis Palmate Begg, her two girls were Adriana Circe and Juliana Aphrodite and her youngest boy, her favourite child, was Hubert Alhambra born on 18 January, 1855, after his father's fatal fall at Balaclava.

A youthful disciple of Eastlake, by the late 1870s Hubert Begg was a practising architect whose largest single commission was Castle Bothwell on the shores of Loch Ness (his sister had married James Bothwell) which became a victim of the Glasgow blitz. 'But it was little more than a bit of quasi-Eastlake and no rival for instance to the V and A,' Edwin Begg had told me. He did not share my admiration for his great-uncle's achievement. 'Quite frankly, his best work was always his furniture.' He was proud of his complete bedroom suite in Begg's rather spare late style but he did not delight in living in 'an art nouveau wedding cake'. He claimed the Square's buildings cost up to ten times as much to clean as Oakwood Mansions, for instance, at the western end of Kensington High Street. 'Because of the crannies and fancy mouldings, those flowing fauns and smirking sylphs the late Victorians found so deliciously sexy. Dust traps all. It's certainly unique, my dear, but so was Quasimodo.'

Hubert Begg never struggled for a living. He had married the beautiful Carinthia Hughes, an American heiress, during his two years in Baltimore and it was she who suggested he use family land for his own creation, tearing down that ramshackle old firetrap, the Sporting Club Tavern, which together with a smallholding was rented to a family called Foulsham whom Begg generously resettled on prime land, complete with their children, their cow, their pig and various other domestic animals, near Old Cogges.

The North Star land was cleared. North Star Square was named but lasted briefly as that. It was designed as a true square with four other smaller squares around it to form a sturdy box cross, thus allowing a more flexible way of arranging the buildings, ensuring residents plenty of light, good views and more tennis. Originally there were plans for seven tennis courts. By the 1880s tennis was a social madness rather than a vogue and everybody was playing. Nearby Queen's Club was founded in Begg's shadow. Begg's plans were altogether more magnificent and soon the projected settlement blossomed into Sporting Club Square. The name had a slightly raffish, romantic reference and attracted the more daring young people, the financiers who still saw themselves as athletic privateers and who were already patrons to an artist or two as a matter of form.

Clients were encouraged to commission favourite styles for Begg to adapt. He had already turned his back on earlier influences, so Gothic did not predominate, but was well represented in Lohengrin Villas which was almost an homage to Eastlake, commissioned by the Church to house retired clergy who felt comfortable with its soaring arches and mighty buttresses. Encouraged by the enthusiasm for his scheme, the architect was able to indulge every fantasy, rather in the manner of a precocious Elgar offering adaptations of what Greaves called, in the *British Architect*, 'Mediterranean, Oriental, Historical and Modern styles representing the quintessence of contemporary taste.' But there were some who even then found it fussy and decadent. When the queen praised it as an example to the world Begg was knighted. Lady Carinthia, who survived him by many years, always credited herself as the Square's real procreator and it must be said it was she who nudged her husband away from the past to embrace a more plastic future.

Work on Sporting Club Square began in 1885 but was not entirely completed until 1901. The slump of the 1890s destroyed the aspirations of the rising bourgeoisie, who were to have been the likely renters; Gibbs and Flew had bankrupted themselves building the Olympia Bridge, and nobody who still had money felt secure enough to cross into the new suburbs. Their dreams of elevation now frustrated, the failed and dispossessed took their new bitter poverty with them into the depths of a North Star development doomed never to rise and to become almost at once a watchword for social decrepitude, populated by loafers, psychopaths, unstable landladies, exploited seamstresses, drunkards, forgers, beaten wives, braggarts, embezzlers, rat-faced children, petty officials and prostitutes who had grown accustomed to the easy prosperity of the previous decade and were now deeply resentful of anyone more fortunate. They swiftly turned the district into everything it remained until the next tide of prosperity lifted it for a while, only to let it fall back almost in relief as another generation lost its hold upon life's ambitions. The terraces were occupied by casual labourers and petty thieves while the impoverished petite bourgeoisie sought the mews and parades. North Star became a synonym for wretchedness and miserable criminality and was usually avoided even by the police.

By 1935 the area was a warren to rival Notting Dale, but Sporting Club Square, the adjoining St Mary's Convent and the churchyard, retained a rather dreamy, innocent air, untouched by the prevailing mood. Indeed locals almost revered and protected the Square's tranquillity as if it were the only thing they had ever held holy and were proud of it. During the last war the Square was untouched by incendiaries roaring all around, but some of the flats were already abandoned and then taken over by the government to house mostly Jewish political exiles and these added to the cosmopolitan atmosphere. For years a Polish delicatessen stood on the corner of North Star Road; it was possible to buy all kinds of kosher food at Mrs Green's grocery, Mandrake Terrace, and the Foulsham Road French pâtisserie remained popular until 1980 when Madame Stejns retired. According to Edwin Begg, the War and the years of austerity were their best, with a marvellous spirit of co-operation everywhere. During the War and until 1954 open-air concerts were regularly performed by local musicians and an excellent theatrical group was eventually absorbed into the Lyric until that was rationalised. A song, 'The Rose of Sporting Club Square', was popular in the 1930s and the musical play it was written for was the basis of a Hollywood musical in 1940. The David Glazier Ensemble, perhaps the most innovative modern dance troupe of its day, occupied all the lower flats in Le Gallienne Chambers.

Edwin Begg was not the only resident to become famous with

the general public. Wheldrake's association with the old tavern, where he spent two years of exile, is well known. Audrey Vernon lived most of her short life in Dowson Mansions. Her lover, Warwick Harden, took a flat in Ibsen Studios next door and had a door built directly through to her bedroom. John Angus Gilchrist the mass murderer lived here but dispatched his nearest victim three miles away in Shepherd's Bush. Others associated with the Square, sometimes briefly, included W. Pett Ridge, George Robey, Gustav Klimt, Rebecca West, Constance Cummings, Jessie Matthews, Sonny Hale, Jack Parker, Gerald Kersh, Laura Riding, Josef Kiss, John Lodwick, Edith Sitwell, Lord George Creech, Angela Thirkell, G.K. Chesterton, Max Miller, Sir Compton Mackenzie, Margery Allingham, Ralph Richardson, Eudora Welty, Donald Peers, Max Wall, Dame Fay Westbrook, Graham Greene, Eduardo Paolozzi, Gore Vidal, Bill Butler, Jimi Hendrix, Jack Trevor Story, Laura Ashley, Mario Amayo, Angela Carter, Simon Russell Beale, Ian Dury, Jonathan Carroll and a variety of sports and media personalities. As its preserves were stripped, repackaged and sold off during the feeding frenzy of the 1980s only the most stubborn residents refused to be driven from the little holdings they had once believed their birthright, but it was not until Edwin Begg led me back to his bedroom and raised the newly installed blind that I understood the full effect of his nephew's speculations. 'We do not rest, do we,' he said, 'from mortal toil? But I'm not sure this is my idea of the new Jerusalem. What do you think, dear?'

They had taken his view, all that harmony. I was consumed with a sense of unspeakable outrage! They had turned that beautiful landscape into a muddy wasteland in which it seemed some monstrous, petulant child had scattered at random its filthy Tonka trucks and Corgi cranes, Portakabins, bulldozers in crazed abandon, then in tantrum stepped on everything. That perfect balance was destroyed and the tranquillity of Sporting Club Square was now forever under siege. The convent was gone, as well as the church.

'I read in the *Telegraph* that it required the passage of two private members' bills, the defiance of several preservation orders, the bribery of officials in thirteen different government departments and the blackmailing of a cabinet minister just to annex a third of the cemetery and knock down the chapel and almshouses,' Begg said.

Meanwhile the small fry had looted the cemetery of its saleable masonry. Every monument had been chiselled. The severed heads of the angels were already being sold in the antique boutiques of Mayfair and Saint-Germain-des-Prés. Disappointed in their share of this loot, others had daubed swastikas and obscenities on the remaining stones.

'It's private building land now,' said Begg. 'They have dogs and fences. They bulldozed St Swithold's. You can't get to the Necropolis, let alone the river. Still, this is probably better than what they were going to build.'

The activities of Barbican Begg and his associates, whose enterprises claimed more victims than Maxwell, have been discussed everywhere, but one of the consequences of BBIC's speculations was that bleak no man's land standing in place of Edwin Begg's familiar view. The legal problems of leases sold to and by at least nine separate companies mean that while no further development has added to the Square's decline, attempts to redress the damage and activate the Council's preservation orders which they ignored have failed through lack of funds. The project, begun in the name of freedom and civic high-mindedness, always a mark of the scoundrel, remains a symbol and a monument to the asset-stripped '8os. As yet only Frank Cornelius, Begg's close associate, has paid any satisfactory price for ruining so many lives.

'Barbican was born for that age.' Edwin Begg drew down the blind against his ruined prospect and sat on his bed, his frail body scarcely denting the great Belgian pillows at his back. 'Like a fly born to a dungheap. He could not help himself, my dear. It was his instinct to do what he did. Why are we always surprised by his kind?'

He had grown weak but eagerly asked if I would return the following Wednesday when he would tell me more about his visions and their effect upon his life. I promised to bring the ingredients of a meal. I would cook lunch. He was touched and amused by this. He thought the idea great fun.

I told him to stay where he was. It was easy to let myself out.

'You know,' he called as I was leaving, 'there's a legend in our family. How we protect the Grail which will one day bring a reconciliation between God and Lucifer. I have no Grail to pass on to you but I think I have its secret.'

Chapter Three

Astonishing Revelations of the Clapham Antichrist;
Claims Involvement in the Creation of a New Messiah;
His Visions of Paradise & Surrendering His Soul for Knowledge;
Further Description of the Sporting Club Square Madonna;
Final Days of the Antichrist;
His Appearance in Death.

'PERHAPS THE CROWNING irony,' said the Clapham Antichrist of his unfrocking, 'was how devoted a Christian I was then! I argued that we shouldn't wait for God or heroes but seek our solutions at the domestic level. Naturally, it would mean empowering everyone, because only a thoroughly enfranchised democracy ever makes the best of its people. Oh, well, you know the sort of thing. The universal ideal that we all agree on and never seem to achieve. I merely suggested we take a hard look at the systems we used! They were quite evidently faulty! Not an especially revolutionary notion! But it met with considerable antagonism as you know. Politics seems to be a war of labels, one slapped on top of another until any glimmer of truth is thoroughly obscured. It's no wonder how quickly they lose all grip on reality!'

'And that's what you told them?'

He stood in his dressing gown staring down at a square and gardens even BBIC had failed to conquer. The trees were full of the nests crows had built since the first farmers hedged the meadow. His study, with its books and big old-fashioned stereo, had hardly changed but had a deserted air now.

I had brought the ingredients of our lunch and stood in my street clothes with my bag expecting him to lead me to the kitchen, but he remained in his window and wanted me to stay. He pointed mysteriously towards the Duke's Elm and Gilbert's

War Memorial, a fanciful drinking fountain that had never worked.

'That's what I told them, my dear. In the pulpit first. Then in the travelling shows. Then on the street. I was arrested for obstruction in 1937, refused to recognise the court and refused to pay the fine. This was my first brief prison sentence. Eventually I got myself in solitary.

'When I left prison I saw a London even more wretched than before. Beggars were everywhere. Vagrants were not in those days tolerated in the West End, but were still permitted in the doorways of Soho and Somers Town. The squalor was as bad as anything Mayhew reported. I thought my anger had been brought under control in prison but I was wrong. The obscene exploitation of the weak by the strong was everywhere displayed. I did whatever I could. I stood on a box at Speakers' Corner. I wrote and printed pamphlets. I sent letters and circulars to everyone, to the newspapers, to the BBC. Nobody took me very seriously. In the main I was ignored. When I was not ignored I was insulted. Eventually, holding a sign in Oxford Street, I was again arrested but this time there was a scuffle with the arresting policeman. I went into Wormwood Scrubs until the outbreak of the Blitz when I was released to volunteer for the ambulance service. Well, I wasn't prepared to return to prison after the War and in fact my ideas had gained a certain currency. Do you remember what Londoners were like then, my dear? After we learned how to look after ourselves rather better than our leaders could? Our morale was never higher. London's last war was a war the people won in spite of the authorities. But somewhere along the line we gave our achievements over to the politicians, the power addicts. The result is that we now live in rookeries and slum courts almost as miserable as our nineteenth-century ancestors', or exist in blanketed luxury as divorced from common experience as a Russian Tsar. I'm not entirely sure about the quality of that progress, are you? These days the lowest common denominators are sought for as if they were principles.'

'You're still an example to us,' I said, thinking to console him.

He was grateful but shook his head, still looking down at the old elm as if he hoped to see someone there. 'I'll never be sure if I did any good. For a while, you know, I was quite a celebrity until they realised I wasn't offering an anti-Christian message and then they mostly lost interest. I couldn't get on with those Jesuits they all cultivated. But I spoke to the Fabians twice and met Wells, Shaw, Priestley and the rest. I was very cheerful. It appeared that I was spreading my message. I didn't understand that I was merely a vogue. I was quite a favourite with Bloomsbury and there was talk of putting me on Radio Luxembourg. But gradually doors were closed to me and I was rather humiliated on a couple of occasions. I hadn't started all this for fame or approval, so as soon as I realised what was happening I retired to the travelling shows and seaside fairgrounds which proliferated in England in the days before television.

'Eventually I began to doubt the value of my own pronouncements, since my audiences were dwindling and an evil force was progressing unchecked across Europe. We faced a future dominated by a few cruel dictatorships. Some kind of awful war was inevitable. During my final spell in clink I made up my mind to keep my thoughts to myself and consider better ways of getting them across. I saw nothing wrong with the message, but assumed myself to be a bad medium. In my free time I went out into the Square as much as I could. It was still easy to think there, even during the War.'

He took a step towards the window, almost as if he had seen someone he recognised and then he shrugged, turning his head away sharply and pretending to take an interest in one of his Sickerts. 'I found her there first, as you know, in 1933. And that one sight of her inspired a whole series of sermons. I came back week after week, but it always seemed as if I had just missed her. You could say I was in love with her. I wanted desperately for her to be real. Well, I had seen her again the evening I was "unfrocked". Of course I was in a pretty terrible state. I was praying. Since a boy I've always found it easy to pray in the Square. I identified God with the Duke's Elm – or at least I visualised God as a powerful old tree. I never understood why we placed such peculiar prohibitions on how we represented God. That's what they mean by "pagan". It has nothing to do with one's intellectual sophistication. I was praying when she appeared for the second time. First there was that strong scent of roses. When I looked up I saw her framed against the great trunk and it seemed a rose drew all her branches, leaves and blooms together and took human form!'

His face had a slight flush as he spoke. 'It seemed to me I'd been given a companion to help me make the best use of my life. She had that vibrancy, that uncommon beauty; she was a sentient flower.

'Various church examiners to whom I explained the vision understood my Rose either as an expression of my own unstable mind or as a manifestation of the Devil. It was impossible for me to see her as either.

'She stepped forward and held out her hand to me. I had difficulty distinguishing her exact colours. They were many and subtle – an unbroken haze of pink and green and pale gold – all the shades of the rose. Her figure was slim but it wasn't easy to tell where her clothes met her body or even which was which. Her eyes changed in the light from deep emerald to violet. In spite of her extraordinary aura of power, her manner was almost hesitant. I think I was weeping as I went to her. I probably asked her what I should do. I know I decided to continue with my work. It was years before I saw her again, after I'd come out of prison for the last time.'

'But you did see her again?'

'Many times. Especially during the Blitz. But I'd learned my lesson. I kept all that to myself.'

'You were afraid of prison?'

'If you like. But I think it was probably more positive. God granted me a dream of the universe and her ever-expanding realities and I helped in the procreation of the new messiah!'

I waited for him to continue but he turned from the window with a broad smile. He was exhausted, tottering a little as he came with me to the kitchen and sat down in my place while I began to cook. He chatted amiably about the price of garlic and I prepared the dishes as he had taught me years before. This time, however, I was determined to encourage him to talk about himself.

He took a second glass of wine, his cheeks a little pinker than usual, his hair already beginning to rise about his head in a pure white fog.

'I suppose I needed her most during the War. There wasn't much time for talk, but I still came out to the Duke's Elm to pray. We began to meet frequently, always in the evenings before dark, and would walk together, comparing experience. She was from a quite different world – although her world sort of included ours. Eventually we became lovers.'

'Did she have a name?'

'I think so. I called her the Rose. I travelled with her. She took me to paradise, my dear, nowhere less! She showed me the whole of Creation! And so after a while my enthusiasm returned. Again, I wanted to share my vision but I had become far more cautious. I had a suspicion that I made a mistake the first time and almost lost my Rose as a result. When my nephew, who was in BBC Talks, offered me a new pulpit I was pretty much ready for it. This time I was determined to keep the reality to myself and just apply what I had experienced to ordinary, daily life. The public could not accept the intensity and implications of my pure vision. I cultivated an avuncularity which probably shocked those who knew me well. I became quite the jolly Englishman! I was offered speaking engagements in America. I was such a show-off. I spent less and less time in the Square and eventually months passed before I realised that I had lost contact with my Rose and our child! I felt such an utter fool, my dear. As soon as I understood what was happening I gave everything up. But it was too late.'

'You haven't seen her since?'

'Only in dreams.'

'What do you believe she was? The spirit of the tree?' I did my best to seem matter-of-fact, but he knew what I was up to and laughed, pouring himself more wine.

'She is her own spirit, my dear, make no mistake.'

And then the first course was ready, a *pâté de foie gras* made by my friend Loris Murrail in Paris. Begg agreed that it was as good as his own. For our main course we had Quantock veal in saffron. He ate it with appreciative relish. He had not been able to cook much lately, he said, and his appetite was reduced, but he enjoyed every bite. I was touched by his enthusiasm and made a private decision to come regularly again. Cooking him lunch would be my way of giving him something back. My spirits rose at the prospect and it was only then that I realised how much I had missed his company.

'Perhaps,' he said, 'she was sent to me to sustain me only when I most needed her. I had thought it a mistake to try to share her with the world. I never spoke of her again after I had told the bishop about her and was accused of militant paganism, primitive nature-worship. I saw his point of view but I always worshipped God in all His manifestations. The bishop seemed to argue that paganism was indistinguishable from common experience and therefore could not be considered a religion at all!'

'You worshipped her?'

'In a sense, my dear. As a man worships his wife.'

I had made him a *tiesen sinamon* and he took his time with the meringue, lifting it up to his lips on the delicate silver fork which Begg's Cotswold benches had produced for Liberty in 1903. 'I don't know if it's better or worse, dear, but the world is changing profoundly, you know. Our methods of making it safe just aren't really working any more. The danger of the simple answer is always with us and is inclined to lead to some sort of Final Solution. We are affected by turbulence as a leaf in the wind, but still we insist that the best way of dealing with the fact is to deny it or ignore it. And so we go on, hopelessly attempting to contain the thunder and the lightning and creating only further confusion! We're always caught by surprise! Yet it would require so little, surely, in the way of courage and imagination to find a way out, especially with today's wonderful computers?'

I had been depressed by the level and the outcome of the recent British election and was not optimistic. He agreed. 'How we love to cling to the wrecks which took us onto the rocks in the first place. In our panic we don't even see the empty lifeboats within easy swimming distance.'

He did not have the demeanour of a disappointed prophet. He remained lively and humorous. There was no sense of defeat about him, rather of quiet victory, of conquered pain. He did not at first seem disposed to tell me any more but when we were having coffee a casual remark set him off on a train of thought which led naturally back to that most significant event of his life. 'We aren't flawed,' he said, 'just as God isn't flawed. What we perceive as flaws are a reflection of our own failure to see the whole.' He spoke of a richly populated multiverse which was both within us and outside us. 'We're all reflections and echoes, one of another, and our originals, dear, are lost, probably for ever. That was what I understood from my vision. I wrote it in my journal. Perhaps, very rarely, we're granted a glimpse of God's entire plan? Perhaps only when our need is desperate. I have no doubt that God sent me my Rose.'

I am still of a secular disposition. 'Or perhaps,' I suggested, 'as God you sent yourself a vision?'

He did not find this blasphemous but neither did he think it worth pursuing. 'It's much of muchness, that,' he said.

He was content in his beliefs. He had questioned them once but now he was convinced. 'God sent me a vision and I followed her. She was made flesh. A miracle. I went with her to where she lived, in the fields of colour, in the far ether. We were married. We gave birth to a new human creature, neither male nor female but self-reproducing, a new messiah, and it set us free at last to dwell on that vast multiplicity of the heavens, to contemplate a quasi-infinity of versions of ourselves, our histories, our experience. That was what God granted me, my dear, when He sent me my Rose. Perhaps I was the Antichrist, after all, or at least its parent.'

'In your vision did you see what became of the child?'

He spoke with light-hearted familiarity, not recalling some distant dream but describing an immediate reality. 'Oh, yes. It grew to lead the world upon a new stage in our evolution. I'm not sure you'd believe the details, my dear, or find them very palatable.'

I smiled at this, but for the first time in my life felt a hint of profound terror and I suppressed a sudden urge to shout at him, to tell him how ridiculous I considered his visions, a bizarre blend of popular prophecy and alchemical mumbo-jumbo which even a New Age traveller would take with a pinch of E. My anger overwhelmed me. Though I regained control of it he recognised it. He continued to speak but with growing reluctance and perhaps melancholy. 'I saw a peculiar inevitability to the process. What, after all, do most of us live for? Ourselves? And what use is that? What value? What profit?'

With a great sigh he put down his fork. 'That was delicious.' His satisfaction felt to me like an accolade.

'You're only describing human nature.' I took his plate.

'Is that what keeps us on a level with the amoeba, my dear, and makes us worth about as much individual affection? Come now! We allow ourselves to be ruled by every brutish, greedy instinct, not by what is significantly human in our nature! Our imagination is our greatest gift. It gives us our moral sensibility.' He looked away through the dining-room window at the glittering domes of Gautier House and in the light the lines of his face were suddenly emphasised.

I had no wish ever to quarrel with him again. The previous argument, we were agreed, had cost us both too much. But I had to say what I thought. 'I was once told the moment I mentioned morality was the moment I'd crossed the line into lunacy,' I said. 'I suppose we must agree to understand things differently.'

For once he had forgotten his usual courtesy. I don't think he heard me. 'Wasn't all this damage avoidable?' he murmured. 'Weren't there ways in which cities could have grown up as we grew up, century adding to century, style to style, wisdom to wisdom? Isn't there something seriously wrong with the cycle we're in? Isn't there some way out?'

I made to reply but he shook his head, his hands on the table. 'I saw her again, you know, several times after the birth. How beautiful she was! How much beauty she showed me! It's like an amplification, my dear, of every sense! A discovery of new senses. An understanding that we don't need to discard anything as long as we continue to learn from it. It isn't frightening, what she showed me. It's perfectly familiar once you begin to see. It's like looking at the quintessential versions of our ordinary realities. Trees, animals – they're there, in essence. You begin to discover all that. The fundamental geometry's identified. Well, you've seen this new maths, haven't you?'

He seemed so vulnerable at that moment that for once I wasn't frank. I was unconvinced by what I judged as hippy physics made possible only by the new creative powers of computers. I didn't offer him an argument.

'You can't help but hope that it's what death is like,' he said. 'You become an angel.'

He got up and returned slowly to his dusty study, beckoning me to look out with him into the twilight gathering around the trees where crows croaked their mutual reassurances through the darkening air. He glanced only once towards the old elm then turned his head away sharply. 'You'll think this unlikely, I know, but we first came together physically at midnight under a full moon as bright and thin and yellow as Honesty in a dark blue sky. I looked at the moon through those strong black branches the moment before we touched. The joy of our union was indescribable. It was a confirmation of my faith. I made a mistake going back into public life. What good did it do for anyone, my dear?'

'We all made too many easy assumptions,' I said. 'It wasn't your fault.'

'I discovered sentimental solutions and comforted myself with them. Those comforts I turned to material profit. They became lies. And I lost her, my dear.' He made a small, anguished gesture. 'I'm still waiting for her to come back.'

He was scarcely aware of me. I felt I had intruded upon a private moment and suggested that I had tired him and should leave. Looking at me in surprise but without dispute he came towards me, remarking in particular on the saffron sauce. 'I can't tell you how much it meant to me, my dear, in every way.'

I promised to return the following Wednesday and cook. He licked his pink lips in comic anticipation and seemed genuinely

delighted by the prospect. 'Yum, yum.' He embraced me suddenly with his frail body, his sweet face staring blindly into mine.

I had found his last revelations disturbing and my tendency was
to dismiss them perhaps as an early sign of his senility. I even considered putting off my promised visit, but was already planning
the next lunch when three days later I took a call from Mrs Arthur
Begg who kept an eye on him and had my number. The Clapham
Antichrist had died in his sleep. She had found him at noon with
his head raised upon his massive pillows, the light from the open
window falling on his face. She enthused over his wonderful
expression in death.

In memoriam, Horst Grimm

Cake

I FELL IN love with Mrs Male long before she went into national politics. She was married to Victor Male, who was on Streatham Borough Council. She worked in an East Croydon solicitor's office when I first met her but she found her degree to be more useful at Gault Thomson, who were quite a small accountancy firm in those days. When Vic burnt out on the Council, she stood for the same seat and won it easily. I still saw her if she had time for me, though I was living north of the river by then. We generally met at lunchtime in the sparkling anonymity of the Kensington Gardens Hotel, always walking in the park for a bit after we'd made love.

Even then she was usually fitting me in between other errands. She visited Westminster every four days or so, was friendly with all the right people. When she became an MP she dropped me. She had too much at stake now, she said. I remember her last determined, regretful kiss.

She was never the shrew the cartoonists drew. Never the arrogant maîtresse of *Spitting Image*. I always found her a bit sentimental. I think that's why she went on seeing me, long after she had the baby.

I got married, bought a flat in Notting Hill and became a happy, loving husband, the doting father of two girls. We still had lunch together, most frequently at the House of Commons, but there was never anything undercover about it. I was working for *The Spectator* by then and briefly, before the other party's victory, she was Home Secretary. It suited her to keep in with me, of course. My political loyalties were so flexible I was tempted to vote Lib Dem in more than one election. I felt a strong personal loyalty to her and defended her policies fairly passionately. My colleagues used to joke that I was in love with her and in some ways, of course, I still was.

I continued to feel awkward around Vic Male, whom I bumped into on occasion. He had long since gone back into the building business, though his rhetoric remained that of the economic revolutionary he had once considered himself. His attitude to me was so familiar I sometimes suspected he knew everything about us, but in the end I decided he was too ordinarily friendly to suspect anything. I met him amidst the smell and glare of well-polished mahogany at the Royal Overseas League one evening last year. We had both been invited to hear about some new bit of policy. 'They want me to be the party's new Secretary.' He was very pleased about it. 'What do you think?'

'You know me, Vic. I'm not one to commit myself.'

'Oh, come off it, Jonny. You work on *The Spec*, write for the *Chronicle* and you ghosted that column in the *Express*.' He grinned. 'So what does that make you?'

'An old-fashioned conservative liberal populist,' I said. 'I haven't liked anyone in your party since Jack Taylor died.'

'That's not what I heard.' He gave me a hard stare.

'Oh, okay,' I replied. 'I quite like Eric Moses. And your good lady wife, of course.' I wondered if he was trying to draw me. Connie hadn't said anything, had she? It wouldn't be like her to let that sort of cat out of the bag. She relished secrets more than she valued her offshore bank balances. Had we been spotted at the KPH all those years ago?

He shook his head at me and then raised disgusted eyebrows. 'David Gregory, George Smith and Jill Baldock ring any bells?'

All I knew was that they were up-and-coming backbenchers. More or less on the party's right wing. Not likely to be my bosom buddies these days. I shrugged and took a canapé from a passing tray.

Vic pressed on. 'Okay, what if my spies tell me they're planning to back Jimmy Pilgrim and that you're about to do a big profile on him in *The Spec*?'

'I'd say you needed a new set of spies. Honest, Vic, I have no plans to do anyone favours – neo-cons or neo-libs or raving loony. I'm the original neutral. You couldn't get me any more neutral unless you had me spayed.'

He had begun to believe me. He frowned. 'That's very odd.' What had he heard?

Vic was suddenly steered away by the obnoxious Denby Jones whom I could never look at without remembering his weedy legs and horrible underpants, dripping wet as he came out of the flamingo pool at Derry & Toms roof garden on a famous occasion in 1997. He brayed horribly: 'Sorry to butt in, old boy. I'm going to have to take Vic off your hands.' They crossed to the big window overlooking the park and began talking intensely to Lord Northborough, who seemed a bit baffled. Once the mild-mannered greybeard glanced over at me, perhaps hoping I'd rescue him. Or maybe I was the subject of their conversation.

That was the night I learned the names of the runners in the party's leadership race. Connie Male was an outsider, of course, but since support for the others was evenly divided, there was a chance she might be everyone's compromise and get to take the party into the next election.

I was not particularly surprised when she called me a couple of days after the announcement. I thought she was trying to get my support. She suggested we meet at the KPH. That did surprise me. When I got there and entered the bright dining room, blinking in the glare of white linen and cream gloss, she was already at the table, smiling rather sweetly when she saw me.

It could have been twenty years ago, except she didn't peck me on both cheeks as she used to. I sat down and picked up the massive menu. It hadn't changed much, either. 'You're looking good,' I said. 'The power struggle's brought the roses back.'

She grinned and made a brushing gesture. 'I've decided I needed a sexier image. Gets the odd boy-voter, you know. Can't do any harm, can it?' She was recognised, these days. People in the restaurant kept pretending they weren't looking at her.

'I wouldn't have thought so. What's up?'

She glanced shiftily around the room, taking a ladylike sip of her Kir Royale. 'She's written to me, Jonny. From Florida. She wants to meet us. Well, me, really.'

'How did she find out who you were?'

'She didn't. The agency forwarded the letter. Sea-mail. My father got it. He took over the Fulham flat after Mummy died. Bit of a shocker.'

'You'll just have to ignore it, surely? Or tell her it's not on?'

'I know. I've made iffier decisions, after all.' Her eyes narrowed in that way familiar to anyone who had seen her clashing with her opposite number in the Commons.

'Why are you telling me, Connie? Do you want me to do something?' It had been a long time since she had gone off to the States and taken what to everyone else but me was a surprise vacation in Florida. 'The child must be – what – a teenager by now? Sixteen?'

'Seventeen. Haven't you wondered? Aren't you curious about her?'

'I suppose I am.' In fact I hated the emotions I was beginning to experience all over again. They were horrible. Like drowning. I ordered a stiff Glenlochy.

'You know. You might want to see her. Tell her why it's impossible. I've never regretted not having an abortion. But I still wonder if I shouldn't have told Vic she was his. He'd never have guessed. But he might have divorced me.'

'I thought you weren't – you know – having sex with Vic…'

'I could have forced myself. I never made love to him again after you and I split up.'

'Oh.' I couldn't think of anything to say. 'Sorry.'

'It didn't suit me. He never minded much. Politics was more important to us both. I think he kept the odd floozie, but he was discreet. He dumped the last one when I became Home Secretary.' She picked up her glass and then put it down again. She raised her eyebrows at me.

Being honest with myself, I had to admit I still fancied her. She'd thickened a bit and used a lot more make-up, but she was still a pretty woman in her soft, round, Slavic sort of way. Her father had been Polish, in the RAF, flying with the British during the War.

'You're not going to tell Vic, though?'

'I've no idea how he'd react. With his prostate problems and everything. I wouldn't want to make him worse. He's been a total brick, backing me every way he can. Just shows you. Serves me right.' She studied her silverware.

'Well, we always agreed there were no free lunches.'

She looked up in surprise.

'You can't,' I added relentlessly, 'have your cake and eat it.'

This broke her mood and she began to beam. She chuckled, shaking her head at me. 'Well, if I ever get to be PM, I'll show you that there *can* be free lunches. And free cake, too!'

I was baffled. I wasn't used to her having mood swings. 'But realistically, Connie, in ordinary life…'

'That's right,' she said. It was almost as if she were shutting me up. As if she'd reached a conclusion, closed the subject.

I remembered a rare afternoon we'd had at Mitcham fair one Easter. She usually loved the bumper cars but that day wouldn't go on them. We walked back to the bus stop. When I asked her why she hadn't ridden the dodgems, she told me she was pregnant and that she was planning to stand for Streatham South. My emotional response then was identical to how I felt now. I wanted her to be a success. I really hadn't wanted the kid. She was against abortion. She kept saying how Vic wouldn't understand. They'd agreed from the beginning not to have children. They enjoyed politics too much. I understood they'd had some sort of prenup agreement with a no kids clause. We'd discussed all this, of course, but it had been some eighteen years ago.

In the end she'd gone to the US on that lecture tour. In Florida she visited a slightly iffy adoption agency run by Cuban nuns. When it was all over she'd come home and instantly set about seriously climbing the political ladder until she got where she was now. In three years, as things stood, she could be PM.

'Let's face it, we've neither of us lost a lot of sleep over the kid, have we?' I sipped the Scotch. We'd imagined our daughter growing up in a nice Middle American suburb doing all the things little girls in Florida do – Girl Scouts, soccer, getting braces, cheer-leading, the high school prom. We knew the kind of people who adopted. They were always the best qualified to have children. Connie had often joked that if she ever got the chance she'd make people take a breeding licence test, like a driving test only more rigorous.

'You needn't worry,' she said. 'I'm not going to do anything stupid. She can't come here. My guess is she thinks her natural mother's American, anyway,' again the glance touching every-thing but me, 'anyway, I thought you should know about it. I'd appreciate it if –'

'Don't be silly.' I was rather irritated by her presumption. 'I'd be an idiot to give in to sentimental impulses.' I could imagine how my wife would take it. I'd never told her about Connie. 'It wouldn't be fair to anyone.'

'I agree, but that's the trouble.' Now she looked me full in the face and I saw a shocking longing in her eyes. 'I'm afraid I might. It's awful, Jonny. I mean it's making my stomach hurt. I never expected –'

'It would finish you if the papers smelled a rat. You'll never get this chance again. It's not something you can wait out, make some sort of public apology and expect the party to take you back after a reasonable show of falling on your sword. You'd let every-one down. Yourself included.'

'It's ridiculous, isn't it?'

I must admit her emotion was infecting me. I risked a hand across the table. She gripped it briefly before she looked up at the waiter and asked for a salad.

Never one to starve in a crisis, I ordered the steak-and-kidney pudding, even though I guessed it would still be terrible. I found myself lost in her familiar perfume. Shalimar. I had bought her enough bottles of the stuff. She seemed younger even than when we'd first met at that party in Hampstead thrown by some mil-lionaire socialist. I hadn't known she was married when I first saw her on the other side of the room, sitting awkwardly on a chair and chatting to a silly young man with a quiff who squatted at her feet. She looked a bit out of place in her Sloane-ish costume. Powder blue, like today. It wasn't an affectation, just her favourite colour. It went so well with her blonde, neatly permed hair and her wonderful aquamarine eyes. Now, glancing at her across the lunch table, I was seized with the same desire I had felt then. In spite of myself, I was on the brink of suggesting the impossible, that we get a room upstairs and afterwards walk in the park again.

I was shocked at myself. Was it because she seemed so vulnerable, just as she had that night in Hampstead? She wasn't a bit vulnerable, even then, of course. She had been uncertain of herself, that was all, and unhappy at Vic for copping out of going with her at the last moment. When she agreed to come back to my awful flat in Balham I thought she was only wearing a wedding ring for appearances, as a sort of protection. She only told me she was married when she was under me on the couch and I already had my hand on her unresisting leg. She asked me if I minded. I didn't, of course. By then I wouldn't have worried about it if Vic had been standing on the landing checking his watch.

Realistically I'd never seen myself married to Connie. The only time I proposed she laughed full in my face, but I was a little surprised, as the months became years, that she never considered leaving Vic. She was much brighter than he was and braver. But it would be totally against everyone's interest, she said. They had careers planned together. They were a team. The family business. It would seriously interfere with the momentum of their climb up their respective ladders. I occasionally thought of breaking it off, but I never met anyone I loved as much as Connie.

The adoption had finished it, of course. That was the beginning of the end. I saw her a couple of days after she came home to England. She'd told Vic she'd caught some sort of bug and they'd kept her in hospital for a check-up. That explained the bills, if he ever noticed. I'd paid my share. She would have expected nothing less. And that had been that. No solace. No free lunch. Within the year we had broken up and she had won her seat. Another year and I met my wife.

'Yes,' I complied bleakly. 'Ridiculous.'

For a few seconds we sat staring at one another, helplessly sad.

'PM, eh?' I pulled myself together. 'It seems only yesterday they made you a junior minister. Will you have to drop me, do you think? No more tête-à-têtes?'

'Oh, we'll work something out.' She looked away and threw one of those sickeningly artificial smiles at someone giving her a thumbs up from the bar. Then her attention returned to what was really concerning her. 'Jill and David are wavering. I'd say it's between me and Ken.'

'Not what the papers are saying.'

'That's because it's the reality. They think they create the news, but of course they don't.'

'You're the expert,' I conceded. 'You'll make a spectacular PM.'

'You'll support me?'

I laughed. 'I didn't say that.'

'You're so old-fashioned, Jonny.' She allowed herself a touch of that mockery which served her so successfully in debate.

A couple of weeks later the vote was out and she had disappeared. Her husband said she had gone to the country to stay with friends, to rest and avoid the publicity. I got an invitation at the office to attend a party at the Males' massive mock Georgian mansion and I went out of curiosity, not expecting her to be back. Everyone else thought it was to rally the last of the floating voters.

She wasn't there when I arrived. Vic saw me through the glass doors and came forward, shaking my hand as someone took my coat. I managed to get a good view of their big pale green reception room. I recognised quite a few of the other guests. And it did look as if she was courting the undecideds. 'Where's Connie been staying?' I asked Vic casually.

'Oh, it'll be no secret soon,' he said. He began to grin. 'She's just back from Florida. Family matter, that's all.'

'You have family in Florida?'

'She went to pick up our god-daughter. An old friend's kid. She hasn't seen her in years.'

'God-daughter? Who?' I have to admit I was hard put to speak.

Vic slapped my shoulder. 'You'll find out when everyone else does, Jonny.'

When Connie finally made her appearance, she had Cydney with her. Connie brought her over to where I stood at the buffet with an empty plate. She introduced us. Cydney was about Connie's height. She had my looks and Connie's eyes, but not so you'd guess; a smiling, open young woman who charmed everyone and was already the hit of the evening. Somehow she helped give Connie a subtly maternal air. We shook hands. Cydney called me 'sir'. I approved of her good manners. Nice kid. An asset to any parent.

'Are you staying long?' I asked.

'Three years!' Her face was a happy mask. 'It's so kind of them. They're sending me to Oxford. It's like I have a whole other family over here. Isn't it wonderful?'

I couldn't think of anything intelligent to say. 'It certainly is.' I waved vaguely at the centrepiece of the table, an enormous gâteau decorated in red, white and blue. 'Can I get you anything?'

Connie eyed me a little nervously.

'Cake?' I asked.

CALLAHAN'S, WHITECHAPEL HIGH STREET, E1

In 1909 Prince Kropotkin travelled to London to give a series of lectures on 'The Tyranny of Government'. He was refused admission into Britain until some Fabians, including Hubert Black, Edith Nesbit and James 'Big Jim' Callahan, interceded on his behalf, offering personal sureties for his good conduct, and the use of Callahan's Meeting Rooms, previously known for their association with Keir Hardie's Independent Labour Party.

Callahan became increasingly involved in questions of Irish Home Rule, returning to Dublin in 1914. He died, largely forgotten, in a botched robbery (or guerrilla attack) on Amiens Street Station, in 1921.

The Meeting Rooms, flourishing under their original name, continued to welcome anarchists (some of whom were to die in Spain). By the 1940s, Callahan's lost its political aspect and became a dancehall. When it was demolished in 1968, it was best known as a venue for 'Old Time' dancing and bingo. It enjoyed one final episode of public controversy when Frank Cornelius, standing as a Liberal candidate in the 1959 election, attacked the long-serving local member, Ian Rinkoff, for ballot-rigging, involvement with dubious property deals (under the guise of slum clearance), and part-ownership of a Maltese-run café/brothel in Cable Street. The café features in Alexander Baron's novel *The Lowlife*.

MARRIAGE'S WHARF, E6

Marriage's Wharf lay across the river from Marriage's Old Wharf at Gallions Reach. The old wharf was destroyed in the Arsenal fire of 1843 and William Marriage, grandson of the company's founder, rebuilt the wharf and warehouse so that it would be more convenient for the Custom House on the other side of the Woolwich Basin. Marriage was the chief importer and exporter of opium and the rarer spices. He financed a fleet of his own 'Poppy Clippers' and founded a hospice for destitute Chinese women in Albert Road. In the mid-twentieth century Marriage's eccentric mansion, attached to the old warehouse, was still standing – but, by 1970, it had been demolished to make way for the GLC's Gallions Street development.

MARRIAGE'S WHARF, E6. About 1930

London Bone

For Ronnie Scott

Chapter One

My NAME IS Raymond Gold and I'm a well-known dealer. I was born too many years ago in Upper Street, Islington. Everybody reckons me in the London markets and I have a good reputation in Manchester and the provinces. I have bought and sold, been the middleman, an agent, an art representative, a professional mentor, a tour guide, a spiritual bridge-builder. These days I call myself a cultural speculator.

But, you won't like it, the more familiar word for my profession, as I practised it until recently, is *scalper*. This kind of language is just another way of isolating the small businessman and making what he does seem sleazy while the stockbroker dealing in millions is supposed to be legitimate. But I don't need to convince anyone today that there's no sodding justice.

'Scalping' is risky. What you do is invest in tickets on spec and hope to make a timely sale when the market for them hits zenith. Any kind of ticket, really, but mostly shows. I've never seen anything offensive about getting the maximum possible profit out of an American matron with more money than sense who's anxious to report home with the right items ticked off the *been-to* list. We've all seen them rushing about in their overpriced limos and minibuses, pretending to be individuals: **Thursday: Changing-of-the-Guard, Harrods, Planet Hollywood, Royal Academy, Tea-at-the-Ritz,** *Cats*. It's a sort of tribal dance they are compelled to perform. If they don't perform it, they feel inadequate. **Saturday: Tower of London, Bucket of Blood, Jack-the-Ripper talk,**

Sherlock Holmes Pub, Sherlock Holmes tour, Madame Tussaud's, Covent Garden Cream Tea, *Dogs*. These are people so traumatised by contact with strangers that their only security lies in these rituals, these well-blazed trails and familiar chants. It's my job to smooth their paths, to make them exclaim how pretty and wonderful and elegant and *magical* it all is. The street people aren't a problem. They're just so many charming Dick Van Dykes.

Americans need bullshit the way koala bears need eucalyptus leaves. They've become totally addicted to it. They get so much of it back home that they can't survive without it. It's your duty to help them get their regular fixes while they travel. And when they make it back after three weeks on alien shores, their friends, of course, are always glad of some foreign bullshit for a change.

Even if you sell a show ticket to a real enthusiast, who has already been forty-nine times and is so familiar to the cast they see him in the street and think he's a relative, who are you hurting? Andros Loud Website, Lady Hatchet's loyal laureate, who achieved rank and wealth by celebrating the lighter side of the moral vacuum? He would surely applaud my enterprise in the buccaneering spirit of the free market. Venture capitalism at its bravest. Well, he'd applaud me if he had time these days from his railings against fate, his horrible understanding of the true nature of his coming obscurity. But that's partly what my story's about.

I have to say in my own favour that I'm not merely a speculator or, if you like, exploiter. I'm also a patron. For many years, not just recently, a niagara of dosh has flowed out of my pocket and into the real arts faster than a cat up a Frenchman. Whole orchestras and famous soloists have been brought to the Wigmore Hall on the money they get from me. But I couldn't have afforded this if it wasn't for the definitely iffy *Miss Saigon* (a triumph of well-oiled machinery over dodgy morality) or the unbelievably decrepit *Good Rockin' Tonite* (in which the living dead jive in the aisles), nor, of course, that first great theatrical triumph of the new millennium, *Schindler: The Musical*. Make 'em weep, Uncle Walt!

So who is helping most to support the arts? You, me, the lottery?

I had another reputation, of course, which some saw as a second profession. I was one of the last great London characters. I was always on late-night telly, lit from below, and Iain Sinclair couldn't write a paragraph without dropping my name at least once. I'm a quintessential Londoner, I am. I'm a Cockney gentleman.

I read Israel Zangwill and Gerald Kersh and Alexander Baron. I can tell you the best books of Pett Ridge and Arthur Morrison. I know Pratface Charlie, Driff and Martin Stone, Bernie Michaud and the even more legendary Gerry and Pat Goldstein. They're all historians, archaeologists, revenants. There isn't another culture-dealer in London, oldster or child, who doesn't at some time come to me for an opinion. Even now, when I'm as popular as a pig at a Putney wedding and people hold their noses and dive into traffic rather than have to say hello to me, they still need me for that.

I've known all the famous Londoners or known someone else who did. I can tell stories of long-dead gangsters who made the Krays seem like Amnesty International. Bare-knuckle boxing. Fighting the fascists in the East End. Gun-battles with the police all over Stepney in the 1900s. The terrifying girl gangsters of Whitechapel. Barricading the Old Bill in his own barracks down in Notting Dale.

I can tell you where all the music halls were and what was sung in them. And why. I can tell Marie Lloyd stories and Max Miller stories that are fresh and sharp and bawdy as the day they happened, because their wit and experience came out of the market streets of London. The same streets. The same markets. The same family names. London *is* markets. Markets are London.

I'm a Londoner through and through. I know Mr Gog personally. I know Ma Gog even more personally. During the day I can walk anywhere from Bow to Bayswater faster than any taxi. I love the markets. Brick Lane. Church Street. Portobello. You won't find me on a bike with my bum in the air on a winter's afternoon. I walk or drive. Nothing in between. I wear a camelhair in winter and a Barraclough's in summer. You know what would happen to a coat like that on a bike.

I love the theatre. I like modern dance, very good movies and ambitious international contemporary music. I like poetry, prose, painting and the decorative arts. I like the lot, the very best that London's got, the whole bloody casserole. I gobble it all up and bang on my bowl for more. Let timid greenbelters creep in at weekends and sink themselves in the West End's familiar deodorised shit if they want to. That's not my city. That's a tourist set. It's what I live off. What all of us show-people live off. It's the old, familiar circus. The big rotate.

We're selling what everybody recognises. What makes them feel safe and certain and sure of every single moment in the city. Nothing to worry about in jolly old London. We sell charm and colour by the yard. Whole word factories turn out new rhyming slang and saucy street characters are trained on council grants. Don't frighten the horses. Licensed pearlies pause for a photo opportunity in the dockside Secure Zones. Without all that cheap scenery, without our myths and magical skills, without our whorish good cheer and instincts for trade – any kind of trade – we probably wouldn't have a living city.

As it is, the real city I live in has more creative energy per square inch at work at any given moment than anywhere else on the planet. But you'd never know it from a stroll up the Strand. It's almost all in those lively little side streets the English-speaking tourists can't help feeling a bit nervous about and that the French adore.

If you use music for comfortable escape you'd probably find more satisfying and cheaper relief in a massage parlour than at the umpteenth revival of *The Sound of Music*. I'd tell that to any hesitant punter who's not too sure. Check out the phone boxes for the ladies, I'd say, or you can go to the half-price ticket booth in Leicester Square and pick up a ticket that'll deliver real value – Ibsen or Shakespeare, Shaw or Churchill. Certainly you can fork out three hundred sheets for a fifty-sheet ticket that in a justly ordered world wouldn't be worth two pee and have your ears salved and your cradle rocked for two hours. Don't worry, I'd tell them, I make no judgements. Some hard-working whore profits, whatever you decide. So who's the cynic?

I went on one of those tours when my friends Dave and Di from Bury came down for the Festival of London in 2001 and it's amazing, the crap they tell people. They put sex, violence and money into every story. They know fuck-all. They soup everything up. It's *Sun*-reader history. Even the Beefeaters at the Tower. Poppinsland. All that old English duff.

It makes you glad to get back to Soho.

Not so long ago you would usually find me in the Princess Louise, Berwick Street, at lunchtime, a few doors down from the Chinese chippy and just across from Mrs White's trim stall in Berwick Market. It's only a narrow door and is fairly easy to miss. It has one bottle-glass window onto the street. This is a public house that has not altered since the 1940s when it was very popular with Dylan Thomas, Mervyn Peake, Ruthven Todd, Henry Treece and a miscellaneous bunch of other Welsh adventurers who threatened for a while to take over English poetry from the Irish.

It's a shit pub, so dark and smoky you can hardly find your glass in front of your face, but the look of it keeps the tourists out. It's used by all the culture pros – from arty types with backpacks, who do specialised walking tours, to famous gallery owners and top museum management – and by the heavy-metal bikers. We all get on a treat. We are mutually dependent in our continuing resistance to invasion or change, to the preservation of the best and most vital aspects of our culture. We leave the bikers alone because they protect us from the tourists, who might recognise us and make us put on our masks in a hurry. They leave us alone because the police won't want to bother a bunch of well-connected middle-class wankers like us. It is a wonderful example of mutuality. In the back rooms, thanks to some freaky acoustics, you can talk easily above the music and hardly know it's there.

Over the years there have been some famous friendships and unions struck between the two groups. My own lady wife was known as Karla the She-Goat in an earlier incarnation and had the most exquisite and elaborate tattoos I ever saw. She was a wonderful wife and would have made a perfect mother. She died on the A1, on the other side of Watford Gap. She had just found out she was pregnant and was making her last sentimental run. It did me in for marriage for a while. And urban romance.

I first heard about London Bone in the Princess Lou when Claire Rood, that elegant old dike from the Barbican, who'd tipped me off about my new tailor, pulled my ear to her mouth and asked me in words of solid gin and garlic to look out for some for her, darling. None of the usual faces seemed to know about it. A couple of top-level museum people knew a bit, but it was soon obvious they were hoping I'd fill them in on the details. I showed them a confident length of cuff. I told them to keep in touch.

I did my Friday walk, starting in the horrible pre-dawn chill of the Portobello Road where some youth tried to sell me a bit of scrimshawed reconstitute as 'the real old Bone'. I warmed myself in the showrooms of elegant Kensington and Chelsea dealers telling outrageous stories of deals, profits and crashes until they grew uncomfortable and wanted to talk about me and I got the message and left.

I wound up that evening in the urinal of the Dragoons in Meard Alley, swapping long-time-no-sees with my boyhood friend Bernie Michaud who begins immediately by telling me he's got a bit of business I might be interested in. And since it's Bernie Michaud telling me about it I listen. Bernie never deliberately spread a rumour in his life but he's always known how to make the best of one. This is kosher, he thinks. It has a bit of a glow. It smells like a winner. A long-distance runner. He is telling me out of friendship, but I'm not really interested. I'm trying to find out about London Bone.

'I'm not talking drugs, Ray, you know that. And it's not bent.' Bernie's little pale face is serious. He takes a thoughtful sip of his whisky. 'It is, admittedly, a commodity.'

I wasn't interested. I hadn't dealt in goods for years. 'Services only, Bernie,' I said. 'Remember. It's my rule. Who wants to get stuck paying rent on a warehouse full of yesterday's faves? I'm still trying to move those *Glenda Sings Michael Jackson* sides Pratface talked me into.'

'What about investment?' he says. 'This is the real business, Ray, believe me.'

So I heard him out. It wouldn't be the first time Bernie had brought me back a nice profit on some deal I'd helped him bankroll and I was all right at the time. I'd just made the better part of a month's turnover on a package of theatreland's most profitable stinkers brokered for a party of filthy-rich New Muscovites who thought Chekhov was something you did with your lottery numbers.

As they absorbed the quintessence of Euro-ersatz, guaranteed to offer, as its high emotional moment, a long, relentless bowel movement, I would be converting their hard roubles back into Beluga.

It's a turning world, the world of the international free market, and everything's wonderful and cute and pretty and *magical* so long as you keep your place on the carousel. It's not good if it stops. And it's worse if you get thrown off altogether. Pray to Mammon that you never have to seek the help of an organisation that calls you a 'client'. That puts you outside the fairground for ever. No more rides. No more fun. No more life.

Bernie only did quality art, so I knew I could trust that side of his judgement, but what was it? A new batch of Raphaels turned up in a Willesden attic? Andy Warhol's lost landscapes found at the Pheasantry?

'There's American collectors frenzied for this stuff,' murmurs Bernie through a haze of Sons of the Wind, Motorchair and Montecristo fumes. 'And if it's decorated they go through the roof. All the big Swiss guys are looking for it. Freddy K. in Cairo has a Saudi buyer who tops any price. Rose Sarkissian in Agadir represents three French collectors. It's never catalogued. It's all word of mouth. And it's already turning over millions. There's one inferior piece in New York and none at all in Paris. The pieces in Zurich are probably all fakes.'

This made me feel that I was losing touch. I still didn't know what he was getting at.

'Listen,' I say, 'before we go any further, let's talk about this London Bone.'

'You're a fly one, Ray,' he says. 'How did you suss it?'

'Tell me what you know,' I say. 'And then I'll fill you in.'

We went out of the pub, bought some fish and chips at the Chinese and then walked up Berwick Street and round to his little club in D'Arblay Street where we sat down in his office and closed the door. The place stank of cat-pee. He doted on his Persians. They were all out in the club at the moment, being petted by the patrons.

'First,' he says, 'I don't have to tell you, Ray, that this is strictly double-schtoom and I will kill you if a syllable gets out.'

'Naturally,' I said.

'Have you ever seen any of this Bone?' he asked. He went to his cupboard and found some vinegar and salt. 'Or better still handled it?'

'No,' I said. 'Not unless it's fake scrimshaw.'

'This stuff's got a depth to it you've never dreamed about. A lustre. You can tell it's the real thing as soon as you see it. Not just the shapes or the decoration, but the quality of it. It's like it's got a soul. You could come close, but you could never fake it. Like amber, for instance. That's why the big collectors are after it. It's authentic, it's newly discovered and it's rare.'

'What bone is it?'

'Mastodon. Some people still call it mammoth ivory, but I haven't seen any actual ivory. It could be dinosaur. I don't know. Anyway, this bone is *better* than ivory. It's in weird shapes, probably fragments off some really big animal.'

'And where's it coming from?'

'The heavy clay of good old London,' says Bernie. 'A fortune at our feet, Ray. And my people know where to dig.'

Chapter Two

I HAD TO be straight with Bernie. Until I saw a piece of the stuff in my own hand and got an idea about it for myself, I couldn't do anything. The only time in my life I'd gone for a gold brick I'd bought it out of respect for the genius running the scam. He deserved what I gave him. Which was a bit less than he was hoping for. Rather than be conned, I would rather *throw* the money away. I'm like that with everything.

I had my instincts, I told Bernie. I had to go with them. He understood completely and we parted on good terms.

If the famous Lloyd Webber meltdown of '03 had happened a few months earlier or later I would never have thought again about going into the Bone business, but I was done in by one of those sudden changes of public taste that made the George M. Cohan crash of '31 seem like a run of *The Mousetrap*.

Sentimental fascism went out the window. Liberal-humanist contemporary relevance, artistic aspiration, intellectual and moral substance and all that stuff was somehow in demand. It was *better* than the '60s. It was one of those splendid moments when the public pulls itself together and tries to grow up. Jones's *Rhyme of the Flying Bomb* song-cycle made a glorious comeback. *American Angels* returned with even more punch.

And Sondheim became a quality brand name. If it wasn't by Sondheim or based on a tune Sondheim used to hum in the shower, the punters didn't want to know. Overnight, the public's product loyalty had changed. And I must admit it had changed for the better. But my investments were in *Cats*, and *Dogs* (Lord Webber's last desperate attempt to squeeze from Thurber what he'd sucked from Eliot), *Duce!* and *Starlight Excess*, all of which were now taking a walk down *Sunset Boulevard*. I couldn't even get a regular-price ticket for myself at *Sunday in the Park*, *Assassins* or

Follies. Into the Woods was solid for eighteen months ahead. I saw *Passion* from the wings and *Sweeney Todd* from the gods. *Five Guys Named Mo* crumbled to dust. *Phantom* closed. Its author claimed sabotage.

'Quality will out, Ray,' says Bernie next time I see him at the Lou. 'You've got to grant the public that. You just have to give it time.'

'Fuck the public,' I said, with some feeling. 'They're just nostalgic for quality at the moment. Next year it'll be something else. Meanwhile I'm bloody ruined. You couldn't drum a couple of oncers on my entire stock. Even my E.N.O. side-bets have died. Covent Garden's a disaster. The weather in Milan didn't help. That's where Cecilia Bartoli caught her cold. I was lucky to be offered half-price for the Rossinis without her. And I know what I'd do if I could get a varda at bloody Simon Rattle.'

'So you won't be able to come in on the Bone deal?' said Bernie, returning to his own main point of interest.

'I said I was ruined,' I told him, 'not wiped out.'

'Well, I got something to show you now, anyway,' says Bernie. We went back to his place.

He put it in my hand as if it were a nugget of plutonium: a knuckle of dark, golden Bone, split off from a larger piece, covered with tiny pictures.

'The engravings are always on that kind of Bone,' he said. 'There are other kinds that don't have drawings, maybe from a later date. It's the work of the first Londoners, I suppose, when it was still a swamp. About the time your Phoenician ancestors started getting into the upriver woad-trade. I don't know the significance, of course.'

The Bone itself was hard to analyse because of the mixture of chemicals that had created it and some of it had fused, suggesting prehistoric upheavals of some kind. The drawings were extremely primitive. Any bored person with a sharp object and minimum talent could have done them at any time in history. The larger, weirder-looking Bones had no engravings.

Stick-people pursued other stick-people endlessly across the fragment. The work was unremarkable. The beauty really was in the tawny ivory colour of the Bone itself. It glowed with a wealth of shades and drew you hypnotically into its depths. I imagined the huge animal of which this fragment had once been an active part. I saw the bellowing trunk, the vast ears, the glinting tusks succumbing suddenly to whatever had engulfed her. I saw her body swaying, her tail lashing as she trumpeted her defiance of her inevitable death. And now men sought her remains as treasure. It was a very romantic image and of course it would become my most sincere sales pitch.

'That's six million dollars you're holding there,' said Bernie. 'Minimum.'

Bernie had caught me at the right time and I had to admit I was convinced. Back in his office he sketched out the agreement. We would go in on a fifty-fifty basis, funding the guys who would do the actual digging, who knew where the Bonefields were and who would tell us as soon as we showed serious interest. We would finance all the work, pay them an upfront earnest and then load by load in agreed increments. Bernie and I would split the net profit fifty-fifty. There were all kinds of clauses and provisions covering the various problems we foresaw and then we had a deal.

The archaeologists came round to my little place in Dolphin Square. They were a scruffy bunch of students from the University of Norbury who had discovered the Bone deposits on a run-of-the-mill field trip in a demolished Southwark housing estate and knew only that there might be a market for them. Recent cuts to their grants had made them desperate. Some lefty had come up with a law out of the Magna Carta or somewhere saying public land couldn't be sold to private developers and so there was a court case disputing the Council's right to sell the estate to Livingstone International, which also put a stop to the planned rebuilding. So we had indefinite time to work.

The stoodies were grateful for our expertise, as well as our cash. I was happy enough with the situation. It was one I felt we could easily control. Middle-class burbnerds get greedy the same as anyone else, but they respond well to reason. I told them for a start-off that all the Bone had to come in to us. If any of it leaked onto the market by other means, we'd risk losing our prices and that would mean the scheme was over. 'Terminated,' I said significantly. Since we had reputations as well as investments to protect there would also be recriminations. That was all I had to say. Since those V-serials kids think we're Krays and Mad Frankie Frasers just because we like to look smart and talk properly.

We were fairly sure we weren't doing anything obviously criminal. The stuff wasn't treasure trove. It had to be cleared before proper foundations could be poured. Quite evidently L.I. didn't think it was worth paying security staff to shufti the site. We didn't know if digging shafts and tunnels was even trespass, but we knew we had a few weeks before someone started asking about us and by then we hoped to have the whole bloody mastodon out of the deep clay and nicely earning for us. The selling would take the real skill and that was my job. It was going to have to be played sharper than South African diamonds.

After that neither Bernie nor I had anything to do with the dig. We rented a guarded lock-up in Clapham and paid the kids every time they brought in a substantial load of Bone. It was incredible stuff. Bernie thought that chemical action, some of it relatively recent, had caused the phenomenon. 'Like chalk, you know. You hardly find it anywhere. Just a few places in England, France, China and Texas.' The kids reported that there was more than one kind of animal down there, but that all the Bone had the same rich appearance. They had constructed a new tunnel, with a hidden entrance, so that even if the building site was blocked to them, they could still get at the Bone. It seemed to be a huge field, but most of the Bone was at roughly the same depth. Much of it had fused and had to be chipped out. They had found no end to it so far and they had tunnelled through more than half an acre of the dense, dark clay.

Meanwhile I was in Amsterdam and Rio, Paris and Vienna and New York and Sydney. I was in Tokyo and Seoul and Hong Kong. I was in Riyadh, Cairo and Baghdad. I was in Kampala and New

Benin, everywhere there were major punters. I racked up so many free air-miles in a couple of months that they were automatically jumping me to first class. But I achieved what I wanted. Nobody bought London Bone without checking with me. I was the acknowledged expert. The prime source, the best in the business. If you want Bone, said the art world, you want Gold.

The Serious Fraud Squad became interested in Bone for a while, but they had been assuming we were faking it and gave up when it was obviously not rubbish.

Neither Bernie nor I expected it to last any longer than it did. By the time our first phase of selling was over we were turning over so much dough it was silly and the kids were getting tired and were worrying about exploring some of their wildest dreams. There was almost nothing left, they said. So we closed down the operation, moved our warehouses a couple of times and then let the Bone sit there to make us some money while everyone wondered why it had dried up.

And at that moment, inevitably, and late as ever, the newspapers caught on to the story. There was a brief late-night TV piece. A few supplements talked about it in their arts pages. This led to some news stories and eventually it went to the tabloids and the Bone became anything you liked, from the remains of Martians to a new kind of nuclear waste. Anyone who saw the real stuff was convinced but everyone had a theory about it. The real exclusive market was finished. We kept schtoom. We were gearing up for the second phase. We got as far away from our stash as possible.

Of course, a few faces tracked me down, but I denied any knowledge of the Bone. I was a middleman, I said. I just had good contacts. Half a dozen people claimed to know where the Bone came from. Of course they talked to the papers. I sat back in satisfied security, watching the mud swirl over our tracks. Another couple of months and we'd be even safer than the house I'd bought in Hampstead overlooking the Heath. It had a rather forlorn garden the size of Kilburn, which needed a lot of nurturing. That suited me. I was ready to retire to the country and a big indoor swimming pool.

By the time a close version of the true story came out, from one of the stoodies, who'd lost all his share in a lottery syndicate, it was just one of many. It sounded too dull. I told newspaper reporters that while I would love to have been involved in such a lucrative scheme, my money came from theatre tickets. Meanwhile, Bernie and I thought of our warehouse and said nothing.

Now the stuff was getting into the culture. It was chic. *Puncher* used it in their ads. It was called Mammoth Bone by the media. There was a common story about how a herd had wandered into the swampy river and drowned in the mud. Lots of pictures dusted off from the Natural History Museum. Experts explained the colour, the depths, the markings, the beauty. Models sported a Bone motif.

Our second phase was to put a fair number of inferior fragments on the market and see how the public responded. That would help us find our popular price – the most a customer would pay. We were looking for a few good millionaires.

Frankly, as I told my partner, I was more than ready to get rid of the lot. But Bernie counselled me to patience. We had a plan and it made sense to stick to it.

The trade continued to run well for a while. As the sole source of the stuff, we could pretty much control everything. Then one Sunday lunchtime I met Bernie at the Six Jolly Dragoons in Meard Alley, Soho. He had something to show me, he said. He didn't even glance around. He put it on the bar in plain daylight. A small piece of Bone with the remains of decorations still on it.

'What about it?' I said.

'It's not ours,' he said.

My first thought was that the stoodies had opened up the field again. That they had lied to us when they said it had run out.

'No,' said Bernie, 'it's not even the same colour. It's the same stuff – but different shades. Gerry Goldstein lent it to me.'

'Where did he get it?'

'He was offered it,' Bernie said.

We didn't bother to speculate where it had come from. But we did have rather a lot of our Bone to shift quickly. Against my will,

I made another world tour and sold mostly to other dealers this time. It was a standard second-wave operation but run rather faster than was wise. We definitely missed the crest.

However, before deliveries were in and cheques were cashed, Jack Merrywidow, the fighting MP for Brookgate and East Holborn, gets up in the House of Commons on telly one afternoon and asks if Prime Minister Bland or any of his dope-dazed cabinet understand that human remains, taken from the hallowed burial grounds of London, are being sold by the piece in the international marketplace? Mr Bland makes a plummy joke enjoyed at Mr Merrywidow's expense and sits down. But Jack won't give up. They're suddenly on telly. It's *The Struggle of Parliament* time. Jack's had the Bone examined by experts. It's human. Undoubtedly human. The strange shapes are caused by limbs melting together in soil heavy with lime. Chemical reactions, he says. We have – he raises his eyes to the camera – been mining mass graves.

A shock to all those who still long for the years of common decency. Someone, says Jack, is selling more than our heritage. Hasn't free-market capitalism got a little bit out of touch when we start selling the arms, legs and skulls of our forebears? The torsos and shoulder blades of our honourable dead? What did we used to call people who did that? When was the government going to stop this trade in corpses?

It's denied.

It's proved.

It looks like trade is about to slump.

I think of framing the cheques as a reminder of the vagaries of fate and give up any idea of popping the question to my old muse Little Trudi, who is back on the market, having been dumped by her corporate suit in a fit, he's told her, of self-disgust after seeing *The Tolstoy Investment* with Eddie Izzard. Bernie, I tell my partner, the Bone business is down the drain. We might as well bin the stuff we've stockpiled.

Then, two days later the TV news reports a vast public interest in London Bone. Some lordly old queen with four names comes on the evening news to say how by owning a piece of Bone, you own London's true history. You become a curator of some ancient ancestor. He's clearly got a vested interest in the stuff. It's the hottest tourist item since Jack-the-Ripper razors and O.J. gloves. More people want to buy it than ever.

The only trouble is, I don't deal in dead people. It is, in fact, where I have always drawn the line. Even Pratface Charlie wouldn't sell his great-great-grandmother's elbow to some overweight Jap in a deerstalker and a kilt. I'm faced with a genuine moral dilemma.

I make a decision. I make a promise to myself. I can't go back on that. I go down to the Italian chippy in Fortess Road, stoke up on nourishing ritual grease (cod roe, chips and mushy peas, bread and butter and tea, syrup pudding), then heave my out-of-shape, but mentally prepared, body up onto Parliament Hill to roll myself a big wacky-baccy fag and let my subconscious think the problem through.

When I emerge from my reverie, I have looked out over the whole misty London panorama and considered the city's complex history. I have thought about the number of dead buried there since, say, the time of Boudicca, and what they mean to the soil we build on, the food we still grow here and the air we breathe. We are recycling our ancestors all the time, one way or another. We are sucking them in and shitting them out. We're eating them. We're drinking them. We're coughing them up. The dead don't rest. Bits of them are permanently at work. So what am I doing wrong?

This thought is comforting until my moral sense, sharpening itself up after a long rest, kicks in with – *But what's different here is you're flogging the stuff to people who take it home with them*. Back to Wisconsin and California and Peking. You take it out of circulation. You're dissipating the deep fabric of the city. You're unravelling something. Like, the real infrastructure, the spiritual and physical bones of an ancient settlement...

On Kite Hill I suddenly realise that those bones are in some way the deep lifestuff of London.

It grows dark over the towers and roofs of the metropolis. I sit on my bench and roll myself a further joint. I watch the silver rising from the river, the deep golden glow of the distant lights, the plush of the foliage, and as I watch it seems to shred before my eyes, like a rotten curtain. Even the traffic noise grows fainter. Is the city sick? Is she expiring? Somehow it seems there's a little less breath in the old girl. I blame myself. And Bernie. And those kids.

There and then, on the spot, I renounce all further interest in the Bone trade. If nobody else will take the relics back, then I will.

There's no resolve purer than the determination you draw from a really good reefer.

Chapter Three

S O NOW THERE isn't a tourist in any London market or antique arcade who isn't searching out Bone. They know it isn't cheap. They know they have to pay. And pay they do. Through the nose. And half of what they buy is crap or fakes. This is a question of status, not authenticity. As long as we say it's good, they can say it's good. We give it a provenance, a story, something to colour the tale to the folks back home. We're honest dealers. We sell only the authentic stuff. Still they get conned. But still they look. Still they buy.

Jealous Mancunians and Brummies long for a history old enough to provide them with Bone. A few of the early settlements, like Chester and York, start turning up something like it, but it's not the same. Jim Morrison's remains disappear from Père-Lachaise. They might be someone else's bones, anyway. Rumour is they were KFC bones. The Revolutionary death-pits fail to deliver the goods. The French are furious. They accuse the British of gross materialism and poor taste. Oscar Wilde disappears. George Eliot. Winston Churchill. You name them. For a few months there is a grotesque trade in the remains of the famous. But the fashion has no intrinsic substance and fizzles out. Anyone could have seen it wouldn't run.

Bone has the image, because Bone really is beautiful.

Too many people are yearning for that Bone. The real stuff. It genuinely hurts me to disappoint them. Circumstances alter cases. Against my better judgement I continue in the business. I bend my principles, just for the duration. We have as much turnover as we had selling to the Swiss gnomes. It's the latest item on the *been-to* list. 'You *have* to bring me back some London Bone, Ethel, or I'll never forgive you!' It starts to appear in the American luxury catalogues.

But by now there are ratsniffers everywhere – from Trade and Industry, from the National Trust, from the Heritage Corp, from half a dozen South London councils, from the Special Branch, from the CID, the Inland Revenue and both the Funny and the Serious Fraud Squads.

Any busybody who ever wanted to put his head under someone else's bed is having a wonderful time. Having failed dramatically with the STOP THIS DISGUSTING TRADE approach, the tabloids switch to offering bits of Bone as prizes in circulation boosters. I sell a newspaper consortium a Tesco's plastic bagful for two and a half mill via a go-between. Bernie and I are getting almost frighteningly rich. I open some bank accounts offshore and I become an important anonymous shareholder in the Queen Elizabeth Hall when it's privatised.

It doesn't take long for the experts to come up with an analysis. Most of the Bone has been down there since the seventeenth century and earlier. They are the sites of the old plague pits where, legend had it, still-living people were thrown in with the dead. For a while it must have seemed like Auschwitz-on-Thames. The chemical action of lime, partial burning, London clay and decaying flesh, together with the broadening spread of the London water table, thanks to various engineering works over the last century, letting untreated sewage into the mix, had created our unique London Bone. As for the decorations, that, it was opined, was the work of the pit guards, working on earlier bones found on the same site.

'Blood, shit and bone,' says Bernie. 'It's what makes the world go round. That and money, of course.'

'And love,' I add. I'm doing all right these days. It's true what they say about a Roller. Little Trudi has enthusiastically rediscovered my attractions. She has her eye on a ring. I raise my glass. 'And love, Bernie.'

'Fuck that,' says Bernie. 'Not in my experience.' He's buying Paul McCartney's old place in Wamering and having it converted for Persians. He has, it is true, also bought his wife her dream house. She doesn't seem to mind it's on the island of Las Cascadas about six miles off the coast of Morocco. She's at last agreed to divorce him. Apart from his mother, she's the only woman he ever had anything to do with and he isn't, he says, planning to try another. The only females he wants in his house in future come with a pedigree a mile long, have all their shots and can be bought at Harrods.

Chapter Four

I EXPECT YOU heard what happened. The private Bonefields, which contractors were discovering all over South and West London, actually contained public bones. They were part of our national inheritance. They had living relatives. And stones, some of them. So it became a political and a moral issue. The Church got involved. The airwaves were crowded with concerned clergy. There was the problem of the self-named bone-miners. Kids, inspired by our leaders' rhetoric and aspiring to imitate those great captains of free enterprise they had been taught to admire, were turning over ordinary graveyards, which they'd already stripped of their saleable masonry, and digging up somewhat fresher stiffs than was seemly.

A bit too fresh. It was pointless. The Bone took centuries to get seasoned and so far nobody had been able to fake the process. A few of the older graveyards had small deposits of Bone in them. Brompton Cemetery had a surprising amount, for instance, and so did Highgate. This attracted prospectors. They used shovels mainly, but sometimes low explosives. The area around Karl Marx's monument looked like they'd refought the Russian Civil War over it. The barbed wire put in after the event hadn't helped. And, as usual, the public paid to clean up after private enterprise. Nobody in their right mind got buried any more. Cremation became very popular. The borough councils and their financial managers were happy because more valuable real estate wasn't being occupied by a non-consumer.

It didn't matter how many security guards were posted or, by one extreme authority, landmines, the teenies left no grave unturned. Bone was still a profitable item, even though the market had settled down since we started. They dug up Bernie's mother. They dug up my cousin Leonard. There wasn't a Londoner who didn't have some intimate unexpectedly back above ground. Every night you saw it on telly.

It had caught the public imagination. The media had never made much of the desecrated graveyards, the chiselled-off angels' heads and the uprooted headstones on sale in King's Road and the Boulevard Saint-Michel since the 1970s. These had been the targets of first-generation grave-robbers. Then there had seemed nothing left to steal. Even they had baulked at doing the corpses. Besides, there wasn't a market. This second generation was making up for lost time, turning over the soil faster than an earthworm on E.

The news shots became clichés. The heaped earth, the headstone, the smashed coffin, the hint of the contents, the Leader of the Opposition coming on to say how all this has happened since his mirror image got elected. The councils argued that they should be given the authority to deal with the problem. They owned the graveyards. And also, they reasoned, the Bonefields. The profits from those fields should rightly go into the public purse. They could help pay for the Health Service. 'Let the dead,' went their favourite slogan, 'pay for the living for a change.'

What the local politicians actually meant was that they hoped to claim the land in the name of the public and then make the usual profits privatising it. There was a principle at stake. They had to ensure their friends and not outsiders got the benefit.

The High Court eventually gave the judgement to the public, which really meant turning it over to some of the most rapacious borough councils in our history. A decade or so earlier, that Charlie Peace of elected bodies, the Westminster City Council, had tried to sell their old graveyards to new developers. This current judgement allowed all councils at last to maximise their assets from what was, after all, dead land, completely unable to pay for itself, and therefore a natural target for privatisation. The feeding frenzy began. It was the closest thing to mass cannibalism I've ever seen.

We had opened a fronter in Old Sweden Street and had a couple of halfway presentable slags from Bernie's club taking the calls and answering enquiries. We were straight up about it. We called it *The City Bone Exchange*. The bloke who decorated it and did the sign specialised in giving offices that long-established look. He'd created most of those old-fashioned West End hotels you'd never heard of until 1999. 'If it's got a Scottish name,' he used to say, 'it's one of mine. Americans love the skirl of the pipes, but they trust a bit of brass and varnish best.'

Our place was almost all brass and varnish. And it worked a treat. The Ritz and the Savoy sent us their best potential buyers. Incredibly exclusive private hotels gave us taxi-loads of bland-faced American boy-men, reeking of health and beauty products, bellowing their credentials to the wind, rich matrons eager for anyone's approval, massive Germans with aggressive cackles, stern Orientals glaring at us, daring us to cheat them. They bought. And they bought. And they bought.

The snoopers kept on snooping but there wasn't really much to find out. Livingstone International took an aggressive interest in us for a while, but what could they do? We weren't up to anything illegal just selling the stuff and nobody could identify what – if anything – had been nicked anyway. I still had my misgivings. They weren't anything but superstitions, really. It did seem sometimes that for every layer of false antiquity, for every act of Disneyfication, an inch or two of our real foundations crumbled. You knew what happened when you did that to a house. Sooner or later you got trouble. Sooner or later you had no house.

We had more than our share of private detectives for a while. They always pretended to be customers and they always looked wrong, even to our girls.

Livingstone International had definitely made a connection. I think they'd found our mine and guessed what a windfall they'd lost. They didn't seem at one with themselves over the matter. They even made veiled threats. There was some swagger came in to talk about violence but they were spotties who'd got all their language off old '90s TV shows. So we sweated it out and the girls took most of the heat. Those girls really didn't know anything. They were magnificently ignorant. They had tellies with chips that switch channels as soon as they detect a news or information programme.

I've always had a rule. If you're caught by the same wave twice, get out of the water.

While I didn't blame myself for not anticipating the Great Andrew Lloyd Webber Slump, I think I should have guessed what would happen next. The tolerance of the public for bullshit had become decidedly and aggressively negative. It was like the Bone had set new standards of public aspiration as well as beauty. My dad used to say that about the Blitz. Classical music enjoyed a huge success during the Second World War. Everybody grew up at once. The Bone had made it happen again. It was a bit frightening to those of us who had always relied on a nice, passive, gullible, greedy punter for an income.

The bitter fights that had developed over graveyard and Bone-field rights and boundaries, the eagerness with which some borough councils exploited their new resource, the unseemly trade in what was, after all, human remains, the corporate involvement, the incredible profits, the hypocrisies and politics around the Bone brought us the outspoken disgust of Europe. We were used to that. In fact, we tended to cultivate it. But that wasn't the problem.

The problem was that our *own* public had had enough.

When the elections came round, the voters systematically booted out anyone who had supported the Bone trade. It was like the sudden rise of the anti-slavery vote in Lincoln's America. They demanded an end to the commerce in London Bone. They got the Boneshops closed down. They got work on the Bonefields stopped. They got their graveyards and monuments protected and cleaned up. They got a city that started cultivating peace and security as if it was a cash crop. Which maybe it was. But it hurt me.

It was the end of my easy money, of course. I'll admit I was glad it was stopping. It felt like they were slowing entropy, restoring the past. The quality of life improved. I began to think about letting a few rooms for company.

The mood of the country swung so far into disapproval of the Bone trade that I almost began to fear for my life. Road and anti-abortion activists switched their attention to Bone merchants. Hampstead was full of screaming lefties convinced they owned the moral high ground just because they'd paid off their enormous mortgages. Trudi, after three months, applied for a divorce, arguing that she had not known my business when she married me. She said she was disgusted. She said I'd been living on blood money. The courts awarded her more than half of what I'd made, but it didn't matter any more. My investments were such that I couldn't stop earning. Economically, I was a small oil-producing nation. I had my own international dialling code. It was horrible in a way. Unless I tried very hard, it looked like I could never be ruined again. There was no justice.

I met Bernie in the King Lyar in Old Sweden Street, a few doors down from our burned-out office. I told him what I planned to do and he shrugged.

'We both knew it was dodgy,' he told me. 'It was dodgy all along, even when we thought it was mastodons. What it feels like to me, Ray, is – it feels like a sort of a massive transformation of the zeitgeist – you know, like Virginia Woolf said about the day human nature changed – something happens slowly and you're not aware of it. Everything seems normal. Then you wake up one morning and – bingo! – it's Nazi Germany or Bolshevik Russia or Thatcherite England or the Golden Age – and all the rôles have changed.'

'Maybe it was the Bone that did it,' I said. 'Maybe it was a symbol everyone needed to rally round. You know. A focus.'

'Maybe,' he said. 'Let me know when you're doing it. I'll give you a hand.'

About a week later we got the van backed up to the warehouse loading bay. It was three o'clock in the morning and I was chilled to the marrow. Working in silence we transferred every scrap of Bone to the van. Then we drove back to Hampstead through a freezing rain.

I don't know why we did it the way we did it. There would have been easier solutions, I suppose. But behind the high walls of my big back garden, under the old trees and etiolated rhododendrons, we dug a pit and filled it with the glowing remains of the ancient dead.

The stuff was almost phosphorescent as we chucked the big lumps of clay back onto it. It glowed a rich amber and that faint rosemary smell came off it. I can still smell it to this day when I go in there. My soft fruit is out of this world. The whole garden's doing wonderfully now.

In fact London's doing wonderfully. We seem to be back on form. There's still a bit of a Bone trade, of course, but it's marginal.

Every so often I'm tempted to take a spade and turn over the earth again, to look at the fortune I'm hiding there. To look at the beauty of it. The strange amber glow never fades and sometimes I think the decoration on the Bone is an important message I should perhaps try to decipher.

I'm still a very rich man. Not justly so, but there it is. And, of course, I'm about as popular with the public as Percy the Paedophile. Gold the Bone King? I might as well be Gold the Graverobber. I don't go down to Soho much. When I do make it to a show or something I try to disguise myself a bit. I don't see anything of Bernie any more and I heard two of the stoodies topped themselves.

I do my best to make amends. I'm circulating my profits as fast as I can. Talent's flooding into London from everywhere, making a powerful mix. They say they haven't known a buzz like it since 1967. I'm a reliable investor in great new shows. Every year I back the Iggy Pop Awards, the most prestigious in the business. But not everybody will take my money. I am regularly reviled. That's why some organisations receive anonymous donations. They would refuse them if they knew they were from me.

I've had the extremes of good and bad luck riding this particular switch in the zeitgeist and the only time I'm happy is when I wake up in the morning and I've forgotten who I am. It seems I share a common disgust for myself.

A few dubious customers, however, think I owe them something.

Another bloke, who used to be very rich before he made some frenetic investments after his career went down the drain, called me the other day. He knew of my interest in the theatre, that I had invested in several West End hits. He thought I'd be interested in his idea. He wanted to revive his first success, *Rebecca's Incredibly Far Out Well* or something, which he described as a powerful religious rock opera guaranteed to capture the new nostalgia market. The times, he told me, they were a-changin'. His show, he continued, was full of raw old-fashioned R&B energy. Just the sort of authentic sound to attract the new no-nonsense youngsters. Wasn't it cool that Madonna wanted to do the title rôle? And Bob Geldof would play the Spirit of the Well. *Rock and roll, man! It's all in the staging, man! Remember the boat in* Phantom? *I can make it look better than real. On stage, man, that well is W.E.T. WET! Rock and roll!* I could see that little wizened fist punching the air in a parody of the vitality he craved and whose source had always eluded him.

I had to tell him it was a non-starter. I'd turned over a new leaf, I said. I was taking my ethics seriously.

These days I only deal in living talent.

Stories

THIS IS THE story of my friend Rex Fisch who blew out his complicated brains in his Lake District library all over his damned books one Sunday afternoon last September. Naturally the place was a horror to clean, but Rex never really cared much about the mess he left in his wake. What pissed me off was the waste: each blasted cell was a story he'd never tell; a story no-one else would ever tell. Rex knew how to hurt himself and the old friends who loved him. Only a few of us are now left. Cancer took Hawthorn, Hayley, Slade and Allard that same year. The first three had shared digs with Rex when he first lived in London. It didn't seem fair of the bastard to deliberately deplete what remained of our joint memory.

As I said at his funeral Rex had more fiction in him than could ever come out, no matter how long he'd lived. A superb raconteur, he produced stories in every form, from dry, funny narrative verse to self-dramatising social lies. Novels, plays, short stories, comic strips, operas, movies, RPGs: throughout his career he was never stuck for a narrative. In that respect we were pretty much alike and shared a kind of discomfort at our own facility. We both identified with Balzac, sharing a fascination for Jacques Collin, his sinister and ubiquitous many-named master villain who set out to ruin La Torpille in *Splendeurs et misères des courtisanes*. Rex discovered that most people prefer a good story and a bit of conventional prejudice to honest ambiguity; they made their most profound life decisions based on tales they saw in the tabloids or on reality TV. That didn't stop Rex telling the truth when it frequently occurred to him. Truth was always in there somewhere, even when he thought he was lying. For all his later right-wing posturing, he had, like Balzac, a way of tapping into poor people's dreams and understanding what they wanted most in the world. I envied him his empathy, if not his ambition. There was one story he couldn't write. I think it was what we were all waiting for and which might have brought him the literary recognition he longed for. But he believed *Paris Review* editors could 'smell the pulp writer on you', while as an editor I rejected stories because I could smell *Paris Review* on them. I believed we were too good for the reviews even when we appeared in them. The conventions of genre were staler in literary writing than Harlequin romances: exactly why Rex turned out to be the writer we most needed on *Mysterious*.

We were both six-two and shared the same colouring and humour, though Rex was already balding. I guess our differences came from our backgrounds. I was a Londoner. Rex had been born and raised in Wrigley, Texas, pop. 1,204, about forty miles from Waco. He'd believed everything they told him until he went to Austin where he found out how to doubt his small-town certainties, trading them for the snobberies of the UT literary enclave. Dumping his provincialism a little late, he never lost his reverence for academia. Furiously cynical, he was determined to tell readers what fools they were to believe his stories. Despite this, he seemed oddly innocent when he turned up in London fresh from the UT campus via Spain, with the remnants of his jaundice, an uncompleted creative-writing degree and a few sales to the American crime and sci-fi digests, to be disgusted by our rates, even lower than the US, but delighted when we bought whatever he wrote, at whatever length he did it. When we met we were both twenty-five. Literary powers like Julie Mistral had already called him the James M. Cain of his generation. Angus Wilson had compared me to Gerald Kersh and Arnold Bennett.

The 'digests' were the pulps' attempts to look more sophisticated, with abstract expressionist covers and cooler titles, but I had grown up reading the real pulps with their powerful pictures and raving shout lines (*Donna was a dame who dared to be different – Kelly was a cop who craved to kill!*). The quality of the fiction didn't alter, just the presentation.

I found it hard to come in at the end of that era, working on the Falcon and Sexton Blake Library, but it had proved one thing to me. There were no such things as pulp writers. Bad writers like Carroll John Daly and brilliant ones like Dashiell Hammett just happened to write for the pulps. Mostly their reputation had to do with context. Jack Trevor Story would write a novel for Sexton Blake then, with minor modifications, turn it into a novel for Secker & Warburg.

By the time I took it over, Hank Janson's *Mystery Magazine* was about the last of the UK thriller digests and I had some crack-brained notion to lift it away from genre altogether and make it into something addressing the widest possible readership. By 1964 there were few short-story mags left and most of those were generic. They ran romances, military adventures, mysteries and sci-fi. To get published and paid you had to adapt your work, usually by inserting a clunky rationalised plot. That way you earned a bit as you learned a bit. We didn't want to write what we called Englit-fic: the styles and themes of which came out of universities in sad imitation of the great modernists. We wanted to write something that had the vitality of good commercial fiction and the subtle ambition of good literary fiction, reflecting the sensibilities and events of our times: stuff that would get us high with the sense of enthusiasm and engagement of Proust or Faulkner but with the disciplined vitality of genre fiction pulsing from every page.

A few of us talked about a 'two-way street' to reunite junk, middlebrow and highbrow fiction. Some people out there had to be as frustrated as us, dissatisfied by pretty much everything on offer, literary or commercial. For ages people had discussed the 'two cultures'. We might just be the guys to unite them: writing for a reader who knew a bit about poetry, painting and physics, enjoyed Gerald Kersh, Elizabeth Bowen and Mervyn Peake, merging realism with grotesquerie and doing it elegantly, eloquently. By 1963 we were publishing a few examples in the digests and with Billy Allard and Harry Hayley, my two closest writer friends, we made plans for a 'slick' quarto magazine bringing together designers, artists, scientists, poets, but of course the cost of the art paper alone made publishers shake their heads.

Then Len Haynes, the decent old drunk who ran it for ever, proposed that I take over Janson's when he retired to live with his daughter in Majorca.

Married less than a year, Helena Denham and I lived in Colville Terrace, still Rachman's Notting Hill fiefdom. We'd had our first daughter, Sally, and Helena, beautiful as ever with her pageboy chestnut hair framing a heart-shaped face, was furiously pregnant with Kitty, our second. I'd been fired from *Liberal Topics*, the party magazine whose wages I'd taken in spite of promising Winston Churchill, when I was little, never to become a Liberal. So I needed Janson's money. More important, it would be a chance to do what we'd been saying we should do for so long. I talked it over with Helena and the others.

When I went back to Dave and Howard Vasserman, the publishers, I made only three conditions: that I decide policy, that they let me change the title gradually and if our circulation went up they give me the paper and size I wanted. I would help them get mainstream distribution with their more upmarket titles. I convinced them I could make their imprint respectable enough to be taken on by the high street retailers. Then I got my friends busy. We lacked a decent designer but I did my best. Our first issue would not merely offer a manifesto, we would attempt to demonstrate policy – and we'd have a lot of illustrations, one of the secrets, in my experience, of a successful periodical. They were Jack Hawthorn's job.

Hayley started finishing a novella he'd been talking about, a weird thing in which the detective's dreams informed his case. Allard began writing us a new serial, full of brooding metaphysical imagery borrowed from Dalí and Ernst. Helena finished her alternate-world Nazi creeper. I drafted my editorial about pulp influences on William Burroughs, and Burroughs gave us a chapter from his new book. American beats and British pop artists had something in common with noir movies, our other great enthusiasm. Allard produced a guest editorial arguing that 'the space age' needed a new lexicon, new literary ideas. I did a short under a regular pseudonym and the rest came from Janson's stable of favourites.

All three of us were English but had known little conventional upbringing. Hayley had been orphaned by a buzz bomb, taken a job on a local paper before being conscripted into the RAF, studied metaphysics at Oxford where he'd met Allard who'd been raised in occupied France with an Anglo-Jewish mother who'd been on one of the last transports to Auschwitz, worked for the Resistance as a kid then come home not to prewar Mayfair fantasy but despairing suburban austerity, the world Orwell captured. After his conscription served in the RAF, he did physics at Oxford, where he met Harry. They both dropped out after a few terms, writing features and noirish sci-fi stories for mags like *Authentic* or *Vargo Statten's*. Allard was qualified to fly obsolete prop planes, Hayley was a qualified radio operator and I'd done a couple of miserable ATC years before they abolished conscription about a nanosecond before I was due to be drafted, edited juvenile story papers, trade mags and Sexton Blake, so I had loads of editorial experience but little formal education.

We'd spent half our lives in the pub discussing why modern fiction was crap and why it needed an infusion of the methods and concerns of popular fiction, all of us having sold a bit to the surviving thriller and science fantasy pulps. I think we felt we knew what we were talking about, having been raised in the social margins, thanks to one trick of fate or another, and loved surrealism, absurdism, French New Wave movies as well as Pound, Eliot, Proust and the rest. In common with a few other restless autodidacts of our day we loved anything containing Gabin's smoking .38, Mitchum's barking .45 or Widmark's glittering knives, all mixed up with Brecht and Weill, Camus's fascist *Caligula* screaming 'I'm still alive' and the black bars crossing the faces of Sartre's *Huis Clos*, emphasising the prisons in which we place ourselves. Into that mix we threw James Mason in *Odd Man Out*, Harry Lime, Gerald Kersh's *Night and the City*, Bester's *Demolished Man*, Bradbury's *Fahrenheit 451*, Household's *Rogue Male*, Lodwick's

Brother Death. We'd met the likes of Francis Bacon, Somerset Maugham and Maurice Richardson at the Colony, read Beckett, Miller and Durrell in Olympia Press and generally got our education from the best novelists, journalists and artists of our day. Allard liked Melville more than I did, Hayley preferred Kafka and I loved Meredith. We were agreed that their lessons needed to be brought back into contemporary culture via the popular arts. Borges, too, though his stuff was only just being done into English via Ferlinghetti's City Lights press. We also thought that fiction should be able to carry as many narratives per paragraph as possible, using techniques borrowed from absurdism, futurism and combined with new ideas of our own. We'd thought there were hundreds of writers dying for the chance to do the same as us, but though a lot more readers welcomed what we made of *Mysterious*, contributors were slow in coming.

By 1965 we'd at least laid the foundations of the two-way street. Pop art came one way, pulp the other. The Beatles and Dylan were doing the soundtrack. They broke new ground and got paid for it, but most people had no real idea what we meant when we talked about combining 'high' and 'low' arts, in spite of the two cultures being as popular a subject in features pages as the big bang and planet-size computers. We wanted to rid pop fiction of its literalism, taking exaggeration for granted in ambitious work. We were only slowly developing a critical vocabulary, trying to bring a deeper seriousness to the novel. We were still frustrated, reckoning we were still missing a piece in the equation. Whittling the title slowly down to one word hadn't been enough. We needed writers desiring to emulate modern classicism to help build a genuine bridge able to take the weight of our two-way traffic.

It took Rex turning up in 1965 to show us what we needed to convince readers and writers of our authority. Like Allard or Hayley, he wrote better than any other contemporary I knew. His sardonic style was deceptively simple. He, too, was a Balzac fan with a special love of Jacques Collin/Vautrin. We were almost exactly the same age. Like me, he'd supported himself since the age of sixteen. He'd climbed out of a family of father-dominated

German Catholic drunks, dropping out of the University of Texas after selling a few stories to the digests which got him a couple of book contracts to fund the trip to Europe he felt was the next rung on his career ladder, which he planned with his friend Jack Slade, a fellow Texan Catholic and a master ironist.

I was only familiar with Rex's world through what little fiction I'd read of Jim Thompson or what he'd described himself in *Paine in Congress* or *The Clinic*. I'd certainly never been to Texas and only knew Manhattan. Jack's stories had never seen print; they were dry, sly and ticking with the energy of unexploded bombs. Rex's were like Henry James on speed. Quick-mouthed contemporary clarity; good fast fiction fresh off the calendar and with plenty of class. Rooted in our familiar world.

Jack and Rex had planned to write a mystery together in Spain, travel around Europe for a while, then return either to Austin or to New York. But they hadn't anticipated catching jaundice from bad acid in Spain and having to stay with friends in London until they could finish the book. Rex, having read about us in Julie Mistral's *NYT* column, came to see me in the hope of raising some living money. He also brought some of Jack's manuscripts and I immediately knew we were in luck. Neither had come from populist traditions but they thirsted for pulp. They brought the best academic ambitions to the subject matter we featured. They were exactly what I'd been looking for, roaring down from the other end of the two-way street and bringing a bunch of new writers and readers after them. Two for the price of one. Murder and the human soul. The face of society and the fabric of the future. Their intensity and intelligence lacked the hesitancy or vulgarity I'd rejected when posh literary agents thought they'd found somewhere to dump their clients' awful bits of generic slumming, neither did they stink of the creative-writing class.

Sociable, a little formal, a knowing catalyst, Rex introduced me to friends he had known at UT, including the talented fine artists Peggy Zorin, Jilly Cornish and her husband, Jimmy, as well as others who were yet to leave Texas en route for *Mysterious* and London. At last we had a full set of talented contributors who could give us a substantial inventory, interacting with increased gravity, attracting other writers who added superb stories to our contents list, the best anyone had read in ages, combining a sophistication and vitality taken for granted today but representing a quantum jump at the time and making us the most celebrated fiction magazine of our day. The debate was suddenly over. We could demonstrate everything we'd discussed. That was what Rex Fisch did for *Mysterious* and the rough-and-ready movement we'd always denied was a movement. We entered a Golden Age. Almost every story we published was anthologised. A good many won prizes.

I knew of course that our little revolution would collapse rapidly once we achieved what we hoped for and our individual careers were made. Real life grew darker after those good years. The first tragedy was Jane Allard's death on a trip back to the family home near Nantes. Billy moved to Streatham to bring up his kids. We drove over with our own to visit from time to time. Next, Rex took part in a poetry tour with several well-known poets, including the notoriously omnisexual Spike Allison. He came back gay (no surprise to his friends) and monstrously troubled about it after Spike dumped him on their return to London. Our relationships were only just surviving the divorces, rearrangements and general infighting. People join revolutions until they get what they want as individuals, then start quarrelling over the spoils, however imaginary. I was surprised by how many of our friendships remained intact. Writing mostly non-fiction, Jack settled down with a local girl, Daisy Angelino, in Portobello Road, near our offices. Rex met Chick Archer, who was from Maine, at an S&M bar in Paris. They fell in love, travelled for a few years, then bought their lovely freezing old house in the English Lakes. The place couldn't be more Wordsworthy with its hard, driving cloud banks bringing relentless rain, rewarding you with bursts of sunshine, the whole fell moving like a living body in its contours and shadows, over which Rex presided with a rather proprietorial air at his huge sitting-room windows. Sometimes the wind bawled against the long scar of Wattendale Edge, creating waves across the black tarn. You can see those landscapes, beautifully drawn by Chick in the *Mary Stone* comic. They're still syndicated. Almost nobody knew Rex wrote that great, gritty newspaper strip which made them more money than anything else and which explained why their home smelled so strongly of well-loved wealth.

Rex and I still made each other laugh uncontrollably, much to Chick's silent disgust. This of course drove the sadistic Rex to increase Chick's discomfort. I suspect that's why we didn't get invited up so often. Harry went to live in Ireland with his Dublin-born wife, to look after her mother who lived on a miserable council estate just outside Cork. Stuck there, Harry grew increasingly depressed and began a long book on Nietzsche. I saw him occasionally when he came to do research at the British Library. Jimmy and Jill Cornish settled near the old mill in Tufnell Hill. He wrote reviews, criticism for the *LRB* and non-fiction guides. She produced commercial posters to supplement her gallery shows. Others continued to get novels published and exhibitions arranged with increased success. Pete Bates disappeared on a cycling holiday in France. His bike was found at the bottom of a sea cliff in Brittany. Other good writers and artists came and went. Charlie Ratz joined us as our designer. I performed and made records with the Deep Fix.

I thought we were extending the '60s Golden Age but really it was the end. I continued to publish *Mysterious* but now it was edited by others as affairs and relationships collapsed dramatically across four continents. Gender rôles rolled in every possible direction. Stable quartets became full orchestras; ramshackle duets became rock-solid trios. If you visited friends in San Francisco, you needed a complicated chart to know who was with whom, why, when and where. As he and Rex settled in to do the old Alan Bennetts, Chick now wore the slightly self-conscious air of a resting chorus boy down from London for the weekend. Rex had exchanged his Texan brogue for a rather attractive Cowardian drawl which disappeared on the few occasions he phoned home. Chick's tones grew increasingly clipped. They were models of moral righteousness, so thoroughly faithful that when AIDS came it gave them no hint of anxiety. They adopted a very superior attitude to everyone else, of course. And particularly, it turned out, to me. With three much-loved offspring to care for, I weakly divorced Helena, married again and moved across the street with my child bride, Jenny.

Though I had suffered with Rex through his sexual transition and every minor treachery practised on and by him, he chose to see my break-up with Helena as perhaps the most infamous deed since Eddie's in *Death of the Heart*. My separation from Helena was reasonably amicable, I thought. I was still supporting everyone. I'd done it pretty straightforwardly. But the first time I took Jenny up to Wattendale to see them and a group of friends they'd invited, I thought the murmured commentary from Rex would never end. If Kim and Di Stanley hadn't as usual conned me into giving them a lift up from Bury I would have gone back on the Saturday morning. I was furious and very close to ending our friendship on the spot.

Jenny talked me out of it. 'I love hearing you and Rex tell your stories.' She grinned. 'You're such great liars.'

I hardly saw Rex or Chick for the next three years. Chick sent a card at Christmas with just his signature on it. Jenny sent one from us. But I'd had enough. Rex wasn't the only moody bastard writing for *Mysterious* and I just didn't have the energy to work at anything more. At least he was still sending his stuff in, via Charlie Ratz, the new editor. Charlie still saw him regularly. His parents had retired to a massive house outside Keswick, only a couple of miles from Rex and Chick. Whenever Charlie returned to London, he had a new story or two with him. Or Jack Slade would go up and bring something back.

Rex knew the prestige of publishing in the mag. The public saw no ruptures. We were getting more praise than was probably healthy. In fact, a critic brought about our reconciliation. Julie Mistral, the *NYT* reviewer who had been our early champion, now lived about half the year in England. She threw one of her so-called A-list parties and we were all invited. The party was held in the huge run-down hotel restaurant she rented.

Jenny and I were amongst the first to arrive. Rex and Chick were already there, sipping Jacquesson from dusty flutes. Rex spotted me, came over and greeted us with all his old, amused affection. The Great Big Hi as Jack called it. We were embraced. We were kissed. We were mystified.

I was wise enough not to ask how or why this had happened but Jenny found out later from Chick. Rex had come across a review written by Helena for *Tribune*, which had a circulation of about twenty. She had failed to praise *Lost Time Serenade*, Rex's Proustian parody, as much as Rex felt it should be praised. It wasn't a bad review, given I knew she'd found the whole thing pretentious and unworthy of such a good writer, but with Rex you were expected as a friend either to praise him to the skies or not review him at all. Now I knew why Helena hadn't been invited and since I'd never made that particular error of diplomacy I was back in favour again. Then Chick came up and gave me that look of wordless disgust, which was his way of maintaining friendships when Rex blew hot and cold. I was still unsure of him. I was a bit unsure of everything, in fact, because Jenny was just getting into what she'd call her experimental phase, which would enliven our sex-life and destroy our marriage. Fourteen years younger than me, she felt she hadn't experienced enough of the world.

I have to admit our sexual experiments were funny to me at first. There's not a lot of sexual pleasure to be got from hopping shouting around your bedroom having failed to wallop your wife's bottom and whacked your own leg instead. I had no instinct for it. Eventually though I was able to play the cruel Sir Charles with reasonable skill. A bit like faking an orgasm.

Ever since we'd been together Jenny had a fantasy about me watching one of my friends fuck her. There were a thousand scenarios in her little head and scarcely one in mine. I think I used up all my stories while I was working. I didn't dream either. I needed a rest from tale-spinning at the end of the day. But I did my best. I hated to disappoint her.

I had an idea of the scenario she planned one evening when Rex turned up holding a bottle of Algerian red in one hand and his dripping cap and overcoat in the other, beaming. 'Hi!' A wild giggle at his own physical discomfort. Charming. On his best and happiest behaviour. He embraced us in his soft gigantic arms. He had some meetings with Universal Features and wanted to stay for a bit. I thought the evening was to be a celebration of our reborn friendship. Jenny was all over him, flirting like a fag hag, bringing Rex out all a-twitter. So we dined. While I washed up, she whispered in his ear.

It turned out Jenny loved threesomes but mostly with her looking on frigging herself blind while waiting to get fucked by the least exhausted bloke. Mostly that was me, as Rex jerked off. That image is no more appealing to me than to you. After three or four nights and days of this, I realised that Rex was getting most of his buzz from knowing Chick had no suspicion of what he was up to.

Of course, to add to his own wicked relish Rex told Chick what he'd done with us. He had to. He never could resist a good story, particularly if he was telling it. Our few nights of passionless sex had become a means of manipulating Chick. This time Chick cut us.

Inevitably Jenny and I grew further apart as our games got more fantastic. Rex had already been through all that with Chick in Paris. Real-life fantasies are distractions for a working writer. Years before Rex told me that himself. 'It's as bad as going to law. The story starts to take over. Like falling in love. All sentimentality and melodrama. The scenarios are repetitive, conventional. All they offer are the comforts of genre.' He was right. Sex games are more boring than an Agatha Christie novel.

Anyway Jenny, despite our investment in special clothing and sex aids, wasn't getting a big enough buzz out of my efforts. It's like horror movies or superhero comics, you either stop and give them a rest or you have to keep heightening the action. Even if the games didn't bore me, our widening circle of acquaintances did. I wasn't finding enough time alone. Individuals, couples, whole fucking communes got involved. If they gave me a good paragraph or two, I wouldn't have minded so much, but there was an infantile sameness about their scenarios. Jenny and I were driven further apart by what the courts call intimacy. I tried to get to see Rex and Chick on their own, desperately needing to find out how they had rescued themselves from the crack of the crop, the smell of damp leather, the spell of repetition. Did you just grow out of it? Sometimes Jenny seemed to be flagging until some fresh variation on a familiar theme perked her up again. She was a natural addict. I've never been seriously addicted to anything. So I started trying to get her off the habit. It didn't work. She made excuses, started doing stuff in secret. I hate ambiguity in my day-to-day life. There's enough in my work. A writer needs routines and certainties. What can I say? As well as losing real intimacy with old friends, I lost it with Jenny. In a half-arsed attempt to restore our earlier closeness, she told me some of her new adventures. Then I got hooked for a while. I started pumping her for more revelations. She owed me that, I decided. They added nothing but did become pretty chilling. The seduction of under-age girls. Things my friends liked to do. It amazed me how so many women took the odd rape for granted. Too many secrets revealed. Friendships frayed. Rex came back in the picture. I moved out.

I took my kids, whom I'd been missing anyway, on a long trip round the USA. It made us feel better. To my relief we grew back together. Feeling my old self I got home, bought a short lease on a little flat in Fulham, just when Notting Hill turned into a gentri-fied suburb. I saw enough of Jenny to know it was thoroughly over. I didn't like what she'd done to herself. She'd dyed her hair bright blonde and her brown eyes had a vaguely dazed, mirrorlike quality, as if they only reflected and no longer saw anything. She'd lost her sense of humour, too, and was into various odd relation-ships, still searching for the good life. When I shifted the last of my stuff she made a half-hearted attempt to patch things up. She wanted to have a baby, she said, and get back into our old domes-tic routine. Even while she proposed this deal, a bloke I vaguely knew was sleeping upstairs in what had been our bed, where once, like Proust, I'd done most of my writing. From being a place of concentration in which I conceived stories it had become a place of distraction, where real stories died. I said she could keep the place. All she had to do was pay the mortgage.

'But I love you.' She wept. She made an awkward attempt to remind me of the old days. 'I love just lying in your arms at night while you tell me a story.'

I was sad. 'It's too late, Jenny.' Those stories were over.

I went up to Windermere, phoned Rex and Chick, but Chick was frosty. Did I know I had almost broken them up? I apologised. I said how much I regretted what had happened. Rex, just as distant and haughty, put the phone down on me. I saw them in Kendal once or twice and in Grasmere. They wouldn't speak to me. Once, over his shoulder, Rex gave me the most peculiar leer. Did he wish we were still deceiving Chick? It made me shudder. Was something wrong with him?

Of course I longed to be back with Helena but she'd settled down with a jolly Scottish chef and was doing her best work. Why would she want to change that?

Even though our pillow talk inspired a couple of shorts, I really hated having been part of Jenny's daisy chain. Some of those people I never wanted to see again, others I needed distance from; I wasn't ready to see Charlie Ratz or Jonny Fowler yet. Pete was still missing in France, presumed dead. I gave up any interest in *Mysterious*, which was now doing fine without me, bought a house near Ingleton, West Yorks, and settled in first with Emma Mac-Ewan, who couldn't stand the rain and cold, and then started seeing a local woman who disapproved of central heating. I desperately hoped to restore my friendship with Rex, even after I met Lucinda, to this day the love of my life. Lu found my obsession weird, I know, until she eventually met Rex in Leeds, at a Ted Hughes literary weekend we'd all been invited to. Lu's teenage daughter loved Rex's work and wanted him to autograph her books. She was too shy to ask him, so Lucy, her fair hair flying and blue eyes blazing, marched up to the table where he was sitting and said: 'I gather you're Mike's old friend. Well, I'm his new wife and this is my daughter, who's read most of your work and loves it. I think it's pretty good, too. So what about some autographs and while you're at it why don't you two shake hands?' And, that being just one of her powers, we did.

Later at the bar Rex told me Chick blamed me for the infamous 'seduction'. At that idea we continued to laugh for the rest of the day, until the next, when Chick turned up, glaring when he saw us, and Lucinda, nearly six feet herself, took him in hand as well. 'It's all over,' she said. 'If you're going to blame anyone, blame that poor, barmy bitch Jenny. She got you all involved in her folly and now look at you.' And when Chick grumbled that Rex was still seeing Jenny, which surprised me, Lu said: 'Well, she's poison as far as I can tell, and he doesn't need her now he has Mike back.' Chick teared up then. He told her I was the best friend Rex had ever had but I had betrayed them both. Which again I admitted. And the following weekend Lu and I went up and stayed with them. On our way home she said: 'You two could make Jeremiah roll about on the floor laughing himself sick.'

I didn't know why Rex went on seeing Jenny, unless he simply enjoyed wounding Chick. He still had that cruel streak in him. Chick and I talked about it. Chick thought it had to be directed at him, too. He guessed Jenny was a substitute for me, especially when Rex dropped Jenny so soon after we were reconciled. She still phoned him.

I saw Jenny myself a few times after that. She seemed more her old self in some ways. She'd had twins and was living with her mother in Worthing, on the Sussex coast. She had the washed-out look of so many single mothers, said she was happy, if poor, and even suggested my 'sexual conservatism' had dulled me down. Next time I bumped into her in Kensington High Street she was again pale, overpainted, dyed up. She looked as if all the vitality had been sucked from her. I thought she was doing junk. Her eyes were back to blank. Was she living in London? Did she have someone? She laughed and looked even more devitalised. 'None of your business,' she said. I couldn't argue with that.

Of course, I was curious to know what she and Rex had been up to. I guessed she hadn't accepted that he'd dropped her. At a party in Brighton a year or two later she looked worse than ever, clinging to Rupert Herbert, one of those new Low Tories on *The Spectator*. More make-up, too blonde and getting through a packet of Gauloises a minute. I did really feel sorry for her. Then Rex turned up and snubbed her so royally he pissed me off, so I made a point of going over to talk to her but she snubbed me in turn. Lucinda came over and murmured 'poor bitch' and meant it. Between us the *Mysterious* crew had ruined a nice, unimaginative girl, she thought. Not entirely fair. You could hear Jenny over the general buzz talking about some famous film producer she'd lived with. He'd been the one who bought *The Vices of Tom* from Rex and then turned it into that pot of toss. 'The bastard…' she was saying. You could guess the rest. Maybe Lu was right.

For the next ten years or so life settled into routines nobody felt like messing with though Rex grew increasingly unreasoning in his arguments with editors, then publishers, then agents until almost nobody would work with him. His books didn't sell enough for any editor to bother keeping him sweet. He took offence easily and frequently and, through his vengeful verse, publicly. Chick said he could no longer manage him. I would have thought this a good thing. I believed Chick's natural leanings towards convention and literary respectability pushed Rex away from his saving self-mocking vulgarity. Balzac and Vautrin were less his models than Proust or Albertine. His work seemed to apologise for itself. He lost his popular touch without gaining critical prestige. Only *Mary Stone* went on making money for them. His short stories came out less frequently, but he kept his habit of phoning and often reading the whole thing to you. And he still enjoyed inventing a story when he got your answering machine. 'Oh, I know what you're doing. You've met that good-looking farmer again and gone badger-watching with him.' Usually the time would be up before he could complete his fantasy. His new novels tended to peter out after a few chapters. I'd get frustrated and consider continuing them for him. They were wonderful ideas. Occasionally they would re-emerge when a way of telling them occurred to him. His aptitude for ironic narrative verse never left him. I'd labour for hours to get anything close to what usually took him minutes. Chick helped him develop his taste for classical music. which is how he came to write his three operas, one of which he based on Kersh's *The Brazen Bull* and another on Balzac's *Illusions perdues* but he became snobbish about popular music or he'd have written some great lyrics. I used a few of his verses in my own music stuff. I inserted another into one of my hack thrillers, its redeeming feature. His only opera to reach the stage was a version of Firbank's *Cardinal Pirelli*. Rex delighted in upsetting Catholics, although his attacks meant little to most of us.

Then, as we limped into our sixties, we began to suffer from real illnesses, as opposed to passing scares. Rex was diabetic, arthritic. Chick was the first of us to be diagnosed with cancer. I think it was colon, he wouldn't say. Even Rex refused to betray him on that occasion. His surgery seemed to cure him. We heard Jenny survived a stroke. By that time she hardly saw any old friends. When she had an operation, I'm not sure what it was for. Rex didn't speak of the years when he'd seen her regularly, even as we grew closer than ever, all living up in those northern hills, from Todmorden to Kendal. Harry, of course, was still in Ireland. Billy Allard went to Corfu after his children grew up. Pete continued to be presumed dead. Peggy Zorin returned to New York and was very successful. The Cornishes moved to Kirkby Lonsdale. I had a hernia operation which went wrong. Bad stitching cut off an artery and caused problems in my leg. I couldn't walk or climb any more. Rex's diabetes was complicated by drinking. Chick successfully got him on the wagon. In 2005, while we were at our place in Paris, I got an e-mail from Rex referring casually to Chick's return to Airedale General, so I phoned the hospital at once. 'It's spread a bit,' Chick said. 'I'll be out in a few days.' So we flew home and drove over. Chick had lost a lot of weight. He was ghastly white but Rex pretended nothing was wrong. A lot of surgery was involved. Chick started a short story called 'Over the Knife'. He showed it to us. Very mystical and sardonic. He got me to ask Jack Hawthorn if he'd take over *Mary Stone*, but Jack wasn't up to it. The next thing we knew he was admitted again and we made the first of several trips to Skipton. Chick was bitter about friends who couldn't find time to visit or phone. 'Or send a bloody Hallmark card and a bunch of fucking flowers.' Rex, sometimes there when I was, echoed all this. I did what I could to make friends visit. Very few did. People were fighting to keep some sort of income, I suppose. At the hospital we made the usual jokes, complimented Chick on his courage. He found this amusing. 'You're just thanking me for not making you feel bad. It's easy to be brave when everyone's attention's focused on you.' He could do the best wan smile, remembered Rex, giggling later. Chick asked us to stop sending flowers. The smell reminded him too much of funerals. I remembered my mother making the same complaint.

Rex was still pretty much in denial. Who could blame him? His responses became more and more monosyllabic, either because he didn't want to cry or because he didn't want to be reminded of what was happening. His partner of nearly forty years, however, spoke more freely. He had so little time. Subsequent operations were done to 'repair' his intestines. When he went home he was only there for a matter of weeks, even days, before they sent him back again. Another series of surgeries was proposed but Chick refused any more. He wanted to die with a semblance of dignity. A quietly practising Anglican for some years, he was ready to go. I asked if he was scared. 'In a way,' he said, 'as if I were going for a job interview.' He chiefly needed promises that we'd keep an eye on Rex, make sure he paid bills, had repairs done, all the jobs Chick had taken on so Rex could write without worry. 'I know it's hard, but you're the best friends he has.' A kind of blackmail. I didn't resent it. He probably said the same to others. 'He mustn't start drinking. He won't look after the place unless you pester him. There's still a bit on the mortgage. He'll let the pool go. Make sure he gives you a key. Oh, and he has a gun. Get the bullets if you can. You know what a drama queen he can be.' Next time we saw him he had written out a list in his educated American hand. Where the stopcocks were, what needed watering when, the names and numbers of the oil-delivery people, the gas and electricity people, the best plumber, the most reliable electrician. Their handyman, the local rates office: all the details of their domestic lives. We promised to do all we could.

His thin, grey face with its grey toothbrush moustache became earnest. 'In spite of anything Rex says?'

We promised.

'Or anything he tells you? Or I tell you?' This was puzzling, but we agreed. Once he had our promises, he drew a long breath. Then: 'You know, don't you, what he was doing with Jenny?'

'We don't want to.' Lucinda spoke before I could answer. Of course I wanted him to tell me.

'Okay.' Chick turned on his pillows. 'Probably just as well.'

Lu and I drove home in unspeaking silence.

Chick died a few days later. In late August many friends were on holiday and couldn't make it to the funeral. Rex blamed them, of course. If Chick's frail old dad could make the trip, then surely...? I went to stay with him. He was dazed. He'd found Chick's diaries before we could. 'I never realised what he gave up. Why he was so unhappy.' I pointed out that journals are almost always misleading. We use them to record miseries, frustrations of the moment, anger we don't want to put into the air. We didn't need them when we were content. But he refused to be comforted. He had failed Chick. That's all he had to say. He was drinking again.

Rex was very particular about the funeral, insisting we wear what he called 'full mourning', which meant black hats and veils for women, suits and ties for men. There were only seven of us in the Grasmere cemetery where Chick wanted to be buried. Rex bore his grief through his familiar haughty disguise. Lucinda had organised the funeral meats, such as they were. Rex had insisted on everything being simple. Chick had wanted the same. After we had all gone to bed or home, Rex sat down in his study and phoned everyone who hadn't been able to make it. If they didn't pick up, he left messages on their machines. Not the usual whimsical tales. He told them what he and Chick had always said behind their backs about their lack of talent, their ugly child, their gigantic ego, their terrible cooking, their bad taste. When Rex hurt, everyone got hurt. Next day, high on his own vengeance, he told me in a series of vignettes what he'd done. Some of the people phoned me next. Many were in tears. Almost all tried to forgive him. Several wanted to know if he was right. My daughter Kitty had given him Helena's regards and been snubbed so badly by Rex she was still crying when she got through to me. She was readier to forgive him than I was.

About a week later, while Lu visited her hypochondriacal mother, I went over to see how Rex was doing. He'd been drinking heavily. 'I'm glad you came,' he said. 'I wanted you to know about a favour I did you a few years back.' I cooked us dinner, after which he told me what he'd done for me. He was sure I'd be pleased, he said. I didn't know who he was mocking. Gasping and yelping with pain from the arthritis brought on by the booze, he poked up the fire and poured us cognacs. Then he started with the slow, dramatic relish he reserved for his readings. I suppose you could call it a revenge tale, with all the elements he enjoyed in Balzac and the Jacobeans. Soon after Jenny and I split up, and blaming her for 'luring' him into the threesome with which he had taunted Chick, Rex became, in his words, her confessor, suggesting ideas to her for sexual adventures, often helping her make specific contacts and introducing her to what he called his list of 'forty famous perverts'. He had sometimes accompanied her to dinners and parties, encouraging her to risks she'd never have dared take on her own. 'I drove her farther and farther down that road, Mike. You'd have loved it! Whenever she faltered I was there encouraging her to stay the course. I told her heroin wasn't addictive!' (Luckily he'd only been able to persuade her to snort it.) 'I convinced her she was a natural whore. I became her best friend, just as Vautrin took Emma under his wing!' That terrible, self-approving chuckle followed as he sat there in his big leather chair overlooking the darkening fell, staring in sardonic satisfaction at the sky, speaking in the tones of measured mockery usually reserved for his satirical verse. 'I knew you wanted to do it but couldn't. So I took your revenge *for* you, Mike!'

'Jesus, Rex. She didn't deserve... I would never...'

'Oh, Mike, you *know* what she deserved. *You'd* never do it, but Vautrin could, eh? I learned the lessons of Balzac better than you ever did!' At that point, as the world grew darker and the fire reflected on his face, he was every inch Balzac's monster, apparently completely mad. I felt physically sick, concerned for his sanity, deeply sorry for Jenny. I wondered if Lucinda had guessed what had gone on. Was that why she had refused to let Chick tell us anything? Rex relished every revelation. Giggling, he explained how he persuaded her to do something particularly demeaning. I was no sadist but of course he was. He could hate women. He went on for ages, offering chapter and verse, names, places, bringing all the horror and misery back. He explained little mysteries, offered anecdotes, consequences, a whole catalogue of betrayal. Chick could not have known the half of it. I wanted to walk out on him there and then but I was too fascinated. Besides, I had promised Chick I would stand by Rex. I couldn't abandon him. This was Rex's way of being my friend. I knew how much he relished revenge. He sincerely believed others merely pretended not to take the same pleasure in it.

I had promised to stay the night. By the time I went to bed, I had nothing to say to him. I knew how kind he could often be, how kind he had been to Jenny. I could hardly imagine such complicated, elaborate cruelty. Around three a.m. I took a couple of sleeping pills and woke up at eight on a wonderful sunny morning. Under a clear grey-blue sky the granite glittered and the grass glowed. Rex was down in the big, stone-flagged kitchen making breakfast. I ate it as if it might be poisoned. Standing in his drive beside my car, I hugged him. 'I love you, Rex,' I said. And I did, even at that moment, when I could barely look at him. He paused, appearing to consider this. Then he teared up, making that muted humming sound I became used to hearing when he searched for an appropriate word, the little smack of his lips and intake of breath when he'd found it.

'I love you, too,' he said at last.

I got home that afternoon. I'd had to pull over twice to collect myself. Lucinda was still out. I'd hoped so much she would be home before me. The message light was flickering on the phone. I had a sickening premonition something had happened to her.

But it was Rex sounding dramatically cheerful, a sure sign he'd been drinking. 'Hi, Mike! I know you're off ratting with your friend the vicar and your Jack Russells. Clearly you've no time to spend for poor old Rex...' And so on until the machine cut him off. I was relieved I'd taken longer getting home. When Lu finally arrived with fish and chips from the local, she was too full of her own frustrations with her mother to notice my mood so I explained how I was tired from staying up all night with Rex.

We saw a bit more of Rex after that. Because I would never know anything different, I decided to treat most of what he'd told me that night as an elaborate fiction. I was probably right. A couple of months later, as if he had been practising on me with the Jenny story, he began writing again. At first I was relieved, but we eventually realised he was unable to finish anything. He had lost his gift for narrative, his sense of the future. We did all we could to encourage him, to keep him engaged. The ideas themselves were as brilliant as ever. He phoned to read me a couple of opening paragraphs over the answering machine and they were so good, so typical of Rex at his best, Lucinda wouldn't let me erase them. When I was home he might read several pages, even a chapter. But two chapters were the most he could manage of anything. Chick had always been the one to help with construction. After I stopped editing he wouldn't let me do it any more. He claimed Chick's diary had left him unable to complete a story. 'Maybe because I know how it finishes. How they all finish.'

Rex had spent his whole life telling stories. There wasn't much I could say. He was still writing narrative verse and every fortnight or so he would phone again with the start of a new story, still leaving it on the machine if we weren't in.

Then his troubles began to increase. Phoning him I learned how he was threatened by the VAT authorities because of his failure to send in his forms or how a builder had gone off on a second job in the middle of fixing the library roof, how rain was drenching his books. I'd go over and do what I could but eventually I'd have to return home. I felt horribly guilty, recalling my promise to Chick. Not that I failed to remind Rex of what Chick had mentioned, but I couldn't be there the whole time. Often he seemed to resent our help. I suppose the boxed wine he bought by mail-order didn't help. He ate a lot, but badly for a diabetic, and for all the various domestic disasters, which his friends coped with pretty well among us, things appeared to improve with time. If anything his grasp on reality seemed to strengthen. He broke down less and began going to a few parties and conferences. He made his peace with the friends he'd insulted and was mostly forgiven. Optimistically, we spoke of him as becoming his old self again. He was introspective in a positive way.

When another August came round he seemed pretty positive. He might start off feeling miserable but conversation soon cheered him up. We'd share a piece of gossip or make fun of a good friend. That was how we were. He joked about Chick, too. I saw that as another sign of healing. Lucinda could always tell who was on the phone because of the laughter. I spoke to him on the first Monday in September. He was drunk, but no more than usual. He'd sent me an e-mail, he said. This was unusual. He hated e-mail as a rule. So I went to my PC and there it was. Rex rarely offered that amount of self-revelation and this had the feel of a continuing conversation, maybe with himself. It knocked me back a bit. So much that I made plans to see him the following weekend. It was as short as it was shocking:

'The story I never wrote was the story of my life, my unhappiness at failing to convince my father of my worth. I tried so hard, but I never had the courage or the method to tell that story. I wrote to impress. The verses always had to be witty, the prose clever. You remember me telling you, when we were young, how scared I was about dropping my guard. Truth wasn't as important as success to me. I needed to impress the people my dad approved of. Nobody else's opinion meant much. Either he saw me in the *Saturday Evening Post* or I simply didn't exist as a writer.' I think he'd planned to say more, but that's all there was.

On the Thursday, Jimmy Cornish called and told me Rex was dead. The rest was in the obits. Gone but not forgiven.

I had failed to keep my word to Chick. I hadn't found the

bullets. I should have spoken to his accountant. I should have helped him back to AA. I've never understood booze. People have to be rolling in the gutter singing 'Nellie Dean' before I get the picture. I missed all the signs and fell down on a solemn promise. Not for the first time. I never gave a promise to a child I couldn't keep, but I made a habit of breaking them to adults. Rex knew exactly what he was doing. I'm not the only survivor still running scenarios through their head. If I'd found the gun and stolen it... If I'd checked to see how much he was drinking... If I'd listened more closely…

Rex wrote some great ghost stories. When it came to haunting his friends, he was a bloody expert. What he'd done to Jenny told me he knew exactly what he was up to. People say all ghost stories are optimistic because they show a belief in life after death. Equally, all artists are optimists because the act of creation is optimistic in itself. Rex's poems and openings are still on our machine. Lu won't erase them. On a bad night I'll pour myself a glass of wine and press the button until I hear his voice. I'll listen to his gentle mockery as he invents an outrageous tale about my getting my toe stuck in the bath's hot tap or being arrested for vagrancy on my way back from a climb. He always gets cut off. If I'm feeling up to it, I'll listen the way you listen to a sweet, familiar tune.

I think that was the real reason why, after Chick's death, Rex never completed anything. There was only one story he really had to tell and from deep habit he had repressed it, choosing suicide rather than write it. 'The Story of Rex and Chick'. Even under such dreadful stress he couldn't let it come out. It would never be known. He had destroyed Chick's journals. And then he had destroyed himself.

Rather than dwell on that I'll listen to his familiar fantasies once again. Then I'll turn off the machine, curse the bastard for a liar and a coward and a calculating fucking sadist, pick up one of his books and head for bed, glad enough, I guess, that I still have a few stories of my own to tell and some rotten bloody friends to remember.

TRIPCOCK FLATS, SE28

Probably the best-known 'mudlarking' territory, once the domain of boys and girls who, until the 1900s, made a living digging in the oily mud along the Thames. Tripcock Flats was also notorious as a burial ground for murdered sailors who had the misfortune to drink at the Lady Margaret public house in Goldfinch Lane. The publican, James Sale, and his wife, Hannah, were thought to have killed more than forty 'homeward bounders'. The ghosts of the sailors are said to dance a hornpipe on the flats every summer solstice, to celebrate the hanging of the Sales at Southwark on 21 June, 1824; an event witnessed and recorded by the poet John Clare on his third and final visit to London.

THE TERMINAL CAFÉ, BRIXTON, SW18

Designed and fitted by Mendelsohn and Chermayeff (modernist architects of Bexhill-on-Sea's De La Warr Pavilion), the Terminal Café was originally established for the exclusive use of tramworkers. It was attached to the celebrated Brixton terminus. Now rebranded, it is the flagship restaurant of former screen star Una Persson, and remains a favoured late-night dining experience with customers of the Roxy and other local venues.

CAMBERWELL COLISEUM, HIGH STREET, SE12

One of the largest of the South London music halls, the Coliseum was built in 1890, became a cinema and bingo hall in 1970, and was demolished to make way for Enron's London headquarters in 1995. In its heyday the Coliseum featured Marie Lloyd, Gus Elen, Little Tich, Dan Leno, Una

Persson, Gloria Cornish, Albert Chevalier, J.K. Elliot, Sonny Hale, Max Peters, Harry Lauder, Max Miller, Tommy Cornelius, Max Wall and Arthur Askey. It served as the setting for the BBC's *Stars of the Past* show, which ran from 1962 to 1969. Following the collapse of Enron, an attempt was made by the Society for the Preservation of Historical Comedy to acquire the building as a museum. The Coliseum proved to be an unsuccessful finalist in the television programme that decided, by popular vote, which British folly should be restored and retained.

TURNER'S COTTAGES, STREATHAM, SW16

On the south side of Streatham Green, set back from London Road, this row of cottages (along with St Stephen's Church) is all that remains of the original village street – which, in 1924, was razed to make way for the new road to Tooting Bec (and the Cricketers at Mitcham). Protected by a preservation order since 1974, thanks to the efforts of Helena Mitford-Begg, long-time resident of Step Cottage (No. 7), the row has recently come under threat from an attempt to obtain planning permission for a canalside office/residential development. The canal, long buried, is being excavated and dressed as a sculpture park: the 'Genevieve Way'. Classic cars will be positioned as art objects along the old road from London to Brighton. A plaque in honour of Henry Cornelius, director of the 1953 film *Genevieve*, will be unveiled by his nephew Sir Frank Cornelius (a major investor in the development).

THE NOAH'S ARK, LONDON ROAD, NORBURY, SW16

Torn down to make way for office development, this pub was popular with between-wars 'race gangs', especially the Nicholsons (Joe and Jim). By the mid 1950s it was a Teddy Boy hangout and the scene of a bloody affray among members of the Brixton Chain Gang (whose weapon of choice, after the open razor, was a bicycle chain). Two were left for dead, twenty others required hospital treatment. Derek Bentley, Chris and Neville Craig were regular under-age drinkers.

But the most famous Noah's Ark 'face' is alive and well. He runs a restaurant in Portals Nous (Majorca) under his real name of Moses Collier. In the 1940s he was better known as 'Two Gun' Collier. He was an associate of the Notting Dale Cornell family and a rumoured enforcer for the Nicholsons. His restaurant is called the Gunslinger Saloon and serves Tex-Mex cuisine. His collection of Walther PPK .38 automatics is on display in the foyer.

In its final days, in the mid 1960s, the Ark hosted poetry and jazz evenings and was a haunt of countercultural dope dealers. The Carshalton poet (and parks' gardener) Chris Torrance launched his mimeographed collection *Diary of an Assassin* in a reading there with Lee Harwood and Zen monk Bill Wyatt.

London Flesh

Chapter One

DANIEL DEFOE WAS the first to write about 'London Flesh', the legendary meat of the hern supposed to 'confer Magical Powers upon those who Partook of it'. Defoe, in fact, invested money in its unsuccessful commercial production. Perhaps that was why he wrote his famous pamphlet which, while pretending scepticism, actually gave the impression that the meat, sold mostly in the form of a paste, had supernatural properties.

De Quincey, Lamb, Dickens, and Grossmith all claimed to have sampled London Flesh, usually in pies, sausages or patés, but only Lamb was convinced that he had briefly become invisible and known the power of flight (over Chelsea Gardens). The Flesh was rumoured, of course, to be human, and Dickens raised the name of Sweeney Todd in *Household Words*, but Doctor 'Dog' Donovan of Guy's was convinced that the meat was 'undoubtedly that of the female hern'. That said, the rumour persisted.

The hern was never abundant. The last pair in the London area was seen in Kew in 1950. Legend had it they were raised in captivity in Hackney Marshes up until the Second World War. Patrick Hamilton and Gerald Kersh both claimed to have been taken to a hern farm (Kersh was blindfolded) and seen dozens of the creatures penned in cages hidden behind trees and bushes, where they were offered hern paté on cream crackers. 'London Flesh,' reports Hamilton, 'as sweet and smooth as your mother's cheeks.'

'There's a book in heaven,' said Coleridge, who was convinced that the Flesh was human, 'in which is recorded the names of all who dishonour the Dead. Graveyard Desecrations and any form of Cannibalism, including the eating of London Flesh.'

London believes it remembers the horrible story of the cannibal tramwaymen of Hampstead Heath and how they devoured on Christmas Day the passengers and crew of the Number 64 tram which mysteriously returned empty to the Tudor Hamlets terminus. This is the true story of that event.

No complete list of passengers has ever been made, but we do know that a party of some dozen revellers left the Red Mill public house on Tufnell Hill and made their way to the tram stop to board the 64. Witnesses saw and heard them, commenting on their cheerful drunkenness and the somewhat lewd behaviour of the young women who, removing hats and veils, bared their entire heads at passers-by. We also know that the vicar of St Alban's, Brookgate, was last seen boarding at the Tessie O'Shea stop, because his brother walked him there. A young mother with three rather boisterous children also boarded, though it was possible they disembarked before the 64 began its crossing of the Heath. The night was foggy. The gas was out across a fairly wide area, due to air in the pipes at Highgate, the GLC said. Indeed the Gas Light & Coke Co. were held partially responsible for police officers not at once investigating after the tram failed to reach Tudor Hamlets. The gas being restored, the tram mysteriously returned to its own terminus. All that was found aboard was a leverman's uniform cap and two ladies' hats, which told their own grim story.

At that time there was no fashion for elaborate headgear or, indeed, the casual doffing of it as there is today. At least two young women had been aboard, yet at first the police tried to treat the case as one of simple abandonment. They thought the overhead power rail had come adrift from its connector and passengers had decided to walk home. But neither the leverman nor the conductor reported for duty. The Home Office decided to investigate the mystery and sent Sir Seaton Begg and his friend Dr 'Taffy' Sinclair relatively late on Boxing Day. Unhappy at being called away from their festivities, the two men came together at Tudor Hamlets, in the office of Mr Thorn, the regional manager of the Universal Transport Company.

Best known for its stories of Billy Bunter and the boys of
Greyfriars, *The Magnet* ran many 'Tramway' romances during
the 1920s. Almost always set in London and its environs,
tram tales were enormously popular.

Thorn was a red-faced, anxious man whose perspiration made dark stains on his scarlet, gold and white uniform. He was somewhat in awe of Begg and Sinclair, their reputations being familiar to all who followed the news.

'It will be my head on the block, gentlemen,' he reminded them, 'if the UTC determine negligence here. Of course, we are used to tram robbers on the Heath, but in all my years we have only known one killing and that was when a barker went off by accident. It has always been prudent of levermen to obey a command when they receive one, especially since we are insured for material loss but not for the death of our employees. Guild tramwaymen never do more than wound. Those flintlock pistols they affect allow for little else. It is to everyone's advantage that their guild, formed in 1759, laid down strict regulations as to weaponry, masks, mounts, uniforms, and so on. Do you have any suspicions, gentlemen?'

Removing his wide-brimmed slouch hat Sir Seaton Begg brushed at the brim with his sleeve. 'It's rare for a tramwayman to disobey his own strict codes. They would soon lose the good will of Londoners and therefore their guarantees of secrecy and shelter. Nor is it like them to abduct women and children. Either this was a gang feigning to be real tramway thieves or we are dealing with rogues who hold their guild honour at nought.'

'It would be yet another sign of the times,' murmured the tall Welshman, the detective's lifelong friend and amanuensis. 'When tramwaymen go against their traditions, then the next thing we'll see will be the looting of graves.'

'Quite so,' said Begg, taking out an enormous briar, filling it with black shag and lighting it from a vesta he struck against the bricks of the terminus. Soon heavy black smoke filled the hall as, puffing contemplatively, he paced back and forth across the stone flags.

'Remarkable,' offered Sinclair, 'that no passengers were reported missing.'

'And only the leverman's wife called in to say he had not come home.' Begg paused frowning. 'The conductor lived alone?'

'A widower,' said Mr Thorn. 'His mother is in Deal with relatives.'

'Young women? A mother with children?' Sir Seaton drew thoughtfully on his briar. 'Could they all have disembarked before the terminus?'

'It's not unheard of, sir.'

'But unlikely, I'm sure you'll agree. I think it's probably time we took a tram back to the Red Mill. Can you spare us a leverman, Mr Thorn?'

'We're still on a skeleton schedule for the holidays, but in these circumstances…' Guild rules usually demanded that every tram carry both a driver and a conductor. 'I can't see anyone objecting here if only the leverman takes out the Special. I'll give the appropriate instructions. We should have her connected in fifteen minutes.'

Chapter Two

GREY CLOUDS REGATHERED over the Heath as the Special began her long climb up Tufnell Hill. The Red Mill's tethered sails strained against air bending foliage across the horizon like mourners in procession.

Snow had melted into the grass, and mud puddles reflected the sky. Crows called with mysterious urgency, and there was a strong, fecund smell. Dr Sinclair remarked on the unseasonable warmth. Only a few roofs and the steeple of St Valentine's, Hampstead Vale, could be seen below until the Mill was reached. There they looked onto Tudor Hamlets and the suburbs beyond Highgate, red roofs, green cedars and pines, the bones of elms supporting untidy nests, all gauzed in smoke from the chimneys.

Disembarking, Begg strolled up the path, through the ornamental metal gates and began to ascend worn granite steps to the Red Mill. Sinclair, examining the soft ground, bent to frown over something. 'Hello! That's odd for this time of the year!' He straightened, now giving his attention to something on the other side of the path. 'I wonder why –?'

A bass voice greeted them from the door of the hostelry attached to the Mill. 'I'm sorry, gents, but we're closed until New Year's Eve.' Sinclair looked up to see the large red-bearded publican standing there.

'Except for guests who ride hunters, it seems.' Dr Sinclair smiled and pointed to the evidence. 'One doesn't have to be a High Mobsman to know that tramway thieves always convene here for the holidays.'

Sir Seaton shared his friend's humour. 'Don't worry, Mr O'Dowd,' he told the publican, 'we're neither peelers nor wildsmen and have no direct business to discuss with your guests.

Would I be wrong if I understood Captain Anchovy to be stabling his horse here for the Season?'

A cheerful, handsome face appeared behind O'Dowd's broad shoulder as, with his famous dashing grace, a man in the white wig and elaborate long waistcoat of a guild member stepped forward, lowering and uncocking a huge horse pistol, the traditional tool of his trade.

'Festive greetings to ye, Sir Seaton. I trust you and your companion will take a glass with us?' He smiled as he shook hands with the detectives. Together they entered the heat of a public bar filled with tobymen of every rank. Any suspicion of the newcomers was swiftly dispelled, and within moments the two investigators were imbibing goblets of mulled wine while Captain Anchovy and his men volunteered their aid in solving the mystery. Their own honour, they said, was at stake.

Tom Anchovy in particular was inflamed with disgust. 'My dear Sir Seaton, that 64 was indeed our intended prize as she came up Tufnell Hill. But it was Boxing Day, and we had no intention of stealing anything but the hearts of the ladies aboard. All were brought here. Three children were given presents, and old men of pleasant humour were presented with a glass of wine. Only a few refused our hospitality – the mother of the children, a good-hearted reverend gentleman whose abstinence we respected – and that sour fellow who had refused to quit the inn on our arrival and refused to share his vitalls with us. On any other occasion we might have taken him for ransom.'

'And he was –?' Sir Seaton lifted the beaker to his lips.

'Henry Marriage, sir. A humourless walking cadaver if ever I met one. Yet even he was permitted to retain his valuables. I don't mind tellin' ye, Sir Seaton, that had it not been Christmas, I would have had his last stitch *and* kept him for ransom!'

'Is that Marriage of Marriage's Opiates by the river?' asked Dr Sinclair, placing his finished beaker on the bar and nodding with approval as O'Dowd refilled it. 'The millionaire who lives in a house on his own wharf?'

'The same, Doctor Sinclair. Do ye know him?'

'Only by reputation,' replied the doctor. 'A solitary individual, they say. A dabbler in the alchemist's art. He's published an interesting book or two. No charlatan, but no great scientist, either. Many of his findings and experiments have been discredited. He's considered a mere amateur by the medical and scientific guilds.'

'I understand nothing of such things, sir. But I'll swear to this – when that tram left last evening he was safe and sound, as was every living soul aboard. Though he chose to go with them, all but Henry Marriage were as cheerful as when they had embarked. If that 64 was taken, then it would have been on the high stretch of track below the ruined village.'

'Why so?' Begg enquired.

'Because we watched her lights until they were out of sight, and young Jaimie Gordon here was on his way to join us, taking the low road up the Vale. He'd have spotted anything untoward.'

Sir Seaton was already slamming down his glass and cramming his hat onto his handsome, aquiline head. 'Then I can guess where the tram was stopped. Come on, Taffy, let's board our Special. I'm much obliged to you, Captain Anchovy.'

'Delighted to have helped, sir.'

After a further quick word with the tramwayman, the two metatemporal investigators were again on their way.

Chapter Three

A BLÉRIOT 'BAT', no doubt taking the day's mail to France, flew high overhead as the Special rattled to a stop below the ruins of Hampstead Model Village which lay on the brow of the hill above the tramline whose branches had once serviced the inhabitants of Lady Hecate Brown's failed evangelical dream of a healthy environment where a good Christian life and enlightened working conditions would be the antidote to all the ills of city life. Her failure to supply the model village with familiar recreations, public houses and fried fish shops caused even the most enlightened artisans to view her idealistic community as a kind of prison. The village had flourished as a middle-class enclave until, without servants or city facilities, the bourgeoisie chose the suburbs of Tudor Hamlets and Lyonne's Greene. The tram service had been discontinued, though the tracks were intact, lost beneath the encroaching weeds and brambles.

As Begg and Sinclair disembarked, the sky clouded darker and it began to rain heavily. Peering with difficulty through the ever-thickening mist, Begg quickly saw that his intuition had been right.

Sinclair was the first to observe how the track had been cleared through the swampy ground leading up to the ruins. 'Look, Begg. There's the shine of brass. A tram was diverted at this very spot and went up Ham Hill towards the old village. What do you make of it?'

'The best place to take a tram off the usual routes, Taffy. The emptied vehicle was sent back on its way, perhaps to divert attention from whatever dark deed was done here. Let us pray we are in time to save those poor souls – victims, no doubt, of some rogue band caring nought for the rules and habits of an old guild!'

With difficulty, they followed the line up the muddy terrain, their boots sinking and sliding in ground normally frozen hard.

As the rain let up, Ham Hill's ruins were seen bleak beneath a lowering sky. The air was unseasonably muggy; thunder rolled closer. Melted snow left pools so that the hill might have been the remains of Hereward's Romney fastness. Sinclair suppressed a shiver as a sudden chill crept up his spine. The afternoon's gloom was illuminated by a sudden sheet of lightning throwing the ruins into vivid silhouette.

'Press on, Taffy,' murmured Seaton Begg, clapping his friend on his sturdy shoulder. 'I sense we're not far from solving this mystery!'

'And maybe perishing as a consequence.' The mordant Welshman spoke only half in jest.

Making some remark about the 'dark instincts of the Celtic soul', Begg tramped on until they at last stood regarding the outskirts of the ruins, looking down at Tufnell Vale whose yellow lights offered distant reassurance.

No such friendly gas burned in the ruins of Hampstead Model Village, yet a few guttering brands lit the remaining glass in the low church chapel, said now to harbour all manner of pagan ritual and devil worship. The nearby Anglican church had been desanctified on orders from Southwark, but the ragged walls remained. Close to the church blazed three or four bonfires built from the wood of old pews and other religious furniture.

Begg and Sinclair kept to the cover of fallen walls and shrubbery. Human figures gathered around the fires.

'Vagrants, perhaps?' murmured Sinclair. 'Do such people still exist?'

Signalling his friend to silence, Begg pointed to a collapsing house sheltering the bulky shapes of horses. Rough laughter and uncultured voices told Begg they had found another tramwayman gang. 'Guildless outcasts, Taffy, by the cut of their coats. Rejected by every mobsmen's association from here to York.'

Keeping well down, the detectives crept closer. Unlike Tom

Anchovy's men, guildless tram thieves were known for their cruel savagery.

'It's been years since such a gang was seen this close to London,' whispered Sinclair. 'They risk life imprisonment if caught!'

Begg was unsurprised. 'I knew Captain Zenith was outside Beaconsfield and suspected of several tram robberies in that region. Quickly, Taffy, drop down.' He flung himself behind a broken wall. 'That's the rogue himself!'

A tall, white-haired man in a black greatcoat sauntered towards one of the fires, eyes burning like rubies in the reflected light. A handsome albino with skin the colour of ivory, Zenith was an old enemy of Begg's. The two were said to be cousins who had often crossed swords.

As they watched, Zenith approached a thin individual, as tall as himself, on the far side of the fire. It was Sinclair's turn to draw in a sharp breath. Henry Marriage, one of the missing passengers, seemed to be on friendly terms with the most notorious tram thief in Europe!

It grew darker until all the inhabitants of the ruins were mere silhouettes.

'We can't take 'em single-handed,' murmured Begg. 'We'd best return to the depot and telegraph to Scotland Yard.'

Picking their way carefully down the hill, they had scarcely gone twenty yards before dark shadows suddenly surrounded them. They heard a horrible, muffled noise.

Moving towards them across the unnaturally damp ground, big pistols threatening, came an unsavoury circle of leering tram robbers.

'Good evening, gentlemen!' The leader doffed his cocked hat in a mocking bow. 'Always pleased to welcome a few more guests to our holiday harum-scarum!' He removed the shutter from his night lamp, showing the face of their unfortunate tram-driver. The leverman's hands were tied before him, and a gag had been forced into his mouth. He had been trying to warn his passengers of his own capture.

Chapter Four

THE MOBSMEN HAD not reckoned with the two detectives being armed. In a flash Begg and Sinclair produced the latest repeating Webleys! 'Stand, you scum,' levelly declared the investigator. 'You no doubt recognise this revolver which I intend to use to advantage.'

Triumph draining from their decadent features, the mobsmen fell back, knowing full well the power and efficiency of the Webleys over their own antique barkers. Then a voice cut through the misty air. Sharp as a diamond, it bore the tone of a man used to obedience.

'Fire one chamber, Sir Seaton, and count yourself responsible for the death of an innocent woman.'

Turning their heads, the investigators saw Captain Zenith, a bright lantern in one hand, pressing his barker against the head of a dishevelled coster-girl grinning stupidly from under her raised veil, her hat at an unseemly angle.

Sinclair stifled a cry of outrage. 'You fiend!' He did not let his Webley fall, nor did he disengage the safety catch. 'What have you done to that poor young creature?'

'I, sir?' An almost melancholy smile played across the mobsman's pale lips. 'What d'ye think I've done? Murdered her?' The light from the lantern gave his red eyes a savage sparkle.

'Drugged her!' Sinclair muttered in disgust. 'You're cowards as well as kidnappers.'

Captain Zenith's face clouded for a moment before resuming its habitual mask. 'She's unhurt, sir. However, aggressive action on your part might alter her circumstances.'

'No doubt one of the missing passengers, but where are the children?' demanded Sir Seaton.

'Safe and sound with their mother and full of mince pies,' Zenith assured him.

'Then show them to me.'

'I'd remind you, Sir Seaton, that you are at a disadvantage.'

'And I'd remind you, Captain Zenith, that I am a servant of the Crown. Harm me or those under my protection and you'll answer to Her Majesty's justice.'

'I have been escaping that justice, sir, for longer than you and I have travelled the moonbeam roads. Put that fancy barker aside and be my welcome guest.' He stepped away from the giggling young woman as Begg and Sinclair reluctantly reholstered their weapons. Then, tucking the woman's somewhat limp arm into his, Captain Zenith led them back to the central fire, built just outside the ruined chapel where more of his gang and their captives could clearly be seen.

All but the wide-eyed children were in artificially good humour. Another pair of young women wore their hats on the backs of their heads. Sinclair guessed they had been well supplied with alcohol, but Begg shook his head, saying softly, 'Not beer or spirits, I think, Taffy, old man. I suspect another hand in this, don't you?'

Sinclair nodded gravely. 'Do we share the suspicion of who it was put Zenith up to this crime?'

'I think we do, Taffy.'

Standing among the other prisoners they noticed that only the young mother showed signs of concern. Even the reverend gentleman cheerfully led the leverman, the conductor and a youth wearing the cadet uniform of the Farringdon Watch in a rather jolly hymn.

'See how our guests enjoy their Boxing Day?' Captain Zenith offered Begg and Sinclair a somewhat cynical grin. 'And all with their pocket books in place.'

'Drugged with laudanum.' Sinclair picked up an empty black bottle and was sniffing it, just as tall, lugubrious Henry Marriage stepped into the firelight and extended his hand. Sinclair ignored the gesture, but Begg, ever the diplomat, bowed. 'Good evening, sir. Are these villains holding you to ransom?'

Marriage's hearty manner thinly disguised an evasive expression. 'Not at all, sir.' He stared around him somewhat helplessly.

'Or is Captain Zenith in your employ?' demanded Sinclair. 'Why do you only bind our driver?'

'He'll be released at once.' Captain Zenith signed for the leverman to be freed. 'He offered my men violence. Whereas these other good fellows accepted our hospitality –'

'And were drugged into doltishness.'

'Please, sir, are you here to help us?' The young mother clutched imploringly at Sir Seaton's sleeve.

With his usual gentle courtesy towards the fair sex, Sir Seaton smiled reassurance. 'I am indeed, madam. What charming children! Is their father here?'

'I am a widow, sir.'

'My dear lady!'

'We have not been mistreated, sir.'

'I should hope you have not!' interjected Henry Marriage. 'I doubt if your children have ever eaten so well!'

'You have been feeding them, Mr Marriage?' Dr Sinclair offered the thin man an intense glare of inquisition.

'I returned from visiting a generous relative who gave me the hamper. It was meant for my family at home.'

'Indeed, sir,' said Sir Seaton. With the toe of his shoe he touched a large, open basket. Stencilled on its side were the words MARRIAGE'S OPIATES, MARRIAGE'S WHARF, LONDON E. 'This is the Christmas Box, eh?'

'The same, sir.'

'You were sharing it on the tram before Captain Zenith appeared?'

'He was very generous, sir.' The conductor looked up from where he sat beside the fire. 'I know it's against regulations, but the company generally turns a blind eye at Christmas. Of course, we didn't take any alcoholic beverage.'

'Quite so. What did you enjoy from Mr Marriage's hamper?'

'Just a piece of game pie, sir. Some ginger beer. And a couple of sandwiches.'

'Whereupon you reached the old Hampstead Model Village stop, broke down and, at Mr Marriage's suggestion, continued up here, eh, conductor?'

'Such merry yule fires, sir. Who could resist 'em? It was commonly agreed, sir, even by that reverend gent, there could be no happier way of celebrating Boxing Day until rescue came.' A stupid, sentimental grin crossed the conductor's long face.

'Except by you, madam, I take it?' Again Sir Seaton turned to the mother.

'I've been pained by a bit of a dicky tummy since we had the goose at my husband's brother's house. I'd rather hoped the children and me'd be home by now. But it was either come here or stay on the tram.' She was close to tears. Again Begg laid a gentlemanly hand on her arm. 'And Mr Marriage promised you his protection.'

'He did, sir. The tramwaymen have offered us no harm. But they're a bad example, sir, and –'

'Captain Zenith and his men make no threats. They keep the traditional tramwaymen's Christmas truce.' Marriage was insistent. 'I offered them a handsome fee to act for our safety when the tram broke down. They helped us guide it up the old line to this spot where we could find some sort of shelter.'

'How on earth did the tram find its own way back to the terminus?' Dr Sinclair was clearly not entirely convinced by this story.

'She slipped backwards, sir, once the horses were untethered,' offered the conductor. 'Somehow she must have reconnected to the overhead power line and continued her journey. It has been known, sir, for such things to happen.'

'So I understand.'

'Stranding us here, of course,' explained Henry Marriage. 'Well, it seems you've brought another vehicle to take everyone home, and no harm done. We are all grateful to you, Sir Seaton and Doctor Sinclair. I am prepared to stand guarantee for Captain Zenith. My honour depends upon promising safe conduct to all parties. I shall elect to stay as evidence of good faith and come morning shall board a fresh tram on the regular morning route. This will give Captain Zenith and his men time to make themselves scarce. A fair bargain, eh, Sir Seaton?'

'Very fair. And very noble of you, Mr Marriage.' Speaking with a certain irony, Sir Seaton was careful not to challenge anything. They were seriously outnumbered and had many innocents to consider. Since Zenith the Albino was mixed up in this affair Begg was convinced not everything could be above board. He had several reasons to suspect Marriage's tale. Nevertheless he did not object when the tramwaymen lit the way with their lanterns to lead the happy party back down the hill. At last the passengers were safely aboard and the leverman reinstalled at his controls.

The passengers cheered as the overhead power rail sparked in the darkness. The magnificent Special hummed, lurched and began to move forward. 'A generous soul, that Mr Marriage,' declared the conductor. 'We'd be mighty hungry by now had he not been so free with his pies.' He reacted with a muttered explanation as Dr Sinclair's eyes stared sternly into his own. 'I speak only the honest truth, sir. I've done nothing against Company tradition.'

'Of course you haven't, conductor,' interrupted Sir Seaton, his hand on his friend's shoulder. 'You must now ensure your charges arrive safely at the terminus.'

'My duty, sir.' The conductor saluted, shaking off his euphoria.

The two detectives returned swiftly to the tram's boarding plate. 'We have to go back, of course,' said Begg.

'Absolutely, old man!'

As soon as the tram took a bend, they dropped quietly from the platform. Ankle-deep in marshy ground, they moved rapidly back to the village.

'You noticed their eyes, I take it, Taffy?'

'Drugged! All but the mother and children. Something in those meat pies, eh?'

'Opium or Indian hemp. That preposterous story of a generous relative!'

'And at least two of the party were not returned to the tram.'

'Two young women? Exactly!'

'No doubt they imbibed more freely from the hamper's contents than any of the others.'

'Hurry, old man! Knowing Marriage's obsessions, you can guess as readily as I what the fiend intends.'

The detectives rapidly regained the camp, creeping carefully up to the ruined chapel where Zenith's gang continued to make merry. Yet of the leader or Henry Marriage there was no sign.

Drawing his Webley, Begg motioned towards the ruined Anglican church. Sinclair had already noticed lights shining through the broken stained glass. They heard voices, what might have been laughter, a stifled cry and then a piercing scream. Caution abandoned, they rushed the building, kicking open the rotting doors.

'Oh, for the love of God!' Sinclair was almost forced backward by the horrible smell. The scene's bestial reality was unfit to be seen by anyone save the curator of Scotland Yard's Black Museum. Two young women hung in ropes above the remains of the church altar. One was bleeding from deep wounds in her lower extremities. Her blood dripped into two large copper basins placed there for the purpose. She had fainted, but her companion shrieked in terror, through her gag. Henry Marriage, long razor in hand, prepared to perform the same operation upon the friend as the gloating albino placed bowls in readiness.

Marriage seemed completely deranged, but Zenith was fully alert, his face a mask of hatred as he saw Begg and Sinclair. His long white hair hanging loose to his shoulders, he snarled defiantly, lifting a copper bowl to his lips.

Levelling his pistol, Begg snapped off a single shot spinning the bowl from Zenith's hands. Sinclair darted forward and with an expert uppercut knocked Marriage to the floor. The razor fell with a clatter from the opiate merchant's hands.

Growling like a wild animal, Zenith produced his own pistol, but Begg's revolver sounded again, and Zenith's weapon went flying. Sinclair jumped up to the altar and, using Marriage's razor, severed the cords, lowering the two young women gently down as he kicked the bowls of blood clear.

Next Begg leapt forward to press the barrel of his Webley

against Zenith's heart. The albino raised his hands, his ruby eyes glaring.

Knowing that his shot had probably alerted Zenith's men, Sinclair turned to face the door.

Motioning with his revolver, Begg forced Zenith to stand between them and the entrance. Henry Marriage groaned and came to his senses as the first outlaws appeared in the doorway.

'Stand back, there!' The metatemporal investigator held his Webley against the albino's head. But Zenith's gang was already circling the altar.

His lips rimmed with blood, mumbling curses, Marriage climbed to his feet, his eyes staring into space.

'As you guessed, Taffy, he believes he possesses supernatural powers.' Begg motioned with his pistol.

'Let's hope we are not alone, old man. We decidedly need help from those who promised it…'

'Without them we're dead men, I agree. Have you any spare ammunition?'

'None.'

Grimly Begg and Sinclair prepared for the worst. Aware of their dilemma, Zenith grinned even as Sir Seaton's pistol pressed against his head.

The investigator knew his captive too well to demand he call his men off. Whatever dark evil Zenith practised, he was no coward and would die before allowing the two detectives to escape.

Ironically Henry Marriage came to their aid. Drugged eyes rolling in his head, he lifted up his arms and ran for the door. 'I am free!' he cried. 'Free! Invisible, I shall climb like an eagle into the sky.' His long arms flapping at his sides, he stumbled towards the entrance and, before the astonished outlaws, ran wildly into the night. Zenith laughed grimly. 'He believes the spell has worked. He forgets our ritual was interrupted.'

'Silence, you monster!' Sinclair covered as many outlaws as he could. Savouring their anticipated triumph they tightened the circle.

From outside came a fusillade of shots and sounds of Marriage screaming in frustrated rage. 'No! No! I am invisible. I fly. You cannot –' There descended a sudden silence.

Taking advantage of this unexpected turn, Zenith broke free to join the mass of his own men. Grabbing a pistol from one of them, his red eyes blazing, he curved his pale lips in a snarling grin. 'You're lost, Begg! Arming the leverman and a drugged vicar won't save you!'

Then a figure appeared in the smashed doorway. A gold-trimmed tricorn on his bewigged head, a black domino hiding his upper face, he had pushed back his huge three-caped coaching coat, two massive barkers in either beringed hand. Captain Tom Anchovy laughed as the guildless tramwaymen fell back in fear. Behind him, in the fancy coats and three-cornered hats of their trade, pressed his men, contemptuous of the guildless outlaws bringing their trade into disrepute.

'Drop your arms, lads, or we'll blow you all to the hell you thoroughly deserve!' rapped Anchovy.

But Captain Zenith, using the cover of his men, disappeared through the far door.

'After him, quickly!' ordered Tom. Some mobsmen followed the albino into the night.

Realising how outnumbered they were, the remaining outlaws gave up their pistols with little resistance, leaving Sir Seaton Begg, Doctor Sinclair and Tom Anchovy to bind the young women's wounds and get them decently covered.

'Their hats will be waiting for them at the terminus, no doubt,' said Dr Sinclair. 'They owe their lives to that lost headgear.'

'Indeed they do, Taffy. It was our clue that two young women were still held by Marriage and Zenith. All the others we saw still had their hats, even if worn at a rather unladylike angle!' He warmly shook hands with the tobyman. 'You turned up in the nick of time, Captain Tom. Thanks for keeping your word to help us. We remain on opposite sides of the law, but I think we share a moral purpose!'

'Probably true, sir.' Captain Anchovy prepared to leave. 'We'll truss those rogues thoroughly. Should we catch Zenith, he'll also be left for the peelers to pick up. Boxing Day's almost over, and we must return to our regular trade if we're to eat. Marriage's hamper out there was sadly empty of all its vitalls.'

'Just as well. You'd best warn your men that those pies and sausages were poisoned with hern meat and opium. They won't die, but they'll be unable to ride for a day or two should they try any.'

'I'll tell 'em at once. Good luck to ye, gentlemen!' The daring tramwayman disappeared into the night.

'That's what I saw at the Red Mill,' said Sinclair. 'The tiny tracks of the crested hern. I've studied the little creatures a fair bit and was surprised to find some still around London. Brought too early out of hibernation by the unseasonal weather and easily caught by Marriage while staying at the inn. Some opiates, and his food was ready for those unsuspecting passengers.'

'From what I know of his debased brand of alchemy, Taffy, hern meat is only thought efficacious if fed to female virgins first. Partaking of the flesh, or preferably your victim's freshly drawn blood, imparts great supernatural powers, including those of invisibility and flight. Luckily he proved himself a liar with that tale of his hamper being a relative's gift. It clearly came from his own warehouse.'

The doctor shuddered. 'Thank God we were able to stop him in time.'

The two men strolled from the ruined church to see that Anchovy's band had already bound Zenith's followers. Anchovy, astride his magnificent black Arab, saluted them as they appeared. 'If I know Zenith, he'll be long gone in the direction of London, to lose himself in the twittens of Whitechapel. No doubt our paths will cross again! As for Henry Marriage, I could have sworn my men filled him with enough lead to sink the HMS *Victory*, yet he, too, has disappeared. Perhaps his beliefs had substance, eh?' With that the gallant tramwayman doffed his tricorn in a deep bow, then turned for distant Waymering where Begg knew he lived a double life as Septimus Grouse, a Methodist parson.

Though weak from their experience, the two young victims

had recovered somewhat by the time another Special arrived towing a hospital car and a prison van full of peelers. Attended by expert doctors, the women were made comfortable in the hospital car while Zenith's gang were manacled to hard benches, destined for Wormwood Flats.

Thus the tale garbled by the yellow press as 'The Affair of the Hampstead Cannibals' was brought to a successful conclusion and all innocent lives saved. Enjoying their pipes the detectives relaxed in the first-class section of the tram's top deck.

'I think I'll be returning to the Red Mill as soon as possible,' murmured Sinclair thoughtfully.

'You're curious to retrace the stages of the case, Taffy?'

'What's more interesting, old man, was finding those London hern tracks when all naturalists are agreed the species became extinct during the latter part of the last century. I'd like to find another specimen.'

'And vivisect it?' enquired Sir Seaton in some disapproval.

'Oh, not at all. I want to see it in the wild for myself and confirm that Henry Marriage, God rest his soul wherever he may be now, did not destroy the entire species. After all, it isn't every day one discovers that part of the past can yet be recovered, however small that part might be.'

With a sudden rattle the tram began to move forward. Its buzzing electric engine could not quite disguise the sound of Sir Seaton Begg's approving grunt.

The Cairene Purse

For Robert Nye

Chapter One
Her First Fond Hope of Eden Blighted

O N T H E E D G E of the Nile's fertile shadow, pyramids merged with the desert and from the air seemed almost two-dimensional in the steady light of late morning. Spreading now beyond the town of Giza, Cairo's forty million people threatened to engulf, with their old automobiles, discarded electronics and every dusty non-degradable of the modern world, the grandiose tombs of their ancestors.

Though Cairo, like Calcutta, was a monument to the enduring survival of our race, I was glad to leave. I had spent only as much time as I needed, seeking information about my archaeologist sister and discovering that everyone in the academic community thought she had returned to England at least a year ago. The noise had begun to seem as tangible as the haze of sand which hung over the crowded motorways, now a mass of moving flesh, of camels, donkeys, horses, mules and humans hauling every variety of vehicle and cargo, with the occasional official electric car or, even rarer, petrol-driven truck.

I suppose it had been a tribute to my imagined status that I had been given a place on a plane, rather than having to take the river or the weekly train to Aswan. Through the porthole of the little VW8 everything but the Nile and its verdant borders were the colours of sand, each shade and texture of which still held meaning for the nomad Arab, the Bedouin who had conquered the First Kingdom and would conquer several others down the millennia.

In the past only the Ptolomies, turning their backs on the Nile and the Sahara, ever truly lost the sources of Egypt's power.

My main reason for accepting the assignment was personal rather than professional. My sister had not written for some months and her letters before that had been disconnected, hinting at some sort of emotional disturbance, perhaps in connection with the dig on which I knew she had been working. An employee of UNEC, I had limited authority in Egypt and did not expect to discover any great mysteries at Lake Nasser, which continued to be the cause of unusual weather. The dam's builders somewhat typically had refused to anticipate this. They had also been warned by our people in the 1950s that the New High Dam would eventually so poison the river with bilharzia that anyone using its water would die. The rain, some of it acid, had had predictable effects, flooding quarries and washing away towns. The local Nubians had long since been evicted from their valleys to make way for the lake. Their new settlements, traditionally built, had not withstood the altered environment, so the government had thrown up concrete shells for them. The road to Aswan from the airport was lined with bleak, half-built structures of rusted metal girders and cinder blocks. Today's Egyptians paid a high price for regulated water.

From the airport my horse-drawn taxi crossed the old English dam with its sluices and gigantic gauges, a Victorian engineer's dream of mechanical efficiency, and began the last lap of the journey into town. Aswan, wretched as much of it is, has a magic few Nile settlements now possess, rising from the East Bank to dominate the coppery blue waters and glinting granite islands of the wide river where white-sailed feluccas cruise gracefully back and forth, ferrying tourists and townspeople between the two sides. The heights, massive grey boulders, are commanded by a beautiful park full of old eucalyptus, poplars and monkey-puzzle trees. Above this, the stately Edwardian glory of Cook's Cataract Hotel is a marvellous example of balconied and shuttered rococo British orientalism at its finest.

The further upriver one goes the poorer Aswan becomes,

though even here the clapboard and corrugated iron, the asbestos sheeting and crumbling mud walls are dominated by a splendid hilltop mosque in the grand Turkish style. I had asked to be billeted at a modest hotel in the middle of town, near the souk. From the outside, the Hotel Osiris, with its pale pink and green pseudo-neon, reminded me of those backstreet Marseilles hotels where once you could take your partner for a few francs an hour. It had the same romantic attraction, the same impossible promises. I found that, once within its tiny fly-thick lobby – actually the communal hallway leading directly to the courtyard – I was as lost to its appeal as any pop to his lid. I had discovered a temporary spiritual home.

The Osiris, though scarcely more than a bed-and-breakfast place by London standards, boasted four or five porters, all of them eager to take my bag to the rooms assigned me by a Hindu lady at the desk. I let one carry my canvas grip up two flights of dirty stairs to a little tiled, run-down apartment looking into the building's central well where two exhausted dogs, still coupled, panted on their sides in the heat. Giving him a five-pound note, I asked my porter on the off chance if he had heard of an Englishwoman called Noone or von Bek living in Aswan. My sister had used the poste restante and, when I had last been here, there were few Europeans permanently living in town. He regretted that he could not help. He would ask his brother, who had been in Aswan several months. Evidently, now that I had as it were paid for the information in advance he felt obliged to me. The *bakshish* custom is usually neither one of bribery nor begging in any European sense, but has a fair amount to do with smooth social intercourse. There is always, with legitimate *bakshish*, an exchange. Some measure of mutual respect is also usual. Most Arabs place considerable emphasis on good manners and are not always tolerant of European coarseness.

I had last been in Egypt long before the great economic convulsion following that chain reaction of destruction or near-exhaustion of so many resources. Then Aswan had been the final port of call for the millions of tourists who cruised the Nile from dawn to dusk, the sound of their dance music, the smell of their barbecues, drifting over fields and mud villages which had remained unchanged for five thousand years.

In the '80s and '90s of the last century Aswan had possessed, among others, a Hilton, a Sheraton, a Ritz-Carlton and a Holiday Inn, but now the luckiest local families had requisitioned the hotels and only the State-owned Cataract remained, a place of pilgrimage for every wealthy enthusiast of 1930s detective stories or autobiographies of the twentieth-century famous. Here, during wartime, secret meetings had been held and mysterious bargains struck between unlikely participants. Today on the water below the terrace some tourists still sailed, the Israelis and the Saudis on their own elegant *schoomers*, while other boats carried mixtures of Americans, Italians and Germans, French, English, Swedes, Spaniards, Japanese and Hungarians, their women dressed and painted like pagan temptresses of the local soap operas, displaying their bodies naked on the sundecks of vast slow-moving windliners the size of an earlier era's ocean-going ships, serving to remind every decent Moslem exactly what the road to Hell looked like. No eighteenth-century English satirist could have provided a better image.

As an officer of the UN's Conservation and Preservation Department I knew all too well how little of Egypt's monuments were still visible, how few existed in any recognisable state. Human erosion, the dam raising the water table, the volume of garbage casually dumped in the river, the activities of archaeologists and others, of tourists encouraged in their millions to visit the great sites and bring their hard currency, the two-year Arabian war, all had created a situation where those monuments still existing were banned to everyone but the desperate restorers. Meanwhile replicas had been made by the Disney Corporation and located in distant desert settlements surrounded by vacation towns, artificial trees and vast swimming pools, built by French and German experts and named 'Rameses City', 'Land of the Gods' or 'Tutankhamen World'. I was sure that this was why my sister had been secretive about her team's discoveries, why it was important to try to avoid the circumstances which now made Abu Simbel little more than a memory of two great engineering miracles.

When I had washed and changed I left the Osiris and strolled through busy alleys in the direction of the corniche, the restored Victorian riverfront promenade which reminded me more than anywhere of the old ocean boulevard at Yalta. Without her earlier weight of tourists, Aswan had developed a lazy, decayed glamour. The foodstalls, the fake antiquities, the flimsy headdresses and gelabeas sold as traditional costume, the souvenir shops and post-card stands, the 'cafetrias' offering 'Creme Teas' and 'Mix Grile', were still patronised by a few plump Poles and tomato-coloured English who had been replaced in the main by smaller numbers of blond East Africans, Swedes and Nigerians affecting the styles and mannerisms of thirty or forty years earlier and drawn here, I had heard, by a Holy Man on the outskirts of Aswan who taught a peculiar mixture of orthodox Sunni Islam and his own brand of mysticism which accepted the creeds of Jews and Christians as well as the existence of other planetary populations, and spoke of a 'pure' form of Islam practised in other parts of the galaxy.

Aswan's latter-day hippies, wearing the fashions of my own youthful parents, gave me a queer feeling at first, for although Egypt offers several experiences akin to time travel, these images of recent history, perhaps of a happier period altogether, were somehow more incongruous than a broken-down VW, for instance, being dragged behind a disgusted camel. There was a greater preponderance of charm-sellers and fortune-tellers than I remembered, together with blank-eyed European men and women, some of them with babies or young children, who begged me for drug-money on the street. With the rise of Islamic-Human-ism, the so-called Arab Enlightenment, coupled to the increasing power of North Africa and the Middle East in world politics, the drug laws, introduced originally to placate foreign tour operators and their governments, had been relaxed or formally abolished. Aswan, I had heard, was now some kind of Mecca for privileged youngsters and visionary artists, much as Haight-Ashbury or Lad-broke Grove had been in the 1960s. Romanticism of that heady, exaggerated, rather mystical variety was once again loose in the world and the comforts it offered seemed to me almost like devilish temptations. But I was of that puritanical, judgemental generation which had rejected the abstractions of its parents in favour of more realistic, as we saw it, attitudes. A good many of us had virtually rejected the entire Western Enlightenment itself and retreated into a kind of liberal mediaevalism not incompatible with large parts of the Arab world. In my own circles I was considered something of a radical.

I had to admit however that I found these new Aswanians attractive. In many ways I envied them. They had never known a time when Arabia had not been a major power. They came here as equals with everyone and were accepted cheerfully by the Nubians who treated them with the respect due to richer pilgrims and potential converts to the divine revelation of Islam.

Again in common with my generation, I was of a secular disposition and saw only damaging, enslaving darkness in any religion. We had even rejected the received wisdoms of Freud, Jung, Marx and their followers and embraced instead a political creed which had as its basis the eminent likelihood of ecological disaster and the slight possibility of an economic miracle. They called us the Anaemic Generation now: a decade or more that was out of step with the progress of history as it was presently interpreted. It suited me to know that I was an anachronism; it afforded me a special kind of security. Very few people took me seriously.

An Egyptian army officer marched past me as I crossed to the river-side of the corniche to look down at the half-completed stairways, the crumbling, poorly mixed concrete and the piles of rat-infested rubble which the Korean engineers, who had put in the lowest tender for the work, had still neither repaired nor cleared. The officer glanced at me as if he recognised me but then went past, looking, with his neatly trimmed moustache and rigid shoulders, the perfect image of a World War Two English Guards captain. Even his uniform was in the English style. I suppose Romans coming to fifth-century Britain after some lapse of time would have been equally impressed to see a Celt striding through the streets of Londinium, impeccable in a slightly antiquated centurion's kit. The whole casual story of the human race seemed to be represented in the town as I paused to look at the hulks of converted pleasure boats, home to swarms of Nubian families impoverished by the altered climate and the shift of tourism towards the Total Egypt Experience found in the comfort of Fort Sadat and New Memphis. Despite the piles of filthy garbage along the shore, Aswan had acquired the pleasant, nostalgic qualities of unfashionable British resorts like Morecambe or Yarmouth, a local population careless of most strangers save sometimes for the money they brought.

About halfway along the corniche I stopped at a little café and sat down on a cane chair, ordering mint tea from a proprietor whose ancient tarboosh might have escaped from the costume department of a touring production of *Death on the Nile*. He addressed me as '*effendi*' and his chosen brand of English seemed developed from old British war movies. Like me, I thought, he was out of step with the times. When he brought the tea I told him to keep the change from a pound and again on the off chance asked after my sister. I was surprised by the enthusiasm of his response. He knew the name 'von Bek' and was approving when I told him of our relationship. 'She is very good,' he said. 'A tip-top gentlewoman. But now, I think, she is unwell. It is hard to see the justice of it.'

Pleased and a little alarmed, I asked if he knew where she lived. 'She lived in *Sharri al Sahahaldeen*, just off the *Sharri al Souk*.' He pointed with his thumb back into town. 'But that was more than a year ago. Oh, she is very well known here in Aswan. The poor people like her immensely. They call her *Saidneh Duukturah*.'

'Doctor?' My sister had only rudimentary medical training. Her doctorate had been in archaeology. 'She treats the sick?'

'Well, not so much any more. Now only if the hospitals refuse help. The Bisharim, in particular, love her. You know those nomads. They trust your sister only. But she moved from Sahahaldeen Street after some trouble. I heard she went to the English House over on the West Bank, but I'm not so sure. Perhaps you should ask the Bisharim.' He raised his hand in welcome to a small man in a dark blue gelabea who walked briskly into the darkness of the shop's interior. 'A customer.' From his pocket he took a cut-throat razor. '*Naharak sa'id,*' he called and, adopting the swagger of the expert barber, waved farewell to me and entered his shop.

'*Fi amani 'llah.*' Picking up my hat I crossed to a rank where the usual two or three ill-used horses stood between the shafts of battered broughams, still the commonest form of taxi in Aswan. I approached the first driver, who stood flicking at flies with his ragged whip while he smoked a cigarette and chatted with his fellows. He wore an American sailor's hat, a faded T-shirt advertising some Russian artpopper, a pair of traditional baggy trousers exposing ulcerated calves and, on his feet, pink and black Roos. From the state of his legs I guess he had retained the habit, against all current warnings, of wading into the Nile to urinate. I asked him to take me first to the dam's administration office where, for courtesy's sake, I presented myself and made an appointment with my old acquaintance Georges Abidos, the Chief Press Officer, who had been called out to the northern end of the lake. His secretary said he was looking forward to seeing me tomorrow and handed me a welcoming note. I then asked the calash driver if he knew the Bisharim camp on the outskirts of town. I had heard that in recent years the tribe had returned to its traditional sites. He was contemptuous. 'Oh, yes, sir. The barbarians are still with us!' I told him I would give him another ten pounds to take me there and return. He made to bargain but then accepted, shrugging and gesturing for me to get in his carriage. I guessed he was maintaining some kind of face for himself. In my travels I had grown used to all kinds of mysterious body language, frequently far harder to interpret than any spoken tongue.

We trotted back to town and jogged beside a river strewn with old plastic water bottles, with all the miscellaneous filth from the boats that no legislation appeared able to limit, past flaking quasi-French façades still bearing the crests of Farouk and his ancestors and each now occupied by twenty or thirty families whose washing hung over the elaborate iron balconies and carved stone sphinxes like bunting celebrating some joyous national holiday. We passed convents and churches, mosques and graveyards, shanties, monuments, little clumps of palm trees sheltering donkeys and boys from a sun which as noon approached grew steadily more intense.

We went by the English holiday villas where hippies nowadays congregated; we passed the burned-out shells of warehouses and storerooms, victims of some forgotten riot, the stained walls sprayed with the emerald-coloured ankh of the Green Jihad, and eventually, turning inland again, reached the old Moslem necropolis, almost a mile long and half a mile across, surrounded by a low, mud wall and filled with every shape and size of stone or sarcophagus. Beyond this, further up the hill, I made out clumps of palms and the dark woollen tents of the Bisharim.

My driver reined in his horse some distance from the camp, beside a gate into the graveyard. 'I will wait for you here,' he said significantly.

Chapter Two

Ah, Whence, and Whither Flown Again, Who Knows?

THE NOMAD CAMP, showing so few outward signs of Western influence, had the kind of self-contained dignity which city Arabs frequently manage to re-create in their homes and yet which is not immediately noticed by those visitors merely disgusted by, for instance, Cairo's squalor.

Sheikh Khamet ben Achmet was the patriarch of this particular clan. They had come in a month ago, he said, from the Sudan, to trade horses and camels. They all knew my sister but she had disappeared. He employed a slow, classical Arabic which was easy for me to understand and in which I could easily respond. 'God has perhaps directed thy sister towards another vocation,' he suggested gently. 'It was only a short time since she would visit us whenever we put down our tents here. She had a particularly efficient cure for infections of the eye, but it was the women who went to her, chiefly.' He looked at me with quiet amusement. 'The best type of Englishwoman, as we say. Sometimes God sends us his beneficence in strange forms.'

'Thou has no knowledge of her present dwelling?' I sipped the coffee a servant brought us. I was glad to be in the cool tent. Outside it was now at least thirty-five degrees. There was little danger of freak rain today.

He looked up at me from his ironic grey eyes. 'No,' he said. 'She always visits us. When we needed her we would send messages to the Copt's house. You know, the carpenter who lives on the street leading from the great mosque to the souk.'

I did not know him, I said.

'He is as gold-haired as thou. They nickname him The German, but I know he is a Copt from Alexandria. I think he is called Iskander. I know that he is easily found.'

'Thou knowest my sister was an archaeologist?' I was a little hesitant.

'Indeed, I do! We discussed all manner of ancient things together and she had the courtesy to say that I was at least as informative as the great Egyptian Museum in Cairo!' He was amused by what he perceived as elegant flattery. My sister, if I still knew her, had done no more than to state her direct opinion.

It would have been ill-mannered of me to have left as soon as I had the information I sought, so I spent two further hours answering the sheikh's questions about current American and European politics. I was not surprised that he was well informed. I had seen his short-wave radio (doubtless full of piles noires) standing on the ivory-inlaid chest on the far side of the tent. I was also unsurprised by his interpretations of what he had learned. They were neither cynical nor unintelligent, but they were characteristic of certain desert Arabs who see everything in terms of power and opportunity and simply cannot grasp the reverence for political institutions we have in the West. For a few minutes I foolishly tried to re-educate him until it became clear I must give offence. Recalling my old rules, I accepted his terms. As a result we parted friends. Any South African apologist for apartheid could not have been more approving of my good manners.

When I got up to leave, the old man took my arm and wished me God's grace and help in finding my sister. 'She was associated with Jews.' He spoke significantly. 'Those who did not like her said that she was a witch. And it is true that two of my women saw her consorting with the spell-seller from the souk. The one called Lallah Zenobia. The black woman. Thou and I art men of the world and understand that it is superstitious folly. But thou knowest how women are. And they are often,' he added in an even lower tone, 'susceptible to Yehudim flattery and lies.'

It was by no means the first time I had to accept such sentiments from the mouth of one who was otherwise hospitality, tolerance and kindness personified. It is still easier to persuade a desert Arab that Jews are not in direct and regular touch with Satan and all his minions than convince a Dixie Baptist that the doors of a Catholic Church are not necessarily a direct gateway to Hell. One is dealing with powerful survival myths which only direct experience will disprove. In such circumstances I never mention my mother's family. I said I would visit Iskander the Carpenter. At this point a braying, bellowing and snorting chorus grew so loud I could barely hear his elaborate goodbyes. The stock was being beaten back from the water. As I emerged from the tent I saw my driver in the distance. He was sitting on the wall of the cemetery feinting with his whip at the boys and girls who flowed like a tide around him, daring one another to run within his range.

Chapter Three
Crystal to the Wizard Eye

I HAD NO difficulty in discovering Iskander the Carpenter. He was a slight man wearing a pair of faded denim overalls. Sanding off a barley-sugar chairleg, he sat just inside his workshop, which was open to the street and displayed an entire suite of baroque bedroom and living-room furniture he had almost completed. He chose to speak in French. 'It is for a couple getting married this weekend. At least they are spending their money on furniture rather than the wedding itself!' He put down his chairleg and shook my hand. He was fair-skinned and blond, as Sheikh Achmet had said, though I could not have taken him for anything but Egyptian. His features could have come straight from the Egyptian Museum's clay statue displays of ancient tradespeople. He might have been a foreman on a Middle Kingdom site. He turned up a chair which still had to have the upholstery over its horsehair seat, indicated that I should sit and sent his son to get us a couple of bottles of Pyramid beer.

'Of course I know Saidneh Duukturah. She was my friend. That one,' he pointed to his disappearing boy, 'owes his life to her. He was poisoned. She treated him. He is well. It is true I knew where she lived and would get messages to her. But for a year or more she went away from us. Until recently she was staying at the English House. There are many rumours. Most of them are simply stupid. She is no witch. She was a woman blessed by God with the healing touch. The other woman, now, is undoubtably a witch. My wife heard that your sister fell in love and went to the Somalin, Zenobia, for a philtre. Certainly, by chance, my wife saw her handing Zenobia a heavy purse. A Cairene purse, she was sure.'

'I do not know what that is.' I moved further into the shade. Outside, Aswan had fallen into a doze as the population closed its shutters until mid-afternoon. The yellow walls of the houses were now almost blistering to the touch.

'A purse of money, that's all. It used to mean a bag of gold. About twenty sovereigns. That is what a witch demands for a very powerful spell. Something very valuable, my friend.'

'My sister was buying a charm from a spell-seller?'

'A powerful one, yes. That negress has been involved with the police more than once. She was suspected of killing a rival suitor at the behest of another, of being responsible for the death of a man who was owed over a thousand pounds by another man. Now, if your sister was disposed to witchcraft, why would she go to a witch and pay her a healthy sum for a job she could as readily do herself?'

I agreed it was unlikely my sister was a witch. I asked how the matter had come to official attention.

'The police went to see her, I think. My wife's friend – friend no more – gossiped. They arrested Zenobia, then let your sister go. You should visit the *mamur* at the *markaz*, the police department. The *mamur* here is a very just man. He never accepts money unless he can do whatever it is he promises. His name is Inspector el-Bayoumi. If anyone knows where your sister is living in Aswan he probably will.'

By the time I had discussed the affairs of the day and thanked the carpenter for the beer, it was already cooler and I walked down to the *Sharri al Souk* which was beginning to open for business again, filling with women in black lacy *milayum* which barely revealed the vivid colours of their house dresses beneath, clutching bright plastic shopping bags and going about their weekend buying. Because it was Friday afternoon the butchers were displaying their calves' heads and bullock tails, their sheep's hearts and heads, their divided carcasses, all protected from an unforgiving sun by the thick coating of black flies which also covered the fish and offal on other stalls. Sellers of turkeys, pigeons and chickens took water in their mouths to force between the beaks of their wares so that they would not dehydrate before they were sold, and seemed to be kissing, tenderly, each one. Cheerful greengrocers called out the virtues of their squash, mangoes, potatoes or green beans. Gas lorries, electro-scoots, bicycles and a few official cars moved in slow competition with rickshaws, donkeys, mules or camels through alleys where, every so often, a bright sign would advertise in English the virtues of unobtainable Panasonic televisions or Braun refrigerators and others would, almost pathetically, alert the passer-by to the Color Xerox machine or Your Local Fax Office. Like every similar souk in the Arab world, the tools and artefacts of the centuries were crowded side by side and functioning in perfect compatibility. Aswan had adapted, far more readily and more cheerfully, to modern energy restraints than had London, for instance, where it had taken an Act of Parliament to reintroduce the public horse trough.

I made my way to the northern end of the street where the police station, the *markaz*, resembling an old British garrison, was guarded by two boys in serge khaki who were armed with the Lee-Enfield .303s with which Lawrence had armed his men for the Desert War and which had, then, been an Arab's prized possession. Now it was unlikely any reliable ammunition existed for these antiques. I understood only the crack militia was allowed to sport the old Kalashnikovs or M16s issued to regular infantry. With the end of international arms trading, almost any well-made gun was valuable, if only as status.

I had no appointment and was informed by the bright young civilian woman on the duty desk that Inspector el-Bayoumi would be back from New Town, the concrete development near the airport, in about an hour. I gave my name, my business, and said I would be back at about five-thirty. Courteously she assured me that the inspector would await me.

Chapter Four

Her Heart All Ears and Eyes, Lips Catching the Avalanche of the Golden Ghost

I HAD FORGOTTEN how much time one had to spend on enquiries of this kind. I returned to my apartment to find an envelope pushed under my door. It was not, as I had hoped, from my sister, but a letter welcoming me to Aswan, a short personal note from my friend Georges, a list of appointments with various engineers and officials, some misleading publicity about the dam, consisting mainly of impressive photographs, a variety of press releases stressing the plans for 'an even better dam' and so on. I went out again having glanced at them. I was obsessed with all the mysteries with which I had been presented in a single day. How had my sister metamorphosed from a dedicated archaeologist to some kind of local Mother Teresa?

Disturbed by my own speculations I forced myself to think about the next day's work when I would be discussing methods of reducing pollution in all its varieties and rebuilding the dam to allow silt down to the arable areas. The signs of serious 'redesertization', as ugly official jargon termed it, were now found everywhere in the Nile valley. In other words, the Aswan Dam was now seriously contributing to ecological damage as well as helping to wipe out our most important links with the remote past. I could not believe how intelligent scientists, who were not those industrial developers motivated only by greed, failed to accept the dreadful psychic damage being done to people whose whole identities were bound up with a particular and very specific landscape. My own identity, for instance, was profoundly linked to a small Oxfordshire village which had remained unchanged for hundreds of years after successfully resisting developers wanting to surround it with high-quality modern properties instead of its existing beeches and oaks.

Few Egyptians were in such comfortable circumstances or could make any choice but the one promising the most immediate benefit, yet they had the same understanding of their tribal homes and what values they represented, and still resisted all attempts to force them to lose their traditional clothes, language and attitudes and make them modern citizens of their semi-democratic society. Unfortunately, this attitude also extended to a dam now much older than many of its staff and never at any time an engineering miracle. UNEC had plans for a replacement. Currently they and the Rajhidi government were arguing over the amounts each would contribute. Happily, that was not my problem.

With a slightly clearer head, I walked to the post office on the corner of Abdel el Taheer Street. Though almost fifty years had passed since the First Revolution, the building still bore the outlines of earlier royal insignia. The elaborate cast-ironwork on doors and windows was of that 'Oriental' pattern exported from the foundries of Birmingham to adorn official buildings throughout the Empire east of Gibraltar. Even by the 1970s the stuff was still available from stock, during the brief period after the death of Britain's imperial age and before the birth of that now much-despised and admittedly reckless Thatcher period known ironically as 'the Second Empire', the period which had shaped my own expectations of life as well as those of uncounted millions of my fellows, the period in which my uncle had died, a soldier in the Falklands cause.

I entered the main door's cool archway and walked through dusty shafts of light to a tiled counter where I asked to speak to the Post Master. After a moment's wait I was shown into his little gloomy mahogany office, its massive fan constantly stirring piles of documents which moved like a perpetually unsettled flight of doves. A small, handsome Arab entered and closed the door carefully behind him. His neat Abraham Lincoln beard suggested religious devotion. I told him that my name was von Bek and I was expecting mail. I handed him an envelope I had already prepared. On the outside was my name and occupation. Inside was the conventional 'purse' – actually another envelope containing a few pounds. I said I would appreciate his personal interest in my mail and hoped he could ensure it was available to me the moment it arrived. Absently, he took the envelope and put it in his trouser pocket. He had brightened at the sound of my name. 'Are you related to that woman of virtue whom we know here in Aswan?' He spoke measured, cultured Arabic with the soft accents of Upper Egypt.

'My sister.' I was trying to locate her, I said. Perhaps her mail was delivered here?

'It has not been collected, Si von Bek, for several months. Yet she has been seen in Aswan recently. There was a small scandal. I understand that El Haj Sheikh Ibrahim Abu Halil intervened. Have you asked him about your sister?'

'Is he the governor?'

He laughed. Clearly the idea of the governor intervening on behalf of an ordinary member of the public amused him. 'No. Sheikh Abu Halil is the gentleman so many come to Aswan to see these days. He is the great Sufi now. We are blessed in this. God sends us everything that is good, even the rain. So much more grows and blooms. People journey to us from all over the world. Here, God has chosen to reveal a glimpse of Paradise.'

I was impressed by his optimism. I told him I would go to see Sheikh Abu Halil as soon as possible. Meanwhile I had an appointment with the police chief. At this his face grew a little uncertain, but his only response was some conventional greeting concerning Allah's good offices.

Police Inspector el-Bayoumi was one of those suave career officers produced by the new academies. His manners were perfect, his hospitality generous and discreet, and when I had replied to his question, telling him where I had been born in England, he confessed affectionate familiarity with another nearby Cotswold village. Together, we deplored the damage tourism had done to the environment and confessed it to be a major problem in both our countries, which depended considerably on the very visitors who contributed to the erosion. He sighed. 'I think the human race has rather foolishly cancelled many of its options.'

Since he preferred to speak it, I replied in English. 'Perhaps our imaginative resources are becoming as scarce as our physical ones?'

'There has been a kind of psychic withering,' he agreed. 'And its worst symptom, in my view, Mr von Bek, is found in the religious and political fundamentalism to which so many subscribe. As if, by some sort of sympathetic magic, the old, simpler days will return. We live in complicated times with complicated problems. It's a sad fact that they require sophisticated solutions.'

I admitted I had been schooled in many of those fundamentalist notions and sometimes found them difficult to resist. We chatted about this for a while. Coffee was brought, together with a selection of delicious *gurrahiya* pastries, whose secret the Egyptians inherited from the Turks, and we talked for another half-hour, during which time we took each other's measure and agreed the world would be a better place if civilised people like ourselves were allowed a greater voice. Whereupon, in that sometimes abrupt change of tone Arabs have, which can mislead Europeans into thinking they have somehow given offence, Inspector el-Bayoumi asked what he could do for me.

'I'm looking for my sister. She's an economic archaeologist who came here two and a half years ago with the Burbank College Project. It was an international team. Only about half were from California and those returned the next year, after the big earthquake. Most of them, of course, had lost relatives. My sister stayed on with the remaining members.' I did not mention her talk of a wonderful discovery out in the Western Sahara. Their sonavids had picked up a New Kingdom temple complex almost perfectly preserved but buried some hundred feet under the sand. My sister had been very excited about it. It was at least on a par with the discovery of the Tutankhamen treasures and probably of far greater historical importance. She and the team kept the discovery quiet, of course, especially since so many known monuments had suffered. Naturally, there were some conflicts of interest. There was little she could tell me in a letter and most of that was a bit vague, making reference to personal or childhood incidents whose relevance escaped me. I added delicately, 'You know about the discovery, naturally.'

He smiled as he shook his handsome head. 'No, Mr von Bek, I don't. I think an elaborate dig would not escape my notice.' He paused, asking me if he might smoke. I told him I was allergic to cigarette smoke and he put his case away. Regretfully, he said: 'I should tell you that your sister is a little disturbed. She was arrested by us about a year ago. There was something we had to follow up. An outbreak of black magic amongst the local people. We don't take such things very seriously until it's possible to detect a cult growing. Then we have to move to break it up as best we can. Such things are not a serious problem in London, but for a policeman in Aswan they are fairly important. We arrested a known witch, a Somali woman they call Madame Zenobia, and with her an Englishwoman, also rumoured to be practising. That was your sister, Mr von Bek. She was deranged and had to be given a sedative. Eventually, we decided against charging her and released her into the custody of Lady Roper.'

'The Consul's wife?'

'He's the Honorary Consul here in Aswan now. They have a large house on the West Bank, not far from the Ali Khan's tomb. You can't see it from this side. It is our miracle. Locally, it's called the English House. More recently they've called it the Rose House. You'll find no mysteries there!'

'That's where my sister's staying?'

'No longer. She left Aswan for a while. When she came back she joined the community around Sheikh Abu Halil and I understand her to be living in the old holiday villas on the Edfu road, near the racecourse. I'll gladly put a man to work on the matter. We tend not to pursue people too much in Aswan. Your sister is a good woman. An honest woman. I hope she has recovered herself.'

Thanking him I said I hoped my search would not involve the time of a hard-working police officer. I got up to leave. 'And what happened to Madame Zenobia?'

'Oh, the courts were pretty lenient. She got a year, doing quarry work for the Restoration Department in Cairo. She was a fit woman. She'll be even fitter now. Hard labour is a wonderful cure for neurosis! And far more socially useful than concocting love potions or aborting cattle.'

He sounded like my old headmaster. As an afterthought, I said, 'I gather Sheikh Abu Halil took an interest in my sister's case.'

He flashed me a look of intelligent humour. 'Yes, he did. He is much respected here. Your sister is a healer. The Sufi is a healer. He sometimes makes an accurate prophecy. He has a following all over the world, I believe.'

I appreciated his attempt at a neutral tone, given his evident distaste for matters psychic and mystical. We shared, I think, a similar outlook.

I found myself asking him another question. 'What was the evidence against my sister, inspector?'

He had hoped I would not raise the matter, but was prepared for it. 'Well,' he began slowly, 'for instance, we had a witness who saw her passing a large bag of money to the woman. The assumption was that she was paying for a spell. A powerful one. A love philtre, possibly, but it was also said that she wanted a man dead. He was the only other member of her team who had remained behind. There was some suggestion, Mr von Bek,' he paused again, 'that he made her pregnant. But this was all the wildest gossip. He did in fact die of a heart attack shortly after the reported incident. Sometimes we must treat such cases as murder. But we only had circumstantial evidence. The man was a drug addict and apparently had tried to force your sister to give him money. There was just a hint of blackmail involved in the case, you see. These are all, of course, the interpretations of a policeman. Maybe the man had been an ex-lover, no more. Maybe she wanted him to love her again?'

'It wasn't Noone, was it?'

'It was not her estranged husband. He is, I believe, still in New Zealand.'

'You really think she got tangled up in black magic?'

'When confused, men turn to war and women to magic. She was not, as the Marrakshim say, with the caravan.' He was just a little sardonic now. 'But she was adamant that she did not wish to go home.'

'What did she tell you?'

'She denied employing the witch. She claimed the Somali woman was her only friend. Otherwise she said little. But her manner was all the time distracted, as if she imagined herself to be surrounded by invisible witnesses. We were not unsympathetic. The psychiatrist from the German hospital came to see her. Your sister is a saintly woman who helped the poor and the sick and asked for no reward. She enriched us. We were trying to help her, you know.'

He had lost his insouciance altogether now and spoke with controlled passion. 'It could be that your sister had an ordinary breakdown. Too much excitement in her work, too much sun. Caring too much for the hardships of others. She tried to cure the whole town's ills and that task is impossible for any individual. Her burden was too heavy. You could see it written in every line of her face, every movement of her body. We wanted her to recover. Some suspected she was in the witch's power, but in my own view she carried a personal weight of guilt, perhaps. Probably pointlessly, too. You know how woman are. They are kinder, more feeling creatures than men.'

Chapter Five

The Seasons of Home – Aye, Now They Are Remembered!

THAT EVENING, WHILE there was still light, I took the felucca across the Nile, to the West Bank. The ferryman, clambering down from his high mast where he had been reefing his sail, directed me through the village to a dirt road winding up the hillside a hundred yards or so from the almost austere resting place of the Ali Khan. 'You will see it,' he assured me. 'But get a boy.'

There were a couple of dozen children waiting for me on the quay. I selected a bright-looking lad of about ten. He wore a ragged Japanese T-shirt with the inscription I LOVE SEX WAX, a pair of cut-off jeans and Adidas trainers. In spite of the firmness with which I singled him out, we were followed by the rest of the children all the way to the edge of the village. I had a couple of packs of old electronic watches which I distributed, to a pantomime of disappointment from the older children. Watches had ceased to be fashionable currency since I had last been in Aswan. Now, from their requests, I learned it was 'real' fountain pens. They showed me a couple of Sheaffers some tourist had already exchanged for their services as guides and companions of the road.

I had no fountain pen for the boy who took me to the top of the hill and pointed down into the little valley where, amongst the sand and the rocks, had been erected a large two-storey house, as solidly Edwardian as any early-twentieth-century vicarage. Astonishingly, it was planted with cedars, firs and other hardy trees shading a garden to rival anything I had ever seen in Oxfordshire. There were dozens of varieties of roses, of every possible shade, as well as hollyhocks, snapdragons, foxgloves, marigolds and all the flowers one might find in an English July garden. A peculiar wall about a metre high surrounded the entire mirage and I guessed that it disguised some kind of extraordinarily expensive watering and sheltering apparatus which had allowed the owners to do the impossible and bring a little bit of rural England to Upper Egypt. The grounds covered several acres. I saw some stables, a garage, and a woman on the front lawn. She was seated in a faded deckchair watching a reader or a video which she rested in her left hand. With her right hand she took a glorious drink from the little table beside her and sipped through the straw. As I drew nearer, my vision was obscured by the trees and the wall, but I guessed she was about sixty-five, dressed in a thoroughly unfashionable Marks and Ashley smock, a man's trilby hat and a pair of rubber-tyre sandals. She looked up as I reached the gate and called 'Good afternoon'. Happy with cash, my boy departed.

'Lady Roper?'

She had a quick, intelligent, swarthy face, her curls all grey beneath the hat, her long hands expressive even when still. 'I'm Diana Roper.'

'My name's Paul von Bek. I'm Beatrice's brother.'

'The engineer!' She was full of welcome. 'My goodness, you know, I think Bea could foretell the future. She *said* you'd be turning up here about now.'

'I wrote and told her!' I was laughing as the woman unlocked the gate and let me in. 'I knew about this job months ago.'

'You're here on business.'

'I'm going through the rituals of sorting out a better dam and trying to do something about the climatic changes. I got sent because I know a couple of people here – and because I asked to come. But there's little real point to my being here.'

'You don't sound very hopeful, Mr von Bek.' She led me towards the back of the house, to a white wrought-iron conservatory which was a relatively recent addition to the place and must have been erected by some forgotten imperial dignitary of the last century.

'I'm always hopeful that people will see reason, Lady Roper.'

We went into the sweet-smelling anteroom, whose glass had been treated so that it could admit only a certain amount of light, or indeed reflect all the light to perform some needed function elsewhere. Despite its ancient appearance, I guessed the house to be using up-to-date EE technologies and to be completely self-sufficient. 'What an extraordinary garden,' I said.

'Imported Kent clay.' She offered me a white basket chair. 'With a fair bit of Kenyan topsoil, I understand. We didn't have it done. We got it all dirt cheap. It takes such a long time to travel anywhere these days, most people don't want the place. It belonged to one of the Fayeds, before they all went off to Malaysia. But have you looked carefully at our roses, Mr von Bek? They have a sad air to them, a sense of someone departed, someone mourned. Each bush was planted for a dead relative, they say.' Her voice grew distant. 'Of course, the new rain has helped enormously. I've survived because I know the rules. Women frequently find their intuition very useful in times of social unrest. But things are better now, aren't they? We simply refuse to learn. We refuse to learn.'

Grinning as if enjoying a game, a Nubian girl of about sixteen brought us a tray of English cakes and a pot of Assam tea. I wondered how I had lost the thread of Lady Roper's conversation.

'We do our best,' I said, letting the girl take tongs to an éclair and with a flourish pop it on my plate. 'I believe Bea lived here for a while.'

'My husband took quite a fancy to her. As did I. She was a sweetie. And so bright. Is that a family trait? Yes, we shared a great deal. It was a luxury for me, you know, to have such company. Not many people have been privileged as she and I were privileged.' She nodded with gentle mystery, her eyes in the past. 'We were friends of your uncle. That was the funny thing we found out. All at Cambridge together in the late '60s. We thought conservation an important subject *then*. What? Fifty years ago, almost? Such a jolly boy. He joined up for extremely complicated reasons, we felt. Did you know why?'

I had never really wondered. My picture of my mother's brother was of the kind of person who would decide on a military career, but evidently they had not been acquainted with that man at all. Finding this disturbing, I attempted to return to my subject. 'I was too young to remember him. My sister was more curious than I. Did she seem neurotic to you, while she was here?'

'On the contrary. She was the sanest of us all! Sound as a bell upstairs, as Bernie always said. Sharp intelligence. But, of course, she had been there, you see. And could confirm everything we had been able to piece together at this end.'

'You're referring to the site they discovered?'

'That, of course, was crucial. Especially at the early stages. Yes, the site was extraordinary. We went out to see it with her, Bernie and I. What a mind-blower, Paul! Amazing experience. Even the small portion they had excavated. Four mechanical sifters just sucking the sand gradually away. It would have taken years in the old days. Unfortunately three of the operators left after the earthquake and the sifters were recalled for some crucial rescue work over in Sinai. And then, of course, everything changed.'

'I'm not sure I'm…'

'After the ship came and took Bea.'

'A ship? On the Nile?'

She frowned at me for a moment and then her tone changed to one of distant friendliness. 'You'll probably want a word with Bernie. You'll find him in his playroom. Nadja will take you. And I'm here if you need to know anything.'

She glanced away, through the glass walls of the conservatory and was at once lost in melancholy reflection of the roses and their guardian trees.

Chapter Six
The Smoke Along the Track

SOME ANTIQUE RADIO programme was playing as I knocked on the oak door and was admitted by a white-haired old man wearing a pair of overalls and a check shirt, with carpet slippers on his feet. His skin had the healthy sheen of a sun-baked reptile and his blue eyes were brilliant with trust. I was shocked enough to remain where I was, even as he beckoned me in. He turned down his stereo, a replica of some even older audio contraption, and stood proudly to display a room full of books and toys. One wall was lined with glass shelves on which miniature armies battled amidst a wealth of tiny trees and buildings. 'You don't look much like a potential playmate!' His eyes strayed towards the brilliant jackets of his books.

'And you're not entirely convincing as Mr Dick, sir.' I stood near the books, which were all well ordered, and admired his illustrated Dickens. The temperature in the room was, I guessed, thoroughly controlled. Should the power fail for just a few hours the desert would fade and modify this room as if it had been a photograph left for an hour in the sun.

My retort seemed to please him. He grinned and came forward. 'I'm Bernie Roper. While I have no immediate enemies, I enjoy in this room the bliss of endless childhood. I have my lead soldiers, my bears and rabbits, my model farm, and I read widely. *Treasure Island* is very good, as are the "William" books, and Edgar Rice Burroughs and, as you say, Charles Dickens, though he's a bit on the scary side sometimes. E. Nesbit and H.G. Wells and Shaw. I enjoy so much. For music I have the very best of *Children's Favourites* from the BBC – a mixture of comic songs, Gilbert and Sullivan, "Puff, the Magic Dragon", "The Laughing Policeman", popular classics and light opera. Flanders and Swann, Danny

Kaye, *Sparky's Magic Piano*, *Peter and the Wolf* and *Song of the South*. Do you know any of those? But I'm a silly chap! You're far too young. They'd even scrapped *Children's Hour* before you were born. Oh, dear. Never to enjoy *Larry the Lamb* or Norman and Henry Bones, the Boy Detectives! Oh!' he exclaimed with a knowing grin. 'Calamity!' Then he returned his attention to his toys for a moment. 'You think I should carry more responsibility?'

'No.' I had always admired him as a diplomat. He deserved the kind of retirement that suited him.

'I feel sorry for the children,' he said. 'The pleasures of childhood are denied to more and more of them as their numbers increase. Rajhid and Abu Halil are no real solution, are they? We who remember the Revolution had hoped to have turned the desert green by now. I plan to die here, Mr –?'

'My name's von Bek. I'm Bea's brother.'

'My boy! Thank goodness I offered an explanation. I'm not nearly as eccentric as I look! "Because I could not stop for Death, He kindly stopped for me. We shared a carriage, just we two, and Immortality." Emily Dickinson, I believe. But I could also be misremembering. "The child is Father to the Man", you know. And the lost childhood of Judas. Did you read all those poems at school?'

'I was probably too young again,' I said. 'We didn't do poetry as such.'

'I'm so sorry. All computer studies nowadays, I suppose.'

'Not all, sir.' The old-fashioned courtesy surprised us both. Sir Bernard acted as one cheated and I almost apologised. Yet it was probably the first time I had used the form of address without irony. I had, I realised, wanted to show respect. Sir Bernard had come to the same understanding. 'Oh, well. You're a kind boy. But you'll forgive me, I hope, if I return to my preferred world.'

'I'm looking for my sister, Sir Bernard. Actually, I'm pretty worried about her.'

Without irritation, he sighed. 'She was a sweet woman. It was terrible. And nobody believing her.'

'Believing what, Sir Bernard?'

'About the spaceship, you know. But that's Di's field, really. Not my area of enthusiasm at all. I like to make time stand still. We each have a different way of dealing with the fact of our own mortality, don't we?' He strolled to one of his displays and picked up a charging 17th Lancer. 'Into the Valley of Death rode the six hundred.'

'Thank you for seeing me, Sir Bernard.'

'Not at all, Paul. She talked about you. I liked her. I think you'll find her either attending Abu Halil's peculiar gymnasium or at the holiday homes. Where those Kenyan girls and boys are now living.'

'Thank you. Goodbye, sir.'

'Bye, bye!' Humming some stirring air, the former Director General of the United Nations hovered, contented, over his miniature Death-or-Glory Boys.

Chapter Seven

Another Relay in the Chain of Fire

Lady Roper had remained in her conservatory. She rose as I entered. 'Was Bernie able to help?'

'I could be narrowing things down.' I was anxious to get back to the East Bank before dark. 'Thank you for your kindness. I tried to find a phone number for you.'

'We're not on the phone, lovey. We don't need one.'

'Sir Bernard mentioned a spaceship.' I was not looking forward to her reply.

'Oh, dear, yes,' she said. 'The flying-saucer people. I think one day they will bring us peace, don't you? I mean one way or another. This is better than death for me, at any rate, Paul. But perhaps they have a purpose for us. Perhaps an unpleasant one. I don't think anybody would rule that out. What could we do if that were the case? Introduce a spy? That has not proved a successful strategy. We know that much, sadly. It's as if all that's left of Time is here. A few shreds from a few ages.'

Again I was completely nonplussed and said nothing.

'I think you share Sir B.'s streak of pessimism. Or realism is it?'

'Well, we're rather different, actually…' I began to feel foolish.

'He was happier as Ambassador, you know. Before the UN. And then we were both content to retire here. We'd always loved it. The Fayeds had us out here lots of times, for those odd parties. We were much younger. You probably think we're both barking mad.' When I produced an awkward reply she was sympathetic. 'There *is* something happening here. It's a *centre*. You can feel it everywhere. It's an ideal place. Possibly we shall be the ones left to witness the birth of the New Age.'

At that moment all I wished to do was save my sister from that atmosphere of half-baked mysticism and desperate faith, to get her back to the relative reality of London and a doctor who would know what was wrong with her and be able to treat it.

'Bea was never happier than when she was in Aswan, you know,' said Lady Roper.

'She wrote and told me as much.'

'Perhaps she risked a bit more than was wise. We all admire her for it. What I don't understand is why she was so thick with Lallah Zenobia. The woman's psychic, of course, but very unsophisticated.'

'You heard about the witness? About the purse?'

'Naturally.'

'And you, too, are sure it was a purse?'

'I suppose so. It's Cairo slang, isn't it, for a lot of money? The way the Greeks always say "seven years" when they mean a long time has passed. Bernie's actually ill, you realise? He's coherent much of the time. A form of P.D., we were told. From the water when we were in Washington. He's determined to make the best of it. He's sweet, isn't he?'

'He's an impressive man. You don't miss England?'

She offered me her hand. 'Not a bit. You're always welcome to stay if you are bored over there. Or the carping materialism of the Old Country gets to you. Simplicity's the keynote at the Rose House. Bernie says the British have been sulking for years, like the Lost Boys deprived of their right to go a-hunting and a-pirating at will. I'm afraid, Paul, that we don't think very much of home any more.'

Chapter Eight

And All These in Their Helpless Days...

THE GREAT EGYPTIAN sun was dropping away to the horizon as, in the company of some forty blue-cowled Islamic school-girls and a bird-catcher, I sailed back to the East. Reflected in the Nile the sky was the colour of blood and saffron against every tone of dusty blue; the rocks, houses and palms dark violet silhou-ettes, sparkling here and there as lamps were lit, signalling the start of Aswan's somewhat orderly nightlife. Near the landing stage I ate some *mulakhiya*, rice and an antique salad at Mahom-meds' Cafetria, drank some mint tea and went back to the Osiris, half expecting to find that my sister had left word, but the Hindu woman had no messages and handed me my key with a quick smile of encouragement.

I slept poorly, kept awake by the constant cracking of a chem-ical 'equaliser' in the basement and the creak of the all but useless wind-generator on the roof. It was ironic that Aswan, so close to the source of enormous quantities of electricity, was as cruelly rationed as everyone.

I refused to believe that my sister, who was as sane as I was and twice as intelligent, had become entangled with a black-magic flying-saucer cult. Her only purpose for associating with such people would be curiosity, perhaps in pursuit of some anthropo-logical research connected with her work. I was, however, puzzled by her secrecy. Clearly, she was deliberately hiding her where-abouts. I hoped that, when I returned the next day, I would know where she was.

My meetings were predictably amiable and inconsequential. I had arrived a little late, having failed to anticipate the levels of security at the dam. There were police, militia and security people everywhere, both on the dam itself and in all the offices and operations areas. I had to show my pass to eleven different people. The dam was under increased threat from at least three different organisations, the chief being Green Jihad. Our main meetings were held in a large, glass-walled room overlooking the lake. I was glad to meet so many staff, though we all knew that any decisions about the dam would not be made by us but by whoever triumphed in the Geneva negotiations. It was also good to discover that earlier attitudes towards the dam were changing slightly and new thinking was being done. Breakfasted and lunched, I next found myself guest of honour at a full-scale Egyptian dinner which must have taken everyone's rations for a month, involved several entertainments and lastly a good deal of noisy toasting, in cokes and grape juice, of our various unadmired leaders.

At the Hotel Osiris, when I got back that night, there was no note for me so I decided next day to visit the old vacation villas before lunching as arranged at the Cataract with Georges Abidos, who had told me that he was retiring as Public Relations officer for the dam. I had a hunch that my sister was probably living with the neo-hippies. The following morning I ordered a calash to pick me up and sat on the board beside the skinny, cheerful driver as his equally thin horse picked her way slowly through busy Saturday streets until we were on the long, cracked concrete road with the railway yards on one side and the river on the other, flanked by dusty palms, which led past the five-storey Moorish-style vacation complex, a tumble of typical tourist architecture of the kind once found all around the Mediterranean, Adriatic and parts of the Black and Red Seas. The white stucco was patchy and the turquoise trim on window frames and doors was peeling, but the new inhabitants, who had occupied it when the Swedish owners finally abandoned it, had put their stamp on it. Originally the place had been designed for Club Med, but had never sustained the required turnover, even with its special energy dispensations, and had been sold several times over the past ten years. Now garishly dressed young squatters from the wealthy African countries, from the Australias, North and South America, as well as Europe and the Far East, had covered the old complex with their sometimes impressive murals and decorative graffiti. I read a variety of slogans. LET THE BLOOD CONSUME THE FIRE, said one. THE TYGERS OF THE MIND RULE THE JUNGLE OF THE HEART, said another. I had no relish for such undisciplined nonsense and did not look forward to meeting the occupants of this bizarre New New Age fortress. Psychedelia, even in its historical context, had never attracted me.

As I dismounted from the calash I was greeted by a young woman energetically cleaning the old Club Med brass plate at the gate. She had those startling green eyes in a dark olive skin which one frequently comes across everywhere in Egypt and are commonly believed to be another inheritance from the Pharaonic past. Her reddish hair was braided with multicoloured ribbons and she wore a long green silk smock which complemented her eyes.

'Hi!' Her manner was promiscuously friendly. 'I'm Lips. Which is short for Eclipse, to answer your question. Don't get the wrong idea. You're here to find a relative, right?' Her accent was Canadian with a trace of something else, possibly Ukrainian. 'What's your name?'

'Paul,' I said. 'My sister's called Bea. Are the only people who visit you trying to find relatives?'

'I just made an assumption from the way you look. I'm pretty good at sussing people out.' Then she made a noise of approving excitement. 'Becky Beak, is it? She's famous here. She's a healer and an oracle. She's special.'

'Could you take me to her apartment?' I did my best not to show impatience with the girl's nonsense.

'Lips' answered me with a baffled smile. 'No. I mean, sure I could take you to one of her rooms. But she's not here now.'

'Do you know where she went?'

The girl was vaguely apologetic. 'Mercury? Wherever the ship goes.'

My irritation grew more intense. But I controlled myself. 'You've no idea when the ship gets back?'

'Now? Yesterday? There's so much time-bending involved. No. You just have to hope.'

I walked past her into the complex.

Chapter Nine

Fast Closing Toward the Undelighted Night...

B Y THE TIME I had spoken to a dozen or so *enfants des fleurs* I
had found myself a guide who introduced himself as Magic
Mungo and wore brilliant face-paint beneath his straw hat. He
had on an old pair of glitterjeans which whispered and flashed as
he walked. His jacket announced in calligraphic Arabic phonetic
English: THE NAME IS THE GAME. He was probably no older than
thirteen. He asked me what I did and when I told him he said he,
too, planned to become an engineer 'and bring back the power'.
This amused me and restored my temper. 'And what will you do
about the weather?' I asked.

'It's not the weather,' he told me, 'not Nature – it's the ships.
And it's not the dam, or the lake, that's causing the storms and
stuff. It's the Reens.'

I misheard him. I thought he was blaming the Greens. Then I
realised, belatedly, that he was expressing a popular notion amongst
the New New Agers, which by the time I had heard it several
times more had actually begun to improve my mood. The Reens,
the flying-saucer people, were used by the hippies as an explanation for everything they couldn't understand. In rejecting Science,
they had substituted only a banal myth. Essentially, I was being
told that the gods had taken my sister. In other words they did not
know where she was. At last, after several further short but keen
conversations, in various rug-strewn galleries and cushion-heavy
chambers smelling strongly of kif, incense and patchouli, I met a
somewhat older woman, with grey streaks in her long black hair
and a face the colour and texture of well-preserved leather.

'This is Ayesha.' Mungo gulped comically. 'She-who-must-be-
obeyed!' He ran to the woman who smiled a perfectly ordinary
smile as she embraced him. 'We encourage their imaginations,'

she said. 'They read books here and everything. Are you looking for Beck?'

Warily expecting more Reen talk, I admitted that I was trying to find my sister.

'She went back to Aswan. I think she was at the Medrasa for a bit – you know, with the Sufi – but after that she returned to town. If she's not there, she's in the desert again. She goes there to meditate, I'm told. If she's not there, she's not anywhere. Around here, I mean.'

I was relieved by the straightforward nature of her answer. 'I'm greatly obliged. I thought you, too, were going to tell me she was taken into space by aliens!'

Ayesha joined in my amusement. 'Oh, no, of course not. That was more than a year ago!'

Chapter Ten

Thoughts of Too Old a Colour Nurse My Brain

I DECIDED TO have a note delivered to the Sufi, El Haj Ibrahim Abu Halil, telling him that I planned to visit him next day, then, with a little time to spare before my appointment, I strolled up the corniche, past the boat-ghetto at the upper end, and along the more fashionable stretches where some sporadic attempt was made to give the railings fresh coats of white paint and where a kiosk, closed since my first time here, advertised in bleached Latin type the *Daily Telegraph*, *Le Monde* and the *New York Herald Tribune*. A few thin strands of white smoke rose from the villages on Elephantine Island; and from *Gazirat-al-Bustan*, Plantation Island, whose botanical gardens, begun by Lord Kitchener, had long since mutated into marvellously exotic jungle, came the laughter of the children and teenagers who habitually spent their free days there.

Outside the kiosk stood an old man holding a bunch of faded and ragged international newspapers under one arm and *Al Misr* under the other. 'All today!' he called vigorously in English, much as a London coster shouted 'All fresh!' A professional cry rather than any sort of promise. I bought an *Al Misr*, only a day old, and glanced at the headlines as I walked up to the park. There seemed nothing unusually alarming in the paper. Even the E.C. rate had not risen in the last month. As I tried to open the sheet a gust came off the river and the yellow-grey paper began to shred in my hands. It was low-density recyke, unbulked by the sophisticated methods of the West. Before I gave up and dumped the crumpled mess into the nearest reclamation bin I had glimpsed references to the UNEC conference in Madagascar and something about examples of mass hysteria in Old Paris and Bombay, where a group called *Reincarnation* was claiming its leader to be a newly born John Lennon. There were now about as many reincarnated

Lennons abroad as there had been freshly risen Christs in the early Middle Ages.

I stopped in the park to watch the gardeners carefully tending the unsweet soil of the flower beds, coaxing marigolds and nasturtiums to bloom at least for a few days in the winter, when the sun would not burn them immediately they emerged. The little municipal café was unchanged since British days and still served only ice creams, tea, coffee or soft drinks, all of them made with non-rationed ingredients and all equally tasteless. Pigeons wandered hopelessly amongst the débris left by customers, occasionally pecking at a piece of wrapping or a sliver of *Sustenance* left behind by some poor devil who had been unable to force his stomach to accept the high-concentrate nutrients we had developed at UNEC for his benefit.

The Cataract's entrance was between pillars which, once stately, Egyptianate and unquestionably European, were now a little the worse for wear, though the gardens on both sides of the drive were heavy with freshly planted flowers. Bougainvillaeas of every brilliant variety covered walls behind avenues of palms leading to a main building the colour of Nile clay, its shutters and ironwork a dark, dignified green, the kind of colour Thomas Cook himself would have picked to represent the security and solid good service which established him as one of the Empire's noblest champions.

I walked into the great lobby cooled by massive carved mahogany punkahs worked on hidden ropes by screened boys. Egypt had had little trouble implementing many of the UN's mandatory energy-saving regulations. She had either carried on as always or had returned, perhaps even with relief, to the days before electricity and gas had become the necessities rather than the luxuries of life.

I crossed the lobby to the wooden verandah where we were to lunch. Georges Abidos was already at our table by the rail looking directly over the empty swimming pool and, beyond that, to the river itself. He was drinking a cup of Lipton's tea and I remarked on it, pointing to the label on the string dangling from his tiny metal pot. 'Indeed!' he said. 'At ten pounds the pot why shouldn't the Cataract offer us Lipton's, at least!' He dropped his voice. 'Though my guess is the teabag has seen more than one customer through the day's heat. Would you like a cup?'

I refused. He hadn't, I said, exactly sold me on the idea. He laughed. He was a small, attractively ugly Greek from Alexandria. Since the flooding, he had been driven, like so many of his fellow citizens, to seek work inland. At least half the city had not been thought worth saving as the sea level had steadily risen to cover it.

'Can't you,' he asked, 'get your American friends to do something about this new embargo? One misses the cigarettes and I could dearly use a new John B.' He indicated his stained Planter's straw and then picked it up to show me the label on the mottled sweatband so that I might verify it was a genuine product of the Stetson Hat Co. of New Jersey. 'Size seven and a quarter. But don't get anything here. The Cairo fakes are very close. Very good. But they can't fake the finish, you see.'

'I'll remember,' I promised. I would send him a Stetson next time I was in the USA.

I felt we had actually conducted our main business before we sat down. The rest of the lunch would be a social affair with someone I had known professionally and as a personal acquaintance for many years.

As our mixed hors d'oeuvres arrived, Georges Abidos looked with a despairing movement of his mouth out towards the river. 'Well, Paul, have you solved any of our problems?'

'I doubt it,' I said. 'That's all going on in Majunga now. I'm wondering if my function isn't as some kind of minor smokescreen.'

'I thought you'd volunteered.'

'Only when they'd decided that one of us had to come. It was a good chance, I thought, to see how my sister was. I had spare relative allowance and lots of energy and travel owing, so I got her a flight out with me. It took for ever! But I grew rather worried. The last note I had from her was three months ago and very disjointed. It didn't tell me anything. I'd guessed that her husband had turned up. It was something she said. That's about all I know which would frighten her that much. My mistake, it's emerged. Then I wondered if she wasn't pregnant. I couldn't make head nor tail of her letters. They weren't like her at all.'

'Women are a trial,' said Georges Abidos. 'My own sister has divorced, I heard. But then,' as if to explain it, 'they moved to Kuwait.' He turned his eyes back to the river which seemed almost to obsess him. 'Look at the Nile. An open sewer running through a desert. What has Egypt done to deserve rescue? She gave the world the ancestors who first offered Nature a serious challenge. Should we be grateful for that? From Lake Nasser to Alexandria the river remains undrinkable and frequently unusable. She once replenished the earth. Now, what with their fertilisers and sprays, she helps poison it.' It was as if all the doubts he had kept to himself as a publicity officer were now being allowed to emerge. 'I listen to Blue Danube Radio from Vienna. The English station. It's so much more reliable than the World Service. We are still doing less than we could, they say, here in Egypt.'

The tables around us had begun to fill with Saudis and wealthy French people in fashionable silk shifts, and the noise level rose so that it was hard for me to hear my acquaintance's soft tones.

We discussed the changing nature of Aswan. He said he would be glad to get back to Cairo where he had a new job with the Antiquities Department raising money for specific restoration or reconstruction projects.

We had met at the reopening of the Cairo Opera House in 1989, which had featured the Houston Opera Company's *Porgy and Bess*, but had never become more than casual friends, though we shared many musical tastes and he had an extraordinary knowledge of modern fiction in English. His enthusiasm was for the older writers like Gilchrist or DeLillo, who had been amongst my own favourites at college.

We were brought some wonderfully tasty Grönburgers and I remarked that the cuisine had improved since I was last here. 'French management,' he told me. 'They have one of the best teams outside of Paris. They all came from Nice after the troubles. Lucky for us. I might almost be tempted to stay! Oh, no! I could not. Even for that! Nubian music is an abomination!'

I told him about my sister, how I was unable to find her and how I was beginning to fear the worst. 'The police suggested she was mad.'

Georges was dismissive of this. 'A dangerous assumption at any time, Paul, but especially these days. And very difficult for us to define here, in Egypt, just as justice is at once a more brutal and a subtler instrument in our interpretation. We never accepted, thank God, the conventional wisdoms of psychiatry. And madness here, as elsewhere, is defined by the people in power, usually calling themselves the State. Tomorrow those power-holders could be overthrown by a fresh dynasty, and what was yesterday simple common sense today becomes irresponsible folly. So I do not like to make hasty judgements or pronounce readily on others' moral or mental conditions – lest, indeed, we inadvertently condemn ourselves.' He paused. 'They say this was not so under the British, that it was fairer, more predictable. Only real troublemakers and criminals went to jail. Now it isn't as bad as it was when I was a lad. Then anyone was liable to arrest. If it was better under the British, then that is our shame.' And he lowered his lips to his wine-glass.

We had slipped, almost automatically, into discussing the old, familiar topics. 'It's sometimes argued,' I said, 'that the liberal democracies actually stopped the flow of history. A few hundred years earlier, as feudal states, we would have forcibly Christianised the whole of Islam and changed the entire nature of the planet's power struggle. Indeed, all the more childish struggles might have been well and truly over by now!'

'Or it might have gone the other way,' Georges suggested dryly, 'if the Moors had reconquered France and Northern Europe. After all, Islam did not bring the world to near-ruin. What has the European way achieved except the threat of death for all?'

I could not accept an argument which had already led to massive conversions to Islam amongst the youth of Europe, America and Democratic Africa, representing a sizeable proportion of the vote. This phenomenon had, admittedly, improved the tenor of world politics, but I still deplored it.

'Oh, you're so thoroughly out of step, my friend.' Georges Abidos smiled and patted my arm. 'The world's changing!'

'It'll die if we start resorting to mystical Islamic solutions.'

'Possibly.' He seemed unconcerned. I think he believed us unsaveable.

A little drunk, I let him take me back to the Osiris in a calash. He talked affectionately of our good times, of concerts and plays we had seen in the world's capitals before civilian flight had become so impossibly expensive, of the Gilbert and Sullivan season we had attended in Bangkok, of Wagner in Bayreuth and Britten in Glyndebourne. We hummed a snatch from *Iolanthe* before we parted.

When I got up to my room all the shutters had been drawn back to give the apartment the best of the light. I recognised the subtle perfume even as my sister came out of the bathroom to laugh aloud at my astonishment.

Chapter Eleven

Saw Life to Be a Sea Green Dream

B EATRICE HAD CUT her auburn hair short and her skin was paler than I remembered. While her blue eyes and red lips remained striking, she had gained an extra beauty. I was overjoyed. This was the opposite of what I had feared to find.

As if she read my mind, she smiled. 'Were you expecting the Mad Woman of Aswan?' She wore a light blue cotton skirt and a darker blue shirt.

'You've never looked better.' I spoke the honest truth.

She took both my hands in hers and kissed me. 'I'm sorry I didn't write. It began to seem such a sham. I *couldn't* write for a while. I got your letters today, when I went to the post office. What a coincidence, I thought – my first sally into the real world and here comes good old Paul to help me. If anyone understands reality, you do.'

I was flattered and grinned in the way I had always responded to her half-mocking praise. 'Well, I'm here to take you back to it, if you want to go. I've got a pass for you on the Cairo plane in four days' time, and from there we can go to Geneva or London or anywhere in the Community.'

'That's marvellous,' she said. She looked about my shabby sitting room with its cracked foam cushions, its stained tiles. 'Is this the best you get at your rank?'

'This is the best for any rank, these days. Most of us don't travel at all and certainly not by plane.'

'The *schoomers* are still going out of Alex, are they?'

'Oh, yes. To Genoa, some of them. Who has the time?'

'That's what I'd thought of, for me. But here you are! What a bit of luck!'

I was immensely relieved. 'Oh, Bea. I thought you might be dead – you know, or worse.'

'I was selfish not to keep you in touch, but for a while, of course, I couldn't. Then I was out there for so long…'

'At your dig, you mean?'

She seemed momentarily surprised, as if she had not expected me to know about the dig. 'Yes, where the dig was. That's right. I can't remember what I said in my letters.'

'That you'd made a terrific discovery and that I must come out the first chance I got. Well, I did. This really was the first chance. Am I too late? Have they closed down the project completely? Are you out of funds?'

'Yes,' she smiled. 'You're too late, Paul. I'm awfully sorry. You must think I've brought you on a wild-goose chase.'

'Nonsense. That wasn't why I really came. Good Lord, Bea, I care a lot for you!' I stopped, a little ashamed. She was probably in a more delicate condition than she permitted me to see. 'And, anyway, I had some perks coming. It's lovely here, still, isn't it? If you ignore the rubbish tips. You know, and the sewage. And the Nile!' We laughed together.

'And the rain and the air,' she said. 'And the sunlight! Oh, Paul! What if this really is the future?'

Chapter Twelve

A Man in the Night Flaking Tombstones

S HE ASKED IF I would like to take a drive with her beside the evening river and I agreed at once. I was her senior by a year but she had always been the leader, the initiator and I admired her as much as ever.

We went up past the ruins of the Best Western and the Ramada Inn, the only casualties of a shelling attack in '02, when the Green Jihad had attempted to hole the dam and six women had died. We stopped near the abandoned museum and bought a drink from the ice-stall. As I turned, looking out at the river, I saw the full moon, huge and orange, in the cloudless night. A few desultory mosquitoes hung around our heads and were easily fanned away as we continued up the corniche, looking out at the lights from the boats, the flares on the far side, the palms waving in the soft breeze from the north.

'I'm quitting my job,' she said. 'I resigned, in fact, months ago. I had a few things to clear up.'

'What will you do? Get something in London?'

'Well, I've my money. That was invested very sensibly by Jack before our problems started. Before we split up. And I can do free-lance work.' Clearly, she was unwilling to discuss the details. 'I could go on living here.'

'Do you want to?'

'No,' she said. 'I hate it now. But is the rest of the world any better, Paul?'

'Oh, life's still a bit easier in England. And Italy's all right. And Scandinavia, of course, but that's closed off, as far as residency's concerned. The population's dropping quite nicely in Western Europe. Not everything's awful. The winters are easier.'

She nodded slowly as if she were carefully noting each

observation. 'Well,' she said, 'anyway, I don't know about Aswan. I'm not sure there's much point in my leaving Egypt. I have a permanent visa, you know.'

'Why stay, Bea?'

'Oh, well,' she said. 'I suppose it feels like home. How's Daddy? Is everything all right in Marrakech?'

'Couldn't be better, I gather. He's having a wonderful time. You know how happy he always was there. And with the new government! Well, you can imagine.'

'And Mother?'

'Still in London. She has a house to herself in West Hampstead. Don't ask me how. She's installed the latest EE generators and energy storers. She's got a TV set, a pet option and a gas licence. You know Mother. She's always had the right contacts. She'll be glad to know you're okay.'

'Yes. That's good, too. I've been guilty of some awfully selfish behaviour, haven't I? Well, I'm putting all that behind me and getting on with my life.'

'You sound as if you've seen someone. About whatever it was. Have you been ill, Bea?'

'Oh, no. Not really.' She turned to reassure me with a quick smile and a hand out to mine, just as always. I nearly sang with relief. 'Emotional trouble, you know.'

'A boyfriend?'

'Well, yes, I suppose so. Anyway, it's over.'

'All the hippies told me you'd been abducted by a flying saucer!'

'Did they?'

I recognised her brave smile. 'What's wrong? I hadn't meant to be tactless.'

'You weren't. There are so many strange things happening around here. You can't blame people for getting superstitious, can you? After all, we say we've identified the causes, yet can do virtually nothing to find a cure.'

'Well, I must admit there's some truth in that. But there are still things we can do.'

'Of course there are. I didn't mean to be pessimistic, old Paul.' She punched me on the arm and told the driver to let his horse trot for a bit, to get us some air on our faces, since the wind had dropped so suddenly.

She told me she would come to see me at the same time tomorrow and perhaps after that we might go to her new flat. It was only a temporary place while she made up her mind. Why didn't I just go to her there? I said. Because, she said, it was in a maze. You couldn't get a calash through and even the schoolboys would sometimes mislead you by accident. Write it down, I suggested, but she refused with an even broader smile. 'You'll see I'm right. I'll take you there tomorrow. There's no mystery. Nothing deliberate.'

I went back into the damp, semi-darkness of the Osiris and climbed through black archways to my room.

Chapter Thirteen

You'll Find No Mirrors in that Cold Abode

I HAD MEANT to ask Beatrice about her experience with the Somali woman and the police, but her mood had swung so radically I had decided to keep the rest of the conversation as casual as possible. I went to bed at once more hopeful and more baffled than I had been before I left Cairo.

In the morning I took a cab to the religious academy, or Medrasa, of the famous Sufi, El Haj Sheikh Ibrahim Abu Halil, not because I now needed his help in finding my sister, but because I felt it would have been rude to cancel my visit without explanation. The Medrasa was out near the old obelisk quarries. Characteristically Moslem, with a tower and a domed mosque, it was reached on foot or by donkey, up a winding, artificial track that had been there for at least two thousand years. I climbed to the top, feeling a little dizzy as I avoided looking directly down into the ancient quarry and saw that the place was built as a series of stone colonnades around a great courtyard with a fountain in it. The fountain, in accordance with the law, was silent.

The place was larger than I had expected and far more casual. People, many obviously drugged, of every age and race sat in groups or strolled around the cloisters. I asked a pale young woman in an Islamic burqa where I might find Sheikh Abu Halil. She told me to go to the office and led me as far as a glass door through which I saw an ordinary business layout of pens and paper, mechanical typewriters, acoustic calculators and, impressively, an EMARGY console. I felt as if I were prying. My first job, from which I had resigned, was as an Energy Officer. Essentially the work involved too much peeping-tomism and too little real progress.

A young black man in flared Mouwes and an Afghan jerkin signalled for me to enter. I told him my business and he said, 'No problem, man.' He asked me to wait in a little room furnished like something still found in any South London dentist's. Even the magazines looked familiar and I did not intend to waste my battery ration plugging in to one. A few minutes later the young man returned and I was escorted through antiseptic corridors to the Sufi's inner sanctum.

I had expected some rather austere sort of Holy Roller's Executive Suite, and was a trifle shocked by the actuality which resembled a scene from *The Arabian Nights*. The Sufi was clearly not celibate, and was an epicurean rather than ascetic. He was also younger than I had expected. I guessed he was no more than forty-five. Dressed in red silks of a dozen shades, with a massive scarlet turban on his head, he lay on cushions smoking from a silver-and-brass hookah while behind him on rich, spangled divans lolled half a dozen young women, all of them veiled, all looking at me with frank, if discreet, interest. I felt as if I should apologise for intruding on someone's private sexual fantasy, but the Sufi grinned, beckoned me in, then fell to laughing aloud as he stared into my face. All this, of course, only increased my discomfort. I could see no reason for his amusement.

'You think this a banal piece of play-acting?' He at once became solicitous. 'Pardon me, *Herr Doktor*. I misunderstood your expression for a moment. I thought you were an old friend.' Now he was almost grave. 'How can I help you?'

'Originally,' I said, 'I was looking for my sister Beatrice. I believe you know her.' Was this my sister's secret? Had she involved herself with a charismatic charlatan to whom even I felt drawn? But the banality of it all! True madness, like true evil, I had been informed once, was always characterised by its banality.

'That's it, of course. Becky Bakka was the name the young ones used. She is a very good friend of mine. Are you looking for her no longer, Dr Bakka?'

I pointed out that 'von Bek' was the family name. The hippies had not made an enormously imaginative leap.

'Oh, the children! Don't they love to play? They are blessed. Think how few of us in the world are allowed by God to play.'

'Thou art most tolerant indeed, sidhi.' I used my best classical Arabic, at which he gave me a look of considerable approval and addressed me in the same way.

'Doth God not teach us to tolerate, but not to imitate, all the ways of mankind? Are we to judge God, my compatriot?' He had done me the honour, in his own eyes, of addressing me as a co-religionist. When he smiled again his expression was one of benign happiness. 'Would you care for some coffee?' he asked in educated English. 'Some cakes and so on? Yes, of course.' And he clapped his hands, whispering instructions to the nearest woman who rose and left. I was so thoroughly discomforted by this out-rageously old-fashioned sexism, which, whatever their private practices, few sophisticated modern Arabs were willing to admit to, that I remained silent.

'And I trust that you in turn will tolerate my stupid self-indul-gence,' he said. 'It is a whim of mine – and these young women – to lead the life of Haroun-el-Raschid, eh? Or the great chiefs who ruled in the days before the Prophet. We are all nostalgic for that, in Egypt. The past, you know, is our only escape. You don't begrudge it us, do you?'

I shook my head, although by training and temperament I could find no merit in his argument. 'These are changing times,' I said. 'Your past is crumbling away. It's difficult to tell good from evil or right from wrong, let alone shades of intellectual preference.'

'But I can tell you really do still think there are mechanical solu-tions to our ills.'

'Don't you, sidhi?'

'I do. I doubt though that they're much like a medical man's.'

'I'm an engineer, not a doctor of medicine.'

'Pardon me. It's my day for gaffes, eh? But we're all guilty of making the wrong assumptions sometimes. Let us open the shut-ters and enjoy some fresh air.' Another of the women went to fold back the tall wooden blinds and let shafts of sudden sunlight down upon the maroons, burgundies, dark pinks, bottle-greens and royal blues of that luxurious room. The woman sank into the shadows and only Sheikh Abu Halil remained with half his face in light, the other in shade, puffing on his pipe, his silks rippling as he moved a lazy hand. 'We are blessed with a marvellous view.'

From where we sat it was possible to see the Nile, with its white sails and flanking palms, on the far side of an expanse of glaring granite.

'My sister –' I began.

'A remarkable woman. A saint, without doubt. We have tried to help her, you know.'

'I believe you're responsible for getting her out of police custody, sidhi.'

'God has chosen her and has blessed her with unusual gifts. Dr von Bek, we are merely God's instruments. She has brought a little relief to the sick, a little consolation to the despairing.'

'She's coming home with me. In three days.'

'A great loss for Aswan. But perhaps she's more needed out there. Such sadness, you know. Such deep sadness.' I was not sure if he described my sister or the whole world. 'In Islam, you see,' an ironic twitch of the lip, 'we share our despair. It is a democracy of misery.' And he chuckled. 'This is blasphemy I know, in the West. Especially in America.'

'Well, in parts of the North maybe.' I smiled. My father was from Mississippi and settled first in Morocco, then in England after he came out of the service. He said he missed the old, bittersweet character of the US South. The New South, optimistic and, in his view, Yankified, no longer felt like home. He was more in his element in pre-Thatcher Britain. When she, too, began a programme of 'Yankification' of her own he retreated into fantasy, leaving my mother and going to live in a working-class street in a run-down north-eastern town where he joined the Communist Party and demonstrated against closures in the mining, fishing and steel industries. My mother hated it when his name appeared in the papers or, worse in her view, when he wrote intemperate letters to the weekly journals or the heavy dailies. But 'Jim Beck' was a contributor to *Marxism Today* and, later, *Red is Green* during his brief flirtation with Trotskyist Conservationism. He gave that up for anarcho-socialism and disappeared completely into the world of the abstract. He now wrote me letters describing the 'Moroccan experiment' as the greatest example of genuinely radical politics in action. I had never completely escaped the tyranny of his impossible ideals. This came back to me, there and then, perhaps because in some strange way I found this sufi as charming as I had once found my father. 'We say that misery loves company. Is that the same thing?' I felt I was in some kind of awful contest. 'Is that why she wanted to stay with you?'

'I knew her slightly before it all changed for her. Afterwards, I knew her better. She seemed very delicate. She came back to Aswan, then went out to the dig a couple more times, then back here. She was possessed of a terrible restlessness she would allow nobody here to address and which she consistently denied. She carried a burden, Dr von Bek.' He echoed the words of Inspector el-Bayoumi. 'But perhaps we, even we, shall never know what it was.'

Chapter Fourteen

On Every Hand – The Red Collusive Stain

S HE ARRIVED AT the Osiris only a minute or two late. She wore a one-piece worksuit and a kind of bush-hat with a veil. She also carried a briefcase which she displayed in some embarrassment. 'Habit, I suppose. I don't need the maps or the notes. I'm taking you into the desert, Paul. Is that okay?'

'We're not going to your place?'

'Not now.'

I changed into more suitable clothes and followed her down to the street. She had a calash waiting which carried us to the edge of town, to a camel camp where, much to my dismay, we transferred to grumbling dromedaries. I had not ridden a camel for ten years, but mine proved fairly tractable once we were moving out over the sand.

I had forgotten the peace and the wonderful smell of the desert and it was not long before I had ceased to pay attention to the heat or the motion and had begun to enjoy a mesmeric panorama of dunes and old rock. My sister occasionally used a compass to keep course but sat her high saddle with the confidence of a seasoned drover. We picked up speed until the heat became too intense and we rested under an outcrop of red stone which offered the only shade. It was almost impossible to predict where one would find shade in the desert. A year ago this rock might have been completely invisible beneath the sand; in a few months it might be invisible again.

'The silence is seductive,' I said after a while.

My sister smiled. 'Well, it whispers to me, these days. But it is wonderful, isn't it? Here you have nothing but yourself, a chance to discover how much of your identity is your own and how much is actually society's. And the ego drifts away. One becomes a virgin beast.'

'Indeed!' I found this a little too fanciful for me. 'I'm just glad to be away from all that…'

'You're not nervous?'

'Of the desert?'

'Of getting lost. Nothing comes out here, ever, now. Nomads don't pass by and it's been years since a motor vehicle or plane was allowed to waste its E.R. on mere curiosity. If we died, we'd probably never be found.'

'This is a bit morbid, isn't it, Bea? It's only a few hours from Aswan, and the camels are healthy.'

'Yes.' She rose to put our food and water back into their saddlebags, causing a murmuring and an irritable shifting of the camels. We slept for a couple of hours. Bea wanted to be able to travel at night, when we would make better time under the full moon.

The desert at night will usually fill with the noises of the creatures who waken as soon as the sun is down, but the region we next entered seemed as lifeless as the Bical flats, though without their aching mood of desolation. The sand still rose around our camels' feet in silvery gasps and I wrapped myself in the other heavy woollen gelabea Beatrice had brought. We slept again, for two or three hours, before continuing on until it was almost dawn and the moon faint and fading in the sky.

'We used to have a gramophone and everything,' she said. 'We played those French songs mainly. The old ones. And a lot of classic Rai. It was a local collection someone had brought with the machine. You wouldn't believe the mood of camaraderie that was here, Paul. Like Woodstock must have been. We had quite a few young people with us – Egyptian and European mostly – and they all said the same. We felt privileged.'

'When did you start treating the sick?' I asked her.

'Treating? Scarcely that! I just helped out with my First Aid kit and whatever I could scrounge from a pharmacy. Most of the problems were easily treated, but not priorities as far as the hospitals are concerned. I did what I could whenever I was in Aswan. But the kits gradually got used and nothing more was sent. After the quake, things began to run down. The Burbank Foundation needed its resources for rebuilding at home.'

'But you still do it. Sometimes. You're a legend back there. Ben Achmet told me.'

'When I can, I help those nomads cure themselves, that's all. I was coming out here a lot. Then there was some trouble with the police.'

'They stopped you? Because of the Somali woman?'

'That didn't stop me.' She raised herself in her saddle suddenly. 'Look. Can you see the roof there? And the pillars?'

They lay in a shallow valley between two rocky cliffs and they looked in the half-light as if they had been built that very morning. The decorated columns and the massive flat roof were touched a pinkish gold by the rising sun and I could make out hieroglyphics, the blues and ochres of the Egyptian artist. The building, or series of buildings, covered a vast area. 'It's a city,' I said. I was still disbelieving. 'Or a huge temple. My God, Bea! No wonder you were knocked out by this!'

'It's not a city or a temple, in any sense *we* mean.' Though she must have seen it a hundred times, she was still admiring of the beautiful stones. 'There's nothing like it surviving anywhere else. No record of another. Even this is only briefly mentioned and, as always with Egyptians, dismissively as the work of earlier, less exalted leaders, in this case a monotheistic cult which attempted to set up its own god-king and, in failing, was thoroughly destroyed. Pragmatically, the winners in that contest re-dedicated the place to Sekhmet and then, for whatever reasons – probably economic – abandoned it altogether. There are none of the usual signs of later uses. By the end of Nyusere's reign no more was heard of it at all. Indeed, not much more was heard of Nubia for a long time. This region was never exactly the centre of Egyptian life.'

'It was a temple to Ra?'

'Ra, or a sun deity very much like him. The priest here was represented as a servant of the sun. We call the place Onu'us, after him.'

'Four thousand years ago? Are you sure this isn't one of those new Dutch repros?' My joke sounded flat, even to me.

'Now you can see why we kept it dark, Paul. It was an observatory, a scientific centre, a laboratory, a library. A sort of university, really. Even the hieroglyphics are different. They tell all kinds of things about the people and the place. And it had a couple of other functions.' Her enthusiasm died and she stopped, dismounting from her camel and shaking sand from her hat. Together we watched the dawn come up over the glittering roof. The pillars, shadowed now, stood only a few feet out of the sand, yet the brilliance of the colour was almost unbelievable. Here was the classic language of the Fifth Dynasty, spare, accurate, clean. And it was obvious that the whole place had only recently been refilled. Elsewhere churned, powdery earth and overturned rock spoke of vigorous activity by the discovering team; there was also, on the plain which stretched away from the southern ridge, a considerable area of fused sand. But even this was now covered by that desert tide which would soon bury again and preserve this uncanny relic.

'You tried to put the sand back?' I felt stupid and smiled at myself.

'It's all we could think of in the circumstances. Now it's far less visible than it was a month ago.'

'You sound very proprietorial.' I was amused that the mystery should prove to have so obvious a solution. My sister had simply become absorbed in her work. It was understandable that she should.

'I'm sorry,' she said. 'I must admit...'

For a moment, lost in the profound beauty of the vision, I did not realise she was crying. Just as I had as a little boy, I moved to comfort her, having no notion at all of the cause of her grief, but assuming, I suppose, that she was mourning the death of an important piece of research, the loss of her colleagues, the sheer disappointment at this unlucky end to a wonderful adventure. It was plain, too, that she was completely exhausted.

She drew towards me, smiling an apology. 'I want to tell you everything, Paul. And only you. When I have, that'll be it. I'll never mention it again. I'll get on with some sort of life. I'm sick of myself at the moment.'

'Bea. You're very tired. Let's go home to Europe where I can coddle you for a bit.'

'Perhaps,' she said. She paused as the swiftly risen sun outlined sunken buildings and revealed more of a structure lying just below the surface, some dormant juggernaut.

'It's monstrous,' I said. 'It's the size of the large complex at Luxor. But this is different. All the curved walls, all the circles. Is that to do with sun worship?'

'Astronomy, anyway. We speculated, of course. When we first mapped it on the sonavids. This is the discovery to launch a thousand theories, most of them crackpot. You have to be careful. But it felt to us to be almost a contrary development to what was happening at roughly the same time around Abu Ghurab, although of course there were sun-cults there, too. But in Lower Egypt the gratification and celebration of the Self had reached terrible proportions. All those grandiose pyramids. This place had a mood to it. The more we sifted it out the more we felt it. Wandering amongst those light columns, those open courtyards, was marvellous. All the turquoises and reds and bright yellows. This had to be the centre of some ancient Enlightenment. Far better preserved than Philae, too. And no graffiti carved anywhere, no Christian or Moslem disfigurement. We all worked like maniacs. Chamber after chamber was opened. Gradually, of course, it dawned on us! You could have filled this place with academic people and it would have been a functioning settlement again, just as it was before some petty Pharaoh or local governor decided to destroy it. We felt we were taking over from them after a gap of millennia. It gave some of us a weird sense of responsibility. We talked about it. They knew so much, Paul.'

'And so little,' I murmured. 'They only had limited information to work with, Bea...'

'Oh, I think we'd be grateful for their knowledge today.' Her manner was controlled, as if she desperately tried to remember how she had once talked and behaved. 'Anyway, this is where it all happened. We thought at first we had an advantage. Nobody was bothering to come out to what was considered a very minor find and everyone involved was anxious not to let any government start interfering. It was a sort of sacred trust, if you like. We kept clearing. We weren't likely to be found. Unless we used the emergency radio nobody would waste an energy unit on coming out. Oddly, we found no monumental statuary at all, though the engineering was on a scale with anything from the Nineteenth Dynasty – not quite as sophisticated, maybe, but again far in advance of its own time.'

'How long did it take you to uncover it all?'

'We never did. We all swore to reveal nothing until a proper international preservation order could be obtained. This government is as desperate for cruise-*schoomer* dollars as anyone…'

I found myself interrupting her. 'This was all covered by hand, Bea?'

'No, no.' Again she was amused. 'No, the ship did that, mostly. When it brought me back.'

A sudden depression filled me. 'You mean a spaceship, do you?'

'Yes,' she said. 'A lot of people here know about them. And I told Di Roper, as well as some of the kids, and the Sufi. But nobody ever believes us – nobody from the real world, I mean. And that's why I wanted to tell you. You're still a real person, aren't you?'

'Bea – you could let me know everything in London. Once we're back in a more familiar environment. Can't we just enjoy this place for what it is? Enjoy the world for what it is?'

'It's not enjoyable for me, Paul.'

I moved away from her. 'I don't believe in spaceships.'

'You don't believe in much, do you?' Her tone was unusually cool.

I regretted offending her, yet I could not help but respond. 'The nuts and bolts of keeping this ramshackle planet running somehow. That's what I believe in, Bea. I'm like that chap in the first version of *The African Queen*, only all he had to worry about was a

World War and a little beam-engine. Bea, you were here alone and horribly overtired. Surely…?'

'Let me talk, Paul.' There was a note of aching despair in her voice which immediately silenced me and made me lower my head in assent.

We stood there, looking at the sunrise pouring light over that dusty red and brown landscape with its drowned architecture, and I listened to her recount the most disturbing and unlikely story I was ever to hear.

The remains of the team had gone into Aswan for various reasons and Bea was left alone with only a young Arab boy for company. Ali worked as a general servant and was as much part of the team as anyone else, with as much enthusiasm. 'He, too, understood the reasons for saying little about our work. Phil Springfield had already left to speak to some people in Washington and Professor al-Bayumi, no close relative of the inspector, was doing what he could in Cairo, though you can imagine the delicacy of his position. Well, one morning, when I was cleaning the dishes and Ali had put a record on the gramophone, this freak storm blew up. It caused a bit of panic, of course, though it was over in a minute or two. And when the sand settled again there was the ship – there, on that bluff. You can see where it came and went.'

The spaceship, she said, had been a bit like a flying saucer in that it was circular, with deep sides and glowing horizontal bands at regular intervals. 'It was more drum-shaped, though there were discs – I don't know, they weren't metal, but seemed like visible electricity, sort of protruding from it, half on the inside, half on the outside. Much of that moved from a kind of hazy gold into a kind of silver. There were other colours, too. And, I think, sounds. It looked a bit like a kid's tambourine – opaque, sparkling surfaces top and bottom – like the vellum on a drum. And the sides went dark sometimes. Polished oak. The discs, the flange things, went scarlet. They were its main information sensors.'

'It was organic?'

'It was a bit. You'd really have to see it for yourself. Anyway, it

stood there for a few minutes and then these figures came out.
thought they were test pilots from that experimental field in Libya
and they'd made an emergency landing. I was going to offer them
a cup of tea when I realised they weren't human. They had dark
bodies that weren't suits exactly but an extra body you wear over
your own. Well, you've seen something like it. We all have. It'
Akhenoton and Nefertiti. Those strange abdomens and elongated
heads, their hermaphroditic quality. They spoke a form of very
old-fashioned English. They apologised. They said they had had
an instrument malfunction and had not expected to find anyone
here. They were prepared to take us with them, if we wished to
go. I gathered that these were standard procedures for them. We
were both completely captivated by their beauty and the wonder
of the event. I don't think Ali hesitated any more than I. I left
note for whoever returned, saying I'd had to leave in a hurry and
didn't know when I'd be back. Then we went with them.'

'You didn't wonder about their motives?'

'Motives? Yes, Paul, I suppose hallucinations have motives. We
weren't the only Earth-people ever to go. Anyway, I never regret
ted the decision. On the dark side of the moon the main ship was
waiting. That's shaped like a gigantic dung-beetle. You'll laugh
when I tell you why. I still find it funny. They're furious because
their bosses won't pay for less antiquated vessels. Earth's not
very important project. The ship was designed after one of the
first organisms they brought back from Earth, to fit in with what
they thought was a familiar form. Apparently their own plane
has fewer species but many more different sizes of the same crea
ture. They haven't used the main ship to visit Earth since we
began to develop sensitive detection equipment. Their time is dif
ferent, anyway, and they still find our ways of measuring and
recording it very hard to understand.'

'They took you to their planet?' I wanted her story to be over.
had heard enough to convince me that she was in need of imme
diate psychiatric help.

'Oh, no. They've never been there. Not the people I know
Others have been back, but we never communicated with them

They have an artificial environment on Mercury.' She paused, noticing my distress. 'Paul, you know me. I hated that von Däniken stuff. It was patently rubbish. Yet this was, well, horribly like it. Don't think I wasn't seriously considering I might have gone barmy. When people go mad, you know, they get such ordinary delusions. I suppose they reflect our current myths and apocrypha. I felt foolish at first. Then, of course, the reality grew so vivid, so absorbing, I forgot everything. I could not have run away, Paul. I just walked into it all and they let me. I'm not sure why, except they know things – even circumstances, if you follow me – and must have felt it was better to let me. They hadn't wanted to go under water and they'd returned to an old location in the Sahara. They'd hoped to find some spares, I think. I know it sounds ridiculously prosaic.

'Well, they took us with them to their base. If I try to pronounce their language it somehow sounds so ugly. Yet it's beautiful. I think in their atmosphere it works. I can speak it, Paul. They can speak our languages, too. But there's no need for them. Their home planet's many light years beyond the Solar System which is actually very different to Earth, except for some colours and smells, of course. Oh, it's so lovely there, at their base. Yet they complain all the time about how primitive it is and long for the comforts of home. You can imagine what it must be like.

'I became friends with a Reen. He was exquisitely beautiful. He wasn't really a he, either, but an androgyne or something similar. There's more than one type of fertilisation, involving several people, but not always. I was completely taken up with him. Maybe he wasn't so lovely to some human eyes, but he was to mine. He was golden-pale and looked rather negroid, I suppose, like one of those beautiful Masai carvings you see in Kenya, and his shape wasn't altogether manlike, either. His abdomen was permanently rounded – most of them are like that, though in the intermediary sex I think there's a special function. My lover was of that sex, yet he found it impossible to make me understand how he was different. Otherwise they have a biology not dissimilar to ours, with similar organs and so on. It was not hard for me to adapt. Their food is delicious, though they moan about that, too. It's sent from home. Where they can grow it properly. And they have extraordinary music. They have recordings of English TV and radio – and other kinds of recordings, too. Earth's an entire department, you see. Paul,' she paused as if regretting the return of the memory, 'they have recordings of events. Like battles and ceremonies and architectural stuff. He – my lover – found me an open-air concert at which Mozart was playing. It was too much for me. An archaeologist, and I hadn't the nerve to look at the past as it actually was. I might have got round to it. I meant to. I'd planned to force myself, you know, when I settled down there.'

'Bea, don't you know how misanthropic and nuts that sounds?'

'They haven't been "helping" us or anything like that. It's an observation team. We're not the only planet they're keeping an eye on. They're academics and scientists like us.' She seemed to be making an effort to convince me and to repeat the litany of her own faith, whatever it was that she believed kept her sane. Yet the creatures she described, I was still convinced, were merely the inventions of an overtaxed, isolated mind. Perhaps she had been trapped somewhere under ground?

'I could have worked there, you see. But I broke the rules.'

'You tried to escape?' Reluctantly I humoured her.

'Oh, no!' Her mind had turned backward again and I realised then that it was not any far-off interstellar world but her own planet that had taken her reason. I was suddenly full of sorrow.

'A flying saucer, Bea!' I hoped that my incredulity would bring her back to normality. She had been so ordinary, so matter-of-fact, when we had first met.

'Not really,' she said. 'The hippies call them Reens. They don't know very much about them, but they've made a cult of the whole thing. They've changed it. Fictionalised it. I can see why that would disturb you. They've turned it into a story for their own purposes. And Sheikh Abu Halil's done the same, really. We've had arguments. I can't stand the exploitation, Paul.'

'That's in the nature of a myth.' I spoke gently, feeling foolish and puny as I stood looking down on that marvellous construction.

I wanted to leave, to return to Aswan, to get us back to Cairo and from there to the relative sanity of rural Oxfordshire, to the village where we had lived with our aunt during our happiest years.

She nodded her head. 'That's why I stopped saying anything.

'You can't imagine how hurt I was at first, how urgent it seemed to talk about it. I still thought I was only being taught a lesson and they'd return for me. It must be how Eve felt when she realised God wasn't joking.' She smiled bitterly at her own naïveté, her eyes full of old pain. 'I was there for a long time, I thought, though when I got back it had only been a month or two and it emerged that nobody had ever returned here from Aswan. There had been that Green Jihad trouble and everyone was suddenly packed off back to Cairo and from there, after a while, to their respective homes. People assumed the same had happened to me. If only it had! But really, Paul, I wouldn't change it.'

I shook my head. 'I think you were born in the wrong age, Bea. You should have been a priestess of Amon, maybe. Blessed by the gods.'

'We asked them in to breakfast, Ali and me.' Shading her eyes against the sun, she raised her arm to point. 'Over there. We had a big tent we were using for everything while the others were away. Our visitors didn't think much of our C-Ral and offered us some of their own rations which were far tastier. It was just a scout, that ship. I met my lover later. He had a wonderful sense of irony. As he should, after a thousand years on the same shift.'

I could bear no more of this familiar modern apocrypha. 'Bea. Don't you think you just imagined it? After nobody returned, weren't you anxious? Weren't you disturbed?'

'They weren't away long enough. I didn't know they weren't coming back, Paul. I fell in love. That wasn't imagination. Gradually, we found ourselves unable to resist the mutual attraction. I suppose I regret that.' She offered me a sidelong glance I might have thought cunning in someone else. 'I don't blame you for not believing it. How can I prove I'm sane? Or that I was sane then?'

I was anxious to assure her of my continuing sympathy. 'You're not a liar, Bea. You never were.'

'But you think I'm crazy.' All at once her voice became more urgent. 'You know how terribly dull madness can be. How conventional most delusions are. You never think you could go mad like that. Then maybe it happens. The flying saucers come down and take you off to Venus, or paradise, or wherever, where war and disease and atmospheric disintegration are long forgotten. You fall in love with a Venusian. Sexual intercourse is forbidden. You break the law. You're cast out of paradise. You can't have a more familiar myth than that, can you, Paul?' Her tone was disturbing. I made a movement with my hand, perhaps to silence her.

'I loved him,' she said. 'And then I watched the future wither and fade before my eyes. I would have paid any price, done anything, to get back.'

That afternoon, as we returned to Aswan, I was full of desperate, bewildered concern for a sister I knew to be in immediate need of professional help. 'We'll sort all this out,' I reassured her, 'maybe when we get to Geneva. We'll see Frank.'

'I'm sorry, Paul.' She spoke calmly. 'I'm not going back with you. I realised it earlier, when we were out at the site. I'll stay in Aswan, after all.'

I resisted the urge to turn away from her, and for a while I could not speak.

Chapter Fifteen

Whereat Serene and Undevoured He Lay...

THE FLIGHT WAS leaving in two days and there would be no other ticket for her. After she went off, filthy and withered from the heat, I rather selfishly used my whole outstanding water allowance and bathed for several hours as I tried to separate the truth from the fantasy. I thought how ripe the world was for Bea's revelation, how dangerous it might be. I was glad she planned to tell no-one else, but would she keep to that decision? My impulse was to leave, to flee from the whole mess before Bea started telling me how she had become involved in black magic. I felt deeply sorry for her and I felt angry with her for not being the strong leader I had looked up to all my life. I knew it was my duty to get her back to Europe for expert attention.

'I'm not interested in proving what's true or false, Paul,' she had said after agreeing to meet me at the Osiris next morning. 'I just want you to *know*. Do you understand?'

Anxious not to upset her further, I had said that I did.

That same evening I went to find Inspector el-Bayoumi in his office. He put out his cigarette as I came in, shook hands and, his manner both affable and relaxed, offered me a comfortable leather chair. 'You've found your sister, Mr von Bek. That's excellent news.'

I handed him a 'purse' I had brought and told him, in the convoluted manner such occasions demand, that my sister was refusing to leave, that I had a ticket for her on a flight and that it was unlikely I would have a chance to return to Aswan in the near future. If he could find some reason to hold her and put her on the plane, I would be grateful.

With a sigh of regret – at my folly, perhaps – he handed back the envelope. 'I couldn't do it, Mr von Bek, without risking the peace of Aswan, which I have kept pretty successfully for some years. We have a lot of trouble with Green Jihad, you know. I am very short-staffed as a result. You must convince her, my dear sir, or you must leave her here. I assure you, she is much loved and respected. She is a woman of considerable substance and will make her own decisions. I promise, however, to keep you informed.'

'By the mail packet? I thought you wanted me to get her out of here!'

'I had hoped you might *persuade* her, Mr von Bek.'

I apologised for my rudeness. 'I appreciate your concern, inspector.' I put the money back in my pocket and went out to the corniche, catching the first felucca across to the West Bank where this time I paid off my guides before I reached the English House.

The roses were still blooming around the great brick manor and Lady Roper was cutting some of them, laying them carefully in her bucket. 'Really, Paul, I don't think you must worry, especially if she doesn't want to talk about her experiences. *We* all know she's telling the truth. Why don't you have a man-to-man with Bernie? There he is, in the kitchen.'

Through the window, Sir Bernard waved with his cocoa cup before making a hasty and rather obvious retreat.

Chapter Sixteen

Your Funeral Bores Them with Its Brilliant Doom

A WAKING AT DAWN the next morning I found it impossible to return to sleep. I got up and tried to make some notes but writing down what my sister had told me somehow made it even more difficult to understand. I gave up. Putting on a cotton gelabea and some slippers I went down to the almost empty street and walked to the nearest corner café where I ordered tea and a couple of rolls. All the other little round tables were occupied and from the interior came the sound of a scratched Oum Kalthoum record. The woman's angelic voice, singing the praises of God and the joys of love, reminded me of my schooldays in Fèz, when I had lived with my father during his brief entrepreneurial period, before he had returned to England to become a Communist. Then Oum Kalthoum had been almost a goddess in Egypt. Now she was as popular again, like so many of the old performers who had left a legacy of 78 rpms which could be played on springloaded gramophones or the new clockworks which could also play a delicate LP but which few Egyptians could afford. Most of the records were re-pressed from ancient masters purchased from Athenian studios which, fifty years earlier, had mysteriously manufactured most Arabic recordings. The quality of her voice came through the surface noise as purely as it had once sounded through fractured stereos or on crude pirate tapes in the days of licence and waste. 'Inte el Hob', wistful, celebratory, thoughtful, reminded me of the little crooked streets of Fèz, the stink of the dyers and tanners, the extraordinary vividness of the colours, the pungent mint bales, the old men who loved to stand and declaim on the matters of the day with anyone who would listen, the smell of fresh saffron, of lavender carried on the backs of donkeys driven by little boys crying '*Balek!*' and insulting, in the vocabulary of a professional soldier, anyone who refused to move aside for them. Life had been sweet then, with unlimited television and cheap air-travel, with any food you could afford and any drink freely available for a few dirhams, and every pleasure in the reach of the common person. The years of Easy, the years of Power, the paradise from which our lazy greed and hungry egos banished us to eternal punishment, to the limbo of the Age of Penury, for which we have only ourselves to blame! But Fèz was good, then, in those good, old days.

A little more at peace with myself, I walked down to the river while the muezzin called the morning prayer and I might have been back in the Ottoman Empire, leading the simple, steady life of a small landowner or a civil servant in the family of the Bey. The débris of the river, the ultimate irony of the Nile filling with all the bottles which had held the water needed because we had polluted the Nile, drew my attention. It was as if the water industry had hit upon a perfect means of charging people whatever they wanted for a drink of *eau naturelle*, while at the same time guaranteeing that the Nile could never again be a source of free water. All this further reinforced my assertion that we were not in the Golden Age those New New Aquarians so longed to re-create. We were in a present which had turned our planet into a single, squalid slum, where nothing beautiful could exist for long, unless in isolation, like Lady Roper's rose garden. We could not bring back the Golden Age. Indeed we were now paying the price of having enjoyed one.

I turned away from the river and went back to the café to find Sheikh Abu Halil sitting in the chair I had recently occupied. 'What a coincidence, Dr von Bek. How are you? How is your wonderful sister?' He spoke educated English.

I suspected for a moment that he knew more than he allowed but then I checked myself. My anxiety was turning into paranoia. This was no way to help my sister.

'I was killing time,' he said, 'before coming to see you. I didn't want to interrupt your beauty sleep or perhaps even your breakfast, but I guessed aright. You have the habits of Islam.' He was flattering me and this in itself was a display of friendship or, at least, affection.

'I've been looking at the rubbish in the river.' I shook his hand and sat down in the remaining chair. 'There aren't enough police to do anything about it, I suppose.'

'Always a matter of economics.' He was dressed very differently today in a conservative light-and-dark blue gelabea, like an Alexandrian businessman. On his head he wore a discreet, matching cap. 'You take your sister back today, I understand, Dr von Bek.'

'If she'll come.'

'She doesn't want to go?' The Sufi's eyelid twitched almost raffishly, suggesting to me that he had been awake most of the night. Had he spent that time with Bea?

'She's not sure now,' I said. 'She hates flying.'

'Oh, yes. Flying is a very difficult and unpleasant thing. I myself hate it and would not do it if I could.'

I felt he understood far more than that and I was in some way relieved. 'You couldn't persuade her of the wisdom of coming with me, I suppose, sidhi?'

'I have already told her what I think, Paul. I think she should go with you. She is unhappy here. Her burden is too much. But she would not and will not listen to me. I had hoped to congratulate you and wish you Godspeed.'

'You're very kind.' I now believed him sincere.

'I love her, Paul.' He gave a great sigh and turned to look up at the sky. 'She's an angel! I think so. She will come to no harm from us.'

'Well –' I was once again at a loss. 'I love her too, sidhi. But does she want our love, I wonder?'

'You are wiser than I thought, Paul. Just so. Just so.' He ordered coffee and sweetac for us both. 'She knows only the habit of giving. She has never learned to receive. Not here, anyway. Especially from you.'

'She was always my best friend.' I said. 'A mother sometimes. An alter ego. I want to get her to safety, Sheikh Abu Halil.'

'Safety?' At this he seemed sceptical. 'It would be good for her to know the normality of family life. She has a husband.'

'He's in New Zealand. They split up. He hated what he called her "charity work".'

'If he was unsympathetic to her calling, that must be inevitable.'

'You really think she has a vocation?' The coffee came and the oversweetened breakfast cakes which he ate with considerable relish. 'We don't allow these at home. All those chemicals!' There was an element of self-mockery in his manner now that he was away from his Medrasa. 'Yes. We think she has been called. We have many here who believe that of themselves, but most are self-deluding. Aswan is becoming a little over-stocked with mystics and wonder-workers. Eventually, I suppose, the fashion will change, as it did in Nepal, San Francisco or Essaouira. Your sister, however, is special to us. She is so sad, these days, doctor. There is a chance she might find happiness in London. She is spending too long in the desert.'

'Isn't that one of the habitual dangers of the professional mystic?' I asked him.

He responded with quiet good humour. 'Perhaps of the more old-fashioned type, like me. Did she ever tell you what she passed to Lallah Zenobia that night?'

'You mean the cause of her arrest? Wasn't it money? A purse. The police thought it was.'

'But if so, Paul, what was she buying?'

'Peace of mind, perhaps,' I said. I asked him if he really believed in people from space, and he said that he did, for he believed that God had created and populated the whole universe as He saw fit.

'By the way,' he said, 'are you walking up towards the Cataract? There was some kind of riot near there an hour or so ago. The police were involved and some of the youngsters from the holiday villas. Just a peaceful demonstration, I'm sure. That would be nothing to do with your sister?'

I shook my head.

'You'll go back to England, will you, Dr von Bek?'

'Eventually,' I told him. 'The way I feel at the moment I might retire. I want to write a novel.'

'Oh, your father was a vicar, then?'

I was thoroughly puzzled by this remark. Again he began to laugh. 'I do apologise. I've always been struck by the curious fact that so much enduring English literature has sprung, as it were, from the loins of the minor clergy. I wish you luck, Dr von Bek, in whatever you choose to do. And I hope your sister decides to go with you tomorrow.' He kissed me three times on my face. 'You both need to discover your own peace. *Sabah el Kher.*'

'*Allah yisabbe'h Kum bil-Kher.*'

The holy man waved a dignified hand as he strolled down towards the corniche to find a calash.

By now the muezzin was calling the mid-morning prayer. I had been away from my hotel longer than planned. I went back through the crowds to the green-and-white entrance of the Osiris and climbed slowly to my room. It was not in my nature to force my sister to leave and I felt considerably ashamed of my attempt to persuade Inspector el-Bayoumi to extradite her. I could only pray that, in the course of the night, she had come to her senses. My impulse was to seek her out but I still did not know her address.

I spent the rest of the morning packing and making official notes until, at noon, she came through the archway, wearing a blue cotton dress and matching shawl. I hoped this was a sign she was preparing for the flight back to civilisation. 'You haven't eaten, have you?' she said.

She had booked a table on the Mut, a floating restaurant moored just below the Cataract. We boarded a thing resembling an Ottoman pleasure barge, all dark green trellises, scarlet fretwork and brass ornament, while inside it was more luxurious than the Sufi's 'harem'. 'It's hardly used, of course, these days,' Bea said. 'Not enough rich people wintering in Aswan any more. But the atmosphere's nice still. You don't mind? It's not against your puritan nature, is it?'

'Only a little.' I was disturbed by her apparent normality. We might never have ridden into the desert together, never have talked about aliens and spaceships and ancient Egyptian universities. I wondered, now, if she were not seriously schizophrenic.

'You do seem troubled, though.' She was interrupted by a large man in a dark yellow gelabea smelling wildly of garlic who embraced her with affectionate delight. 'Beatrice! My Beatrice!' We were introduced. Mustafa shook hands with me as he led us ecstatically to a huge, low table looking over the Nile, where the feluccas and great sailing barges full of holidaymakers came close enough to touch. We sat on massive brocaded foam cushions.

I could not overcome my depression. I was faced with a problem beyond my scope. 'You've decided to stay, I take it?'

The major-domo returned with two large glasses of Camparisoda. 'Compliments of the house.' It was an extraordinary piece of generosity. We saluted him with our glasses, then toasted each other.

'Yes.' She drew her hair over her collar and looked towards the water. 'For a while, anyway. I won't get into any more trouble, Paul, I promise. And I'm not the suicide type. That I'm absolutely sure about.'

'Good.' I would have someone come out to her as soon as possible, a psychiatrist contact in MEDAC who could provide a professional opinion. 'You'll tell me your address?'

'I'm moving. Tomorrow. I'll stay with the Ropers if they'll have me. Any mail care of them will be forwarded. I'm not being deliberately mysterious, dear, I promise. I'm going to write. And meanwhile, I've decided to tell you the whole of it. I want you to remember it, perhaps put it into some kind of shape that I can't. It's important to me that it's recorded. Do you promise?'

I could only promise that I would make all the notes possible.

'Well, there's actually not much else.'

I was relieved to know I would not for long have to suffer those miserably banal inventions.

'I fell in love, you see.'

'Yes, you told me. With a spaceman.'

'We knew it was absolutely forbidden to make love. But we couldn't help ourselves. I mean, with all his self-discipline he was as attracted to me as I was to him. It was important, Paul.'

I did my best to give her my full attention while she repeated much of what she had already told me in the desert. There was a kind of biblical rhythm to her voice. 'So they threw me out. I never saw my lover again. I never saw his home again. They brought me back and left me where they had found me. Our tents were gone and everything was obviously abandoned. They let their engines blow more sand over the site. Well, I got to Aswan eventually. I found water and food and it wasn't too hard. I'm not sure why I came here. I didn't know then that I was pregnant. I don't think I knew you could get pregnant. There isn't a large literature on sexual congress with semi-males of the alien persuasion. You'd probably find him bizarre, but for me it was like making love to an angel. All the time. It was virtually our whole existence. Oh, Paul!' She pulled at her collar. She smoothed the tablecloth between her knife and fork. 'Well, he was wonderful and he thought I was wonderful. Maybe that's *why* they forbid it. The way they'd forbid a powerful habit-forming stimulant. Do you know I just this second thought of that?'

'That's why you were returned here?' I was still having difficulty following her narrative.

'Didn't I say? Yes. Well, I went to stay with the Ropers for a bit, then I stayed in the commune and then the Medrasa, but I kept going out to the site. I was hoping they'd relent, you see. I'd have done almost anything to get taken back, Paul.'

'To escape from here, you mean?'

'To be with him. That's all. I was – I am – so lonely. Nobody could describe the void.'

I was silent, suddenly aware of her terrible vulnerability, still convinced she had been the victim of some terrible deception.

'You're wondering about the child,' she said. She put her hand on mine where I fingered the salt. 'He was born too early. He lived for eight days. I had him at Lallah Zenobia's. You see, I couldn't tell what he would look like. She was better prepared, I thought. She even blessed him when he was born so that his soul might go to Heaven. He was tiny and frail and beautiful. His father's col-ouring and eyes. My face, I think, mostly. He would have been a

317

wunderkind, I shouldn't be surprised. Paul…' Her voice became a whisper. 'It was like giving birth to the Messiah.'

With great ceremony, our meal arrived. It was a traditional Egyptian *meze* and it was more and better food than either of us had seen in years. Yet we hardly ate.

'I took him back to the site.' She looked out across the water again. 'I'd got everything ready. I had some hope his father would come to see him. Nobody came. Perhaps it needed that third sex to give him the strength? I waited, but there was not, as the kids say, a Reen to be seen.' This attempt at humour was hideous. I took firm hold of her hands. The tears in her eyes were barely restrained.

'He died.' She released her hands and looked for something in her bag. I thought for a frightening moment she was going to produce a photograph. 'Eight days. He couldn't seem to get enough nourishment from what I was feeding him. He needed that – whatever it was he should have had.' She took a piece of linen from her bag and wiped her hands and neck. 'You're thinking I should have taken him to the hospital. But this is Egypt, Paul, where people are still arrested for witchcraft and here was clear evidence of my having had congress with an *ifrit*. Who would believe my story? I was aware of what I was doing. I'd never expected the baby to live or, when he did live, to look the way he did. The torso was sort of pear-shaped and there were several embryonic limbs. He was astonishingly lovely. I think he belonged to his father's world. I wish they had come for him. It wasn't fair that he should die.'

I turned my attention to the passing boats and controlled my own urge to weep. I was hoping she would stop, for she was, by continuing, hurting herself. But, obsessively, she went on. 'Yes, Paul. I could have gone to Europe as soon as I knew I was pregnant and I would have done if I'd had a hint of what was coming, but my instincts told me he would not live or, if he did live, it would be because his father returned for him. I don't think that was self-deception. Anyway, when he was dead I wasn't sure what to do. I hadn't made any plans. Lallah Zenobia was wonderful to me. She said she would dispose of the body properly and with respect. I couldn't bear to have some future archaeologist digging him up. You know, I've always hated that. Especially with children. So I went to her lean-to in Shantytown. I had him wrapped in a shawl – Mother's lovely old Persian shawl – and inside a beautiful inlaid box. I put the box in a leather bag and took it to her.'

'That was the Cairene Purse? Or did you give her money, too?'

'Money had nothing to do with it. Do the police still think I was paying her? I offered Zenobia money but she refused. "Just pray for us all," was what she said. I've been doing it every night since. The Lord's prayer for everyone. It's the only prayer I know. I learned it at one of my schools.'

'Zenobia went to prison. Didn't you try to tell them she was helping you?'

'There was no point in mentioning the baby, Paul. That would have constituted another crime, I'm sure. She was as good as her word. He was never found. She made him safe somewhere. A little funeral boat on the river late at night, away from all the witnesses, maybe. And they would have found him if she had been deceiving me, Paul. She got him home somehow.'

Dumb with sadness, I could only reach out and stroke her arms and hands, reach for her unhappy face.

We ate so as not to offend our host, but without appetite. Above the river the sun was at its zenith and Aswan experienced the familiar, unrelenting light of an African afternoon.

She looked out at the river with its day's flow of débris, the plastic jars, the used sanitary towels, the paper and filth left behind by tourists and residents alike.

With a deep, uneven sigh, she shook her head, folded her arms under her breasts and leaned back in the engulfing foam.

All the *fhouls* and the marinated salads, the *ruqaq* and the meats lay cold before us as, from his shadows, the proprietor observed us with discreet concern.

There came a cry from outside. A boy perched high on the single mast of his boat, his white gelabea tangling with his sail so that he seemed all of a piece with the vessel, waved to friends on the shore and pointed into the sky. One of our last herons circled overhead for a moment and then flew steadily south, into what had been the Sudan.

My sister's slender body was moved for a moment by some small, profound anguish.

'He could not have lived here.'

A popular spot with working-class Londoners from the Edwardian era to the 1920s, especially on weekends and bank holidays. Trams terminated here. The Mill at one stage incorporated extensive dining rooms, a mosaic hall and an hotel. After the tram route was discontinued, the Mill and its outbuildings fell into disrepair – until it was inherited by the reclusive Dorian 'Tubby' Ollis in 1970 and converted to a recording studio with living accommodation. It has been used by, among others, Bob Dylan, Dave Stewart, Elvis Costello, Martin Stone and Jah Wobble. Ollis gave up touring with the Deep Fix but continued to record for this and other rock bands as a session musician. He restored the Mill to full working condition. Passengers on the upper decks of buses can sometimes catch a glimpse of the sails turning, high above the trees (they supply some of the studio's electricity). Public access has been denied for some years.

Furniture

For Jewell Hodges

T HERE'S SOMETHING TO be said, she thought, for spending
money on old-fashioned furniture. Most of this modern
stuff's rubbish. Just look at the joints. Dovetailing's a forgotten
art. All wire staples and hardboard. And the price! She'd had her
table since she and Mo got married. Just like her mum's. *That
oak's hard as iron.* Vi Corren smiled.

She'd be dead now if it wasn't for good furniture. When this
bomb went off, her table had somehow been lifted across her
chair, protecting her from the collapsing walls. It was pitch-dark,
so she knew there'd be a lot on top of her. But she didn't think
she was in any immediate danger. And her chair was solid as
a rock.

The suite was in perfect condition when she bought it at Mac-
Murtry's. Hardly used. It cost a fraction of that spindly modern
stuff. Okay for a coffee bar, but you wouldn't want it in your home.

MacMurtry's furniture was *better* than new. Made by real
craftsmen, like her dad. Sound as a bell. Good prices. Of course,
she had everything thoroughly cleaned.

Give me what you want to spend, she'd tell Mo. And then let
me go and find what I want. He'd been glad of her savings when
his back went out that time.

Over the years most of her furniture came from MacMurtry's.
That lovely sideboard, her cabinets. Mick MacMurtry had a big
shop on the corner of Old Sweden Street. When his lease ran out
they knocked the whole block down and erected some sort of
insurance building. She couldn't get on with all these new feature-
less skyscrapers.

Her dad had been a joiner and worked for Heal's. Mo's dad had

323

been a Princelet Street tailor. 'You tell me about three-piece *suits*,' she'd say, 'and I'll tell you about three-piece *suites*.'

He'd always liked her humour. He was a couple of years younger. The only kid she had, she told people affectionately. He'd be retiring soon and she'd be glad of it. He wanted a clean break from Brookgate. He'd set his heart on Tudor Hamlets. There wouldn't be any argument from her now. She'd love a little garden.

The big armchair moved under her like a living monster.

Oh!

Huge stones groaning in the darkness overhead. Then a terrible stillness.

Dust fell. Something squeaked and scraped and juddered, but the table held.

'No time for panic, Vi.'

She breathed slowly and easily, the way she did at the dentist. She refused to think of all the rubble that had to be on top of her.

Another noise. Not a shot. Guns made a simultaneous *crack, thud, bang*. This was like something snapping.

'Calm down, Vi.'

Most of her childhood Brookgate was already gone. Buried under glassy concrete. Streets you didn't recognise. People you didn't know. No proper shops. Really, it would be a relief to move. Their insurance would easily cover them, though finding the furniture would be a problem. Everything decent was an antique, these days. Those old parlour drawleafs, still with their wartime utility marks, were selling to Americans for hundreds.

All their married life Mo had complained about her taste. Being a cabby, he picked up the latest trends. She'd bowed to him on decorations but she'd been firm about the furniture.

A second-hand table saved my life in 1945. They'd had an indoor shelter – steel sheeting and wire screens around your ordinary table. She felt so safe sleeping under it. Then the V2 hit Bacon Street. Mum at the pictures. Dad catching a few hours upstairs. The ARP dug her out. Bruised, stiff and wheezing, but unhurt. Just this permanent allergy to dust. She could feel her skin coming up now. The *Mirror* had called her The Miracle Girl. There'd been quite a few miracles in 1945. She loved to see the sun come up over St Paul's. If she had a wish it would be to enjoy one more London sunrise without all these new buildings in the way.

Mo had insisted on buying their flat. He'd seen ahead. You could ask any price you liked for a ground floor since the boom. Business people wanting somewhere near the City. Not much of the flat left now! Just the table, the chair and her. The basics.

She was surprised by her own spontaneous laughter. She was almost relieved. She spoke aloud, into the settling dust.

'I could do with a cup of tea.'

Still, then she'd need to go to the toilet. So it was probably for the best. She wondered what the time was. She'd find out soon from the wireless. When she knew they were searching for her, she'd turned it off to save the battery. These new headphones were so good she hadn't heard the loudspeakers outside. What a fool! Everyone safe but her. Even the cat. People thought she'd left in the first evacuation. Mistaken her for the other Mrs Corren. Ticked her off the residents' list. The other Mrs Corren wouldn't have said anything.

They'd double-checked. But even if you stuck your head round the door you couldn't see a person sitting in this big chair. So while everybody else responded to the bomb warning, she'd been in a world of her own, looking out of her window at the grey drizzle, the slow, reflective concrete, listening to her tape. *Velia, O, Velia, the witch of the wood…* Looking forward to Mo bringing in their usual Friday fish and chips.

According to the news, it had been a huge explosion centred on the bank next door. As warned, it had gone off at exactly eight p.m. She must have blacked out when it happened.

Terrible devastation. All the surrounding office blocks affected. The wireless had said Mo was on his way home when he heard the news. He usually rang her on his mobile. A real worrier, Mo. She felt so sorry for him. He hadn't had her happy childhood.

Her mum had just been glad she was alive. Aunties all over the place. So much space. So much freedom. Ruins to play in. A vast adventure playground. And something more: that rediscovery of a wise, safe, dreaming, dignified, permanent London only made visible again by Hitler's bombs.

A high price to pay, though.

She remembered when she'd run barefoot over grass, through the rosebay willowherb and dandelions and cow parsley down to St Paul's. Good old St Paul's. Thanks to the bombs you had a clear view across the city. Ludgate Circus. The Old Bailey. The way it had been centuries ago. The Tower. The Mint. Not much in the way of tourists, then. She'd known so many people. She'd loved it, running everywhere she wanted to go, cycling over footpaths trodden down to Smithfield, the river, the Custom House, Billingsgate. Wild flowers blooming. All the markets doing noisy business. In the evening, when the office workers had gone to their stations, you could sit on a ruined roof and watch the sun set over great stretches of river. Timeless security in the heart of the city.

As a girl she'd volunteered for the hardest paper round just so she could get up before dawn and stand on a pile of weed-grown rubble to watch the sun rise over St Paul's. You couldn't do that any more, now that they'd built those big, brutal barbicans.

What kind of happy childhood was it, she wondered, that made you so nostalgic for ruins? Ruins were all she'd really known. And there were so few records of them. Lots of pictures of Brookgate before the War, when all the old buildings were still standing. Lots of stuff afterwards, with the big cranes and the permanent scaffolding. By then she was working at the old cigarette factory and the big changes all went on behind hoardings. Then they closed the factory and turned it into executive offices. She got a job at Mullards, Clerkenwell, until that went, too, under that computer tower.

Her childhood had been wonderful. They never really left London. After staying in Wales for a week, they'd all come home. Mum said she'd rather die of an air raid than die of boredom. The peace and quiet got on your nerves. Made you think about things too much. Better to be in it and doing something than out of it and worrying all the time. She'd wanted to be near Dad.

Vi's hands were numb. She wished she could get up and move around. She turned on the wireless.

Radio Five. Some chat about sports, then, abruptly, the news. It was five in the morning. Rescue workers still had hopes of finding her alive. A real drama.

Her chair shook and the table overhead scraped a bit lower. She could feel its pressure on her left shoulder. Like the weight of the earth.

A long moment. It seemed like an hour.

Something fell towards her and seemed to land at her feet. There was a rushing sound, a human yell. Then a surprising gap in the darkness. Lights. Dogs barking. Distant voices. She drew a deep breath of the cool air and shouted. 'Here. I'm here.' Her voice was too hoarse. 'Here!'

Exclamations. More scrabbling. The sound of a motor. Urgent tones. Instructions. Something moved. The table shifted again, but this time the pressure eased.

The patch of pale grey widened. It was the outside. Shadows. Torch-beams. Something flashed in her eyes. 'Are you okay, love?'

'Well, I could do with a cup of tea.'

'We're just bracing all this rubbish up so we can get you out properly.' The face in the torchlight was heavily bearded, wearing a turban. Was it Doctor Singh?

He smiled. 'And I'll tell Tom to put the kettle on.'

Suddenly she was freezing. The morning air. She was only wearing a pair of light slacks and a cotton sweater.

Another squeak and the table was off her shoulder altogether. The bearded man was crawling carefully towards her. 'We're going to make it. We're going to make it, love.' He seemed to be reassuring himself. She wasn't worried at all. She had faith in her furniture.

But when he reached her she almost cried, gripping his lovely warm hand.

'Now we're both under the table,' she said. He smiled, checking this, feeling that.

'Nothing wrong with me, doc.'

'Amazing.'

He murmured rapidly and calmly into his mobile phone.

'We shan't have any trouble getting you clear. The explosion blew most of the heavy stuff away from you. This table formed a sort of shelter. You're a lucky woman, Mrs Corren.'

'Oh, I know that, dear,' she said. 'This isn't the first time I've been stuck in a bit of rubble. Could you ring my husband and tell him I'm all right?'

'He knows by now, love, don't worry. He's out there waiting.'

'It's done terrible damage, hasn't it?'

He was bleak. 'You wouldn't recognise anything. All in ruins. Your chances were a million to one. Like winning the lottery.'

The big steel arms were dragging the concrete back, as if a curtain lifted. Dawn light. Dawn breezes on her face. It was like being born.

'Oh!'

Suddenly she could see her rescuers, the sky, the broken landscape, the vast, shallow crater, the rubble beyond.

The light revealed more and more. Through a smoky haze she could see all the way to St Paul's.

'It's a miracle,' he said. 'A genuine miracle.'

She watched as the sun began to rise, a radiant harmony of pale golds and reds, behind the cathedral's glittering dome.

'Yes,' she said. 'You can always rely on good furniture.'

Through the Shaving Mirror;

or, How We Abolished the Future

(after Maurice Richardson)

'**H**AS ANYONE NOTICED,' Monsignor Cornelius spoke urgently, hoping to divert Sir Perkin Float, on his third bottle of claret, from developing that familiar litany about discovering Chaos Maths years before Mandelbrot, thus being cheated of his place in history and his video royalties, 'how cats can turn off time? With a suitable lens, of course.'

Engelbrecht, the dwarf metaphysical boxer, grew alert. Professional curiosity. A founder of the Surrealist Sporting Club, he refused to fight anything lighter than a cathedral clock. Against advice he'd challenged Big Ben to a 'no quarter' fin-de-millennium celebratory bout. Serious Soho backers. Chinese calendar promoters. That the parliamentary clock had accepted was surprising, that it lost was suspicious. Strong rumbles in the sporting fancy. Someone had slipped the monster timepiece a heavy envelope to lie down. London was now on Chinese time with all serious punters refusing mah-jongg bets involving politicians.

'It reminds me,' said the time-battered pug, 'of that night in New York I almost lost to the Union Square Clock Tower. My career would have been over if it hadn't been for some fancy photon-work.'

Tactfully, the Corinthian Jesuit drew us into Engelbrecht's confidence. 'Your mother discovered that time isn't a dimension of space, but a field whose properties are affected by the nature of space existing within it?'

'Space a quality of time?' Sir Perkin snorted into his wine. Glinting rubies fell to the linen. But Cornelius's clever sourcing meant outright disagreement would be dangerous.

Clearing the cloth, Engelbrecht used a carpenter's pencil and the condensed mathematical logic developed at his famous Marrakech ashram to illuminate us. 'Time alters when it interacts with space. In common with all observable nature, the universe, or multiverse, grows organically and is best imagined as a vast tree, or perhaps even a forest with common roots.'

'And the soil for this tree?' Float's reckless scepticism terrified us. Expensive watches would only be the first victims of our dwarf's distemper.

The tiny slugger observed philosophically that this was the level of logic he must commonly suffer. 'An analogy,' he growled. 'There's a theory that the multiverse is created by the common will, but as to its origins...?' He cracked his knuckles. 'I think, therefore I thump.'

Float's timid attention returned to the claret. The merest whisper of big bangs had him reaching for his jug.

Engelbrecht scowled reminiscently. 'We're familiar with the disappearing neutron, we've recently learned how light can travel faster than light. Conventional method produces Heath Robinson physics turned into formulae by crazed Euclidians. At some point, as Columbus told the Pope, we have to let go of the premise that the world is flat.'

'Can we see these alternative worlds?' 'Prof' Aspinall had been kicking the gong around and wasn't ready for further shocks.

Cornelius embellished smoothly. 'I understand it's a question of scale and mass. Put simply, millions of subtly different versions of our reality are separated by size. Each version, though scarcely different in terms of the multiversal compass, is as invisible to us as if we were only seeing a single magnified pixel out of a complex computer image. We never see the whole. It is either too small or too large. We coexist in the same space through scale. Each alternative world has greater or lesser density and is invisible to the others.'

'Proliferating to infinity. Whales, fairies,' Engelbrecht paused. 'Dwarves.'

'Space curves,' mumbled 'Prof' into his spoon. 'Don't it?'

'Organically and often, as a branch curves.' Cornelius smiled. 'Like ourselves, space consists of spheres, but isn't itself spherical. Nature would be contradicted if it were. Certain entities somehow adjust their mass and move "intrabranally". For instance, few creatures are as expert at varying their size as cats. Thus their mysterious "disappearances". Happily the phenomenon hasn't occurred with dogs.'

'Bigfoot, however...' 'Prof' began.

'Cats,' said Cornelius hastily, 'see space invisible to us, coming and going through the multiverse pretty much at will.'

'Bunkum,' hiccupped Float. 'We were supposed to hear about that New York match our dwarf won by a whisker. In funny circumstances.'

Engelbrecht swelled. 'A classy clock fighting for a consortium of Istanbul high-rollers backing the Julian calendar. Twice my form and landing some tricky Byzantine jabs. By Round Sixty I'd borrowed all available time. I'm on my back looking like someone just unwrapped the Mummy.

'I've already squared the ref, of course. While shaving I've also dreamed up some insurance. Fortunately I have a prism hidden in one glove, a photon in the other. Resting on the count with my hands invisible I pull Harness's old baffled-quantum trick. On nine. Works like a charm. Time hesitates. My seconds Coleman and Benford produce the mirror, rescaling mass and size to shrink the heavy bastard enough so I can stagger up and deliver the dynamite. Gravity completes the job. Down he goes. Dead weight. Space-time readjusts. It's all over. The new reality! The Yankee Boomer's stretched full-size on the canvas, his gobsmacked hands chasing themselves round his face. Cheering punters. GMT keeps the title!'

'Convincing,' admitted Aspinall. 'Except no way would Coleman and Benford help snatch a fix.'

Engelbrecht winked. 'Prof, you can't name a physicist in the multiverse who isn't in my pocket. Now, padre, your cats?'

'Oh, another time, I think,' said Cornelius, contentedly filling his pipe.

Float was at last profoundly asleep.

CONVENT OF THE POOR CLARES,
LADBROKE GROVE, W11

The convent was built during the 1880s, at the time of the Notting Dale development. It was demolished, ninety years later, to make way for blocks of GLC flats. The nuns were moved to Putney. Local legend had it that a tunnel ran from beneath the convent to a mysterious subterranean world known as the 'Middle March'.

THE ALHAMBRA, COLVILLE TERRACE, W11

This magnificent public house, with exceptional fabrics in the art nouveau style, was designed by Voysey and built in 1900. For many years it doubled as a theatre, putting on much of the early experimental work of the Notting Hill group of playwrights (Wilson, Locke, Hare, Hopkins, etc.), as well as poetry-and-performance events promoted by Michael Horovitz and Heathcote Williams. Emma Tennant's 'Banana Follies' were a feature of the mid-1970s. It is now a fashionable restaurant.

THE HEARST CASTLE, LADBROKE GROVE, W10

Possibly the most grandiose project of property developer Sir Frank Cornelius. He bought William Randolph Hearst's Californian folly and transported it, stone by stone, to London – where he had it reassembled on the site of the Convent of the Poor Clares. For several years the Castle stood empty as Cornelius became embroiled in planning disputes with the Greater London Council – who eventually took over the land for the construction of high-rise flats (designed by Ernő Goldfinger).

Hearst Castle was broken up in 2001 and rebuilt at Battle,

near Hastings, East Sussex – where Sir Frank now lives in retirement. Castle and grounds are vigorously policed with no public access (despite attempts by the Ramblers Association to establish a right of way across the Deer Park). Sir Frank acquired a great deal of dilapidated property in the Ladbroke Grove area (along with much of James Burton's crumbling marine speculation in St Leonards-on-Sea). He placed fourth in the latest *Sunday Times* Rich List of British-domiciled plutocrats.

SPORTING CLUB SQUARE, W6

Escaping the flying bombs which spread so much destruction in the area, this extraordinary project, the brainchild of Sir Hubert Begg, was built, between 1885 and 1901, by Gibbs and Flew. The open square once contained half a dozen tennis courts. Each mansion was named for one of Begg's favourite artists – with the exception of Begg Mansions itself, where the architect lived above studios and workshops staffed by a variety of artisans. The mansions were designed in eclectic styles that varied from French Gothic and Arab Baroque to English Art Nouveau. Even the ornamental ironwork of this early gated community was in the complicated 'naturalism' Begg favoured. Completion was delayed, in 1896, when the original builders were declared bankrupt. Begg, through contacts in the City, raised the private finance to see his dream realised. The Square never attracted the respectable 'New Money' for which it had been conceived. It soon became associated with London's bohemian element. The list of music-hall artists, actors, comedians, painters, illustrators, writers, journalists, script-doctors and film persons who lived there, from 1890 to the present day, is astonishing and comprises a secret history of British intellectual life. The Square has been lightly fictionalised in a number of Michael Moorcock's writings: 'The Clapham Antichrist' (*London Bone*, 2001), 'Crimson Eyes' (*Fabulous*

Harbours, 1995) and *King of the City* (2000). Moorcock lived there himself until bankrupted by the Inland Revenue. He moved to his uncle's Old Circle Squared ranch in Lost Pines, Texas, and continued to write stories of the real and imaginary inhabitants of his beloved and post-temporal Square.

Lost London Writers

For Iain Sinclair

Few modern Londoners are willing to die for their city's honour like John Scott, passionate editor of the LONDON MAGAZINE, who published Leigh Hunt, Lamb, Hazlitt, Shelley, Keats and the Opium Eater in the 1820s. Scott was killed in a duel with a representative of his bitter Edinburgh rival, the aggressively Tory BLACKWOOD's, which derided his London writers as 'Cockneys'. There wasn't a happier name for those eloquent radicals who shared London's profound sense of democracy. In 1813, Hunt got two years for describing the Prince of Wales as a libertine 'without one claim on the gratitude of his country or the respect of posterity'. In Horsemonger Road jail, Southwark, Hunt made himself defiantly at home, almost ethereal in the vast, loose-flying nightgown he always wore for work, entertaining his friends and decorating his cell.

Hunt's amiable LONDON JOURNAL, according to a contemporary, 'illumined the fog and smoke of London with a halo of glory, and peopled the streets and buildings with the life of past generations'. But it was the modern world that really fascinated the Cockneys. By 1820, when George IV ruled at last, Byron's Don Juan saw 'a mighty mass of brick, and smoke, and shipping' – a city we recognise as our own.

While Shakespeare's plays addressed Londoners with familiar references, it took the likes of Thomas Dekker (*The Shoemaker's Holiday*, *The Bel-man of London*) and Ben Jonson (*Bartholomew Fair*) to make London a subject as much as a scene and begin a literary relationship with the capital herself. In *A Journal of the Plague Year*, Defoe was perhaps the first to create London as fiction, with all his convincing tricks of invented detail. Then, somewhere between Defoe and Dickens, between the Age of Satire and the Age of Sentiment, certainly via Blake, 'the Towne' became The City. A sentient, often threatening monster, bigger than the sum of her parts.

'Blake showed Southey a perfectly mad poem called "Jerusalem". Oxford Street is in Jerusalem,' said Crabb Robinson, a founder of London University. 'Oxford-street, stony-hearted stepmother! Thou that listenest to the sighs of orphans, and drinkest the tears of children,' said the Opium Eater. Hardly an ideal location for Mothercare, the Virgin Megastore, or even Waterstone's.

Not all De Quincey's contemporaries shared his opinion. For them Oxford Street was mere background to tales of high society. Thackeray satirised these so-called 'Silver Fork' novelists whose doyen was the witty, readable Mrs Gore (*Modern Chivalry, Peers and Parvenus*). Serialised in BELGRAVIA and LONDON SOCIETY, they shared shelves at Mudie's Library with their Gothic and sometimes more questioning sisters Mrs Radcliffe, Mrs Reeve, Mrs Shelley and the lively Maria Edgeworth (*Belinda*). My own literary ancestress, Rachel Moorcock (*Gleanings from the Apocalypse, Poland, The Death of Cobden*) supported parliamentary reform and universal suffrage. A convinced dissenter, she had no time for the anti-Romish fiction written by militant Protestants like Mrs Craven (who dedicated a novel '*TO THE ALMIGHTY!!*'), Mrs Sewell (*Hawkstone*), or Catherine Sinclair whose *London Homes* sounds so pleasantly genteel in contrast to its contents – 'The Murder Hole', 'The Drowning Dragoon', 'The Priest and the Curate' &c.

Dickens was the greatest writer to turn London into a creature, but he had many imitators and rivals. Massive best-sellers in their day, they contributed to the idea of the Thames as a stinking, murky Styx, its surrounding slums the city's corrupted, fascinating heart.

Some, like Harrison Ainsworth, specialised in bloody historical melodramas that would later feed Hollywood (*The Tower of London, Old St Paul's*). Others, like the unfairly neglected Sir Walter Besant (*The Chaplain of the Fleet, St Katherine's by the Tower*), tried to paint an accurate picture of London through fact and fiction from earliest times. Steeped in Scott, often inspired by De Quincey's opium extravagances, imitated by scores of popular serial writers (*Night Rider of London Fields*, *Mysteries of London*) they created an authentic myth, more potent than fact.

The myth becomes derisory when sentimentalised by Hollywood, but easily survives assault. In that invented city Holmes and the Ripper, Jekyll and Hyde, struggle for ever in a foggy Whitechapel never bombed or redeveloped and the whole stew of English class, repression and neurosis, achieves a universal symbolism.

Almost buried under that heavy myth lies the equally authentic city we recognise in Steele, Smollett, Fielding, Gay and Thackeray. It is a domestic city, a vulgar city, a cruelly snobbish and comically arrogant city, a busy, greedy, good-humoured, generous city, a trading city, a supremely articulate and democratic city. A jolly jeering fishwife rather than a leering whore.

Whether describing London society (Mrs Ritchie's excellent *Old Kensington*), barge life on the Thames (Marryat's *Jacob Faithful*, whose spontaneous-combustion scene rivals Dickens's) or the 'gay' world of London's pleasure gardens and gambling houses (Pierce Egan's *Life in London*, introducing the original Tom & Jerry) it's a place generally more familiar to us than George Gissing's Grub Street, Edgar Wallace's Limehouse or even Peter Ackroyd's haunted Spitalfields. It's frequently salacious, as in the low-life tales and fake autobiographies of famous rakes and courtesans. That exemplary hack, Michael Cornelius O'Crook, saw his *London Rakehell*, *London By Night* and *Love Frolics of a Young Scamp* bought eagerly, swiftly enjoyed and as casually binned as a modern tabloid.

In the last quarter of the nineteenth century, and thanks to the reforming efforts of her writers, London changed. The worst slums were cleared, public health improved and education was made universal. Authors emerged whose literary values were often shared with Wilde, Beerbohm and the *fin de siècle*, but whose work was driven more by social conscience. They'd taken advantage of idealistic educational ventures like the People's

Palace, the Normal School of Science, University College and the Birkbeck Institute, all set up to provide people without means with a first-class education.

The impeccable Walter Besant was a founder of the Palace (suggested in his novel *All Sorts and Conditions of Men*) and his passion for social reform was their inspiration. Coming from impoverished backgrounds, they were determined to look at London's problems with unsentimental eyes. Admiring Gissing, they were temperamentally indisposed to examine his depths. Their writing shared something with the best music-hall songs, 'My Old Man', 'The Houses in Between' or 'The Future Mrs 'Awkins', sung by observant wits like Marie Lloyd or Gus Elen.

After Arthur Morrison, whose *Tales of Mean Streets* remains the best portrait of East End life before the slum clearances, my own favourite is the prolific W. Pett Ridge, champion of social causes and creator of *Maud Em'ly*, who in the 1890s begins her determined career in one of South London's infamous girl gangs. Pett Ridge is an invaluable memoirist. With a score or two of highly readable novels, he left us *A Story Teller, Forty Years a Londoner*, and other unique reminiscences of his world. He worked with W.T. Stead, campaigning editor of the PALL MALL GAZETTE, who would go down in the *Titanic*. Soon after H.G. Wells's first sale to the GAZETTE, Pett Ridge introduced him to J.M. Barrie, then best known as a novelist. Barrie's published advice had encouraged a hopeless Wells to sell his first article to the *PMG*.

Featuring Conan Doyle, Grant Allen, L.T. Meade and the great urban adventure-story writers, the illustrated monthlies, LONDON, STRAND and PALL MALL, ran some other outstanding contributors – the likes of Leonard Merrick (*The Actor Manager*), Richard Whiteing (*No. 5 John Street*), E. Nesbit (*Daphne in Fitzroy Street, Harding's Luck*), W.W. Jacobs (*A Master of Craft, The Lady of the Barge*), Arthur Morrison (*A Child of the Jago, The Hole in the Wall*), Barry Pain (*De Omnibus*), Israel Zangwill (*The King of Schnorrers*), H.M. Tomlinson (*Old Junk*), and a little later Compton Mackenzie (*Our Street*) evoke a London of cobbles, fierce class divisions, sardonic humour, killing disease, vicious crime, knockers-up and blanket-funds which even then, through their efforts, was vanishing. Characteristically, these writers offered their readers an ordinary domestic mirror rather than Dickens's dark reflective river. Ordinary Londoners were seen to be sarcastic, sympathetic, quick-witted and profoundly democratic.

We've known Trollope's, Disraeli's and Galsworthy's London, the Westminster of *Mrs Dalloway*, Shaw Desmond's sporting and night-time London, Michael Arlen's languid Mayfair, Wodehouse's fantasy clubland, Waugh's demi-monde. The menaced Fitzrovia of Bowen's *The Heat of the Day*, Greene's surrealistic *The Ministry of Fear* and Hamilton's *Hangover Square* merge with fog-diffused images of Allingham's convincing parables, *Tiger in the Smoke* and *Hide My Eyes*, the half-real Notting Hill of MacInnes's *City of Spades*, the crooked Soho and East End of Frank Norman's *Bang to Rights* and the shabby-genteel Kensington of Angus Wilson's *Such Darling Dodos*. As non-fiction William Kent's *London for Everyman*, Elliott's *Heartbeat London*, Raban's *Soft City* or Nicholas Shakespeare's *Londoners* perpetuate Besant's enquiring tradition. London's transformed again in the hands of so many enthusiastic modern writers, but few display the same obsessed, complicated creative relationship with the city as do Ackroyd and Sinclair.

If Ballard's symbolic suburbs could be anywhere and aren't strong on slapstick, Jack Trevor Story's suburbs and dormitory towns are rooted in comic reality. They give an ironically affectionate picture of the aspiring postwar lower middle class. Story put phrases into the language. He wrote *The Trouble with Harry* and was typically ruined when Hitchcock bought it. He wrote *Live Now, Pay Later* and *The Urban District Lover*, whose film versions sometimes re-emerge on cable. He wrote the best of Adam Faith's *Budgie*. For years he described his life and adventures in a weekly column for THE GUARDIAN. Women loved him. He had an innocent, knowing, honest eye. His worlds and Mike Leigh's have much in common. The Jack Trevor Story Memorial Prize, given in conjunction with Nicholas Royle's *Time Out Book of New Writers*, is awarded on condition that the money be blown in two weeks and the recipient not have a thing to show for it. His exhilarating, unguardedly autobiographical *One Last Mad Embrace* is only matched by my other lasting favourite, Gerald Kersh's *Fowlers End*.

Unspeakably depressing, Fowlers End, NE, has a mephitic cinema. The manager's struggles with his quarrelsome punters make this perhaps the funniest of Kersh's marvellous books. Self-invented, Kersh came from Twickenham but painted a rich, detailed picture of postwar bohemian/criminal London. He wrote chilling short stories ('The Horrible Dummy' is one) and his best work is unmatched. Reprinted recently, his moody, ambiguous *Night and the City* has been filmed twice.

London inspires wonderful poetry. Like Blake, Aidan Dunn's epic *Vale Royal* has a mystical idealism entirely focused on the city. The most moving narrative poem to emerge from the War was Mervyn Peake's *Rhyme of the Flying Bomb* – which Langdon Jones set to music with its hallucinatory vision of the city as a living creature, tortured and ruined, but still, in the character of the sailor who finds a baby in the rubble, full of the will not merely to survive but to triumph with dignity. Peake's own drawings of Londoners are superb, reminding us how much Hogarth, Leach, Gilray, Browne, May, Topolski and so many other illustrators contributed to the city's lasting image.

A capital city is civilisation's ultimate expression. What we do with it is the best test of our collective creativity and humanity. Disraeli said London is a nation, not a city. While some smugly declare that she isn't the 'real' England, London, like Washington, Tokyo or Berlin *is* the quintessence of her nation's history and aspirations. She's the best of our virtues, the worst of our vices – the true measure of our morality. Despite continuing injustices and irritations, London – thanks in large part to her writers – has always been the richest, most coherent, civilised, tolerant and inspiring cosmopolitan megapolis in the world.

With an inconstant future, a malleable past, a questionable present, London is forever volatile, forever the same.

If you don't believe me, go to Charing Cross Road, find

yourself some Thomas Dekker, Leigh Hunt, Arthur Morrison, Jack Trevor Story or Gerald Kersh, then sit in the Embankment gardens and read to the tranquil hum of traffic until it rains or the resident loony decides you're his significant other. After that, you could always try an afternoon with Pett Ridge and the BIG ISSUE on the Northern Line. You'll be surprised how little's changed.

Acknowledgements

'A Child's Christmas in the Blitz' was first published in DODGEM LOGIC No. 8 (courtesy Alan Moore), April 2011.

'Lost London' and 'London Flesh' were first published in *London: City of Disappearances* (courtesy Iain Sinclair), Hamish Hamilton, 2006.

'A Winter Admiral' was first published in the DAILY TELEGRAPH (courtesy John Coldstream), 1994.*

'The Third Jungle Book' was first published in *ParaSpheres* (courtesy Rusty Morrison & Ken Keegan), Omnidawn, 2006.

'London Blood' was first published in *The Time Out Book of London Short Stories Volume 2* (courtesy Nicholas Royle), Penguin, 2000.

'A Portrait in Ivory' was first published in *Logorrhea: Good Words Make Good Stories* (courtesy John Klima), Bantam, 2007.*

'Doves in the Circle' was first published in *The Time Out Book of New York Short Stories* (courtesy Nicholas Royle), Penguin, 1997.

'A Twist in the Lines' was first published in *Multiverse Expanded* (courtesy Ole Hagen), Akershus Kunstsenter, 2011.

'The Clapham Antichrist' was first published in *Smoke Signals* (courtesy the London Arts Board), Penguin, 1993.*

'Cake' was first published in PROSPECT No. 111 (courtesy David Goodhart), June 2005.

'London Bone' was first published in *New Worlds* (courtesy David Garnett), White Wolf, 1997.*

'Stories' was first published in *Stories: All-New Tales* (courtesy Neil Gaiman & Al Sarrantonio), Morrow/Headline, 2010.*

'The Cairene Purse' was first published in *Zenith 2* (courtesy David S. Garnett), Orbit, 1990. The chapter quotes are from poems or lyrics by: 1 Hood; 2 Khayyám/FitzGerald; 3 A.E.; 4

343

Dylan Thomas; 5 Wheldrake; 6 Yokum; 7 Aeschylus/Mac-Neice; 8 Vachel Lindsay; 9 F. Thompson; 10 Peake; 11 Treece; 12 Duffy; 13 Nye; 14 C.D. Lewis; 15 E. St V. Millay; 16 Nye.

'Furniture' was first broadcast by BBC Radio 4 on *Book at Bedtime*, 1999.*

'Through the Shaving Mirror' was first published in NATURE No. 6,803 (courtesy Philip Campbell), September 2000.*

'Lost London Writers' was first published in WATERSTONE'S MAGAZINE (courtesy Andrew Holgate), 1999.

* Exists in audio or Net audio versions.